Agnes & Molly

MERETE MORKEN ANDERSEN

ALSO BY MERETE MORKEN ANDERSEN

Oceans of Time

Agnes & Molly

MERETE MORKEN ANDERSEN

Translated from the Norwegian by
Barbara J. Haveland

For Janike

Published in 2008 by
The Maia Press Limited
82 Forest Road
London E8 3BH
www.maiapress.com

First published in Norwegian as *Mandel* by Gyldendal in 2005
Copyright © 2005 Gyldendal Norsk Forlag AS
English-language translation by Barbara J. Haveland

Merete Morken Andersen asserts her moral right to be
identified as the author of this work
Barbara J. Haveland asserts her moral right to be identified
as the translator of this work

ISBN 978 1 904559 28 3

A CIP catalogue record for this book is available from the
British Library

Printed and bound in Great Britain by Thanet Press on paper
from sustainable managed forests

Translation supported by NORLA
(Norwegian Literature Abroad)  NORLA

The Maia Press is supported by Arts Council England

Now, as I leave . . . at this hour of farewell
when I must part from a friend, a place,
how the longing rises for those I have loved,
and the regret over those I have hurt . . .
O, now I know all life's pain,
so this is what it is to be mortal . . .

Indra's daughter in *A Dream Play*
by August Strindberg

I

AGNES

I fell through the air, from high above.
My hair streamed out behind me like a sail.
I felt a deep, sinking sensation.

I woke up crying:
'Daddy!'

When I woke that morning I could tell that something new was about to happen. My head felt fresh and clear, like after a shower of rain. I lay among the white bedclothes and was conscious of having a body, that it was strong, that it could stretch out in lots of directions at once; bend towards the light like a living plant. I was trembling. That was new. I hadn't trembled like that since I was a young girl.

And Aksel wasn't there, he was on his summer holidays, so it couldn't be because of him. Suddenly it dawned on me: my willpower was finally starting to work. It was time to get well.

Strictly speaking, it's Aksel who's supposed to be here in the mornings. He's the one I'm used to. He's the one with the gentle hands and the nicest voice when he tells me about what he's heard on the morning news. Compared to him, the temp is useless. The temp has colourless eyes and doesn't know me the way I really am, she mumbles her words and scuffs her feet when she walks. Shuffles and scuffs.

Shuffle, scuff. Shuffle, scuff.

Aksel is sharp and clear, he walks with a light, firm step; he has such a nice walk, such good diction. Aksel can make me forget myself. Or rather: Aksel can both remind me of myself and make me forget myself.

Remind me of myself in a good way, isn't that what we say. A tender way.

I have a body, and it's a jolly good one, I always think to myself when I hear Aksel walk through the door.

This was at the very beginning of the summer holidays. I lay and listened to the sounds outside the window in the big bedroom. The morning was light and transparent, and my ears were shaped like the flared bells of trumpets to catch every sound. It had been an almost soundlessly lovely night, the busy roads only a few blocks away might have been in another world. This street on which my house sits seemed to have drawn back in order to listen better.

Not a car to be heard all night, apart from one which pulled up down at the end of the street around three o'clock and dropped off someone wearing soft-soled shoes. It drove away, I heard brisk footsteps, a key was inserted into a lock in the building next door and turned with a little click. Then came the rush of water through a pipe, a creak, a sigh from a window one floor above mine. It's amazing what I can hear, I thought, my hearing must have become even keener lately. Feel these ears: they're positively glowing.

It was as if, all through the bewildered dream-ridden hours before daybreak, I had known that at any moment I might wake up, and when I opened my eyes everything around me would be fresh and vital. I vaguely remembered having cried out something, but couldn't remember what.

I felt as though a little flap had fallen into place: this is where I am now. I must live with this as it is and the healing will naturally follow. Live in this town, this house, this room, this bed, this body, these thoughts. No need to feel sorry for me, this is not about my illness at all. How wrong I have been all these years. Everything is as it is. Why did no one ever tell me this?

Then it struck me that maybe this was what Granny was trying to tell me, that time when I was slumped, naked and crying, on the stool in her bathroom. She wanted to say it to me, but there was no way of saying it. This was six months after I first became ill, I was only nineteen, I had begun to see how helpless I could become. My body could wither away, it *would* wither away, I could lose my memory, the power of speech, everything. I was aware that it had already begun: that indescribable weariness was creeping over me. I looked down at my thighs, they were white and flabby. An acrid odour rose from my armpits; and my arms, with their powerless hands, lay heavy and passive in my lap. They didn't seem to be connected to me, they no longer trusted me. My stomach hung down over them in folds, like a sagging accordion, an empty little pouch.

Granny walked over to me, tilted my chin upwards with a crooked index finger and stared at me for a moment with that strange, inward-looking gaze of hers, then released me and turned away with an irresolute shrug. It occurred to me that what was happening to me was something she knew about, but could not talk about. At least not to me.

But now I can't help feeling that it couldn't have been that hard. Fate had begun to work on me. Maybe Granny didn't know how to deal with the workings of fate. If she had, surely she would have told me then, at that moment.

What she should have said was: My dear. Things are as they are.

She could have wrapped a blanket round me.

And then, earlier this summer, I was sitting in bed in quite another room, with a body that was the same and yet quite different. I was no longer nineteen, I was 36, and much of what the doctors had said could happen, had happened. Things had slid slowly and relentlessly into place, as is always the way with fate.

I pulled up my nightie and studied my stomach and thighs again. There was no doubt that I had aged considerably. My stomach was still a saggy pouch, and my thighs were even flabbier than they had been back then. My skin was white as paper and the black pubic hair sprouted in an unsightly little tuft. And yet everything was different now. I was overwhelmed by a quiet sadness for myself; for the first time it was really brought home to me that this was my body, the only one I had, and that it had been with me right from the start. It had really stuck by me. But had I ever thanked it? I ran a hand over my stomach, rounding off with a little pat. I whispered:

'I'm feeling better now, thanks. Thanks.'

My nightie smelled nice. It was of brushed cotton, freshly washed, it settled softly over my skin when I let it fall back. Molly gave it to me, she gives me nothing but the best. Sometimes, when we were younger, she would spend a whole week's pay on a present for me if she thought it might cheer me up.

My body responded by kind of chuckling at me, it wanted to show me that it bore no grudge. It made me aware that legs, arms and back were definitely stronger now than they had been when I was nineteen. That lovely, tremulous thrill ran through me when I thought of how, for over a year Aksel had been helping me with my training programme. He has plans for me, I thought to myself. Before I know it he'll be back, with a surprise for me, he just has to get his summer holidays out of the way first. He's probably looking forward to starting back at work, so that we can get on with my training.

I was ashamed to recall all the times when I had been somewhat loath to do those exercises, as if they didn't really have anything to do with me. As if I had every right to suppose that it was Aksel's job to coax the strength back into my muscles, and mine to be unwillingly consigned to a hard fate.

I pushed myself up in the bed, propped myself on my arms while I swung my legs over the edge. The rug felt soft and distinct under my feet, I sat for a moment, thinking: it's definitely there, I really can feel the rug today. All those strands of wool knotted together by a little needle, there had to be thousands of them, maybe hundreds of thousands of woollen strands.

'And it's going to become even more distinct!' I told myself out loud.

I hoisted myself over into the wheelchair and rolled down the side of the room to the window. As I passed the chest of drawers I lifted the box of chalk out of the top drawer.

I opened the old-style double window with the aid of a little stick with a hook at the end of it which someone who knows about such things has left there, probably on orders from Aksel.

The smell of the street wafted in at me. I could feel it on my nose, my mouth, on my closed eyes. It was so clear, but it hadn't really warmed up yet, I could feel a draught.

I thought to myself that I wished I had a garden. Or a child. A garden I could wheel myself out into, maybe one with a gazebo; I could sit in the gazebo and feast my eyes on all the growing things, and on the child hopping and skipping among all the greenery. And the temp could do the weeding, if she was still set on making herself useful, I thought. Do the weeding, and fetch a glass of blackcurrant squash for the radiant child on the grass.

But outside there was just the street. Sadly, there are no trees in this street, only parked cars. At the bottom of the street is the hospital.

Out of habit I drew my head carefully back into the room. I trundled over to the bed and lifted myself into it with the chalk between my teeth.

I have a picture of Jesus hanging above my bed. It's a touchingly naïve picture: Jesus' hands are hovering peacefully over the white lambs, his arms slanting downwards, his palms upturned. The lambs seem to be in a world of their own, going about their business, just as I go about my business in the bed underneath them. I managed, with great difficulty, to turn myself around and propped myself up on one arm so that I could lift down the picture with the other. There was a yellow rectangle on the wallpaper where it had hung.

After these exertions I had to rest for a while. I flopped on the bed and ran an eye over the room. I thought of how the light had been quietly working away and had already bleached everything around me, dulled the sharpness of the colours. This is an example of the slow, but indefatigable workings of fate, I thought to myself. Fate has a plan, it is incredibly patient, it has set the light to work in here. And the light has followed orders and had an effect, not just on the wallpaper, but on everything in here; also on Jesus and the lambs, also on me. Oh, yes, on Jesus too, and on me, I was bound to conclude, we too have grown paler. The light always wins in the end. In the end, although it's still a very long way off; both Jesus and I, and all the lambs will have become invisible, we will have blended with the faded wallpaper. Aksel will need to feel his way to me when he gets here in the mornings, and I will need to make a noise to let him know where I am. A grunting sound, or a little cluck. Aksel, too, will be paler, when we finally catch sight of one another. It's time something happened! There has to be some way of speaking with this fate.

In the yellow rectangle on the wallpaper left by Jesus and the lambs, I drew a little double window with the chalk. The window looked exactly like the one out of which I had just stuck my head: two tall, narrow oblongs intersected by a cross, but much smaller than the real window. I'm good at drawing. Not as good as Molly, but good.

Then I put the picture back and turned myself round into the proper position in bed again.

It had taken longer than I had expected to do all this. I was worn out, I had a little ache, but it was a good ache. The first good ache of my new life, I told myself. There I sat, under the peaceful lambs and Jesus' upturned palms and smiled to myself before sliding back down under the duvet. A wave of happiness and warm, salt water washed over me. A fine, damp film coursing down over cheeks and throat.

It's important to remember that it is Molly whom Aksel is seeing now. They met one another here, in my bathroom, just over six months ago, and there was little I could do to prevent him from being drawn to her like a moth to a bright light. The inevitable happened: he flapped his wings frantically and wasn't himself for a long while, he simply went around in a daze. He looked to me as though he was beating himself against a window. But it wasn't in my power to help him, there was no window to open.

To say that Molly is my closest friend would be no exaggeration. We are incredibly well synchronised. I am Molly's head, she is my feet. I think, remember and plan, she travels around the world, putting vast distances behind her. She creates things wherever she goes, and then she moves on. But it's me who tells her where to go and what to do.

Molly can fly. She has such a broad wingspan, it can carry her anywhere. And each evening she calls to tell me what she has seen out there in the world. In this way she lives for me.

She is good at describing things. Sometimes she lies a bit, but that doesn't matter. The difference between truth and lies is not always what counts, at least not for two people who know each other as well as Molly and I do.

Whoosh, she says when she takes off.

Aksel and I were in the bathroom when she walked in that day, we had just finished the day's work-out. She hadn't rung the bell first, but through the running water I had heard her footsteps on the stairs. My ears are sharper than Aksel's, and I can pick those footsteps out from all other footsteps. Molly is not the sort to shuffle her feet. She is invincible, the sort of person to whom one simply surrenders. She opens her mouth and laughs and you feel yourself soften.

Aksel was standing over me, washing my hair with a light, warm spray from the hand-held shower when she barged in, striding across the tiled floor with her shoulderbag swinging from its worn strap. Through the steam on the mirror I saw their eyes meet: that rather sudden, baffled flash of tenderness which passes between two people who don't know one another, but who realise that something is going to happen between them very soon. I knew with all of my being that this was a fateful moment. I shut my eyes, groped blindly in the air with my hand and asked for a towel.

So you could say that it was me who brought them together. And I don't know whether she means to drop him, despite all that has happened in recent weeks.

As far as Aksel is concerned, it's hard to say anything for certain. I used to think that he was the sort of man who is too married, even though he is divorced, and too loyal, too devoted a father to his children to be able to bear living with Molly. But it stands to reason: he must get something from her, and he certainly won't be free of her until she lets go. It's always Molly who has to let go first, it's been that way since she was nineteen.

Aksel went on coming here to help me even after he and Molly started seeing one another: well, he still has his job to do. We work out, he helps me from my chair on to the exercise mat and demonstrates the exercises for me. The physiotherapist has designed a programme specially for me and has no doubt given him detailed instructions on how to coach me, to motivate and encourage me. The physiotherapist is a woman, she has only been here once and I couldn't decide whether I liked her or not, she had the most enormous breasts. You might say that she and Aksel have ganged up together, all in a good cause, of course. I assume that they have regular meetings at her office in the community centre, where they drink coffee out of her chunky, flowery mugs while she tells him all about me and my recalcitrant limbs, all the sorry details. She sets her mug down firmly on the table and leans eagerly towards him, so eagerly that her breasts brush the top of the desk. The temp pretends to be pottering about at the back of the open-plan office, ears straining to catch every word they say. She hasn't been invited to take part in these discussions about me and my body, she just has to keep abreast as best she can, come to her own conclusions about me with very little to go on.

I don't think Aksel keeps case notes on me. He's happiest on the exercise mat, we don't have time for much else. He shows me the correct positions, cheers me on. 'Well done, Agnes,' he says. 'Very well done. There now! That's great!' I sweat and strain and get frustrated, but he has the patience of a saint. After a while he slips off his nurse's shoes, lies down beside me on the mat and shows me the exercise from my angle. He points out how good this is for my strength, my balance, my posture. And he has a thing about breathing exercises. We sit together on the mat, breathing in sync: long, deep breaths with eyes closed. When I open my eyes again his are already open, they are sparkling, and he says: 'There. I bet you feel more relaxed now.'

He's really into it. He smells nice and the skin of his face looks smooth and soft, I suppose he must shave every day.

Aksel has explained to me that good posture is vital not only for those who stand and sit, but also for people who are bed-ridden. In all probability it's the physiotherapist who has told him this, but he acts as though it's something he has come up with himself, and I don't begrudge him that pleasure.

'You seldom hear someone say that a bed-ridden person has beautiful posture,' he said once, with that boyish smile of his. 'But it really does matter. It's not the same to lie there like a stick of wood, all tensed up.'

I knew what he was getting at, of course. I suppose the physio-therapist sketched it out on her flipover chart: a drawing of a skinny woman lying on her back in bed, stiff as a poker. She probably used lines and arrows to explain things, smiling at him all the time, while her upper arms rubbed against her breasts and made them wobble.

On one occasion he promised me a surprise if I managed to complete the entire work-out on the mat without complaining. They took such a long time, those exercises, and they were almost unbearably hard, I prefer to pump away at the dumbbells that I bought by mail order. But Aksel has no time for dumbbells, in fact he went so far as to confiscate them.

The surprise was that he has a kayak, he's had it for years, he goes out in it every summer and well into the autumn. As soon as I'm strong enough and my balance is good enough he's going to arrange for me to go out on the fjord in it.

That's what he said. He said it with rather forced enthusiasm, it's true, and it may well be that he was a bit fed up with me just at that moment, I hadn't exactly been putting my back into my exercises. But I know he meant it, and he's not the type to forget something like that, or make empty promises. Aksel isn't a shirker.

'It's just the thing for you,' he said. 'You'll love it.'

Sometimes, when we're working out he tells me about his children, Eilif and Ine. It's a smart move on his part. When he talks about them I prick up my trumpet ears and put everything I've got into my exercises. Maybe he's noticed that. I have a suspicion he only tells me about them to get me to make more of an effort, but that doesn't matter, I drink in every word and the children go on living inside me after he has gone. I've made some drawings in my sketch-book of how I think they look.

But he never mentions Molly. Not when we're working out, and not at any other time either. Aksel is an extremely tactful person, and he knows me. The word love does not figure in our vocabulary.

On that morning earlier in the summer the air was still crisp and clear. I was waiting for the temp to ring the doorbell.

'*Morning has broken*,' I whispered to myself. '*Like the first morning*!' Before I know it my illness will have been transformed! It can begin to shine like freshly burnished brass, a gleaming instrument on which I can play.

I repeated these last words again, in a slightly louder voice, stressing each and every syllable: *on which I can play*.

The temp does everything differently from Aksel. When Aksel arrives he gives his three sharp, almost fierce rings on the doorbell before coming in. I think of it as a sign of his vitality, his way of arousing the power within me. He gives me a signal which says that now I must greet him, and the day he brings, with everything in me that moves. He wants me to present myself clearly to him. Then he steps into the flat in those efficient white shoes of his. I think: he penetrates the flat in his white shoes, he's feeling virile today, that's good. I have to laugh at myself.

Aksel lays the newspapers on the kitchen worktop and puts on the coffee machine before coming down the hall to the bedroom. He knows what he has to offer, and he is generous. He has powerful forearms which are covered in a blond down, and he sees that I see it. I see that he sees that I see it. That puts him in a good mood.

His gaze never strays and I can tell from the arch above his brow that he has a cheerful nature. Behind him I can hear the gurgle of the coffee machine, and the warm aroma of fresh coffee coils its way down the hall, an all but invisible serpent in the air.

But on this particular morning it was, in fact, the temp. And how was she to know that I was getting better? She doesn't know me, and besides, she doesn't have the antennae for picking up that sort of thing. And even if she had, she wouldn't have had the words with which to talk about it. But she shuffled through the door in her usual fashion, softly bade me good morning, helped me out of bed and into the toilet. She left me alone there for a few minutes while she made the bed, then she came back and lifted me over into the chair in the shower niche.

I said not a word. I didn't want it to be her, I wanted it to be Aksel. I wanted him to lie beside me on the mat first, and show me the exercises as he usually did, and then help me into the bathroom and wash me all over with a soft cloth, as if I were a woman and not a patient. And I wanted it to be him who was there when, for the first time in my new life, I said something about this thing of being washed like a woman. He would put his nicely rounded index finger to my lips and make the same, long-drawn-out shushing sound that you make to little children who look as though they are about to start crying.

The temp helped me get dressed. I tugged at my sweater a bit to make her let go, I wanted to do it myself. But she tugged back, as if she were battling with a recalcitrant three-year-old. When all my clothes were on I wheeled myself pointedly away from her and into the living room, positioned myself at the desk. She stood there dithering for a moment, watching me as I switched on the radio, which was tuned to the news channel, and the computer. She made some remark in a placatory tone about the picture I have installed as a screen-saver. This too shows my bedroom window, I took it with the digital camera Molly gave me for Christmas. The temp called this picture a funny little gimmick, whatever she meant by that. Then she laid the day's papers in a pile on the desk: somehow she has got it into her head that this is what I like. It was probably meant as a gesture. She didn't seem to notice the light-grey model of a house on the desk right next to me.

As she was leaving I said that I wouldn't be needing any more help that day as my arms were so much stronger, I had better movement in my legs and had had more practice in getting out of my chair on my own. I made it clear that from now on I had decided not to be so dependent on other people's help.

'I'm getting better,' I said firmly. 'This morning I distinctly felt the rug under my feet, I haven't done that in a long time.'

But she seemed somehow to elude me, she didn't get the point of what I had said. She merely nodded cheerily in that vague way she has and shuffled out into the hall to find the frumpy coat that she always buttons right up to the chin. I got the impression she felt there was reason to feel sorry for me, that I am hanging on by my fingernails.

With a non-committal nod the temp was out of the door. She had obviously made up her mind that I was sick and that I would go on being sick. Nothing I said or did would change that, she was so totally set in her own ideas. I sniffed at her retreating back and lowered the blinds with a light touch of the button to the right of the window frame; this fills the room with a low humming sound, like a large insect coming in to land. Then I logged on to the computer and switched on the projector that is mounted on a little stand next to the desk. I retrieved some pictures I had found on the internet the previous evening, of a crowd during a demonstration in some South American country, I can't remember which. The spool rotated slowly on its stand, projecting the pictures in a broad, razor-sharp band that glided across the white walls of the flat, swept up to the ceiling and down over walls and floor again before starting a new round.

Then I keyed into the on-line version of the *New York Times* and got ready for the first stage of the day's work on my fate project. I always like to bring myself completely up-to-date on what's going on in the world before I move on to work on my project, and more especially anything connected with the weather. The weather and war. And famine. And terrorism.

There's always something new, something that wasn't there the day before: a tiny shift or a massive upheaval.

But I couldn't concentrate. That feeling of banging my head against the temp's set ideas had settled like a film over my eyes, it made my vision dim and blurred. I knew what could happen next, I had been through this so many times before, and even though I tried to fight it, it went the way it usually does when I bang my head like that.

I should know myself well enough to realise that it doesn't take much to trigger the sense of hopelessness that my illness has brought with it. A person like the temp is a typical release button. It would never have happened if Aksel had been here.

All it takes is for me to have something important to say to someone, and not to have steeled myself beforehand, because I'm so sure that I'll be able to get my message across. And if I then encounter that evasive look in the eye of the person to whom I am attempting to make myself clear, that smooth, indefinable *something* that causes whatever was so important to slip away, leaving no trace of itself, everything inside me is stirred up; I'm aware of a stabbing pain somewhere inside me, and it doesn't matter that I felt strong and happy only minutes earlier, all at once I can feel one foot or the other growing even more lifeless and heavy, or the memory of who I am and what I can do seeps out of my brain to be replaced by images which fill me in that intrusive way that I cannot abide.

I felt that deep sinking sensation again. I seeped out of myself and was filled instead with the image of the black man with the baby on the stairs. There was nothing I could do but abandon myself to it.

The black man had been sitting on the bottom step of the stairs one night last autumn when I came home from an evening at the theatre. I had been to the premiere of one of the plays that Molly had been working on. I was feeling so exhilarated and so happy that night, so proud, for Molly's sake, of all she had done. As it turned out, the play itself received only lukewarm reviews, and I suppose it's true that the actors did seem rather uninspired. But Molly's stage sets had been so beautiful and she had used a number of my ideas, even though everything clearly bore her stamp. I realised how much she had learned about lighting effects over the past year, all the electronic techniques that I have not had the opportunity to learn. She produced an effect with bands of light which I had not seen before: the light seemed to writhe around the figures on the stage and make them jump as if an electric charge was being run through them. I felt enormously inspired, I had the urge to try creating something similar at home, with one of my models. It had to be possible to come up with something: I could do some experimenting with the powerful halogen bulb and different types of perforated foil, and maybe tissue paper too.

It had occurred to me that the play would actually have been better without words. Just Molly's light writhing around and some figures moving convulsively across the stage, that would really have been enough, I would have to remember to tell her that.

The man on the stairs was wearing a slim-fitting leather jacket and he was holding the baby close to his chest as if intent on protecting it from something, from me. I saw them through the glass door while I was waiting for it to open automatically, so I could get through it in the wheelchair. It was a night in late autumn. It was raining, the taxi driver had very kindly held an umbrella over me as I trundled from the taxi to my front door, then he said goodnight, turned and walked back to the car even before I had got out my key and pressed the button to open the door. I couldn't help liking him for the fact that he left me there, I felt that he had taken me for a woman who could manage fine on her own, a woman who could easily cope with a drop of rain even if her legs were rather withered.

As the door swung open and I rolled into the hallway, the man huddled over the child and shrank closer to the wall. He looked scared. I think he must have been African. The child turned its face towards me and sent me a look that made my scalp crawl. It was a look of utter hopelessness. The child did not blink. I had a strong feeling that it was asking me to save it, to take it in.

But I did not reach out my arms to the child. I merely asked the man politely in Norwegian whether he was waiting for someone, if there was anything I could do to help, call the caretaker or something. But he didn't understand what I was saying, and I was so flummoxed by the whole situation, by my own powerful emotions, the child's wide, unblinking eyes. I couldn't think what else to say, it never occurred to me to try speaking to him in English, I just pressed the button for the lift, it was already at the ground floor; the door slid open with a little 'ping', it was simply a matter of rolling into it. And before I knew it the door had slid shut behind me and the lift was drawing me up to the fourth floor, where I live.

The next morning when Aksel arrived I asked him if he had seen an African with a little baby on the stairs, but he hadn't. Once we had finished our work-out and he had gone I sat hunched over the computer, feverishly searching the internet for news of drought in Africa, the movements of refugees, child soldiers on the run under the scorching sun.

By the time Molly finally called on that day just before the summer holidays when, for the first time, I had the feeling that I was going to get well, evening had come again. I hadn't managed to do any work on the model of the summer house, all my time had been taken up with the fate project. I sat at the computer all day, trying to make a breakthrough. I had clicked my way frantically through the various newspapers, scanned the op-ed and features pages, looking for some sign that there was someone out there to act as witness, someone who understood what was happening to us. But it was so glaringly obvious that there were no witnesses, not anywhere. Disasters which were only a few weeks old were already in the process of being forgotten and no one had the wherewithal to deal with future disasters until such time as they presented themselves.

It appeared that everyone out there was living in a kind of benumbed horror; no one had the power to see the whole picture. The image of the distraught mother with her dead child outside the ruins of a house, which had swept the media only two weeks earlier, was already old news. I had had that picture projected on to the wall for a whole morning, but she had eventually been overlaid by other images which had cropped up: a poisonous yellow cloud hanging over the sea, which was threatening to drift towards land, the tent city rising in the desert. I thought: it won't be long before I, too, forget that mother. I won't be able to hold on to her, there's so much else, there's always something worse happening.

The calamities that lay immediately ahead of us did not as yet exist. Not even as vague pictures. No one knew about them yet. And what you don't know anything about, you can't do anything about, that was one of the things I learned from Granny.

Although that in itself is such an elementary fact that I could easily have worked it out for myself.

The sinking feeling was very, very strong that evening. I missed hearing Molly's voice, and somehow my longing for it made the necessity of the fate project more and more apparent to me. I had to keep myself informed, I had to know what fate was doing out there: with all the countries that were at war, with rebel armies and civil wars, with all the storms, the weird movements in the water, with crumbling infrastructures, with acts of terrorism, with the man and the black baby on the stairs, with people on the other side of the world, walking up and down rows and rows of bodies, trying to find their own kith and kin: a familiar T-shirt, a dead, outstretched arm wearing a bracelet they themselves had given as a present, on a day when the face of this corpse was turned to theirs, glowing and alive and framed by pigtails. I had to understand what it is about all these gaunt human ghosts wandering around with nowhere to go and no idea what they are involved in, while the desert creeps up on them. All those people who are looking for their children, their husbands, their belongings, their parents; all those who lug their clattering buckets to a well that they know is almost dry, with one child on the back and another by the hand, while at home their brothers and sisters lie waiting under a tarpaulin. The same ones who, some days later, carry the swaddled body of a child to a hole in the ground, lay down the stiffened form, raise their hands to the heavens and scream out questions the meaning of which they themselves barely understand.

All those who flounder around in this without discerning the grand design. All those who pay for something for which they are not to blame, not knowing when or why it began, not knowing when or how it will end.

I didn't find the answer for which I was looking. But it seemed more obvious to me than ever: fate has a plan for us and someone has to act as witness. No: *I* have to. Fate has a plan for us, it wants to speak to us and I have to act as witness, turn my attentive ears to it. I have to be on the alert.

I found several pictures by photographers and aid workers stationed in one disaster-torn country or another. I brought them up on to the screen, zoomed in on them, then let the projector take over and throw the images up on to the wall, the ceiling and the floor. I saw the faces, the child's bulging eyes, the sharp edges of the skeleton under the tight skin, the flies in the corner of the eye, as if the eye was already dead. The pictures engulfed me, I found myself among the cracks in the hard ground on which they sat, I could feel the fabric draped over the women's shoulders and wound round their heads, the contours of their limp, empty breasts. There was a swooshing sound in my ears: it had to be the sound of my own blood, my breathing was shallow, my chest tight; in desperation I eventually fumbled my way into the website of one of the aid organisations. I projected the giro number on to the wall, red and stark, I felt that deep ache in my chest.

I was left drained and exhausted. I swung the wheelchair sharply away from the desk, trundled into the centre of the room, raised my arms to the ceiling and screamed out something at the top of my voice: questions the meaning of which I myself barely understood. The stark, vivid number covered the whole wall. Slowly it travelled upward towards the ceiling.

Afterwards I sat for a while, slumped over the arm of the wheelchair. I felt the tension trickling out of me and running down on to the floor. A heavy calm crept over me, the way sediment sinks to the bottom as troubled waters gradually regain their tranquillity.

Beyond the window, the light told me that the night was here to stay. In the middle of the summer these shifts from early to late evening are almost imperceptible, but they are there. I rolled out to the kitchen and started to make something to eat, I told myself very firmly that it wouldn't help the world in the slightest if I were to sit here in this flat and starve. On the contrary: you have to get plenty of nourishment, especially the valuable proteins, eat a nutritious diet to encourage the body to keep going. You can't possibly make sense of anything if you have no energy, that's obvious, it goes with saying. You just go on blundering around in a sleepy haze. No food, no awareness, and then fate has no one to talk to.

I felt as though I had undergone a purification process, and the picture of the staring man with the black baby on the stairs was almost gone now, fortunately, just like the pictures which had swept over the ceiling and walls in the living room, accompanied by the quiet hum of the projector.

But although my head was at last feeling almost fresh and clear again, I couldn't find my way back to that tremulous sense of a new life about to begin, which I'd had when I woke that morning.

I called the temp and reminded her that I would not be requiring an evening visit. She was, as usual, amiably uncomprehending, and I did not deign to tell her again that I was getting better, there was no point. I simply gave her the evening off, as one would with a maid, and it did not surprise me that she thanked me as if she were an employee whom I had bought and paid for myself. Everything depends on the authority with which one speaks. It's all a matter of setting the scene.

So, with some difficulty I got myself ready for the night, brushed my teeth and gave my hair the usual hundred strokes with the hairbrush. Aksel has encouraged me to do this, he has shown me what good exercise it is for the arm muscles to give the hair a stiff brushing. It pays to alternate between using the right hand and the left. I gave it my best, telling myself I was working up to handling a kayak paddle.

At last I was back in bed, and to be on the safe side I decided not to watch the evening news, even though the television was ready and waiting on top of the chest of drawers and the remote control was lying on the bedside table as usual, next to my notebook. I told myself that I couldn't absorb any more news right now, that I would rather concentrate on the sun, which was going down behind the hospital at the end of the street: it ought to have been both a heartening and a reassuring sight. The sun and fate are so closely interlinked, I told myself, there can't be much doubt about that, just think of the way they control all life. To understand fate one must also understand the sun.

I gave myself a good shake and imagined that the sun had grown heavier and yellower now that it was evening, that it would slowly and almost imperceptibly go on with its work of bleaching everything in here, even while it was, temporarily and graciously, coming to the conclusion that it would have to give up for the day and sink down into the right-hand corner of the window-pane like a fiery weight.

There's no reason to take on so, just because the sun is setting, I went on in my head. You surely don't doubt that it will rise again tomorrow, in a totally different part of the sky? Well? Because if there is one thing that has willpower, it has to be the sun!

But my body had grown drowsy and listless again. For a moment I doubted whether I would be able to feel the rug under my feet as distinctly the next day as I had that morning. Over the past few years things have, after all, been moving pretty fast in the wrong direction as far as my illness is concerned. All of my senses, apart from my hearing, have become less sharp. But the doubt was too dark, so I fended it off with an almost physical kick.

'Hundreds of thousands of woollen strands in that rug!' I said out loud. 'All secured with a tiny needle! And more to come!'

It had been a hard day, and I simply wasn't up to summarizing it in my notebook as I usually do. I longed to sink back on to the pillows and let sleep wash over me. I recalled my dream from the night before, the one in which I was falling from the sky and Dad was shouting something to me. I wanted to dream on. But it was difficult to let go, I didn't feel I had earned the right to sleep just yet. Heavy-headed, groggy almost, I peered out of the window with half-shut eyes and in my imagination it was actually the sun itself that was trembling as it shed its last, fiery rays on the hospital blocks. With a bit of an effort I could see that it was doing its best to push them to the ground, and that the tall, white, rectangular buildings had absolutely no intention of yielding.

'They're pushing back,' I forced myself to murmur under my breath. 'The hospital blocks are putting up a big fight now, they're quivering with the same almost inhumanly strong will that I feel inside myself. The hospital has not been weakened by this battle, it has been strengthened, just as my own body, with its indomitable willpower and its new insight, pushes against every-thing that is trying to break it down. Look at those buildings, so white and upstanding. Their windows freshly cleaned, as bright and shiny as my eyes. I have the eyes of a hawk, the ears of a little wild animal, I only imagine that all my senses are failing.

Already I was feeling a little better.

'And I've been feeding my body a nutritious diet, it has plenty to run on,' I continued, feeling quite invigorated. 'All sorts of virile proteins, fried eggs, bacon and brown beans with sour cream and chili. It can't possibly fail.'

I forced myself to think about something else that was even more positive and fortifying. One simply cannot over-emphasise the importance of a cheerful nature. If there is one thing I have learned in life it must be that. I flicked through my mental index of happy pictures and finally picked out one of the very best:

In my mind I saw myself at Granny's summer house. The summer house is my natural abode in the summer, I thought to myself. It does me good to have a change of scenery. And now I am there, have been there for some weeks in fact, long enough to have acquired a lovely golden tan. I drove down in my little car, I'm a very good driver, with speedy reflexes and strong, sturdy legs to work the accelerator and the brakes, not to mention the all-important clutch pedal.

Molly is staying there too, I went on. Well, it was actually she who inherited the summer house from Granny; Granny and I aren't really related, you see. But Molly is so happy to have me there, she has told me that I must use the place as much as I want. We love living in the same house, she and I, and we've spent the whole day talking, but now she has decided to take a little nap and I say that I'm going for a swim. I collect my swimming costume and towel from the washing line and set off down the dirt road to the jetty and the bathing hut. And would you believe it, Aksel also happens to be staying at the summer house with Molly and me, and that looks like him coming out of the gazebo at the bottom of the garden. Aksel is on his summer holidays too, of course, I musn't forget that. He and Molly and I make such a jolly little triangle of friends, and now he calls out to me and asks where I'm going, and I say that I'm going down to take an evening dip and watch the sun go down. The sunsets are always so beautiful here, the sun looks so plump and rosy, sinking down into the lovely warm water like a buxom matron.

'The sun's a buxom matron!' I say to Aksel. 'And I'm going to take a dip with her!' And he nods and gives a little chuckle and asks if he can come too and I stop, turn to look at him and laugh back. I tell him I don't need a lifeguard, but that he's welcome to join me if he wants. I walk on, that's what is known as going on ahead, something I'm given to doing. And after a while he comes running up behind me with a pair of blue bathing trunks sticking out of his trouser pocket. We step out smartly, side by side. We don't speak, but it could be that we're smiling. Oh, yes: I'd say we both have big smiles on our faces, I thought.

And how do we look, I asked myself, pursuing my thread. It's not hard to imagine. Aksel is a nice golden-brown too, he has on a freshly ironed shirt which is open at the neck. I'm wearing sandals that fasten with a little buckle at either side. My legs are brown and strong, I have a real spring in my step. Aksel remarks on how light on my feet I've become.

'It gladdens a nurse's heart to see it,' he says and I hoot with laughter again. Aksel is always so full of compliments.

And, I went on, when we get down to the bathing hut, Aksel says there's nothing to stop us going skinny-dipping, there's no one else around. We step inside the little white hut and start to undress. We each lay our clothes on our own bench, against our own wall. Suddenly we're both a little shy. I bend down and unbuckle my sandals, I have no difficulty in bending double, I can do it with almost completely straight legs and I don't lose my balance. Then I slowly unbutton my blouse and slip one arm out of its sleeve, then the other. The blouse drops softly and neatly on to the bench. My arms are strong and lightly tanned, I cross my arms over my chest and cup my hands round my shoulders. I'm not wearing a bra. Then I unbutton my shorts, pull down the zip and let them slide down over my thighs and calves. They flop in a heap around my ankles. I flex one foot, hook up my shorts and send them flying over on to the bench. I can see my stomach and my thighs now: there's a tan line at my waist, where my shorts begin. That's because I've been working so much in the garden around the summer house, in shorts and a bikini top, I've really made myself useful, pushing great barrowloads of steaming topsoil. Load after load.

Only now do I pull down my panties with one hand and toss them, too, on to the bench. I don't look at Aksel, but can tell by his actions that he has got as far as me with his undressing. I walk ahead of him on to the little platform overlooking the sea and start to make my way down the narrow path to the water. Aksel is right behind me now. And as I dip my first foot into the cool water Aksel dives from the bathing hut and lands with a splash a few yards in front of me. The spray from his dive hits me and I scream and laugh and yell at him that he's a beast. Ahead of me, Aksel breaks into a crawl, swimming out across the fjord. He is as swift and powerful as a fish, but I am faster, I glide down into the water and start to swim after him. I'm sure he slows down on purpose, so that I can catch up with him. I swim alongside him, I'll get you for that, you beast, I cry. He grins and turns to face me in the water.

With a bound I'm on top of him, I thought. I sling one arm round his neck and wrap my legs around his waist, all in one smooth movement. We both duck under for a second, but he fights his way back to the surface, coughing and spluttering and spewing out a great jet of water.

'What are you trying to do, drown me!' he yells, pretending to be mad at me.

I sat up in bed and opened my eyes.

And at that very moment Molly called. The intrusive trill of the telephone made me jump three feet in the air, a second later and there was not a trace of the dream left in me.

There was a strained softness to her voice when I at last made it out through all the background noise. Molly's voice always sounds like that when there is something she doesn't understand. She'll get herself mixed up in something, some situation which makes demands on her that she's not sure she can meet, and then she'll call me, drop her voice an octave or two and outline the situation for me in what I can clearly picture are exaggerated movements of her lips. Only once she is back in the same room as me does she remember that it's my muscles that are failing, not my hearing. She has no idea how good my hearing has become lately. I don't tell Molly everything.

Usually, when she calls at that time of night, it has to do with a man. Molly has this theory that all the men she gets involved with have something to teach her, and that she has to hold on to them until she discovers exactly what it is she can learn from them. I know where she has this idea from; she gets it from Granny, she has believed this ever since she was a teenager, and that's fine by me.

Because I was there you see, when Granny told us her theories about men and how to understand them. In fact I was the one who insisted that she should tell us about them. And most of what she said was aimed at me, I think, although Molly wasn't to know that, of course. The idea that men also have something to teach us, and that a certain amount of perseverance is needed to discover what that might be, is quite appealing, even if Molly has so far produced little empirical evidence to back up this theory. Molly is a gem, but where some things are concerned she is a bit dense. A dense gem. Granny would have sighed with exasperation and flapped her hand at her when it came to this particular point, and I would have agreed.

I've been thinking a lot about Granny recently. There's so much I would have liked to ask her: about all these new feelings that are welling up inside me. It has crossed my mind that it might be fate that brings men to us. Maybe that was what she meant. Men and children. I felt it was odd that Granny didn't say anything about what we can learn from children. Her theory probably wasn't fully developed when she died. All theories need honing and polishing, as I know from experience.

Personally, I haven't had much chance to try out Granny's theory about men, my illness saw to that at an early age. I've really only ever had experience of one man. He was Granny's neighbour, and what we had together lasted only half an hour, so it wasn't really what you could call a relationship. If I had had the chance to try out a man for any length of time I'm sure I would have proved to be extremely persevering.

Aksel never talks about Molly, but Molly talks – well, of course she does – and mainly about Aksel. Tact is not her strong suit. She talks about Aksel or, more generally, she talks about men: in long monologues on the phone from her studio in town, while she is busy making something for one project or another: hammering in nails, filing, sanding. The drone of the sewing machine, or the whine of a polisher, and Molly yelling into the phone to be heard over the racket she is making. She has no trouble talking and sewing at the same time, so it seems. Molly is always doing at least two things at once.

'I love you dearly!' she cries. 'But I'm *in love* with Aksel, you understand that, don't you? It's different with a man.'

Sometimes the noise of her machines starts to grate on my nerves, and I have to put down the receiver for a moment, shut my eyes and press the back of my hand to my brow.

I don't think I could bear to lose Molly. I don't want things to pass, at least not those things that relate to her. She and I are one.

That time when she called early in the summer, it did worry me rather. After Granny died and Molly inherited both the flat in town and the summer house a little further south, on the coast, she hadn't called so often. It was as if it hadn't really dawned on her what had happened, that Granny was in fact gone, and that there were signs that fate had a plan for Molly to take Granny's place.

I've missed her lately. I was afraid that this new silence of hers had to do with me being Aksel's patient. That she was unable to divide her love between us, or was confused by the fact that he and I also had a relationship of sorts, if only that of trainer and pupil.

The model I was working on at that time, before the summer holidays, was of Granny's summer house down by the fjord. I was using modelling card, tacks, glue and other bits and pieces which I had asked the temp to buy in the DIY shop. I'd never been to the cottage, it's true, but I had heard so much about it over the years, both from Granny and from Molly, and of course I had seen photographs. I reckoned it must be possible to form a pretty accurate picture of how everything looked. I knew, for example, that the cottage was surrounded by a big garden overlooking the fjord, but that it was a bit of a walk down to the water. Rippling blue tissue paper arranged at one end of the desk, some distance from the model, represented the fjord. Next to the model I had taped a photograph of the house which Molly sent me years ago. The picture had been taken with the light behind the house.

I knew that the cottage had a bathing hut, but I had no picture of it. It sat right next to a little jetty, so I had been told. I thought: the fjord must be sparkling in the background.

But on the evening that Molly called I hadn't yet managed to build either the jetty or the bathing hut. The model was about as big as a medium-sized cardboard box, the sort removal companies use for transporting books. It was light-grey in colour, from the modelling card out of which I had constructed it. But the sun had, of course, already commenced its slow work of rendering it darker. The sun is incredibly patient. The strange thing is that it makes some things darker, while other things become lighter. I haven't yet been able to come up with any good explanation for this.

Molly must have known that she was Granny's closest heir, that a direct line now ran from Granny to her. I, on the other hand, must consider myself lucky that I was allowed to call her Granny. Molly's mother was an only child. She died when Molly was nineteen, and as far as I know there's never been a Grandpa in the picture. But one thing is to know something, another thing is to figure out what to do with that knowledge.

Granny was an institution, a constant in both Molly's life and mine; it was almost unthinkable that she could just be gone, the way death takes people away. And when the unthinkable happens, you need time to yourself, time to think, anyone can see that, I told myself. Molly isn't so used to thinking as I am, sitting here all day long and not able to stop myself thinking even if I wanted to. When Granny dies the person closest to her inherits not only the flat and the summer-house, they also inherit her place. The Granny place. And you have to know how to fill that place.

That's why Molly has become so distanced from me, I told myself firmly. If anyone should know what she's going through, it's me. Molly, too, is trying, though she doesn't know it, to understand what fate has in mind for her. No wonder she needs time to think! That's why I understand her so well; she's in exactly the same situation as me, we're both wondering how the things that are happening to us fit in with everything else. The only difference is that I have more time and more opportunity to study the matter in depth, and that I actually realise what I am doing.

It's even more essential for me to know what I am doing. What if one day I actually did come up with the answer to what fate wants with us, and didn't know what to do with my discovery? How would I get it to shine, like an instrument? Should I call the evening news and let myself be interviewed by some ignorant reporter clutching a quivering microphone, or set up my own website on the internet? There's a whole world of websites out there, run by people who believe they've found the answer to the question of fate. How could I make people see that what I had discovered was different?

Knowledge which you don't know how to use might as well be fly shit.

It had taken Molly a while to get round to installing a telephone and an internet connection in the summer house. But that evening when she finally called, all of the computer equipment she had invested in over the past few years was up and running. What a relief that was for me: I had already made an itty-bitty telephone and computer and added them to the model. I felt it was a good test for my fingers: the fine movement's not so good. I made them out of millboard which I cut to size with the scalpel. In my mind I hooked up these machines to the internet the second I heard Molly's voice on the phone: There. Now everything was as it should be. All the cables connected, and all the good that exists between Molly and me able to flow freely.

For some reason Granny had never put in a telephone at the summer-house. Maybe she didn't want it to be too easy to get in touch with her there. You had to write a letter. Lick the back of a stamp, stick it on the top right-hand corner of the envelope and pop it into a postbox. Have somebody take it from there to the summer-house for you. Somebody in uniform, employed by the state.

I was so happy to hear Molly's voice. All my worries that something had come between us were completely unfounded, I thought. She had just needed time to think, and she'd been busy getting things organised down there, of course. I smiled to myself, certain that, as with her studio here in town, she would soon set her stamp on that summer-house; it would end up as a repository for paint tins, chicken wire, coloured wools, boxes of buttons and ribbons, wooden planks, sheets of plywood, polystyrene, powdered dyes and large baskets full of cloth of every colour and quality. A stained couch, a radio and a Baby Belling. That's how she likes to live. Her brushes, all the unmatched glasses in which she keeps small, sharp objects. Molly doesn't drink from a glass; she drinks straight from the bottle, or from the tap.

I had already included quite a few of these details in the model, I had used all sorts of materials. It wasn't completely lifelike yet, though, there were a lot of things I didn't know about the place, and so couldn't put into the model. But I thought to myself: it's in flux.

We always know more than we know. It seems to me that sometimes it would be a good idea to make models of the future. After all, you have to have something to practise on. Things to come seem somehow more real that way. The future acquires dimension, and you can make little dolls to inhabit it. You can make these dolls look exactly like people you know, and endow them with a will. A direction. You can attach their limbs to garden canes and turn them into stick puppets, you can make them move around in a kind of dance. Bend towards one another, then away from one another. If you've done a good enough job with the garden canes you can even make them put their arms around one another. You can light the scene with a powerful spotlight, and leave them standing like that, wrapped in each other's arms for a long time. You can make this the end of the play, and the audience will think: thank heavens, a happy ending.

Here is something I've been thinking about, something I think has to do with fate:

Sometimes, when you sense something fateful lying waiting out there in the future, something which you know you will have to go through, you form a picture. You can see this picture as clear as clear can be, and then you hurl it ahead of you, into the future.

And it lies up ahead and waits on you, until you are ready to step into it.

Then, when you've stepped into the picture, everything depends on whether you are able to observe things around you with a keen eye. Look straight at them. Live within what is there.

I think this is what I learned on the day when I realised that Mum was going to leave us. I was only ten at the time, but I knew it was going to happen. Dad knew it too, I'm sure. He and I, we saw how it would be, and we knew that we couldn't argue with fate.

Mum had so much that was all her own, that had nothing to do with us: her writing, all the invitations to foreign countries, the lectures she gave, the interviews people wanted to do with her. She wasn't just ours, she belonged to her readers, she was everybody else's. Dad and I didn't deserve her, and even though I thought about it almost all the time, I never did discover what we could have done to merit keeping her to ourselves.

We never talked about it, but I think both Dad and I knew that we knew: Mum would lose patience with us, there would be so many other things pulling at her, she would meet people who would show her things Dad and I knew nothing about. She would want to share herself with all the others. Her books were translated into lots of languages, and the others out there weren't like us at all: it was hard to picture them. Their admiration for her was so much more potent than ours, we who only wanted the everyday side of her. There would be nothing we could do, and in the end she would disappear out of our lives, that was what I told myself back then. If we tried to grab hold of her we would find our hands snatching at thin air.

I needed to make a model of how the new life without Mum would look. But I was only ten, I didn't know how you did that sort of thing, how you prepared yourself for something disappearing. I was too young to be strong, and that made me far too vulnerable, my nights were filled with bad dreams, and these illusions seemed so lifelike: the images in my dreams had smells and sounds and colour and movement, they were even more real than the ones you can make with movable cardboard puppets fixed on to garden canes.

I think Dad may have had the same sort of dreams, although we never talked about it. I heard the loud, plaintive mutterings from the double bed at night. The light in the hall would be burning, I don't remember whether it was him or me who wanted it left on. Dad and I didn't talk to one another the way you have to talk in order to find out which one of you is actually afraid of the dark. I wanted to cry: listen to me! But back then I didn't realise that it was fate I was calling out to, not Dad. And I didn't know that it had been listening to me all along.

This new project of Molly's, the one she started on early this summer, which has its premiere this evening, is her biggest so far. She is in charge of the scenography and lighting for a staging of Strindberg's *A Dream Play* on the main stage of one of the city's biggest theatres. Naturally she's pretty excited about it. Molly's not the type to let it show when she's nervous or worried about a big job, but at such times she is more talkative, she smokes and drinks more than she usually does. Then I know she has got herself wound up and that it will take her a while to come down again. It all comes to a head on the evening of the premiere, of course. And there's nothing for it but to be patient. In all probability she won't come down to earth until tomorrow morning, when the premiere is over and the reviews are out. Which is fine by me.

I have a ticket for the premiere, I always get one. I've made myself thoroughly conversant with the script beforehand and have been considering some possible scenographic effects which I have suggested to her. No doubt, though, I'll find myself being surprised and moved. It happens every time. The stage sets which Molly creates are like worlds all of their own; her work has a unique stamp to it, one that defies imitation: a disturbingly brittle element which gives rise to images unlike anything ever seen before. Images one can step into, be surrounded by. It's really quite creepy.

I think to myself: our art teacher ought to have seen this, the one from fourth grade who gave her free play with a bottle of glue, some rolls of tinfoil and a pile of cardboard boxes while the rest of us had to get on with our potato printing. He saw the spark inside her back then, it only needed a little puff of breath in order to blossom into a flame and he didn't care what the rest of us thought when he was blowing on it. He wasn't very democratic, but he was good.

That art teacher had Molly's best interests at heart, and she was only a child then. It wasn't until she met Strøm, the photographer, and he began to blow on her, that it became dangerous. Strøm blew very hard on her flame, the way a fire extinguisher would do. And she flared up, gazing longingly at him. Then he took her face between his hands and turned it away from him; he forced her to open her eyes wide and look at something she did not want to know about, something ugly. Strøm believes that you have to be familiar with the ugly side of things if you are to create anything truthful. You have to look straight at it. I have heard him say this myself. But I was so young at the time, I didn't understand what he meant.

This evening, though, sitting there in the theatre, I might find myself thinking: he was right. Molly is familiar with the ugly side now, and it shows. It's not pleasant, but it does something to you.

She met Strøm and fell head over heels in love with him around the time when I first fell ill. He was older than her father, she was nineteen. So was I. Now she's a grown woman of thirty-six, now the flame inside her has become so clear that she no longer needs anyone to blow on it. I suppose she has learned to blow on it herself. Maybe it was Strøm who showed her how.

'Me too!' I say out loud to myself. 'I have a flame too! I blow on it myself. And I'm familiar with the ugly side, I discovered it for myself, I didn't need any man to show me.'

Both Molly and I know that I am the person behind some of her best ideas. I am always there for her – if, for example, she needs to discuss a point of interpretation in whatever play she happens to be working on, has practical problems that want solving, or needs help with research. More than once she has arranged for me to be credited in a theatre programme.

It works both ways. I provide her with viable ideas and lines of argument, and she brings my ideas to life for me. She is out in the world, making things happen, she experiences things for me: vibrant, exciting things. While I repay her by keeping alive the memory of who she once was, and show her what she can become. I am her mirror: no matter which way she turns, she sees herself.

I am as faithful as a dog.

She may do more than me, but I have much more time for comprehending things. I am the one who reads and keeps myself informed, and I am the one who poses the good questions.

Through the internet I have access to all the information in the world, it's simply a matter of knowing where to look. Of asking the right questions, coming up with the right key words. Only very rarely do I have to make a phone call or send a letter in order to find out something. Much of the material I have made use of in my fate project has been taken from my work on Molly's productions.

She, on the other hand, probably feels a kind of responsibility for making sure that I have something interesting to do. For as long as I am dependent on this wheelchair . . . I have, for example, never had an ordinary job.

Even so, I believe that I have gained an education and work experience of a sort, albeit indirectly, through Molly. Both when she was at the Academy and later, when she started studying scenography, she shared everything she learned with me. I got myself copies of all her set texts, she lent me the notes from the lectures she had attended and told me what assignments they had been given and when they had to be handed in. Actually it wasn't unusual for me have a go myself at one of her assignments, secretly, at home here in the flat. I felt a bit embarrassed about them in those days, felt almost as though I didn't really have a right to work on them, and I didn't feel that I could show them to anyone, not even to her. In a way this made me seem more pathetic than necessary, doing something like that, and I know it upset her to be reminded of the pathetic nature of my situation. Molly loves me like a sister.

I think I actually still have some of the little models I made when she was working on a college project on *The Seagull.* I tried out various scenographic devices before suggesting them to her, thus saving her, I'm sure, a lot of trial and error. It was while working on that project that I bought a video projector.

Since she started seeing Aksel, this rather complicated aspect of our relationship, my pathetic state and her strength, has become more marked. I suppose that's one of the reasons why I've been doing all I can lately to make myself less dependent on her and her projects. I have devised my own project now. I haven't said anything to her about it, it's good to have something I can keep all to myself.

My fate project would be pretty hard to explain anyway, even to Molly. I'm not sure that even *I* understand exactly what it entails. But it is giving me a life of my own. Not only that, but my legs have grown much stronger recently. I'm hoping that these two things are connected.

I had read Strindberg's *A Dream Play* before, of course, but I ordered a new copy over the internet in the spring when Molly told me that this was what she was going to be working on next. And I was really excited when I started reading the play again, there was so much there with which I could identify. I thought to myself: this is amazing! Why did I never think of it before? This play could almost have been written for me! The dream play is all about suffering, about stepping inside the images and becoming a witness to the sorrows of mankind.

I immediately had some ideas for the set designs which I decided to try out on Molly. A jetty! I thought. Of course, she should set the whole thing on a jetty. The closeness of the sea, the rolling waves underneath, the fact that everything is flowing, the meeting of land and sea, life buoys, the risk of falling into the water and drowning . . . It would be Strindberg distilled. I was sitting at my desk when this thought struck me and my eye fell on the model of the summer house. Of course. I almost had to laugh. The jetty! It's incredible how chance sometimes works in one's favour. I was actually just about to start making the model of the jetty at the summer house. I would have to get hold of a picture of it.

It's as I say: we know more than we know.

I groped around on the desk for the scissors. They were big and solid, they lay heavy and cold in my palm, it took a while for my hand to warm them up. It occurred to me that I used these scissors far too seldom, I'd been lavishing too much attention on the scalpel. The scissors may be bigger and less precise than the scalpel when it comes to the tiny details, but once you've warmed them up they seem to slice through the cardboard of their own accord. It's almost a pity to put them down again.

Six months back I perceived that fate would steer events in the following direction: it had already arranged for Aksel and Molly to meet in my bathroom. Events were now going to speed up as they always do once fate takes a hand. There was little I could do to influence them. I saw how Aksel would gravitate more and more frantically towards Molly because of her mysterious projects, warm generosity and great capacity for forgetting herself. She had something he needed. While she, on the other hand, would be flattered to begin with, but would pretty soon tire of him due to what she would mistakenly regard as his rather clingy, labrador-like love. And so she would leave him before she had learned what he had to teach her, only instantly to reproach herself for not managing to hang on long enough to absorb that particular lesson. It's incredible how dead-set Molly is on sticking to her theories, or rather: the theories she thinks she has come up with, but which in essence actually stem from Granny. Molly doesn't really do any thinking herself, she leaves that work to others.

I felt sorry for Aksel. I thought of how sad he would be when she ended it and left him for all the other things that made calls on her. This twist of fate would render him smaller, not bigger, I thought. He would shrink so much that he would be too small for his children. A father has to be big. He has to make sure that the good forces in the world are given . . . force.

But Aksel was a loving, caring Dad, that wasn't hard to see. He lived and breathed through his children. Nor did it take any great stretch of the imagination to perceive that his life couldn't be all that easy either, like a game of patience that doesn't always work out. I realised early on that he needed someone to confide in, someone who could give him advice and take a slightly more objective view of his life, give him suggestions as to how to lay out his cards. Such a role would fit me like the softest glove, I thought, that's just the job for someone like me. I'm a good listener, and a better tactician than most.

He was very frank when it came to talking about himself and it was almost always the children he told me about when we were working out on the green training mat. I often got that strange trembling in my lips when the conversation came round to Eilif and Ine. I felt as though the stories about them wanted something of me.

Sometimes, after he had gone, I would slump down on to the mat for a bit of a cry. A wet little pool of longing would pour out of me and soak into the green, honeycombed foam-rubber. This can't possible be a coincidence, I told myself. These children. There may well be a connection here.

I had learned that Eilif was a dependable, rather sensitive ten-year-old, always with a baseball cap on his head, tall and slim and blond. Ine was passionate and stubborn, a six-year-old sylph, soon to be seven, she did ballet and had her mother's looks. Aksel had been divorced from the children's mother for almost five years, but there was nothing to indicate that they didn't get along. On the contrary, they still seemed to be close: they had the keys to each other's houses and celebrated Christmas and birthdays together. On birthdays Aksel went over there early in the morning with a flask of cocoa and a tray of cake, he let himself in and woke them, lit candles and sang to them. It wasn't hard to imagine.

He had shown me pictures of the children. Last year this was, just before Christmas; he had been to collect some photos from developing and asked me to help him pick one to use as a Christmas card. We went through them so quickly, I didn't have a chance to study the photographs properly, but I did manage to form some impression of them. My hands were shaking slightly, I suggested that he use a snap from last year's summer holiday in which the children were sitting in a boat, wearing sunglasses and staring solemly at the camera. Eilif was wearing an orange baseball cap.

'That picture has character,' I told him.

But whatever Aksel thought or felt about Molly, or anything else to do with his love life, he kept to himself. This was probably a sign of his particular brand of tactfulness, a tactfulness which I fancy is unique to men. Luckily I am pretty good at putting two and two together, and not easily fooled. You cannot allow yourself to be fooled when you're in my situation. I knew, of course, that he was hopelessly in love with Molly. I knew it before he knew it himself. I only had to take one look in the mirror that day in the bathroom.

Sometimes he would be worried about the kids. He gave a lot of thought to how to arrange things so that they would be affected as little as possible by the fact that he and their mother lived apart. For example, he wanted it to be up to them, as far as was feasible, to say when they wanted to stay with him and when they wanted to be with their mother. He and his ex-wife lived very close to one another and had, as far as I knew, joint custody. Eventually he stopped calling her 'my ex-wife' and started using her name in my presence as if it were the most natural thing in the world: Monika. Her name is Monika. He kind of smiled when he said it, as if it reminded him of something nice.

He has to make sure that it's as simple as possible for the children, I thought to myself. He ought to buy them a mobile phone. Then they can easily get in touch with him or Monika if they should change their minds about which of their parents they want to go home to after school; that would be the simplest thing for them.

He was a bit taken aback by this idea to begin with, he felt the kids were too young to have charge of a mobile phone, and he had read that the radiation from these phones was particularly harmful to children. But I had done a lot of research on the internet, I told him there was no need to worry, he could just buy an earpiece. And I reminded him that Eilif was getting to be a big boy now, it was only natural that he should be in charge of it. A mobile phone would give a child a greater sense of freedom, I said. And it would ensure that both Aksel and Monika would always be within reach, only the touch of a button away. The mobile phone would be a means of keeping the family together. I felt that I presented my case well: skilfully, but with due delicacy. I suppose you could say I was the children's advocate, although they didn't know it.

And in the end he did, in fact, buy them a mobile phone. Not one of the cheapest models, which I had advised him to get, it's true, but one with a built-in camera so that they could also send him pictures. Even better, I thought happily.

They were given the mobile for Christmas. When he came back to work after New Year he told me that they had been absolutely thrilled. Eilif had spent the whole of Christmas Eve reading the instructions for use, and by Christmas Day Aksel had received the first picture of Ine on his own mobile, taken and sent by Eilif.

Everything had turned out as I had imagined, sitting at home in my flat on Christmas Eve, thinking about that little family. Better, almost. I wished Eilif could have sent that picture of Ine to me, too. I could have transferred it to the computer and enlarged it, I could have projected it on to the wall and made something out of it; that would have been a nice thing to do on Christmas Eve.

I immediately started making plans for how the children could use the camera.

Just before fate arranged for Molly to burst into my bathroom and meet Aksel for the first time, I had been thinking of suggesting that he bring the children here one day. We could have found something nice to do together, played a game maybe. I had bought The Hunt for the Lost Diamond, a game I remember from my own childhood. Mum and I played it once on a weekend in the country, sitting at a little folding table one rainy day. We must have played for hours, Mum got really caught up in that game.

And afterwards I could surprise them by inviting all three of them out to dinner at a restaurant. So many good restaurants have now been adapted to accommodate wheelchair users, they're possibly not aware of that, I thought.

But it was not to be.

Molly knows nothing about children. She's just a child herself, with a child's burning curiosity and blatant self-centredness. A warm and happy self-centredness, a self-centredness that makes you want to wag your tail at it, like a dog.

The plan, as far as I could tell from what Molly had told me the last time she called before the long silence earlier in the summer, was that she and Aksel were going to play their little lovebird game for two weeks at the summer house while Eilif and Ine were on holiday in Italy with their mother. After that Aksel was going to take the children camping while Molly got down to some serious work on the dream play.

At the most I gave them those first two weeks of billing and cooing before the cracks started appearing in their relationship. I envisaged, for instance, how Aksel's big, faithful heart would begin very early on to whimper plaintively at what to him would seem like Molly's inattentiveness. I hoped for their sake that they would be able to enjoy their time at the summer house, anything else would be almost too awful to contemplate.

But clearly fate had other plans: suddenly, just before the start of the children's summer holidays, Monika became seriously ill. Or at least, it can't have been that sudden, since the tests showed cervical cancer at an advanced stage, but neither Molly nor I had heard anything about her being ill before that. They had to operate right away, and they wouldn't know until they did the operation exactly how things looked inside this, by Molly's lights, peripheral ex-wife's abdomen, and what the prognosis was.

Monika was rushed into hospital: all of this I had from the temp. The children were taken out of school a week before the end of term, there was no one in the family who could look after them, their surviving grandparents were either too frail or were convalescing in Spain, all their other relatives were scattered across the country and had children of their own who were still in school.

That was how things stood on the evening when, for the first time in weeks, Molly called and I was in bed, trying to keep myself awake by staring at the sun outside the window.

As usual she came straight to the point. Molly has never been one for beating about the bush. There was an awful lot of noise in the background, it was difficult to hear what she was saying.

'Agnes,' she said, then came something I didn't catch: '. . . it's so difficult to . . . I don't know what . . . maybe I should . . . he'll have to . . . men are so . . .'

'What did you say, love?' I said. 'Could you switch off whatever it is that's buzzing in the background, it's so hard to hear what you're saying.'

'What?'

'Could you turn off whatever it is that's making such a racket!'

I heard her slam the receiver down on the tabletop and walk over to the other side of the room. The buzzing sounded as if it was coming from a bandsaw, but that couldn't be right, surely? She didn't have a bandsaw at the summer house, or at least I hadn't put any such thing in the model I was making. Eventually the noise stopped and I heard her feet coming back across the floor to the phone.

'Is that better?'

'Much better,' I said. 'Is that a bandsaw you've got there?'

'Yes, actually,' she said crisply. 'I borrowed one from the theatre, I need it for cutting out some chipboard.'

'Have you started work on the dream play already?'

'Yes, of course. Well, the holiday with Aksel didn't come to anything, did it?'

'I know, I heard about his ex-wife, the temp told me. It's so good to hear your voice again. What was it you were trying to say to me before?'

She dived in:

'Oh, men, they're so unpredictable. Aksel has asked me to have the children here while Monika's in hospital.'

'Oh!' I said. It came out like a little gasp.

'He wants to be with her before and after the operation, he says. I don't know what to think. You'll have to help me think, Agnes.'

I let myself become still and empty for a second.

'Hello? Are you there?' Molly said.

'I'm here,' I said.

'I'm so confused.'

'Look,' I said, 'Aksel's a nurse, right? It's only natural that he would want to tend her himself – after all, she is the mother of his children. It's most certainly in his own interest for her to get well again as quickly as possible. Have you any idea what sort of time frame we're talking about?'

'I've no idea. They're waiting for some surgeon to return from holiday.'

'It must be pretty serious then.'

'I'm sure it is. But I still don't know whether I'm happy about it, him wanting to be with her and asking me to look after the kids. As if she was his wife and I was his next of kin. And it's not that I don't love Aksel, because I do.'

'Of course you do.'

'You don't sound all that convinced.'

'Well, it doesn't really matter what I think or feel about this, does it, if Aksel has already asked you to look after his kids and things are as bad as you say,' I replied. I could hear by my voice that I had struck just the right, matter-of-fact tone. It rather surprised me.

'I knew you would say that.'

'Well if you knew what I would say, why did you call to ask me about it?'

'You don't have to be so nippy. You know how I am.'

'Of course. I know how you are.'

'And you know I don't know the first thing about children.'

'You can learn.'

'So you think I was right to say yes to having them here?'

I had to pause for a moment again.

'So you've already agreed.'

'Yes, but now I'm wondering whether it was a stupid thing to do.'

'I think you said the right thing,' I said, trying to sound sincere. 'I don't think you had any choice.'

I could hear her sitting there quietly, absorbing what I had said. I rested the hand holding the receiver on the duvet for a moment. My arms get so tired sometimes, it's a result of my illness. But I raised it quickly to my ear again when I heard that she was still talking. Her voice came to me from a long way off; suddenly it felt as though she was in another country.

'You're right,' she said. 'I don't have any choice. But it still doesn't feel right.'

'What doesn't feel right?'

'Well, I mean it's not his children I want. It's Aksel.'

'I know,' I said. 'But this is a package deal, you knew that when you got involved with him. He's a man with two children, there's nothing you can do about that. And he has already asked you to look after them for the summer, and you've said you will.'

My words may have sounded a bit stilted, but I hadn't spoken to anyone except the temp the whole day. I cleared my throat, tried to adjust to Molly's inordinately slow, clear speech rhythms.

'I know, but it's not what I had planned!' she wailed.

'Nothing ever turns out the way we've planned,' I said. 'Or, only for neurotics, and you're not what I'd call a neurotic, are you?'

'Don't joke, I'm in no mood for laughing. So you think I just have to accept whatever comes along?'

'The question is whether you have any choice.'

'You're saying it's my lot in life to take on Aksel's children?'

I gave a little start. I was surprised to hear her talking about fate, I'd never heard her speaking in such terms before. I guard myself against saying too much about fate when I'm talking to Molly. I have the feeling that it only annoys her.

'I didn't say that,' I said. 'I'm only saying that you don't have a choice because you're already involved with him. Sometimes one thing leads to another, you know. With love comes responsibility.'

'Okay, I've said they can come,' she said. 'But do I have to like them? I often find it hard to like people. You know that.'

'I'm not saying you won't have to like them,' I said them. 'Or at least try your very best.'

'You mean I'll have to love them? As if they were my own? But what if they're insufferable?'

'It might not be as hard as you think. I don't see them being insufferable.'

I felt around on the bedside table, found my notebook and leafed through it until I came to the pages on which I had tried to draw Eilif and Ine. Not bad portraits, for all that they'd been drawn from memory, copied from the pictures Aksel had shown me.

'I'm sure they'll be very nice,' I said.

'But that's not the point. I don't know them. Aksel hardly ever talks about them. Has he said anything to you?'

I felt a little stab of joy.

'Not much,' I said.

One of the most important questions to which I am trying to find an answer in my fate project is this: can you be a witness to fate when it has its attention directed at you personally? Observe it in the act, as it were?

I think you might at least have some inkling of it. You might, for example, experience it as a trembling of the lips, or a faint burning of the cheeks. You look around, at the other people who are nearby and are, therefore, also part of what fate is bringing about and you think to yourself: I wonder if they realise what is going on? Are their lips trembling too?

That's when it's good to have a notebook on you. You have to have the eyes to see, and make notes as quickly and accurately as possible when something crucial and fateful has occurred. And preferably as it is actually occurring, of course, although in practice this can be tricky: fumbling with pen and paper in all sorts of situations where that sort of thing doesn't seem appropriate. It makes you feel so awkward.

You have to have a little patience, with yourself and with others. It's hard work being a witness, it requires a sort of absolute awareness: in order to do it you have to clarify your thoughts, much the way you would clarify butter. You have to strain off all the impurities. Such things take time, and there are so many things to beware of, it's so easy to slide back into the old, cloudy way of thinking.

The old way of thinking has these sort of tentacles, all sticky with scum, that try to wrap themselves around you, it's rather sinister. Strindberg knew something of this – that is what I thought, the first time I read *A Dream Play*.

The first time I realised that I had the ability to let the impurities sink to the bottom, like sediment, and render myself so clear and sharp that I would be able to see what was going to happen was in the days before Mum left Dad and me. There was something about the atmosphere in the house, the muffled sounds of doors being carefully closed, which was out of all proportion to the terrible dreams I had at night. Nobody said anything, but I knew just the same.

I remember one morning when I had made myself hard and clear, so that I could look straight at what was happening. I sat on the bed in my room and listened to my own breathing, the almost soundless hissing in my nostrils, the passage through the one nostril a little wider than the other. Dad was at the Institute, as usual, and Mum was in her study, working. From the rhythmic tapping of her fingers on the typewriter keys I knew that it would be a long time before she emerged from there: she was on to something, something that lots of people would be able to read.

I tiptoed into their bedroom. It was cool in there, they always kept the window open. I shivered. Her dressing-gown was hanging on a hook on the wall next to the bed. I stood quite still in the centre of the room. Oh, how I longed to press my face against that pale silk, but I didn't do it. I knew what was going to happen. That dressing-gown wouldn't be hanging there for much longer.

I was a breathing creature, I shut my eyes and saw how, in only a few months' time, Mum would be somewhere else and not with us; how she was out travelling, how she came back to her new flat in a strange city after a long trip abroad. I saw quite clearly the way her suitcase still stood in the hall of the new flat, all she had unpacked was two bottles of wine, a bar of Swiss chocolate, a jar of olives and a big, round cheese from the tax-free shop. That was what she always brought home for Dad and me when she had been abroad, but this time she had brought these things home for some other people, people I didn't know.

I pictured how it was only when she walked through the door of the flat that it dawned on her how long she had been away, but that she thought it was lovely to be home again at last. Mum really enjoyed her own company. In her handbag she had a bundle of press cuttings, there were several pictures of her, and interviews which she hadn't bothered to read. She wandered over to a corner cabinet, opened it and took out a wine glass which she filled with red wine from one of the bottles. Then she sank down on to the sofa, her fingers curled around the cool glass. It struck her that she should have gone through to the kitchen and found something to put the olives in, but she couldn't be bothered.

In my mind I saw how it was only after the telephone had rung several times that she got up slowly from the sofa, put her glass down on the table and picked up the receiver.

'Hi,' she said, to a man who was not Dad. 'Yes, that's me home now. The plane was a little bit delayed, but otherwise everything went fine. I'm exhausted. Are you coming over?'

I took a deep breath, I was a ten-year-old girl who kept her eyes shut and walked backwards out of Mum and Dad's bedroom. I backed all the way down the hallway, right into the bathroom. Only then did I come to myself again with a little jolt. I opened my eyes wide, pulled off all my clothes and got out my toothbrush.

I gave my teeth a good, stiff brushing, the strong taste of peppermint washed my mouth clean, turning it into an empty cavern in which my breath could flit about.

It wasn't until after I had filled years of notebooks with observations on the different aspects of fate that it began to dawn on me: to be a witness, that is my project. To be a witness to suffering and, as a natural consequence, to the workings of fate. I have come to the conclusion that fate and suffering are like twins, the Katzenjammer twins of the universe, if you like: you never see one without the other. In not one cartoon frame in the slow turning of the universe will you find Hans without Fritz! No fate without suffering. No suffering without fate. This is one of the conclusions I have so far reached.

And to understand the one twin is, it goes without saying, to understand the other. Fate and suffering, suffering and fate. It doesn't matter what end you start at, with Hans or with Fritz. But for practical purposes one has to make a choice, and for me it was only natural that suffering should come first. If I had to be struck by this illness then the least I could do was to speak with the suffering by being a witness to it, making notes about it, ensuring that it felt it was being heard, that it was not struggling in vain. Because suffering is also going somewhere, I've been pretty certain about that for some time. Suffering needs to know that it is understood, so that it can let go and move on, give the good forces a chance. If suffering doesn't feel that it is being heard, it has to resort to disasters, and we all know what happens then.

My illness has seen to it that I must sit here with all this time on my hands, but I also have a great fund of experience which, for a long time, I did not know how to use: the exhaustion, the pain, the worry, Dad's pale-faced anxiety, all the tests, the bleak prospects, a host of different doctors, the reports, all the pills. This was my world, but I did not grasp the significance of it. It was, after all, so personal, so depressing.

Only now, looking back on it, can I see that my whole life up to this point has been a preparation for the fate project. The new electronic world, affording access at the touch of a few keys to everything that is going on all around the globe, has also enabled me to elevate this project from the individual plane on to the universal one, in a way hitherto unseen in the history of mankind. All information is out there, available to everyone who has the strength to bear witness. At this point in history we have been given a unique opportunity to uncover the greater contexts, and I have more time to spend on this than most. I mean, I don't have to work in order to earn a living, and since Dad died I have no family to look after. I am, for example, much better off than Strindberg was for most of his life. Strindberg had his troubles; I wouldn't be surprised if he had the odd little cry too, lying in his austere bed in the flat in Drottninggatan.

The biggest challenge lies not, therefore, in gaining access to information, or finding time to study it, come to that. The challenge lies, rather, in being a witness to suffering with one's absolute awareness. Looking straight at it, opening one's eyes, daring to take it all in. That is why I set up the projector. It allows me to surround myself with pictures from the outside world, let them glide over my own body; to discover whether, by so doing, they might be able to seep into me.

Over the years I have trained my feeling for fate to such a pitch that I can now make notes in my notebooks only minutes after certain events have taken place. My aim is for the notes to become redundant, for everything to be apprehended and acknowledged even as it is happening. For me to be able to stare straight at the ugliness. It might seem like a Utopian dream, but you have to have something to strive for: to illuminate fate.

Now that I have honed this awareness of the true nature of my undertaking, my life seems to have taken a new and more imperative turn. Everything seems to be moving at a greater rate. I think suffering has understood that I want to speak with it, and it has begun to address itself to me more directly. Maybe it thinks the two of us ought to have one last, serious talk before it lets go of my body and moves on.

And if Hans is there, then Fritz can't be far away, I tell myself. If I can get a grip on suffering, fate will be there right behind it, like two fish on the same hook. The second one has latched on to the first and breaks out of the water and into view, glittering and wriggling as I reel in the line.

The new life has already begun.

A gleaming instrument on which one can play. *Like the first morning.*

'I wish you were here to help me, Agnes.' Molly's voice had become very small, and she had forgotten all about speaking clearly, or maybe she was holding the receiver away from her mouth a bit, I don't know. 'It's hard to know how to act with children,' she went on. 'They seem so . . . unpredictable.'

You're the childish one, dear, I thought to myself, but I said:

'Just be yourself, love. It's always the best way.'

'Couldn't you come down?'

'Well, that might be a bit difficult. I mean, it strikes me that your summer house isn't really designed for somebody in a wheelchair, and I don't have a car.'

'But maybe we could figure something out? I could come and get you. What would you actually need? A lift?'

'No, not a lift,' I say. 'But I would need a ramp, so I could get into the house in the wheelchair unaided. Otherwise, you would have to haul me up the steps like a kid in a pram.'

'I wouldn't mind doing that!'

'Don't be silly. Anyway, apart from the ramp, the doorways would obviously have to be wide enough for me to get through them in the chair.'

Molly thought they were wide enough. She offered to get out her rule and measure them there and then; I could picture how it had to be there already, stuffed into her overall pocket, she always has it handy when she's working.

She hung up with a decisive click, I lay back in bed and shut my eyes. In my mind's eye I saw her whipping the rule briskly out of the tattered pocket, opening it out and taking long, carpenter strides from door to door on the ground floor of the summer house, measuring them. It wasn't hard to imagine what the house looked like, after all I had just been working on the model, cutting out all the doorways. And it is never hard to picture

Molly: her short, tousled hair, her small, efficient hands, the tattered, white overall covered in splotches of indeterminable origin. Those glowing eyes, which often look as though they are peering, especially when she is busy building something, as she almost always is.

The house: the old-fashioned kitchen with the low benches and the deep, dark cupboards, the sort they used to make in the Twenties, as if folk had longer arms back then and better vision, or maybe were simply more used to feeling their way. The tall, mullioned windows. The larder. The two big living-rooms. The double doors on to the large, covered terrace. The steps down to the lovely garden, the white picket fence. The flagpole at the bottom of the gravel path.

I breathed in deeply and slowly, the way Aksel has taught me, and tried to calm down, I could tell that this conversation had taken its toll on me. A rock, I told myself. I am a rock of tranquillity.

It was a only few minutes before Molly called back.

'Okay, I've measured all the doors on the ground floor and I was right, they are all wide enough for a wheelchair,' she said. 'I can build a wheelchair ramp for the front steps in an afternoon. So I don't see what the problem is. I can come and pick you up anytime.'

'Hold on a minute,' I said. 'Not so fast. There's also the bathroom. The bathroom's a problem.'

'How come?' she asked shortly. I could tell by her voice that as far as she was concerned I was already there with her. The ramp was already built, she had formed a mental picture of it. To Molly, thought and action are almost the same thing.

'I'll bet there isn't room for the wheelchair next to the toilet,' I said.

She was quiet for a moment.

'I hadn't thought of that.'

'No, exactly.'

'Yes, I suppose the bathroom is kind of small.'

'Well, we all have to go to the loo every now and again, even invalids like me.'

'So what do you do when you visit other people?'

'I never go any place where there isn't space in the bathroom for a wheelchair,' I said. 'I thought you knew that.'

'What about a potty? I could get you a potty. Or no! I've got it! A commode!'

I shuddered.

'A potty is quite out of the question,' I said. 'I don't have the strength or the balance for sitting on a potty. And commodes are so un-sexy. I've never used a commode in my life.'

'You ought to be a bit more adventurous!'

'Oh, honestly! No, I won't discuss it.'

'I could use the commode too,' Molly said eagerly. 'Everybody in the house could use the commode! Me, you, Eilif, Ine! Aksel, if he comes to see us! We could tape down the lid of the proper toilet, then we'd have no choice! The commode'll be a big hit!'

'Oh, come on!'

'But why not? Actually I think it would be fun to use a commode for a while, I might just buy one anyway.'

'Thanks,' I said drily. 'It's a nice thought, but I don't think it will be necessary.'

'Oh, for heaven's sake, you never get excited about anything! Think about it. You just have to say the word.'

'I don't need to think about it.'

'I don't think you have any right to let a commode come between us just now. I need you here.'

'I told you, a commode is quite out of the question.'

'Okay, that's that decided,' she said, as if the conversation was already finished. 'I'll get hold of a commode, then all that's needed is the ramp, and that'll take no time.'

Sometimes there's just no getting through to her. There's little point in trying. I could hear that she had gone back to hammering away at something or other, it was hard to say what, small tacks being driven into a board covered in felt, perhaps.

'I know you're good at making things,' I said. 'But right now you really should be thinking mainly about the children. It might be that you need to do a bit of tidying up, what do I know? When do they arrive?'

'Don't know. Tomorrow, maybe. Aksel is so brusque on the phone, he seems a bit distracted. I'm not altogether certain that he's as finished with Monika as he says he is.'

'Now don't nag him,' I said. 'He's got enough on his plate right now.'

'I never nag.'

'No, of course you don't. And I'll help you with the children. Let's keep in touch by phone for the time being. Call me right away if there's anything you're uncertain about, and be sure to tell me everything they get up to. I'm really quite good with children.'

I had nothing on which to base this last statement, but it felt right to mention it anyway.

Neither of us hung up. The conversation was not finished, we just didn't quite know what to say next.

'I bought a hammock yesterday,' she suddenly burst out. 'I forgot to tell you.'

I stiffened slightly again. A hammock? I hadn't put any hammock into the model of the summer house.

'A hammock's a great idea!' I cried, trying to sound enthusiastic.

'Do you think so? I didn't know what sort of preparations to make, to show them that they were welcome. A hammock was the only thing I could think of.'

'It seems to me that, strictly speaking, they're not very welcome.'

'Oh, I don't know, Agnes. It's all been so sudden. And it's just occurred to me that they won't know I bought the hammock for them coming. I mean, it's hanging there, but I don't know whether to say that I bought it for them.'

'No, I can see that,' I said. 'But you didn't buy it just for them, did you?'

'Not just them, maybe, but mainly because they were coming. Anybody who wants to can use it. I'm planning on using it myself, once they've gone. And you can use it when you come down.'

'Has Aksel said any more about how long they'll have to stay with you?'

'He's not sure. I suppose it depends on what they say about Monika after the operation. Oh, and he's given them a mobile phone.'

I nodded at the receiver and it was almost as if she had heard the nod.

'Did you know about that?' she asked, surprised.

'Mmm.'

'Did Aksel tell you?'

'I don't really remember. He must have mentioned it in passing.'

'Oh? You said he didn't tell you much about them.'

'No, not much. Like I said, only little things like that. I suppose he just wants to keep in touch with them, maybe he feels easier in his mind, knowing that they have their own phone.'

'But I don't see why they couldn't just use the phone here in the house,' she said.

'He probably didn't know you had one, I expect you forgot to tell him you'd had a phone put in.'

'Maybe I did. Reception for mobiles isn't great out here, I have trouble getting my own mobile to work.'

'I know,' I said. 'That's why I haven't heard from you for so long, isn't it? Your mobile wouldn't work, you had to wait until you could get a phone put in.'

I didn't give her time to answer. 'The children will work something out, don't you worry,' I went on quickly. 'They'll find a spot where they can get a signal, you'll see. Kids know about these things.'

*

But I knew we weren't talking about the children and the mobile. The real point of the conversation was bound to come up soon now. It was time. I simply hadn't been able to bring myself to admit what I already knew: that a fateful moment was approaching. We can't always bring ourselves to know what we know.

'I'm pregnant,' said Molly.

And even though I knew it had to come, I felt a fuse blow in my brain at that moment. Everything went black and I had to struggle to get the emergency generator going. Breathe, I told myself. First you take a good, deep breath, and then you think of something nice. There's nothing to be afraid of. Form a picture!

Gradually the light came back to my brain and it was ready to be filled with pictures. I saw myself standing on a stage. Before me was a piano. A-ha, I thought. Looks like I'm going to play something. That's okay. I play the piano very well!

I saw myself swivel round to look at the other people in the place, because I'm not alone, I thought, there are lots of other people here, they are just waiting for me to play for them. But I am dazzled by the glare of the spotlights that are turned on me, so I can't make out anything but the outlines of them.

They're all there. All the people who care about me, only I can't see them clearly because of the light. The best thing would be for me to start playing right away. I close my eyes just for a second, then I take out my music, set it on the stand on the piano, run two fingers down the centre of the book to make quite sure that the pages will stay put and not be flipped over at the wrong moment by an imperceptible draught running through the auditorium. No tiny whirlwind, no ripple of air, I thought. Nothing like that will be allowed to disrupt things.

Then I make myself comfortable on the piano stool, I continued feverishly. I'm not the slightest bit nervous. My spine is as supple as a snake rising into the air and my shoulders are relaxed. I take two long, deep breaths. Then I lift both my hands at once, hold them in the air for a second before bringing them gently down on to the keys in the first, soft attack, like falling rain.

Arabesque! I play an arabesque by Debussy. The one Granny used to play.

And from then on I simply let it flow. Am aware of nothing else until I hear the little sigh from the people who have been listening. Hear them clapping at my back, as one body.

Applause.

I must have been quiet for a very long time. I was wrenched back into the real world by Molly shouting down the phone. The sound of her voice was hard and sharp, it hurt my eardrums.

'Agnes!' she was shouting. 'Are you there? Is everything okay?'

'Of course everything's okay. I just blanked out for a moment.'

'Blanked out? Have you being doing that a lot recently? Have you spoken to the doctor?'

'Certainly not,' I said. 'It's nothing to worry about, it hardly ever happens. I'm just a bit tired, it's been a hard day, I've had so much to think about.'

'Are you sure? Do you want me to come up? Or call somebody who can look in on you? The temp?'

'I'm not having any temp coming to look in on me,' I said. 'Go on, dear. What was it you were saying?'

'I'm pregnant,' said Molly.

'By Aksel?'

'Wrong question. I only sleep with one man at a time. You know that.'

'Sorry.'

'Don't apologise.'

'No, pet. It was just so unexpected.'

There was silence between us again.

'Have you told Aksel?' I asked at length.

'No. Well, I've only just told you, haven't I?'

'Why not?'

'Because. Oh, God, nothing's gone the way I planned. I was going to tell him now, once we were both on holiday. When we had a bit of peace and quiet. I felt he would need time to think. But then Monika got sick. Not exactly the right time to break it to him, eh? And I don't even know whether I'm going to keep the baby.'

'But why didn't you tell me?'

She didn't answer.

So that was why she'd made such a big thing of having Aksel's children to stay. She was trying to imagine herself as a mother. That was what she was doing.

I felt bad about the fact that she hadn't told me earlier, but to some extent I did understand her. She knew I could never have children, she probably didn't want to remind me of that fact. The pills that I have to take make pregnancy an impossibility, and without my pills I am nothing. And besides: who would I have a baby with? Aksel is the only man who comes here.

The problem is, of course, that we're usually so wrapped up in ourselves and our own little lives that we see neither Hans nor Fritz, neither suffering or fate. We're incapable of looking straight at things as they really are; we know, but don't want to know that we know. We yearn to be insensible.

The set ideas creep in on us gradually along with mother's milk, with our schooling, with our friends' tastes and opinions, with something we heard someone say, with what we read in the papers. Set ideas are like sediment, they render us sluggish, unclear, we go around as if in a deep sleep. We don't have the strength to wake up, open our eyes and look straight at things. Set ideas are like a veil before our eyes. Or something like that.

That is how it looks if you allow yourself to take the gloomy view. And yet it is important not to lose heart, nor to be too hard on oneself. In spite of everything, I can think of a number of situations in my life in which I have looked straight at things, been on the alert when fate made itself known.

Examples: that time in Mum's and Dad's bedroom when I realised that Dad and I were going to find ourselves alone. And some years later in Granny's bathroom, when I was nineteen and understood that I was going to become helpless, that my body was eventually going to stop obeying me. That its aims were different from mine. On such occasions I actually felt a little flutter inside: like a fishtail, which gave me to understand that something was about to happen, something important. Not good, but important. A faint glimpse of Hans down there on the end of the line and, right behind him, all silvery and wriggling: Fritz.

Alone, helpless. At the mercy of others. That is what fate shows you that you are.

*

I've just remembered one other incident. It occurred only a few weeks before the episode in Granny's bathroom, during a conversation which Molly and I had in her room at her parents' house. Looking back on it I can see that fate laid out most of the cards in both Molly's game of patience and my own during those weeks, when we were young and glossy with barely a scratch on us. She was head over heels in love with that devilish photographer, Strøm, at the time, and I was filled with despair, although I didn't really know why. I let Molly down then. I let her down by allowing her to do something she would regret, and I did so even though I knew what would happen. I simply knew. And by not stopping her I helped to shape fate.

I should have stopped her. We are not only responsible for our actions. We are also responsible for the actions we do not take.

I knew back then that suffering was endeavouring to speak to both Molly and me, that Strøm would hurt her, that that might even be why she had been so strongly attracted to him. I knew also that this would have the most terrible consequences, and that because of these consequences I would be left even more alone than I had been. I knew, but I did not want to know that I knew. I pretended to be blind. Or asleep.

But it's strange. As I sit here now, feeling the early autumn sun warm on my face through the open window, everything to do with the past seems hazy, almost unreal. As if the past did not exist, as if the things I am thinking about never were. As if there is only the present. As if I could recreate the past, if I wanted.

I wish I had video recordings of the episodes of which I am thinking. Then I could rewind them to those precise moments and study them in slow motion: make them part of the present. Bring them here. Open my eyes wide.

That evening earlier in the summer when Molly and I were on the phone and she told me she was pregnant: the conversation spluttered into life again. It wasn't easy for us to talk about this business with Aksel, but we had no choice, it was a serious state of affairs, that I knew; it required both of us to step outside of ourselves and try to look at the big picture, at the situation as a whole.

But I don't think Molly tried hard enough. I must have given her a fright when that fuse blew inside my head, it seemed like she was now going to pretend that the subject of her pregnancy had never been mentioned between us. As if she wanted to patch things up between us, rewind and start again.

I was still finding it hard to breathe.

'It's not exactly normal for a divorced man to choose to spend his holiday with his ex-wife,' she said. 'Is it? She can't be that ill.'

'She must be,' I said. I could hear how heavily I was breathing. 'As I understand it she has to be operated on as soon as possible, and no one knows what they will find or how things will go until they open her up.'

'Yes, yes. You know so much more about the body than I do.'

'You can say that again,' I retorted.

There was an odd lump in my throat, I swallowed it, took another deep breath and took charge. I advised her to give Aksel her full support, press his children to her bosom like a warm, substitute Mum and accept without question that he was worried about Monika, and indeed genuinely fond of her.

All at once Molly became very busy; the muffled hammering speeded up. There had to be felt there somewhere, and a very small hammer.

'Don't be mad at me,' she said. 'It's just that I'm so confused. I'll have to get this place tidied up a bit, I can't have it looking like this if two children are going to be staying here. You have a good night.'

There was silence between us for a moment. The hammering stopped. But neither of us hung up.

'Are you feeling better now?' she said softly in that tender way she has, the way she talks to me when I know she really means what she's saying.

'Much better,' I said. 'But I think I'm going to put my head down shortly. I'm worn out.'

'I'm sure you must be,' said Molly. 'Well, goodnight Agnes.'

I hung up and sank back on to the pillows, far too wound up to sleep. Fate was clearly in the act of making a number of quick moves. I could feel my lips trembling. I had to pay attention now and make a note in my notebook right away. If only my arms hadn't been so tired. I would have to get back into the wheelchair and through to the living room again, I would have to take a look at the model and bring it up to date. Make some small cardboard models of Molly, Eilif and Ine: little people to put inside the house, preferably with movable limbs. I would have to make a bandsaw! And a hammock!

Then I would have to see about getting down there as soon as possible to be with them. It was probably best, for Aksel's sake, that I be on hand, I told myself as I turned back the duvet, braced myself and swung my legs over the edge of the bed with a little groan. Well, I did have to keep a bit of an eye on him. And the children.

I gathered all my strength and heaved myself over into the wheelchair.

I couldn't stop thinking while I worked at my desk on the bandsaw and the hammock for the model. It was so glaringly obvious to me: Molly was in the process of taking the children away from me, even before I had had a chance to get to know them. They would become attached to her from the minute they arrived at the summer house, she would teach Ine to swim. She would surprise everybody who had thought she didn't have a way with children, she would be like a mother to them. And as if that weren't enough, she was already carrying a new baby sister or brother for them, she would tell them the news during this summer holiday with her, some day when they'd been having a particularly lovely time and were lazing in the hammock, all three of them, maybe on the day when Ine swims on her own for the first time; she'll whisper it to them, as if it were their secret and they'll laugh at her, happy and surprised. Ine will rub her face against Molly's stomach, her hair will be stiff from the salt water and still wet, it will spread in thick strands across Molly's T-shirt.

After that Molly will automatically slot into place in the children's lives, alongside Monika. Monika will recover and she and Molly will become friends, you only had to say their names one after the other to understand how well suited they were. They would find it only natural to babysit for each other's children, they would go to cafés together, tell each other about Aksel's little foibles, giggle confidentially, share the responsibility. Be happy to have a little break from him every now and again. Send him and his three kids off to the seaside for a few days every summer, remind him that they all had to wear their life vests. Savour their freedom. Be Aksel's little harem. Trust him to take care of everything, to be the best Dad in the world.

'I have eyes like a hawk!' I told myself firmly, out loud. 'And extraordinarily good hearing! Hundreds of thousands of strands in the rug beneath my feet! Images so sharp it's unbelievable! And talk about strong arms!'

I grasped the handles on the wheels of my chair and pushed off, but at that very moment an image came into my mind which I had not made any effort to conjure up. It was a picture of a woman walking down a steep hill with the setting sun behind her. She was tall and slim. She was making her way down to a little kiosk at the foot of the hill. She was fast approaching it. When she reached it, she pushed open the heavy door and stepped inside the crammed little shop. I saw how she was overwhelmed by the golden light in there, the low sun falling through the window dazzling the man behind the counter.

I saw the man squint and laugh at the woman and shade his eyes with his hand. He apologised for not seeing her because he was dazzled, said something to the effect that he ought to have been wearing sunglasses.

The woman picked a newspaper off the stand, she couldn't see what it said on the front page. She had to grope towards the shop-keeper's hand, slipped the coins she had warmed in her palm into it. She stood like that for a moment, until the sun had slipped a couple of inches further to the left of the window and both she and the man could see that in just a few minutes it would disappear behind the parked cars outside.

Only once I had seen all this did I realise that the woman in the kiosk was my mother.

I was conscious that I had hunched down in the wheelchair again. It was so hard to sit up straight.

I think the best thing would be to make a puppet to represent me, too, I thought to myself, in order to blot out this intrusive image. A puppet in a wheelchair, to make it realistic. With finger-less gloves to protect her hands and give her a better grip on the wheels. And I'll have to look at the model, find out what is the best place for a wheelchair ramp. Up the veranda steps, I would guess, as Molly said. It can't be that hard to make a ramp out of card, it should only take a few minutes.

But a commode is out of the question. I'll have to try to manage without. Maybe I could get from the wheelchair over to the toilet on my own two feet? I, who am getting better! I'll have to practise! I've got to get into that kayak of Aksel's anyway, I shall scud across the waves, propelled by smooth, steady strokes of the paddle.

I couldn't stop now. I rang Molly's number. It wasn't like me to be a bother.

It took her ages to answer the phone.

'Hello, Molly here.'

'Sorry,' I said. 'It's me again. Were you in bed?'

''Course not. I'm working.'

'I've been thinking.'

'And? I'm kind of busy right now.'

'You need to know that I'd like to come down to see you as soon as possible,' I said hurriedly. 'You don't have to worry about getting a commode, my legs have become so much stronger lately, I think I'll be able to get myself to the bathroom without any help.'

'Wow!'

'I do realise, though, that it will take some time to build a wheelchair ramp. And there was one thing I was wondering about: I think there may be a camera in the mobile phone that Aksel gave Eilif and Ine.'

'Oh? Did he tell you that?'

'Not exactly, I just sort of worked it out for myself,' I said quickly. 'But I was thinking that the kids are going to need something to keep them occupied while you're working. Maybe you could tell them you have a friend who would like some pictures of how things look at the summer house? You could send them on a photo safari, to take some pictures. Kids like things like that.'

'A photo safari?'

'Uh-huh, although you don't need to call it that exactly.'

'Gosh no, of course I could tell them to go on a photo safari.'

'Yes, you could, couldn't you? You could even tell them this was a little summer job that I would pay them to do. Eilif is good with anything technical, he'll take care of all of that. All he has to do is send the pictures to my phone, you can give him the number.'

'How do you know that Eilif is good with anything technical?' she said.

'Well, all boys of his age are, aren't they,' I said.

'Oh? And how would you know that?'

'Everybody knows that.'

'Yes, yes of course,' she said. It sounded as though she was feeling a bit guilty about having been so sharp with me. She was trying to win me over.

'Right, that's that settled then.'

'Okay. But, Agnes,' she said, all honey now. 'It would be so good if you could help me a little bit with ideas for *The Dream Play*. I'm kind of bogged down at the moment. It's such a tricky piece, and I've had so much else to think about over the past few weeks, I've been feeling so queasy, because of the . . .'

I broke her off, I didn't want to hear her say that word.

'I'm sure you have', I said. 'But you've made your bed, now you'll have to lie in it.'

'I'm getting a bit worried about it now,' she went on unfazed, as if she had not caught the sour note in my voice. 'Jan's been calling from the theatre, wanting to know how far I've got. He keeps telling me time's getting on. As if I didn't know that.'

'You can rely on me,' I said. 'I've read the play thoroughly. We've done this sort of thing together before, haven't we? Just make sure Eilif sends me pictures of how everything looks down there at the house, and I'll work something out, don't you worry. And remember to tell him I'll pay them.'

'I knew I could depend on you,' she said, sounding relieved.

'And I'll come down to stay with you as soon as everything has been organised for the wheelchair and what not. It shouldn't take that long, should it? I'll help you with the children, and we can try out our ideas. And now you've got the bandsaw there, that simplifes things, doesn't it. Makes it easier to work fast.'

'Yes, the bandsaw is . . .'

'Oh, and one last little thing,' I said, cutting her off. 'I've had a thought.'

'Yes?'

'Would you give my best to Aksel and tell him from me that he's most welcome to spend the night here if need be.'

'What do you mean?'

'I mean, what with Monika and so on. Sitting up all night at the hospital – they might not have enough beds there for the relatives of all the patients. And I live right beside the hospital. Right next door, so to speak.'

A warm little wave washed over me when I said those words: *Right next door*.

After we had hung up for the third time that evening, I sat at my desk, staring at the picture which the projector had frozen on to the white wall above the sofa. Niagara Falls.

A decision seemed to come and lodge itself inside me. I got out the white card, a felt-tip pen and the smallest scalpel. Then I drew two big, black birds, each with its own broad wingspan. I drew them with strong, sure strokes; it was as if my hand had a will of its own, as if it had been practising drawing in secret, while I was asleep. The birds looked exactly alike, it was impossible to tell them apart.

I let my ears revel in the lovely crisp sound of steel on card.

She called the next day to ask what she should give Aksel and the children to eat when they came. Neither of us mentioned the baby. She would have to have a meal ready for them, she said, they were coming in the afternoon after taking Monika to the hospital. I had been up half the night, had set the wheelchair ramp and the hammock into the model and made a start on a small cardboard model of Ine, based on the sketch in my notebook. I had left the bandsaw till later, I didn't have the right materials for it.

I was colouring in Ine's hair when she called, I had opted for a shade somewhere between sunshine yellow and light brown. I applied layer after layer, smudging each one with my finger. I'd given Ine moveable joints made from paper fasteners. The long garden canes I was going to attach to her so she could move were lying next to me on the desk.

'They'll need something to eat!' Molly fretted. 'I don't know what to give them.'

I had already given this some thought, so I told her she should make spaghetti with sausage chunks and tomato ketchup. Aksel had once told me the children liked this, and it was important for them to have something they were used to. If nothing else, then at least the food would not be an issue. She could see that that made sense.

I spent the whole day working on the puppets, breaking off only for a stiff work-out on the mat. I really had something to train for now. The temp came and went without my paying her any heed. She wanted to help me; crouched down beside me with her head on one side in that supposedly encouraging way of hers.

'You have to try to take each exercise nice and easy, with pauses in between,' she said. 'And don't forget your breathing. You seem a bit overwrought.'

'Go away!' I cried. I did all I could to make her feel super-fluous.

When I gave her the evening off yet again she shot me a worried look and asked if I was quite sure. She still doesn't seem to have noticed the model on my desk. She really does not have an eye for such things, all she has is a nurse's eye, she sees only poor muscle power and a pallid complexion, the colour of urine, a strong or a weak pulse.

'I've seldom been more sure,' I declared, firing her own look back at her like a ray of steel. I could feel my pulse throbbing all the way to my fingertips: it was very, very strong.

When we spoke on the phone that evening I was given a report on what had happened. Molly told me that Aksel had indeed driven down with the children in the early afternoon. She had just finished making lunch and was setting the table on the veranda when the car pulled up outside the house. Monika had been admitted to hospital to be prepared for her operation, the children had gone with her to wish her luck, she was to be operated on the very next day, it had all happened so quickly.

Molly, Aksel and the children had all had spaghetti with sausage chunks and tomato ketchup together on the veranda. Apparently not much had been said.

It never occured to her to ask how I knew what they liked to eat, I noted this with a little smile which I don't think showed itself in my voice.

'So how are the children doing?' I asked over the phone, as I ran my fingers down the row of coloured pencils in the box beside me on the desk. They were all arranged so nicely and so neatly.

Molly hesitated. It didn't sound as though she had given any thought to how the children were doing until I asked, but that can't be right.

'They don't say anything,' she replied. 'They keep to them-selves. They seem . . . a bit fretful.'

'Well, it's hardly surprising,' I said, deciding on an orange pencil for Eilif's baseball cap. 'How much do they know about what's happening to their mother?'

'I don't know how much Aksel has told them. For the moment we've agreed that they'll stay here with me for the rest of the week. Then we'll see. He'll probably pop down to see them.'

'What do they look like?'

'Ine is slim and blonde. She's the one who seems the most fretful. She looks like her mother, although not as dark.'

'I didn't know you'd met their mother.'

'I saw her in passing once, in a café in town.'

'Oh?'

'She was dancing.'

'Oh, right? Dancing in a café?'

'She's possibly a bit on the skinny side.'

'Monika?'

'No, Ine.'

'Kids are skinny at that age,' I said. 'It's normal. And Eilif?'

'He's skinny too, but wiry with it. He's probably quite athletic. As far as I can see he doesn't resemble either Monika or Aksel. He hasn't looked me in the eye once since they got here.'

'Don't let that worry you. Does he wear a baseball cap?'

'Why do you ask?'

'I was just wondering. Boys his age tend to wear baseball caps.'

'Yes, he does wear a baseball cap. He's a good-looking boy.'

I nodded to myself, it had to be orange, that baseball cap, it was obviously the one he was wearing in that picture from last summer, the one Aksel had shown me.

'Where are they now?' I asked.

'They're out on the veranda, in the hammock. They went for a walk around. Took some pictures, I think. I suppose I'd better tell them soon that it's time for bed.'

I swallowed hard.

'They're lying out there, bickering and sort of hanging on to each other, they look as if all they really want to do is to crawl inside one another,' Molly went on.

'I can just picture it,' I said.

'Do brothers and sisters usually do that sort of thing?'

'I don't know. I don't have any brothers or sisters.'

'Me neither.'

'Tell me more.'

'What can I tell you? I think they're scared of me or something. They keep to themselves.'

'Let them,' I said. 'It's normal.'

'Eilif is so obviously a big brother.'

'What makes you say that?'

'The way he puts out his hands to her. As if he's taking responsibility for what she's feeling.'

'Well, he is ten years old, isn't he?'

'Yes.'

'That's old enough.'

There was a long silence at the other end of the phone. I propped the receiver between my chin and my shoulder while I reached for the box of paper fasteners.

'Molly? Isn't there a jetty near your summer house?' I asked eventually.

'A jetty? Why d'you ask that?'

'I was just wondering. I'm trying to picture how it looks at your place.'

'Yes, there's a jetty down by the bathing hut. But so far I've stayed mainly up here, around the house. And the garden. The garden here is really lovely, but it gets overgrown so quickly. I don't know how I'm going to be able to keep it the way Granny did. I don't know anything about weeding.'

'Didn't Granny teach you anything about gardening when you stayed with her in the summer?'

'Ah, but she didn't actually do the work herself. She always had visitors who did it for her. When I was a little girl I thought that was what summer visitors were there for: to weed the garden and mow the lawn.'

'Well, then you have the choice of learning to do it yourself or finding yourself some summer visitors to do the job for you,' I said.

'Maybe you could help me when you come?'

'I'm not a great hand with a lawn-mower,' I said drily. 'Do you think the children will get round to swimming from the jetty?'

'I haven't thought about it. I don't know if they can swim.'

'You'll have to keep a close eye on them. Don't let them go down to the water alone, whatever you do. Have you got that?'

'Of course I won't.'

'I'm always here, you know that, you just have to pick up the phone,' I said. Then I suddenly thought of something. 'And watch out for that bandsaw!' I said. 'Don't let the children anywhere near that bandsaw!'

'What do you take me for?' she said.

'Pull out the plug! Put a sheet over it!'

'I'm not a complete idiot, you know. And anyway, it's not as if you're such an expert on kids either, is it?' she said.

She was right. I have no idea what it's like to live with a child. I don't remember much about my own childhood, I don't know whether that's one of the effects of my illness. For a long time that was my biggest fear: that I might lose my memory. That my past would be lost to me. I've read everything I could find on the internet about the potential progression of my disease; I know that loss of memory is a possibility and there have been times when I have felt that things were going that way, that my past was becoming more and more of a haze into which significant events have already disappeared.

Lately, though, I've begun to wonder, because who's to say that what I remember is actually what happened when I was a little girl. I mean, there's no way of knowing for certain whether the memories you have are true. Maybe they're just things you've made up later, on the basis of photographs you've seen, for instance, or things someone has told you. I mean we're forever making things up, aren't we.

In any case, I can always turn it around and tell myself that if I lose all memory of who I was when I was young, then I have the chance to be reborn each day. Clean and shining, with no ties of any sort. Create myself anew. New images. *Like the first morning.*

The following morning I made only a quick surf of the internet to bring myself up to date on what fate was up to in the rest of the world. I checked developments on the stock exchange, and had it confirmed that there was indeed some foundation for my suspicions that another crash was in the offing. Then there was the latest refugee disaster, which had not yet burst into full bloom: my bet was that this flower would blossom around the same time as the stock-market crash. And there had been some new terrorist attacks.

I couldn't resist checking, too, what was happening with the miners who had been trapped in a mineshaft. As I had feared things were not looking too good, it seemed unlikely that anyone was still alive in there now. I tried to imagine what it must be like down there: the darkness, the chill dampness. Could they hear sounds outside? Were they able to keep track of time? Did they know which of their mates were dead and which were still alive? Talk to themselves to keep their spirits up?

I spent most of the day working on the model of the summer house and wondering whether Molly would come to collect me. I didn't expect her to, even though I knew the wheelchair ramp was finished. I tried to picture everything. I finished the cardboard puppets of Molly and Eilif, I cut out each part of their bodies separately with the scalpel and joined them together in such a way that they could bend at the elbow-, knee-, hip- and neck-joints. I dressed them in trendy, colourful clothes. Then I started on the puppet of myself in the wheelchair. I made myself just as big and strong as them; stuffed with proteins and with firm, plump breasts. I gave myself as many movable joints as the other puppets. I told myself that I would actually be as well to start on a version of myself without the wheelchair straight away.

Since Molly didn't appear, nor call to tell me more about what was happening at the summer house, I had to make something up. In my mind this is what I saw:

That morning she had risen early and made breakfast for Eilif and Ine. She buttered two slices of bread and put cheese on them, cut each one crosswise into two and laid them on a couple of the green plates with the Twenties-style pattern that she made just after she graduated from the Academy. She gave me two of those plates, too. They're in the cupboard in the kitchen. She poured two glasses of milk, put the whole lot on to a tray and carried it out on to the veranda.

Then she tiptoed up the stairs to the first floor. She paused for a moment, though, outside the spare room door, before knocking. There was no answer. She knocked again. Then she opened the door and peeped in. Both beds were empty. Ine's was neatly made, her nightie had been folded and laid on the chair. The bedclothes on Eilif's bed were all in a tangle; it was easy to see how his firm, angular boy's body had tossed and turned around in them and how he had thrown off the duvet when he woke up, kicked it down to the foot of the bed as if it was an animal that had tried to attack him during the night.

Molly sat down on Ine's bed. All of a sudden she felt sick and dizzy.

She sat like that for some time. She heard the children coming up the stairs, they were talking softly to one another. They stopped short in the doorway when they saw her.

'Good morning,' she said, trying her best to sound bright and cheery. 'Where have you been?'

Eilif gazed mutely at her. Ine was clutching a mobile phone.

'We were calling Dad,' Eilif said.

'Oh? Outside?'

'The signal's so rotten in here, we kept getting cut off. Dad told us to take a walk around outside until we found a spot where he could hear us.'

'And did you get through to him?'

'No. But there has to be some place in the garden where it'll work.'

'Bound to be,' Molly said. 'And you're welcome to use my phone, of course. The one here in the house. I've just had it put in.'

Neither of them said anything. The mobile phone which their father had given them had become a sacred object to them, it wasn't hard to see. Molly thought: It belongs on a household altar.

What Molly didn't realise, I said to myself, was that the children had unwittingly got it into their heads that their parents now inhabited a field of telephone waves somewhere in the garden. They just had to find that spot. And when they found it they would form a colony there, a realm in which everything would be the same as before: Mum and Dad would be together there, and no one would be sick. There would be no Death. The sacred object which Ine clutched in her hand would be the key to this realm.

Molly needed me to understand such things, without me she was pretty helpless. The children sensed this, that was why they didn't trust her, I thought.

They both stared at her as if she were the cause of their mother's cancer-ridden womb. Then they walked over to Eilif's bed and sat down, side by side, on the edge.

'Hmm. So . . .' said Molly. 'Did you sleep well? The first night in a new house can be a bit strange, I know.'

They made no reply, I thought. Molly shifted uneasily.

'You know, I've heard they're really good at doing operations in the hospitals these days,' she ventured.

'What's a shurgeon?' Ine asked. 'Before we left, Daddy was talking about the shurgeon.'

'The *surgeon*,' Eilif corrected her.

'The surgeon is the doctor who operates on patients to make them better,' Molly said.

'Operate – does that mean cutting? Are they going to cut Mum? Eilif says they're going to cut her open with a knife.'

'Yes,' Molly said. 'They use a kind of a knife. A scalpel, it's called. It's very sharp and very clean. But first they'll give her an injection to make her sleep, so she won't feel a thing.'

'Really?'

'Really, truly. It won't hurt a bit, she'll sleep right through the whole operation, and they'll sew her up nicely afterwards. There will be lots and lots of doctors and nurses to look after her when she wakes up. Like your Dad, for instance.'

'Will she dream when she's asleep?'

'No, I don't think so. I think she'll just be in a lovely, deep sleep. A totally blank sleep.'

'Totally blank?'

'Yes, I think so.'

'Will the injection hurt?'

'No, not at all, she'll just feel a little prick, a bit like a mosquito bite.'

'Not exactly like a mosquito bite, though,' said Eilif.

The way I pictured it, there must have been a long silence. And I couldn't imagine that Molly would know how to proceed with this conversation. She's not used to talking to children, I thought, she has no idea what children are capable of understanding, what you can say to them. She's probably afraid of filling their heads with the wrong sorts of ideas, she doesn't realise that they have already started generating terrifying notions of their own, that they can sense death looming up ahead of them like a cold shadow. Like those trapped miners: that chill, dark dampness which . . . I realised that she would never be able to imagine such things. Molly needed me as an interpreter, oh yes.

'No, not exactly like a mosquito bite, perhaps,' she must have said to the children at length. 'But that needle has a tiny, tiny, very fine point, the tiniest and finest there is. Nearly invisible.'

'Invisible?' Ine must have asked.

'Yes, nearly.'

'But she'll definitely wake up afterwards?'

'Certainly. Quite definitely.'

'Will she be all better then?'

'No, it'll probably be a little while before she's all better. The wound has to knit, you see. After the operation your Mum will have to rest and get her strength back. They'll probably want to keep her at the hospital for a while. They might decide to give her something called radiotherapy.'

'Is that dangerous?'

'Not at all. It's just like a sort of sun-lamp.'

'But after that? Can we go on holiday with Mummy then? She promised to teach me to swim this summer.' Ine's voice was shrill and insistent, I could hear it in my mind so clearly.

'I don't know, Ine. What did your Daddy say when you spoke to him on the phone?'

'He sounded so funny. He hardly said anything and then he got cut off. Why do they have to operate on Mummy?'

'Hmm. Has your Dad really not talked to you about this? I don't know that much, but I think it's because your Mum hasn't been feeling very well and nobody really knows why.'

'She's been really crabby. And she just wants to rest all the time. She never wants to go for a bike ride with us.'

'Exactly. So now the doctors have decided to take a look inside her body to see whether there's something there that shouldn't be there, something that's robbing her of all her strength, in the place in her tummy where babies are carried. So she can get well and start going on bike rides again.'

'Is Mummy going to have a new baby!'

'No, no. I mean, where you two were carried when you were babies. Before you came out, I mean.

The two faces stared at her suspiciously.

'What is it?' Ine asked. 'What is it that shouldn't be there?'

'I don't really know. Things called tumours, I think.'

'What do they look like?'

'I'm not altogether sure. Like little lumps, maybe, that grow in places where they're not supposed to be, and are making your Mum feel weak. They can be cut out with a very, very sharp scalpel.'

'Are those lumps sucking up Mummy's strength. Is that why they're growing? Do they have mouths?'

'Come on,' Molly must have said, in an effort to extricate herself from the mess into which she had got herself. 'I've put out breakfast for you on the veranda.'

But both children must have gone on staring silently at her from the bed. No one can have made any move to get up.

'What is it?' Eilif asked.

'How do you mean?'

'What's for breakfast?'

'Milk and sandwiches.'

'I don't like ordinary milk,' Eilif may have said. 'I only like chocolate milk.'

In my mind's eye I saw Molly follow them down the stairs and out on to the veranda. She probably hovered there indecisively, watching them eat in silence, I thought. I knew just how perplexed she could look when she wasn't sure what to do.

Both children must have stuffed the sandwiches she had made into their mouths and started chewing and Ine must have drunk her milk, I continued in my mind. Even at that point I had the impression that Ine was a biddable child; I had guessed as much from what Aksel had told me. But I doubted if Eilif had touched his glass. I imagined Molly saying to herself that she would have to remember to ask me whether she really had to buy cocoa powder for their milk.

'Are you kidding!' I would say when she called to ask me this. 'Tip it in and stir it round. Those kids are staring death in the face. And death throws a cold, damp shadow.'

And the rest of the meal I pictured thus:

'How long do we have to stay here?' Ine asked. I assumed she would be doing the talking both for herself and her brother, after the business with the milk.

'I don't know,' Molly replied. 'Your Dad didn't say?'

'Dad's stupid,' Ine said. Her brother gave her a dirty look, but she stared defiantly back at him and went on chewing deliberately on her sandwich.

'Oh, I'm sure we'll have a lovely few days together here, just the three of us, don't you think?' Molly said. 'Now, what do you like to do during the summer holidays?'

'Be with Mummy and Daddy,' Ine said.

'Play football,' said Eilif.

'And what about swimming?'

'Is it a long way to the beach?' Ine asked.

'Only three minutes' walk.'

'Can we go down there now?'

'Not without me. That's something we have to get straight right away: no going swimming without a grown-up.'

'But you're the only grown-up here,' Ine said.

'Exactly. Which means no going swimming without me. I was thinking we might take a walk down to the beach after lunch. I really ought to do a bit of work in the mornings.'

'With that big thing in the living-room with the sheet over it?'

'That's a band-saw. Yes, with it too. It can be a bit noisy at times. You must never, ever switch it on yourselves. In fact, don't touch it at all. Have you got that?'

'Why not?'

'Because it's very dangerous, Ine. It's an electric saw. It could cut your hand off.'

'Would it hurt?'

'Yes, a lot.'

'Would I have to go to the hospital and have an operation?'

'Yes.'

'Could I die?'

'Oh, I don't think you would die, but you would lose your hand.'

'But what if you cut off your hand?'

'I won't cut off my hand, I've learned how to use the saw.'

'Who showed you how?'

'There are schools for things like that.'

'What are you going to make with it?'

'I'm going to cut some sheets of chipboard to make stage sets for a play that's going to have its premiere after the holidays.'

'What're stage sets?'

But at that point I fancied that Eilif would have snapped at his sister:

'Stop asking so many questions. What are you – stupid? Dad told us all about it, remember?'

*

Molly must have sighed, I thought. I know just how she sighs when she feels she is about to push herself too far.

'Then that's what we'll do,' she may well have said, with strained patience. 'Right? You two find something to do on your own for a while, take a walk round about or something like that, and be back here for lunch at one. After that we can go for a swim. I think you'll find there are lots of nice things to see around here.'

'Like what?' Eilif asked doubtfully.

'Oh, I don't know. That's for you to find out. Maybe you could pick some flowers. I don't know the place all that well either, I've just moved in. It's years and years since I was last here, I'm sure all the houses round here must have changed hands since I was a little girl.'

'Who lived here when you were a little girl then?'

'My grandmother. She stayed here for the whole of the spring and summer and well into the autumn too. The rest of the year she lived in town. I used to be here a lot when I was your age.'

'Is she dead?' Ine asked.

'She died last year.'

'Where?'

'In hospital,' said Molly. It would be just like her to come out with something like that before she had time to think. Not smart. 'Off you go for a walk,' she must have added firmly. 'Eilif, do you have a watch? One o'clock, shall we say that?'

Eilif nodded imperceptibly, the two children got up and walked off down the veranda steps and across the garden. Ine clutched the mobile phone solemnly in one hand. The other she slipped into her brother's.

I pictured Molly following them with her eyes. They did not look back. They disappeared into the lilac bushes then emerged on to the dirt road. They looked scared and cross and vulnerable. It must have been even clearer to Molly, seeing them like that, from behind, that they were not her children. And she knows they never will be either, I thought.

Maybe she picked up Eilif's full glass of milk and was about to tip it over the veranda railing and into the roses below, then thought better of it and raised it to her lips instead. The milk probably tasted sweet and lukewarm. It must be years since she last drank milk, I thought to myself. Molly hates milk, but now that she's pregnant, her tastes could well have changed.

There was a time, just before I fell ill, when Molly and I used to go to parties. We were both rather highly-strung, but it was she who led me on, she didn't draw the line where I did. She didn't seem to have anything holding her back in those days, she didn't have a rubber band in her spine like me.

We experimented with alcohol, of course, with varying degrees of success I would have to say, and occasionally someone would pass round a sweet-smelling cigarette in an ashtray. Everybody took a drag, apart from me; I thought about what Dad would say if he smelled that aromatic scent on my clothes when I got home. There was no saying that he would have associated that scent with anything in particular, but I coughed and spluttered anyway and flapped my hands and tried to look as though I was allergic to the stuff when the ashtray got round to me. I passed it on with a waggish grin which can't have done much for me. You can say a lot of things about me, but one thing I am not is a wag, and I'm certainly not allergic.

Molly always had a boyfriend. She was a lot more forward than me. Sometimes she would disappear into a room with some gangly young man only for them both to reappear some time later looking dishevelled and triumphant. I would stare at them, thinking to myself that they looked as though they had just won a contest, and this made me feel even more stiff and lumpish. I just didn't seem able to drape myself over a sofa, it had something to do with my back, or my arms. The rubber band in my spine tugged at me. I shut my eyes and thought: any minute now they're going to find me out.

I remember one party, in our second year in high school. One of those times when I had drunk too much and Molly was down at the other end of the poorly lit room, sitting on the knee of some long-legged guy in an open shirt, laughing and gesticulating. I couldn't take my eyes off her. I wanted to sit on someone's knee, too, and laugh and wave my hands about, I wanted to be just like her, I wanted to make someone turn to me and shut my mouth with a kiss. Molly had a particular way of kind of sliding down into a boy's lap, almost disappearing completely, like a little girl on the lap of a big uncle. She had a husky laugh. I wanted my laugh to be husky too.

Then somebody passed round the ashtray. I saw Molly pick up the little cigarette between her thumb and index finger and shut her eyes as she inhaled. I turned to the guy who was sitting next to me on the sofa, he was fiddling with an album cover and looked as though he couldn't quite make up his mind about something.

'Put that one on!' I said. 'It's great. D'you want to dance? This place is so dead.'

Then something caught in my throat and I started coughing, I had to bend over and put my hand to my neck, the guy next to me began thumping me on the back.

For a while, after I began to have the first symptoms of my illness, I didn't see so much of Molly. But I did pop over to her house now and again. I remember one time in particular. We were sitting on the stained sofa in her room, leafing through her old photo albums. We had both finished high school; the past six months had been a difficult time for me, with spells in hospital and lots of tests, but no definite diagnosis had yet been reached, so this was before I knew how things were likely to go. It was only a few weeks since I had sat on the stool in Granny's bathroom and looked down at my white thighs and cried. We always know more than we know.

That was the autumn when Molly met Strøm. She had started university, although only so she could get a grant: she would have been hard put to tell you what subject she was studying. My own further education had been postponed indefinitely: I was in the midst of a highly exacting course of study at home and at the hospital, to the extent that it was possible to concentrate. This was, of course, long before I came to understand that what I was actually studying was fate.

Molly had spent the whole summer doing the rounds of festivals and markets, selling the brightly coloured felt hats she was making back then. She made these hats in her room in her parents' house at night and in longer stints that could last for days, when she would lock herself in her room and not come out until she had several sacks full of these weird and wonderful creations. I don't know where she learned how to make them, maybe she picked up the technique from some book, or maybe she had come up with it all by herself. She has always been good with her hands.

She was skinny and brown from all the time spent outdoors, and she walked with a sort of loose-limbed lope. All of her clothes were either jumble-sale finds or things she'd run up herself, and she always went barefoot in clogs in those days, whatever the weather. Her feet were always freezing, of course. But socks were for sissies, that was the sort of thing that only she and I understood.

In those days, Strøm was merely the subject of much gossip. A rather exciting, disreputable man-about-town, a womaniser who tutored selected students, took photographs of wrecked cars and rubbish, made biographical films with a hand-held camera, organised political demonstrations and came to blows with people when he was drunk. Exactly the sort of character whom Molly and I felt it was worth hanging around, but whom we would never have dared to actually approach. Or so I thought.

He had only recently returned home after years abroad, and had had a big exhibition of photographs in one of the top galleries in town. He had a very hectic social life.

Molly was totally fascinated by his pictures, she said they had changed her way of looking at the world. She was planning to spend the money she made from her hats on a Nikon camera, and was seriously considering completely redoing her room, converting it from a milliner's workshop into a darkroom. But she gave up the idea because of certain practical difficulties, such as the fact that there was no running water in the room, and that she also needed a place to sleep. That was so like her, to be planning a darkroom before she even had a camera.

She joined the university photography club, borrowed a camera and was granted temporary use of the club's darkroom. She rarely set foot inside the reading room.

We went to the opening of his exhibition together. I watched her trying, without success, to catch his eye as he stood in the midst of a crowd of culture vultures in designer clothes. When we were reviewing the whole thing the next day at my place she came to the conclusion that the fact that he hadn't noticed her had to be put down to her dress, it had been too long and loose. She would have to make herself something shorter and more figure-hugging and try again later.

Exactly what clinched it for her I do not know. It may have been the short, tight, emerald-green dress she made, but more likely it was the nineteen-year-old body inside the dress that did the trick. In any case, one evening she called me, all-aflutter, to report that she had met Strøm in a café the previous evening, that he remembered her well and that he had invited her over to his place the next day. She had asked if she could show him some of her pictures. Although it can hardly have been her pictures that Strøm was interested in at that point, as she well knew. But I think she meant it when she said she would give anything to have that man as a teacher. He had something she wanted. And she was used to getting what she wanted.

For six months she had hardly been back to the family home at all, except to make hats; no one seemed to know where she was living. But once she had finished that green dress, skin-tight and nicely padded in all the right places, and hooked Strøm, her old room suddenly acquired new value. It's my bet that Strøm wasn't actually so keen on having her moving in with him just like that, and had therefore suggested that she move back home to her parents. That way, he would know where she was and could summon her to him without having to make too much effort. He must have been well aware that shacking up with a nineteen-year-old would be going too far, even for someone with his reputation.

I was glad that she was living with her parents again. I had missed her, it felt good to be back in that chaotic room of hers. I could almost make believe that things were the same as they had been before I fell ill. Everything in that room was certainly just as it had always been: her books and magazines were piled up, as before, in stacks that threatened to topple over at any minute, and the doors of her wardrobe stood wide open. Molly only ever wore the clothes that lay at the very front of the wardrobe shelves. The things at the back were too far out of reach, as far as she was concerned the clothes at the back belonged to her old life. Molly is one of those people who is continually reinventing herself, and she never allows anything of the old persona to cling to her. I've always admired her for this. And there was no question of her mother ever forcing her to tidy up, that's for sure.

The walls were plastered with all her clippings and drawings, and incomprehensible sketches for different projects on which she was working, covered in arrows and figures.

I had missed this place. It was so unlike my own bright, simple room at home with Dad, and could in no way be compared to the sexless hospital wards in which, over the past months, I had lain, fearfully staring into space, with Dad sitting silently in a chair next to the bed, his big hands resting hopelessly on the arms.

I had been hoping that Molly and I would be able to talk about anything and everything, the way we used to do. I couldn't talk to anyone else as easily as I talked to her. With Molly I never had the feeling that I was being misunderstood, or that what I said was simply going in one ear and out the other. Molly was the sort who picked up everything I said and examined it seriously and intently, like a squirrel plucking some interesting titbit off the ground, holding it between its paws and cocking its head from side to side as it inspects it. We often disagreed, but that's quite a different thing.

We felt that we had developed our conversations into an art form. Now and then, when we were deep in discussion, it was as if we had also taken a step back from ourselves, and were listening to what was being said. We were so full of ourselves in those days. In many ways we were pretty naïve; we thought we were so smart in the way we presented our arguments. We exposed lies and phoniness and the hollowness of the world. That was our agenda, we hated everything that smacked of cowardice and apathy.

But as yet we knew little of suffering. Looking back on it I can see of course that by then I had already been steered towards my study of fate, a course which would show me things I could not have learned in any way other than through this disease. Molly's path led in another direction. Molly is not a witness, she is someone who creates moments, someone who stands at the heart of events and lets things happen. She sets the scene. While I explore the scene she has set.

And I tell myself it's just as well I didn't know about this difference between us back then. It would have felt too lonely.

That evening in her room, all Molly wanted to talk about was Strøm. She couldn't stop herself. According to her he was a brilliant photographer, and the most amazing lover, she was sure. She had had no first-hand experience of this latter attribute, it's true, but it probably wouldn't be long before she did. Molly was not a virgin, and she had no inhibitions where that side of things was concerned, not as far as I could tell. All my attempts to change the subject were in vain. I was worn out and felt a little cut off from everything to do with Strøm. Lately, for me, everything had revolved around myself and my own withering body, there was not so much as a flicker of desire to be felt there.

I had only seen Strøm that one time at his exhibition and on a couple of occasions when Molly and I were in our second year at high school, the year when we went to all those parties. That was before I fell ill, the only year I have had as a normal grown-up woman. That was the year when we became aware that we were no longer girls; we saw ourselves as mature women who went to the theatre and exhibitions and frequented cafés and jazz clubs. Took a drag on a joint. Or Molly did.

That was the year when I bought a typewriter on credit and Molly's grandmother gave her a sewing machine. For a while we used to swap machines once a month: I took over the sewing machine and she took over the typewriter. It was hard to say which of the two was the more important, but all of a sudden both sewing and writing by hand seemed unthinkable, it had something to do with taking oneself seriously. It was also around this time that we stopped talking about boys and started talking about men. We were living in a kind of blithe, semi-transparent haze which shielded us, although we didn't know that, we thought we were seeing everything so clearly. We fumble about more now, both of us. And yet I think of us as having been in a kind of slumber back then, and of the time we spent together over the summer as an awakening.

In those days, when we were young, we did all sorts of things to try to consolidate our own reality, that reality which we felt to be harsh and true, by discussing the things we experienced in the long and involved fashion which we had devised. In this way we rendered ourselves invulnerable. Our discussions were our self-developed vaccine against all the things with which we felt we could not live.

But I fell ill, we finished school, Molly went her own way. We lost sight of one another a little, she and I. Neither of us said as much to the other, but it was sort of in the air, and Molly has a way of sensing what is in the air. She was full of concern for me, I grant you; she found out all she could about the disease, wrote long, affectionate letters from wherever she happened to be in the world and when she came home on a visit she took keen note of anything that might indicate a change for the worse or the better in me. But I wasn't particularly interested in discussing my illness with her. I hadn't the energy for it, my symptoms did not fit in with our way of talking. She may have felt that I was pushing her away. I don't know. But something had happened between us.

I felt left out when Molly and Strøm started seeing one another. It made me feel confused and rather angry to think about what the two of them were getting up to. Maybe I had the idea that he was using her, or maybe it was the other way round and she was using him. Be that as it may, the thought of it made me angry; I felt there was something nasty about their relationship.

*

Molly's life had been well documented and almost all of the pictures in the album we were leafing through that evening in her room had been taken on the standard high days and holidays: birthdays, Christmas, Easter holidays in the mountains with oranges and anorak, waving a flag on Constitution Day, end-of term celebrations at school. I was in some of them, too, smiling dutifully at the camera. But Molly looked sulky or cross in just about every snap, as if she was already moving out of frame, and her clothes always hung oddly and wrongly on her. You had the impression that, had it been up to her, she would have been wearing something completely different, or preferably nothing at all.

'In every one of these photos you look as if you hate having your picture taken,' I said, lowering the album on to my lap. A pot of tea and two plastic mugs sat on the little table in front of the sofa. The lid of the teapot was broken, steam rose up through the hole in tremulous spirals. For a cloth the table had a large sheet of tinfoil, artistically scrunched by Molly: part of one of her latest projects, I suppose.

It wasn't very practical, that tinfoil. I hadn't asked her what the point of it was, I felt a bit stupid and rather out of touch with what she was doing. I remember the unpleasant grating sound every time I set the light plastic mug down on the table.

'I hated having my picture taken when I was young, but not any more,' she said.

'What made you change your mind?'

'Strøm.'

'I knew you'd say that. Can't you talk about anything else?'

'I don't think you understand. He has weaned me off hating things.'

'Oh?'

'He helped me to see that there's no point in expending energy on hating.'

'Mmm.'

'Far better to be politically active, he says. If you feel something ought to be changed, then you have to change it, not waste your time in hating.'

'Right. And I suppose he's forever taking pictures of you?'

Molly regarded me with that watchful look which creeps into her eyes sometimes when someone starts to contradict her or tries to take the conversation off at an unexpected tangent. That's when her flame flares up. She looks as though she has the urge to launch herself at whoever is talking, wrestle them to the ground with an exultant whoop, and roll around on the grass, laying into them with her fists. This look of hers is what you might call an integral part of our conversational form, a dramatic device.

'On the contrary,' she said happily, straightening her shoulders. 'It's me who takes pictures of him.'

'Oh, is it?'

'Yes, actually, it is.'

'I didn't know you had a camera.'

'I don't, he's lent me one of his. He's teaching me how to use the darkroom. He has all sorts of equipment.'

I wasn't surprised. I had no reason to doubt that Molly was already a good photographer, it was just the sort of thing she could do almost without having to try.

'How does he feel about that?' I asked.

'About me using his cameras?'

'About you taking pictures of him.'

'To be honest I think he hates it.'

This was my chance and I did not let it go by.

'There, you see, he's contradicting himself!' I said. 'You just said he says there's no point in hating.'

'No, he's not contradicting himself, because he's never said he hated it. But I can see that he does – which is not the same thing at all. He keeps it to himself.'

'Oh, don't be stupid!' I cried, a little too loudly. 'He's contradicting himself! He's just too much of a coward to admit it! How can you go out with a man who's thirty years older than you, and who keeps contradicting himself!'

It was a pointless discussion, of course, but in some fundamental way which we both recognised it had to do with our relationship. It was a way of egging each other on .

I leaned over the rasping cloth and poured more tea into both plastic mugs, playing for time while I worked out my next move. I automatically dropped two lumps of sugar into her mug, I knew her too well to have to ask. Molly took the offered mug. She gazed at me as she stirred her tea briskly with a ballpoint pen.

I heard, of course, the rather too obvious note of jealousy in my voice, and to be jealous would only be to demean myself. I knew I had to take my argument on to a deeper plane.

'When you were a little girl, you weren't a coward,' I said at last, slowly. 'When you were a little girl, you never made any pretence. You were clear and true. You can see it in these photos.'

I nudged the album over to her side of the sofa.

'How do you mean?'

'Look. In none of these pictures are you pretending to be feeling anything other than what you are actually feeling. I am, but you're not. I'm smiling the way I know a child of my age is expected to smile in photographs, but you hate having your picture taken and you make no secret of it.'

'Oh, no?'

'No, see here, you look for all the world as though you're baring your teeth.' I pointed to a snap from some sports meet, of a sullen Molly with her gym bag over her shoulder, glowering at the camera.

'D'you think so?' she said, rather lamely. She didn't look as if she quite understood what I was getting at. Probably all she really wanted to do was to carry on talking about the fabulous Mr Strøm.

'Think about it,' I went on. 'You never pretended when you were a little girl, these photographs prove that. But this man you're so besotted with, he's all pretence.'

'So?'

'So it's rubbing off on you.'

'Agnes! What on earth's got into you today?!'

'Nothing, as far as I know. Why?'

'Strøm is a man of integrity.'

'I know you think that. But the pictures in this album show that *you* possessed the very quality you think he has when you were just a little girl. When you were a little girl you were much more courageous than Strøm is now.'

Molly pushed the album away, flopped back in the sofa and hooted with laughter. Tea sloshed over the lip of her mug, I watched the dark tea stain spread across the orange fabric of the cushion underneath her.

'What's bugging you?' she asked, pretending to sound worried. 'You've changed. Is it your illness that's doing it?'

'I haven't changed a bit. This is simply basic logic. It's got nothing to do with my illness.' I did not take my eyes off the stain.

'But now you're telling me that Strøm is destroying me. I think you're jealous!'

Molly leaned towards me again and stroked my ankle in supposed sympathy, but I kicked out at her with all my strength, with more strength than I had known I had in that leg. I wasn't about to let her sabotage the conversation in this way.

The rest of the tea in her mug went flying in a brown cascade.

At this point we were interrupted by her mother knocking discreetly on the door and asking if we would like a carrot. Her voice coming from the hallway sounded polite, almost subservient. She must have been relieved to have Molly back in her room at home, and probably breathed more easily for every night her daughter spent there, rather than out in town. She had heard about Molly's affair with Strøm, naturally, and doubtless she had her own views on that.

I think Molly's mother always felt she had to offer something to eat when I visited the house, as if she actually worked for the family. She was always plying us with healthy, nutritious snacks – anything loaded with sugar or additives would have been unthinkable.

There really was not a single thing about Molly's mother to indicate that she was Granny's daughter. Molly and I had developed the theory that her mother must have been adopted, but we had never dared to ask Granny straight out about this.

Molly went to the door, mopping tea off her face with an old T-shirt on the way. She unlocked the door, pulled it very slightly ajar, slipped her hand through the chink and took the two peeled carrots with a curt nod, the sort of nod given to butlers in British films.

'I don't give a toss for your logic!' she said with her back to me, turning the key again and trying the handle to make sure the door was properly locked. She handed me one of the carrots. 'Strøm does something to me, and I like it,' she went on. 'He only wants the best for me.'

'Yeah, I'll bet.'

'And I'll tell you what it is he does to me.'

'Oh, please do.'

But the conversation stopped there. Or at least, I can't remember any more. We were so young then, we didn't know what we were talking about, we knew nothing of fate. I have a different view on this now, after all these years. I know now what fate would do to Strøm, and to Molly.

And although I don't remember exactly what was said, it's not hard to make up the part I have forgotten:

'Agnes,' she said. 'He teaches me to see.'

But she was right, of course. I was jealous. I spent a lot of time fantasizing about them, about what they got up to, what they talked about. Some of it I made up, and some of it I had from

Molly. These two sides often got mixed up, and to some extent it came to the same thing. I didn't dream up the idea of the note-book myself at the time, but I know now that Molly kept notes about Strøm. I have read them.

This jealousy of mine was different from the jealous feelings I had had about Molly and the boys we went to parties with in our second year at high school; it was very wearing, in a vague, confusing way that wasn't like anything I had ever experienced before. It could be that I wasn't quite clear as to whether it was her or Strøm I was jealous of.

I got hold of the catalogues for most of his major exhibitions and read all the interviews with him that I came across. In the catalogues I also found a number of supplementary essays in which well-known art critics reflected on his pictures and his films. They were fairly philosophical, those essays; among the first things within that genre that I read. They seemed to have something special to say to me, but I didn't have the strength or the knowledge to absorb ther message.

It goes without saying that even back then I had my own theo-ries as to what had brought Molly and Strøm together. I suppose I thought that Molly was using Strøm as a means of cutting loose from her parents. That's all there is to it! I said to myself. Strøm is Molly's way out, as far as she is concerned her parents are impu-rities, they stand for everything she doesn't want to be, she needs to simply be herself. She needs clarifying, and she thinks Strøm can help her.

But I didn't understand why she had to resort to someone who was so much older than her to be clarified. After all, she'd had other boyfriends of her own age long before she met him. Why couldn't she have stuck to them? I would have been more than content with any one of them. A boy with long legs and an open shirt, a boy whose lap I could slide down into, like a little girl; wave my hands about and laugh huskily as I smoked a joint.

So I went to see him. It was that simple. I called on Strøm. It wasn't difficult. I merely called for a taxi one evening when I knew Molly had a meeting at the photography club and got it to drive me to the address I had found in the catalogue.

He answered the entryphone after only a few seconds and didn't ask who I was when I gave my name: at no time did I have to explain that I was Molly's friend. He must have had some idea of who I was, and that I wasn't as mobile as other nineteen-year-olds, because he came all the way down to the front door and helped me up the stairs to his flat.

He gave me a rather large glass of sherry, but I don't think I got drunk. With what strength I had left I managed to perch myself on a high stool and tried to look as if I was in control, as if I regularly called on people like him. But I couldn't stop myself from looking and looking at his studio. It was very messy, but at the same time very orderly.

I saw right away why Molly felt at home here. This was a place where anything could happen.

He seemed to know why I had come without me having to explain. He knew I was talking about him and Molly, even though the questions I asked were purely about him and the pictures he took.

He was perfectly open. He let me ask him all the questions I had in my head.

I had brought one catalogue with me, from his most recent exhibition, it contained an interview with him. I showed him a place where I had underlined something he had said which I didn't understand. He took the catalogue from me and pointed to an armchair.

'Why don't you sit over there, instead,' he said. 'It's more comfortable. You need to rest.'

Then he read the article, slowly and intently, as if he had never seen it before, as if it were an interview with a stranger. I sank back into the soft leather chair and felt a strange sense of peace stealing over me.

There was perfect silence in the room while he read. Then he asked me what I thought it meant, the quote from the interview. I told him I didn't know, that it was as if I almost understood it, but not entirely, there was something missing, some gap in my comprehension that prevented me from taking in the words on the page. He laughed and said that was just how it was for him, too, he had no idea what it said, and he wasn't even sure he had known what it meant when he said it to the interviewer.

Then he poured us both some more sherry, not a lot, just a little, and proceeded to show me some more recent pictures, taken after the last exhibition. He asked me what I thought of them and I answered him without a moment's thought. Somehow he seemed able to get me to say things I had never said before, things I didn't even understand myself until I heard the words falling from my lips.

Now, looking back on it, I'm not sure I can remember what it was I said. It's on the tip of my tongue, but it's as if it won't come out

It was late. Just before I left he asked me, much to my surprise, why I had come. I didn't answer his question, instead I told him not to let Molly know that I had been there. He promised he wouldn't. Then he asked about Mum. He knew who she was, he wanted to know what I thought of her. Whether I had read her books. The way he asked: no one had ever asked me quite like that before.

Suddenly I was in a hurry to get away. I said I had to be getting home, Dad would be wondering where I'd got to. Strøm gave me a searching look, then nodded and screwed the top on the bottle. He phoned for a taxi and helped me back down to the street.

Just as the taxi was about to drive off he asked me why I didn't have a boyfriend. I didn't answer him, merely gave my address to the taxi driver and asked him to step on it.

Dad couldn't ever find out where I had been. He wouldn't have borne it.

Molly is an only child too, but unlike her mother she has a father. She has never said much about what she thinks of her parents. Not to me, and not to anyone else as far as I know. But I knew them, and I think it would be true to say that they never realised what sort of a child they had brought into the world.

Even back then, when we were nineteen, I understood that what Molly had been doing ever since she was a little girl was to maintain with dogged determination that her reality was every bit as valid as her parents'. More so, in fact. And there wasn't much they could do against such determination.

I said to myself that for her, Strøm was confirmation that she had been right all along about her parents: she didn't belong with them, she never had done. She wanted to show them that they didn't have the faintest idea what had landed in their laps when they had her, and she believed she had the right to punish them for being so . . . stupid. It was her indisputable right to make them aware of their faults.

She did not understand them, they did not understand her. They loved her as best they could and did everything in their power to make her what they considered to be a normal, healthy, well-adjusted child. And Molly, for her part, did everything in her power to oppose this plan.

As she grew older, her sphere of power grew more and more extensive. Her power was greater than theirs and her reality carried more weight than theirs, that much was obvious to everyone who came in contact with the little family.

She was christened Mona Louise, but from the day and hour when she was able to form whole sentences, she refused to let anyone call her by this name. She chose the name Molly herself and as soon as she came of age she applied to have her name changed officially, such that the signature on the dotted lines of all her papers read Molly Madsen. It sounded cool; I was impressed and envious. I would never have dared to change my name like that. I was far too afraid that Dad would be hurt, and besides: I wouldn't have known what name to choose if I didn't use his.

I had a theory that Molly's relationship with Strøm was like an echo of her relationship with our art teacher in primary school. Molly was very bright, as the headmaster put it, but she disrupted classes with an insolence that scared the wits out of the teachers. All except the art teacher to whom, on the other hand, she had taken a liking and whom she richly rewarded.

The art teacher's name was Mr Pedersen, he was a reticent, elderly man, close to retiring age, very different from Strøm, it's true. The word in the playground was that he had once spent some time in a mental hospital. If that were so then at some point he must have got himself out of there, but he was clearly just as unhappy within the supposedly liberal school system as Molly was.

Molly and Mr Pedersen were allies right from the start. He saw straight away that she had a special gift for creating and transforming things, and that she had to be given more to do than just the usual art-class work. She was put in charge of making the sets for the plays we put on for the parents every year at the end of the summer term. The plays were the standard fare from our reading books, and the acting was no better than you might expect: a bunch of children facing stiffly outwards as we stammered out our lines and uttering sighs of relief when we succeeded in reeling them off.

But the sets were magnificent. Molly and Mr Pedersen started planning them immediately after the start of the spring term. Together they could turn the whole classroom into a strange, unknown world; they built things and altered things, using coloured paper, felt, light-bulbs covered with cellophane, garden canes, card, chicken-wire and big, coloured sheets.

They kept the sets in a locked room in the basement, only Mr Pedersen and the janitor had keys to it, so nobody was allowed to see anything until the dress rehearsal. Molly and Mr Pedersen would spend the whole of the evening before this carrying up the scenery they had made and setting it up in the classroom with the aid of sellotape, drawing pins and canvas stretchers. When allowed in, we edged cautiously around the room, terrified of breaking something.

The production didn't really find its form until the dress rehearsal, once the scenery was set up. And somehow those two managed to persuade the school's headmaster to buy a spotlight which Molly worked from the back of the classroom during the play, with Mr Pedersen standing behind her, holding the cable and whispering little instructions in her ear, instructions which she probably did not follow.

I don't know whether even Molly and Mr Pedersen understood the full extent of what they created, but that didn't matter. That is often the way of it in the theatre, I have come to realise: you don't need to understand what you are doing, all that matters is that it works.

Needless to say, these school theatricals did not make Molly or Mr Pedersen any more popular, among the teachers or us pupils. But they did not seem particularly interested in winning our approval, all they were interested in was their projects. And oddly enough, the very fact that they did not care what we thought of them, made them seem interesting to us after all. We instinctively understood that it took a lot of effort to maintain such a lofty attitude.

Some years after she had left the school, Molly went back to the headmaster's office and asked if she could buy the spotlight he had procured for her. It hadn't been used since her time there. Mr Pedersen had taken early retirement, he had sort of faded away after Molly left.

I don't think she ever paid for that spotlight. I assume that even the headmaster regarded it as being hers by rights, and that if she didn't use it nobody would. It has followed her wherever she went for as long as I have known her. It'll be set up in the sitting-room at the summer house now, I suppose. When I made the model I put the spotlight into it. An itty-bitty construction of wire and tinfoil in a summer house with a wheelchair ramp and a veranda.

For the first four years at primary school I wasn't close friends with Molly. No one was, as far as I know. I remember her as being a standoffish, rather restless girl who was always going somewhere. She didn't play the same schoolgirl games as the rest of us and she made no attempt, as we did, to keep up with all the ins and outs of who was friends with whom at any given time.

But then, during the summer when we were in fourth grade, something happened. I remember the last day before the summer holidays, when the class was to perform our play for the parents. I had been making moves towards her for some time, it was a bit like being in love, there was something about her which I thought might rub off on me if only I got to hang around her long enough. An air of freedom, a recklessness which I yearned to possess. But she made no move towards me. Molly made no move towards anyone, no one but herself.

The rest of us kids in the class had donned our costumes and were buzzing frenziedly around the classroom next door as we waited for our own classroom to fill up with parents and brothers and sisters, all there to see the big show. We wound each other up even more by screaming our lines at one another, pretending to be rehearsing. Our teacher dashed frantically from one to another, fastening buttons and straightening costumes on our unruly bodies while trying vainly to quieten us down.

Molly and Mr Pedersen were huddled in a corner, discussing something to which none of the rest of us were privy. I stared at them. They were most likely talking about something to do with the play, something to do with the big spotlight perhaps, I thought to myself. Behind them, through the window overlooking the playground, I could see my mother and Molly's walking through the school gates together. All at once I felt flustered and happy and pink. Did our mothers know one another?

Maybe they had become friends, out of the blue? Maybe they had been sitting together in a cake shop, talking about how their daughters really ought to invite each other home? Maybe Mum wasn't moving away from us after all, maybe she had opted in favour of her family.

I glanced over at Molly again. She hadn't noticed a thing, all her attention was on Mr Pedersen.

The audience had assembled in our classroom. They stood tightly packed along the walls or sat on narrow benches at the back of the room. It was a bit cramped; the set designers had not given much thought to where the audience was supposed to go.

We lined up solemnly in rows, the teacher shushed us for the last time, and this time we actually did fall silent. Then we marched out into the corridor, hand in hand, two by two.

Inside our classroom the windows had been blacked out and the lights were switched off, just like in a proper theatre. Then the door was opened. We marched from the bright summer light in the corridor into the darkness of the classroom, we could only sense the presence of the audience; we filed sedately in, feeling our way, and formed a line in front of the blackboard. It was actually a little bit spooky. Molly brought up the rear and positioned herself next to the spotlight. Then the teacher struck the gong, as Molly had instructed her to do. Molly must have got the idea for the gong from Radio Theatre. The sound of the gong seemed to vibrate around the room and as it died away Molly switched on the spotlight. The effect was staggering: the eyes of those of us who were standing in front of the blackboard had only just grown accustomed to the dark classroom, now all of a sudden we were dazzled. The audience was lost to view, we were enclosed within a world of our own.

But we remembered what we had to do. One by one we bowed or curtsied to the spotlight and gave the name of the character we played in the piece which the audience was about to see.

I was the narrator. I wore a mauve velvet cape and on my head

I had a broad-brimmed velour hat in the same colour. It was a little too big, I had to keep one hand on it to save it from sliding down over my eyes. In my other hand I held a big book constructed out of painted polystyrene: Molly had made it, it didn't weigh a thing.

There was something strangely thrilling about being the narrator. I had the most important role, it was up to me to link the different parts of the play together and explain the whole thing to the audience. Without the narrator none of it would have made sense.

The door at the back of the classroom was left open and, after all the actors had introduced their characters and marched out again with me at their head, the teacher struck a brief fanfare on the piano. And then I entered again, this time alone. Molly kept the spotlight on me as I strode down to the front. I took up my position. It felt as though another person had taken up residence inside me, a real narrator. Where she had come from was a mystery to me, but it was so exhilarating, feeling her there inside me.

'Once upon a time there was a town,' this narrator said in a loud, clear voice. 'And in this town there lived a boy and his little sister. They were very poor, and every day their parents had to go to work in the factory, leaving the two children alone. But one day, something strange happened . . .'

I was aware of the glow from the spotlight all around me. It made me shine. I heard the commanding voice that issued from me, it seemed to come right out of a big hole in my chest. It was so deep and had such volume, I had never heard my voice sound like that before. I thought: now Mum will see me. I'm a different person now. She'll never forget this. She'll see herself in me. I am the narrator.

One by one the other children entered and said their lines on their cue from me. They made simple gestures to one another. I had the feeling that they knew it too: the story had begun. It was bigger than us. Standing there, surrounded by the sets which

Molly had made, we felt something come into being within which we could breathe, in a different way from we normally breathed.

I was the only one who remained on the stage for the whole of the performance. I was conscious of Molly following me with the spotlight from the back of the classroom. She rendered me sharp and clear in a way I had never been before. That clarity lasted for weeks, well on into the summer holidays. By then Mum had left.

Molly wanted nothing to do with her parents, but Granny was another matter. Molly saw herself as Granny's daughter, and although she didn't go to see her all that often, she made no secret of the fact that Granny's world, *that* was her world.

Molly's mother was an only child, too, you see. I don't really know what sort of relationship she had with Granny, she and I never talked about such things. In fact Molly's mother and I scarcely spoke to one another at all; since Molly was so distant with her it was only natural for me to keep her at arm's length too. I remember her as a somewhat fuzzy, well-meaning woman who knitted nice, smart sweaters in toning hues for her daughter and her husband, decked the table with linen napkins on Sundays and played little parlour gems on the piano from memory after dinner.

She had such sad eyes. Sad in that slightly apologetic fashion which is so hard to counter with anything hard and determined.

Always, when I went to see Molly, it was she who opened the door of the flat, then left me to carry on down the hallway and into Molly's bizarre room, which bore conspicuously little resemblance to the rest of the flat, without expecting us to say much to one another. I think she had long since come to terms with the fact that her daughter had no wish to share anything of her life with her.

Molly's father would be sitting somewhere in the background in a deep armchair with one leg crossed over the other and his glasses pushed up on to his forehead, reading some book with no dust-jacket. He would give me a friendly, if somewhat absent-minded, nod as I passed. I felt more at home with him; he reminded me of my own father, although Molly's Dad was more forceful. I knew that sometimes on Sundays he and Molly went hillwalking together; they took rucksacks and mats for sitting on and would be gone for the whole day. Molly was always different when she came back from those walks; she seemed more tranquil and spoke more distinctly.

When you stepped into Molly's room the colours and mess hit you right between the eyes. The orange sofa was littered with red and yellow cushions which she herself had embroidered, using bold decorative stitches of her own invention, and the curtains had a nigh on stupefying effect on you if you stared at them too long. Ever since her confirmation she had had her own kettle and teapot in her room, so she didn't have to use her parents' kitchen any more than was strictly necessary. And from when we were sixteen she made her own wine in a gurgling plastic container under her desk, it was always drunk before it got beyond the must stage.

When we needed to pee we would sneak out of her room and into the bathroom, hoping not to bump into her parents. We hardly ever did. Those two must rarely if ever have gone to the toilet. Or at least, that was how it struck me back then, I never gave much thought as to how, from a purely physical point of view, this could have been possible.

Molly's mother died of cancer. It was while Molly was seeing Strøm that her mother's condition became critical. I was in hospital myself at the time, one floor above Molly's mother and I have never understood why Molly wasn't with her during her last days. She came to see me, but not her mother.

When her mother died, Molly's father was stricken by a grief which he did not understand and with which he did not know how to cope. He grew more distracted and frail, he didn't really seem to see his daughter any more. They stopped going for their Sunday walks, and they no longer sat down together at the dining table to browse through big books full of pictures from archaeological digs.

Her father now lives in a sheltered housing complex for the

elderly. There he tends his library: a collection of books – some quite valuable, some less so – from the inter-war years. Molly seldom visits him, and he makes no complaint. Maybe they are actually relieved to have lost each other.

With Granny it was another story. She was a forceful, strong-willed woman with eyes that bored straight into you, and she usually got her way. Everybody called her Granny, even those of us who weren't related to her. It was said that she had trained as an actress in some Eastern European country where she had lived for some years as a young woman. That must have been where she met the father of her child. But she didn't bring the father home with her, only the newborn baby, and she never spoke of him. And that, as far as I know, was the end of her acting career.

Granny showed a keen, innate sensitivity to everyone who came her way, and held a unique attraction for anyone feeling at odds with themself. She had devised her own special method for taking care of unhappy individuals, a kind of brisk cossetting which called for those whom she took under her wing to put themselves in her hands, to shut their eyes for a while and abide by her benevolent laws.

As a rule, being placed under administration by Granny involved moving in with her for a while, being fed the best of fare and sent to bed early every evening. During the day you were expected to take care of various tasks, large and small, in her flat, all according to your interests and abilities. Granny could very quickly discover a room that needed redecorating, some tiles that wanted changing in the bathroom, a ceiling that required washing, a chest of drawers that needed restoring, or window-frames in need of scraping and painting. Or it might be an old lady's costume or gent's suit from her storage room in the loft which wanted altering, if she found that the depressed, or distressed or secretly pregnant individual whom she had taken under her wing needed to learn to sew. She was an excellent seamstress herself, made all her own clothes from top-quality wools and silks imported from abroad, and she had little time for the cheap, synthetic, mass-produced garments with which the town's department stores were now filled. When one of us showed up wearing some new such item of clothing she would ask us to take it off so that she could inspect it. She would rub a corner of the fabric between her thumb and her index and middle fingers, then whip the garment inside out and check all the seams. Finally she would hand it back to its owner with that well-known sniff of hers and that little wave of her hand.

Granny had heavy, dark hair, which gradually acquired a sprinkling of grey, but never went completely white. She pulled it up into a bun in the morning, but never once during the day did she look at herself in a mirror, and she wasn't the type to always be pinning up strands that had come loose, or adjusting clasps, as women who wear their hair up are wont to do. Her upper lip bore the quite distinct shadow of a dark moustache, her eyes were clear and her neck slender and elegant. She smoked cigarettes through a holder and played patience with a gravity which led you to understand that she dealt not in guesswork, but in genuine predictions. In the autumn and winter she lived in a bright, spacious flat in town, not far from where I live now. As a child Molly visited her often, with her parents and on her own. For my own part I was there on a couple of occasions around the time when I became ill, and as children we helped move her piano.

She always had a guest in the house when we called and whether our own visit was short or long depended on whether Granny had decided that her current lodger was ready to face the world outside her flat again or not.

I remember one time, on a Friday afternoon in late autumn, when Molly and I called at the flat. Granny sounded brusque and rather frosty when she answered the entryphone. We were sent into town to run an errand for her, with instructions not to come back before a certain time. It never occurred to us to protest, so off we slunk to get this particular sort of filler which Granny claimed was only stocked by one paint shop on the other side of town. We walked along in silence, side by side; she hadn't even given us any money.

It took us ages to find the paint shop, and when we did the shopkeeper was just about to close for the day, we had to beg him to let us in and dredged all the small change out of our pockets to pay for the tube of filler. Then we trailed the whole way back through town again.

It was getting dark, our feet were freezing and we were feeling a little woebegone by the time we pressed her buzzer again. But this time when she answered Granny sounded totally different, it was clear that she had achieved her aim with whoever was there with her and we were welcomed with open arms.

Once inside the brightly lit flat we were introduced to her guest. She was a woman in her fifties whom neither of us had met before, her eyes were shining, her hair was mussed up and she had a strange glow about her, the kind of glow you see in people who have experienced something which they cannot put into words, some strange, life-giving experience which they would have loved to share with you if they could. The woman reached out her hands to us both and gave us a smile that was both candid and secretive.

We stood there, shuffling our feet, we didn't know what to say. Behind her in the room I could make out a low table on which lay some masks; they looked as if they were made of papier mâché and each one bore a different expression: an angry face in which both top and bottom teeth were bared, a grinning clown-like face, something resembling a horse's head, a white half mask with a long, hooked beak.

I never did find out what Granny and the lady had been doing with those masks. The next time we called on her they were nowhere to be seen.

Granny never went to see people who had problems. She didn't need to, they came to her of their own accord. People tend to talk to one another about the likes of her, I suppose. Word soon gets around when there is help to be had. A psychologist might perhaps have described a sojourn with her as a sort of combination of work therapy and talk therapy, but it felt as though she was really doing something else and over the past few years Molly and I have spoken a lot about what her treatment actually involved and how we ought to feel about it. We have mapped it out thus:

When the confused or unhappy person got in touch, usually by phone, Granny would invite them for eleven o'clock tea. The procedure was as follows: they pressed the buzzer outside the main door and gave their name, they were then let in to the central courtyard; from here they climbed a broad, bright stairway on to which the light fell through panes of coloured glass, until they came to the flat on the third floor. Even before they reached it, the coloured light on this stairway made the person winding their way upwards in a spiral feel that a change was under way.

When they reached the third floor she would be waiting at the door, her sturdy figure radiating warmth. They would shake her hand, take off their outdoor things, remove their shoes and slip their feet into one of the many pairs of slippers she kept in the hall for her visitors' use. They were then ushered politely into the sitting-room. Everything was strangely hushed in there. They were ensconced in one of the comfy, deep-red armchairs, from where they could watch Granny perform her own wordless little tea ceremony, with a series of exquisite, measured movements of hand and wrist.

The tea was already made, the tea service was of delicate old china and one had the feeling that this was something she had been doing in exactly the same way all her life. She had particular movements for the pouring of the tea, the handling of the tea strainer, the little cotton napkins, and for the way in which she offered the sugar bowl. Once they had all they needed they would sit quietly for a few minutes, watching the flame-like tongues of steam rising from their tea cups. Then they would stir the tea a couple of times with a little silver spoon. Stirring clockwise, never anti-clockwise. And there was not a sound to be heard except the faint tinkle of silver on china. After a while, once the steam from the tea-cups had thinned into tiny coils drifting up past the face of the person blowing gently on the tea, they could put the cup to their lips. And the preliminary conversation could begin. The tea was perfectly ordinary Earl Grey, but it tasted *pure* in a way that I have never experienced since.

In a way, what they were having here was not so much a conversation as an interview. Granny gently steered the talk round to her visitor's personal circumstances and asked a few discreet questions. It was all very undramatic and the interview usually concluded with her and her guest agreeing that it might be a good idea to get away from everything at home for a while, to gain some perspective on their life. Then her guest would thank her for the tea, place their cup down carefully on its saucer, set the slippers back in their place in the hall and go home to make the necessary arrangements, leave instructions and pack a small bag with whatever they were likely to need for a sojourn outside of time.

I believe that even during this preliminary phase most people were aware that something had to change.

And when you were ready, had put the world behind you for a while and presented yourself at Granny's for the second time, you were lodged in the guest room and given a job to do in the flat. You worked all day, breaking only for a hot meal at midday and the obligatory one o'clock siesta.

In the evening you were handed a pile of voluminous bath towels and dispatched to the large and always freshly decorated bathroom to take a hot bath. You were not allowed to come out until Granny knocked on the door, signalling that dinner was ready, so there was no reason not to give yourself up to the hot water.

Granny's bathroom was equipped with every sort of modern convenience, as well as a big cupboard stocked with all manner of oils and creams and soaps, but no mirror. So there was no possibility, when staying with her, of looking at your body from the outside. You had to content yourself with whatever you could see with your own eyes and what you could feel when you rubbed in, massaged, dried and buffed up.

That done, you got dressed and went through to the spacious dining room where you were shown to the table and served a home-cooked dinner by Granny. This always tasted perfectly all right and was doubtless very nutritious, though perhaps not exactly *haute cuisine*, on this Molly and I are agreed. You were also served two glasses, never more, of her home-made red wine: nicely warmed to room temperature, but often rather acidic. All this while Granny steered the conversation in her low, intense voice.

In the middle of the table she would have placed a big, old-fashioned tape-recorder which sat there with its two reels blatantly turning as it recorded the conversation. To begin with, you could almost be hypnotised by those spinning reels, as the tape slowly passed from one spool to the other, regardless of whether you were saying anything or not. But after a while you forgot all about it. This might have had something to do with the wine.

These dinner conversations were very different from the preliminary chat over a cup of tea and often ended with the guest revealing something of their innermost thoughts which came as a surprise even to them: some secret, or the description of some awkward situation in which they felt they had become embroiled; something that had, until now, existed only as a kind of inner pressure which, though not clearly defined, brought with it a sense of gloom and despair, often combined with a feeling of being faced with a choice, although they could not have said what the alternatives might be.

Granny rarely needed any more than one dinner conversation to uncover the real cause of the pressure. She seemed to be conversant with certain laws concerning unhappiness which were known to no one else; it didn't take her long to discern the pattern which applied to the person whom she had taken under her wing. Having thus managed to slot him or her into the right pattern she had an odd way of twisting and turning one's view on things, putting them into an entirely different perspective. Big things became small and a detail could swell and assume quite different proportions.

'Are you really so sure about that?' she was liable to ask, when her guest described his or her situation to her. 'How do you know that's what he's thinking? Are you quite sure that's what you want, and that that is really what happened? Are you quite sure that you're disappointed? Maybe you're actually relieved. Maybe deep down you're not angry, but afraid? Maybe you're not afraid, but angry.'

And when you were no longer sure about the facts surrounding the actual problem, suddenly there were a whole lot of other things which you had taken for granted, but which you weren't nearly so sure about any more. From this point on things tended to move more quickly, you almost felt that the reels of the tape recorder should have been spinning faster in order to catch everything. You could find yourself saying things about your own life and how things actually were which truly surprised you. Maybe Granny was right; maybe the pressure didn't lie where you thought it did at all, but somewhere else entirely, in a spot you had never thought of before. You felt as if you had discovered it all by yourself.

But just as you reached that point, just as fresh insight was about to burst upon you, as you were starting to let go of all your old notions, Granny would press the stop button and bring the meal to an end by raising her glass in a cordial, but decisive, toast. She put the cork back into the wine bottle and sent her guest to bed in the large, cool guest room with instructions to be up early the next morning, there was work to be done. The tape and the tape recorder were never seen again, but it was reassuring to know that some record did exist of what you had said about your life during the meal. That you could ask to listen to it again, if you should start to forget, to slide back into your old ways.

But neither Molly nor I has ever heard of anyone asking to be given their tape.

The stay lasted for as long as it took to scrape and paint the window-frames, put up the new tiles or finish altering the costume. This we know, both Molly and I – it was Granny who taught us to sew. She was very strict when it came to making sure that all hems were double, and that the stitching was neat and even and not puckered. As nice on the right side as on the wrong side.

As soon as the snow had disappeared in the spring, Granny would start preparing for the season at the summer house. She called her son-in-law to come round with a covered trailer which was actually designed for transporting horses, and had it filled up with all the things from the flat that she felt she would need over the spring and summer. These included the piano, pot plants and all the little pots of seedlings and cuttings that had been standing on the window sill and were now ready for planting out in the garden later in the spring.

What a carry-on it was, getting that piano down the stairs. Molly always took part in the removal and from when we were in fourth grade, the year Mum left us and Molly let her light shine on me, I was allowed to come along too. Molly's mother, on the other hand, was never on hand for the piano removal. At the time I never asked why.

Old lodgers were called in to help with the lifting. One of her neighbours, a quiet, flaxen-haired young man was in charge of the operation. Hanging in her storage room in the loft, Granny had harnesses bought specifically for this purpose and she would stand at the top of the stairs, watching her neighbour direct the lifting and shifting of the piano. Somebody said that she gave him free piano lessons and that he was very talented.

In this way, with a lot of fuss and hilarity, the huge instrument was carefully manoeuvred down the three flights of stairs and loaded into the trailer. Molly and I raced up and down the stairs laughing and shouting and getting in everybody's way, Granny came down behind the piano carrying a bottle of port and a tray of little stemmed glasses.

When the piano had finally been made fast inside the trailer everybody clapped and cheered. The port was poured and a toast drunk, folk laughed and wished her a good trip and everybody was invited to come and see her at the summer house whenever it suited them over the summer. Granny wrapped the bottle, tray and glasses carefully in dishtowels, laid them in a little basket and climbed into Molly's Dad's waiting car as if it were a taxi. She waved cheerily to Molly and me as the car disappeared around the block. Her neighbour went with her in the car, he had to get the piano installed in the summer house. Then all the guests who had helped carry the piano shook hands with one another and said thanks for a great day and went their separate ways.

For a number of them, this was how they first met, and they would meet again later on visits to the summer house. Sometimes they kept in touch. They eventually had what you might call their own little club, all the people who had helped move the piano. They knew something that other people did not know.

Molly always knew that she would soon be going to see Granny at the summer house, but I felt as if Granny disappeared into another world when I saw her drive off in the car. It would be months and months before she returned to my neck of the woods. Granny never invited me to the summer house. Not as far as I know, anyway. Sometimes I dreamt that she had got in touch with Dad and asked him to bring me down and he had simply forgotten to tell me. But it seemed unlikely.

The week after Granny moved into the summer house the piano tuner paid her a call, so it was said. Molly saw him once, so she told me. She said he was a blind man, silent and hunched, who, in addition to all his other afflictions, suffered from some sort of bone disease. Apparently he and Granny were totally in accord where the piano was concerned, they referred to it as if it were a living creature.

The piano tuner was accompanied on his rounds by his old mother, a dour character who would show up leading her son by one hand, with a note bearing the name and address of the client in the other. She sat stiffly in a chair while he tuned the instrument. It took half the day, the piano tuner was blessed with perfect pitch and had to have absolute quiet while he worked, his hands feeling their way over the keys and inside the casing. When he was done his mother would get up from her chair and produce a pre-written receipt, always made out for the same amount. She accepted payment, said a curt farewell and led her son down to the hideous blue car which she drove at a speed more befitting an electric wheelchair.

As he was getting into the car the man would raise his voice for the first and only time during his visit and beg Granny most earnestly not to move the piano back and forth between the town and the summer house like this again. It wasn't good for such a fine instrument. His mother would nod sternly, underlining his words, as if it were she who had prompted him to say it. And Granny always smiled warmly at him, but not at his mother, which was odd since, of the two, he was the one who could not see. But she didn't promise to change her ways.

There were rumours that the piano tuner might at some point have lodged with Granny, during a turbulent period after his mother's death.

The summer house had been in Molly's family for generations. In her flat in town it was, so to speak, unthinkable for Granny to put up more than one guest at a time, but at the summer house she could have lots of visitors at once and it was perfectly all right to arrive unannounced. This meant that dinner, which was served on the large, covered veranda, often developed quite naturally into what you might call a lively group-therapy session, in which each guest, while tucking into their helping of salmon with cucumber salad and the obligatory two glasses of slightly acidic wine, was forced to listen to and comment on the problems of the others and their little victories, not to mention giving an account of how things had gone in their own life since their stay in Granny's flat. Granny directed the conversation, exerting the hostess's supreme right to the last word in any possible disagreements between her guests. But I have never heard of her taking the tape-recorder to the summer house.

Molly's mother had spent all her summers among such gatherings. I found it strange to think that she should have grown up to be so quiet and so uncharismatic. She seemed to wither a little with every year that went by from the time I first met her at the age of ten, as if she had no real will to live.

If they decided to stay for a few days, Granny's summer visitors were allocated a bed in one of the guest rooms and one or more jobs to do: usually outdoor tasks such as fixing and painting the garden fence, cutting hedges, mowing the lawn, weeding the rose beds and painting the gazebo.

The garden shed was packed with tools of every description and the property was, not surprisingly, extremely well-kept. If any of her guests happened to play the piano they were always encouraged to perform for the others in the sitting-room after dinner. I don't think Granny ever played when there was anyone there to hear.

All visitors had to take a dip in the sea every day, whatever the weather. But she seldom went down to the water herself. Nothing was ever said, but I don't think Granny could swim.

The next question in the fate project follows on naturally from the first: is it possible to be a witness to fate retrospectively? Can one, by rewinding to certain situations, bring one's pure consciousness to bear on things that lie far back in time and perceive what is happening? Maybe even change it? I don't know.

Lately I've been thinking that maybe it doesn't really matter if I don't manage to reconstruct how it ended, that fateful moment with Molly in her room when we were nineteen and discussing Strøm. For my purposes it is enough that I picture it ending like this:

'Tell me what Strøm does to you that is so ground-breaking,' I said to Molly.

'He teaches me to see,' she answered softly, aiming her carrot at me as if it were a pointer.

'Ah.'

'Why are you so suspicious of him all of a sudden?' she asked. 'You really are jealous, aren't you.'

'Don't talk rubbish. He just interests me. A little.'

'Oh, why?'

'Because he interests you.'

'And why do you think he interests me?'

'You just said it yourself. He helps you to see. He gets you to drop all pretence. And of course it helps that he happens to be a world famous photographer thirty years your senior, and that you snatched him away from all those other women who were hovering around him like moths, every one of whom was older than you.'

'How cold your voice is,' she said. 'I don't recognise you when you talk like that. Don't be like that.'

'Okay. I'll do as you say.'

'I haven't slept with him yet, if that's what you're thinking. And I can tell you this much – he's actually very shy. When I draw him he doesn't know what to do with himself.'

'You draw him too!'

'Of course. I'm working on a drawing of him at the moment. I think it's going to be good. He'll be so surprised. If only I could get him to sit still.'

'Sit still? Oh, I'll bet you know a trick or two.'

'What do you mean?'

'You know exactly what I mean. A trick or two that'll make him sit still. Stick out your tits, wiggle your backside a bit, and he won't budge an inch, you'll see.'

'What a sick, dirty mind you have!' Molly cried gleefully. 'You make me want to go and see him right this minute!'

'You're not serious? I mean, I'm here aren't I? This is our chance to spend some time together.'

'Hah! What did I tell you! You *are* jealous!'

'Don't be so childish.'

'Jealous! Jealous!' she crowed and poked me with the stump of her carrot. 'I'm going over to see him right now! I'll take my toothbrush and tell him that I've been kicked out of the house! Then he'll have to let me stay the night.'

'You wouldn't.'

'D'you think you can stop me?'

'Nobody can stop you.'

'So you're not jealous then?'

'Not at all.'

'Good, then that's settled. Finish your tea and I'll go get my toothbrush. I'll walk home with you and then I'll go over to Strøm's place. I'll get him to sit still, you see if I don't.'

'Lie still, you mean,' I said resignedly.

I heard that happy, slightly too loud laugh of hers. She was invincible. I was numb and heavy.

That was the moment when I let her down. I should have stopped her. But it's hard to think clearly when you're numb and heavy.

And she got her way. As always. I cleared away the tea mugs, Molly fetched her toothbrush, we went out to the hall and put on our jackets. She shouted to her parents in the sitting-room that she was going to walk home with me and that they should just go to bed, she had taken a key. On the way past the sitting-room I caught a glimpse of her mother's sad face where she sat on the sofa: it looked both anxious and resigned, a flower closing up for the night.

I couldn't bring myself to object, I knew that nothing could stop Molly once her mind was made up. Not me, not them. But I felt my lips trembling slightly.

She walked all the way home with me. We walked slowly, neither of us saying anything, I was breathing hard, I was so tired, the pills the doctor had put me on made me feel like I had the 'flu all the time. I found myself thinking they might have been right when they said it would be a good idea to get fitted for a wheel-chair.

Molly's slightly hysterical bravado appeared to have deserted her in the course of our walk. We stopped at the corner of the building where I lived with Dad and gazed up at the wall of windows. We tipped our heads back. Through the bright rectangle of the library window in our fourth-floor flat I could see Dad wandering slowly across the room with a book in his hand. The lamplight surrounding him was warm and yellow, it looked very cosy in there. He didn't appear to be missing me. Nor Mum. He didn't appear to be missing anyone.

Molly gave me a quick peck on the cheek, but didn't meet my eye. She was no longer sparkling. If anything she looked a little lonely. I had a sudden urge to put my arm round her shoulders and ask her to take care of herself, but our relationship at that point didn't really allow for that and I was so exhausted, I dreaded the thought of struggling up those stairs on my own. She didn't offer to give me a hand.

'Sleep tight, Agnes,' she said. 'I'll call you in the morning.'

I couldn't get to sleep that night. I lay on my back in bed, feeling the numbness weighing my body down. The effort of getting up to the flat had been too much for me. I wasn't able to hide my exhaustion from Dad when I finally walked through the door; he had to help me to bed and I heard him calling a doctor when he thought I was asleep, heard his faltering, helpless voice as he tried to describe my weakness in matter-of-fact tones.

As I lay there in bed, staring at the ceiling, I pictured all that was happening between Molly and Strøm. Every detail, every move, every sound, every sigh and creak. I felt as though I was there in the flat with them from the moment she rang the doorbell.

I saw a disconcerted Strøm opening the door to her, saw her push past him and pull off her coat all in one movement. Saw her compose herself, her eyes sparkling; saw his throat grow hot and flushed. Saw him reach out to her and wrench the toothbrush out of her hand as he kissed her, so hard that she was pushed backwards and bumped the back of her head against the wall. Saw him cradle the back of her head in the palm of his hand to protect it. And everything that followed.

The next day, Molly's mother came to see me. I was so surprised to see her at the door. Neither she nor I had slept that night and we were as shy of one another as two little girls. Dad had gone to the office; I showed her into the sitting-room. I was still in my nightie, I hadn't actually been intending to get up that day.

She perched on the edge of the sofa in her coat, with her knees together, the way mothers used to sit in those days. I don't know if mothers sit like that any more. I have the idea that they spread their legs more now.

Hesitantly and very softly she said she would like to ask me a few questions about Molly, if that was okay. She spoke so quietly that more than once I had to ask her to repeat herself.

'Molly isn't going to like me talking behind her back,' I said. It came out more sharply than I had intended. Her mother almost keeled over on the sofa, as if I had given her a nudge. I felt so sorry for her. I hastened to say that of course she could ask me anything at all, I wouldn't say a word to Molly.

I was sure she would want to know everything about Strøm, but that wasn't what she wanted to talk about.

'I don't understand why Molly doesn't want anything to do with us,' she said, even more softly. I had to lean right across to hear her. 'Can't you please try to explain it to me,' she continued. 'I've always done my best to give her all the love I have to give. She's my only child. I don't understand why she doesn't want me.'

I leaned even closer and gently patted her hand. Then she burst into tears.

By the time she left I was another person. It was as if a little hatch had been opened inside me, it seemed to lead to a place where I had not been for a long time. I drifted in to the bathroom and took a shower.

Standing under the stream of hot water I saw Mum again. She was walking along a cobbled street in the old part of some foreign town. Maybe she was on her way to an important appointment with a man who had already been waiting for some time and who was waiting very intently for her. I thought: there will always be someone waiting in just that way for Mum. I can't remember whether anyone has ever waited for me like that.

In my mind's eye I saw how she had come zooming in to this foreign town in a plane. I saw her take a taxi from the airport to the hotel, have a quick, ice-cold shower then slip into the cream-coloured suit which she had carried as hand luggage on a coathanger draped in rubber and plastic. The one with the zip, the one that had hung in our storage room in the loft until she left us.

Mum tucked her blouse into the waistband of her skirt and slid her feet back into her cream sandals. She parted her lips in that bird-like way she had, as she always did when applying fresh lipstick. She left the room and dropped the key on to the desk at reception with a quick smile. The key was attached to a heavy brass bob engraved with the room number: Room 402.

Then she walked out of the door and merged with the crowds on the street.

And all at once it was as if I was her. I felt the fabric of the suit against my skin, felt the way the lining of the skirt had ridden up, I slid my hand under my skirt and tugged at the lining and a little shiver ran through me at the feel of the thin silk grazing my thighs as it fell into place under my skirt. I passed the palm of my hand lightly over my mouth and nose and caught the almost imperceptible whiff of shower gel, the brass of the room key, freshly washed sex.

Suddenly I was back in the shower in my father's flat. I felt myself being filled with a terrible anger: a powerful, incandescent emotion which I did not know how to use. I had to get out. I had to work something out.

*

I told myself I was going to Granny's, but it wasn't true. I rang the doorbell of the flat next to Granny's, which belonged to the young man I had seen helping with the moving of the piano, supervising the process of getting it down the stairs every spring when Molly and I were little.

He was a grown man now, as I had expected. He looked a bit taken aback, but let me in without asking what I wanted. He must have known who I was.

He had been in the kitchen making dinner, I could see the steam rising from a pot of potatoes. He nipped in and turned off the cooker. He appeared to be living alone, there were only his outdoor things in the hall, and only his shoes.

I came straight to the point. I told him that I was undergoing tests to see if I had a serious illness which, if I had it, would leave me disabled for the rest of my life. That I had never had a boyfriend. That I had never slept with anyone. That it was now or never.

'Right now?' he asked. For some reason he didn't seem surprised.

'Right now,' I said.

'Would you like something to eat first?'

'Not really. Maybe I could have something afterwards,' I said.

He was gentle and considerate. His bedroom was messy and stuffy. It didn't hurt, but it wasn't all that great either. He looked happy enough when we were finished. I bled a little. I offered to wash his sheet before I left, but he lay on his back and looked at me and said it wasn't necessary, he would do it himself.

He let me use his shower and afterwards I went through to the kitchen with a bath towel wrapped round me and switched on the ring under the potatoes again. The water immediately started to hiss, it was still hot, it hadn't taken us long. There was a pack of fish fingers on the kitchen bench, and two carrots all ready for grating. I realised I wasn't hungry, not in the slightest.

So I went back through to the bedroom, and I leaned down to him and kissed him. He still showed no surprise.

'Would you like dinner now?' he asked.

'No thanks,' I said. 'It's okay.'

I knew, even as I was struggling back down the stairs, that I was pregnant. It was the right time of the month, and some things you just know. It was a fateful moment.

I knew I could never tell Dad about this.

I carried on with my quiet life at home with Dad, was fitted for a wheelchair and practised using it. I spent a lot of time in my room in my dressing-gown, feeling my body getting on with its work in its own quiet, dogged fashion. There was a human seed inside me now, but I found it impossible to get any perspective on the pregnancy, my thoughts grew muddy whenever I tried to think clearly about the baby. I knew, of course, that I wouldn't be able to keep it.

The one lucid thought I had was that Molly and Strøm were probably getting on very well. There was nothing strange about the fact that Molly hadn't called, I told myself, she was probably just so happy and in love, she was doing fine without me. She would get in touch soon. A good friend like me has to know how to step back when love comes along, I said to myself. A good friend is both discreet and supportive. A good friend knows, but not too much. She listens, but not in a nosy way, she doesn't interfere in her friends' relationships with their mothers, much less their lovers.

After that I had other things to think about. My illness was indeed moving into a new and virulent phase, it was a cruel setback, I had to go back into hospital, undergo more tests. The doctor who discovered that I was pregnant did not make a big deal out of it, and we agreed that there was no point in telling Dad, he was completely devastated as it was, he would never be able to understand how I could have conceived a child. I knew he was in the middle of a major new project at the Institute, but he couldn't think about anything but me, even though I was in hospital and he did in fact have the flat to himself and there was no reason why he shouldn't work. In addition to all my other worries I felt terribly guilty about him.

I can hardly remember the abortion being carried out: everything kind of ran together in the hospital. I was lifted from the bed into the wheelchair and back again, it was around this time that the nurses started washing me as if I were a child and not a young woman. And I dutifully let them lift my arms and run the flannel around my armpits, turned my head from side to side so they could reach all the way round my throat and neck. I thought to myself: these women are my mother. They know me.

I lay in my hospital bed and gazed out of the window while I listened to the news channel on the radio. There were so many dramatic events taking place in the world at that time, the earth seemed to be going through a spate of bad news. And I soaked it all up: images of all those things that were burning, collapsing, plummeting out of the sky, washed back and forth inside my head. I let them wash about, I couldn't bring myself to switch off the radio.

Molly entered the room so softly, I didn't notice her until she was right inside. I was surprised at myself, normally I always knew when she was around. I turned my head sharply towards her. Her face was grey, her hair wasn't all fluffed out, as it usually was, it lay flat and rather lankly against her head.

'Oh, pet,' I said, quite taken aback, and put a hand out to the radio. There, I thought. There, now I've switched it off.

She hurried over to my hospital bed, bent down and hugged me. As her cheek touched mine she burst into tears. She was so hot, it felt as though she had a fever.

'Mum called Strøm,' she said. 'She'd been to the doctor. Apparently she's really ill.'

'Oh, Molly.'

'I don't want to talk about it.'

'But you have to . . .'

'I said I don't want to talk about it.'

'Okay.'

'I knew this would happen. I felt it in my bones. Just when everything was going so well. Trust her.'

'Molly!'

'Don't look at me like that!' she shouted at me. 'I told you, I don't want to talk about it! I won't let her ruin everything for me! Not now, when I'm only just getting started! Just look after me. Let me stay here for a while.'

'Come here,' I said. 'Look, you can have my duvet.'

For a split-second, as she slipped under my duvet I felt like a mother making room for her daughter in her bed. A mother tucking in her feverish daughter with a smooth, grown-up sweep of her hand.

'I'll look after you,' I said. 'There's nothing to be afraid of. You just need to rest a little. It's all been a bit much for you lately.'

The next time she came near my hospital bed was some weeks later. She looked completely different. I didn't tell her about the abortion, I didn't think it was necessary, or maybe I couldn't bring myself to talk about it. There were so many other things wrong with me, they ran into one another, I think perhaps I had lost track a little.

I had heard through Dad that her mother was now in the same hospital as me, in another unit. It sounded as though she was pretty ill. Molly had not been to see her. Dad had looked away when he told me this, as if it was knowledge to which he would rather not admit.

I had been moved to a four-bed ward and had little possibility of any privacy, or of conducting intimate conversations, so I suggested to Molly that we go to the smoking room, where we could talk in peace. But she thought that sounded boring. She said she would rather re-arrange the ward so we could have a little space for ourselves. I suppose she spied an opportunity to put together something that would cheer me up a bit when things were looking so black. In retrospect I think she was probably a bit manic that day.

She strode off, with her usual air of authority, to the duty room. I don't know how she managed it, but only minutes later she and two nurses came in, all laughing and chattering excitedly and each of them wheeling a screen. They looked as though they were already firm friends. Over her arm Molly carried a pile of sheets and with the help of these she soon succeeded in creating a little tent for the two of us around my bed. She got the nurses to help her. The three other patients in the ward who till now hadn't said any more than was absolutely necessary to one another or to me, took a lively interest in the proceedings, making funny comments and coming up with practical suggestions.

'Clothes-pins!' Molly commanded, and one of the nurses promptly trotted off, giggling, to find clothes-pins to hold the sheets in place. One of the other patients had a torch which she insisted we borrow.

In next to no time it was done, and Molly had constructed her own, white-sheeted, little hospital stage-set round about me. I watched in amazement as nurses and patients from other wards came in and applauded her handiwork. It was like being in a play again, I hadn't felt like that since I was in fourth grade. For a few minutes the whole unit was pervaded by a general air of hilarity and vitality. Molly has always had this extraordinary gift for inspiring enthusiasm in others. She reminded me a lot of Granny at that moment, of the way she orchestrated an atmosphere every time the piano had to be moved. I was the only one who saw that she wasn't entirely with us, that she was actually thinking about something totally different.

Once the set was completed, Molly told the others that she and I had something Important to discuss. She pronounced this word in such a way that everyone could hear the capital letter, and also detect the note of cheerful irony in the way she said it.

Then she closed the curtain which had been draped like a tent-opening with a dramatic flourish and stood for a moment, looking perplexed, before climbing into bed beside me. We heard the nurses outside our little tent walking off down the corridor again. Molly pulled the duvet over our heads and switched on the torch.

'There!' she said. 'That's better. Alone at last.'

And so we were. We were in a picture. We whispered. The three patients in the other beds were forgotten. You might think that the situation between us, sitting in bed together like that, might have been a bit tense – and anything but intimate. But her scenery had its effect, it caused the two actors, us, to enter into the play and become part of it.

The play seemed to be about two friends who shared everything. They were so close. One of them, Molly, had a lover who was an artist. Now she was developing into an artist herself, imitating him as it were. Her mother was very ill, she was dying, but Molly didn't want to talk about that.

The other friend was me. She didn't really know what she wanted to be. Her mother had gone off years before, and it certainly didn't look as if this girl would ever be an artist. She was just sick, and she would never be able to have a baby. As yet she had not learned much about fate.

The girl with the lover only wanted to talk about all the things he had helped her to understand.

'He makes me see!' she whispered. 'I know myself much better now, he has made me so aware of myself.'

'You've said that before,' the sick girl whispered back. 'Can't you tell me something new?'

'There won't ever be anything new,' replied the girl who was an artist. 'That's all there is to it: he teaches me to see. That's all it takes.'

'Yes, but see what?'

'It doesn't matter what, don't you see! Everything! With fresh eyes.'

'You don't say?'

'You really don't want to understand,' she said in that rather manic way which I knew so well. 'It's so simple, it's merely a matter of seeing things as they really are. Look, I'll show you. She took a little notebook from her pocket, looking as though she was about to recite something to me, something Strøm had said, no doubt.

'How is your mother?' I asked.

Maybe I shouldn't have said it. At any rate, it was at that point that Molly broke out of our cave with an abrupt, angry flounce. She switched off the torch, threw back the duvet, laid her notebook on the bedside table and got out of the bed. She picked up the large shoulder bag which she had left at the foot of the bed. Out of it she pulled one of the masks I had seen that day at Granny's. I was flabbergasted, I hadn't given a thought to those masks since. The one she had with her was the white half-mask with the big, hooked beak.

'Where did you get that?' I asked.

But she didn't answer. She simply put the beaked mask on her face and pulled the sheets aside, as if they were the curtains on a stage. The three other patients in the ward became real for us again. They stared at her as if hypnotised.

Molly stepped out into the middle of the room and stood there, perfectly still, for some minutes. It was as if the bird mask had transformed her. With one long, graceful flourish she produced a little mirror and held it up in front of her face. And it looked as though the masked figure took on a life of its own when it saw itself in the mirror. It wasn't only Molly's face which had changed, it was her whole body: she began to circle the ward, but I had never seen her move like this before, not with her usual bounce, but quietly, mournfully. The masked figure took up residence inside her and gave expression to all the sadness and fear and confusion we both felt over all that was happening to us. But it did this with such lightness, almost seeming to glide along, moving hesitantly around the room, lifting things, examining everything it saw, including the other patients in their beds. The bird inspected the patients as if they were objects, as if they had no life in them. It lifted an arm in a pale-blue hospital shirt then lowered it gently on to its quilt again, prodded an ear. I had the feeling that this bird was a child that had never set foot in such a strange world before. And it was so very, very sad. It had lost something.

The doorway into the ward gradually filled up with nurses, doctors and patients from other wards who stood there silently watching the bizarre performance which Molly was putting on. No one said a word. I think we all felt transformed, as if we really were objects and not people.

At last it seemed that the bird had inspected the whole room and everything in it, and that this thing had come to its natural conclusion. Again it stood perfectly still in the middle of the room for a few minutes. Then with an upward sweep of the hand it pulled off the beaked mask.

The moment Molly's face appeared the bird was gone. It came as a shock to see that it had been her behind the mask all the time. She looked as if she too were surprised; almost hypnotised.

Still no one in the room said a word. Molly came over to me, bent down and kissed me on the lips. Then she popped the mask and the mirror back into her bag, picked up her jacket and exited the room without a word.

Maybe I should have been worried about her, but I wasn't. I thought to myself: something inside her knows where she's going. She'll go into town now, she'll wander around for a while, until she's cold and hungry. Then she'll go over to Strøm's place. He'll look after her. Strøm and I share the responsibilities. We are like parents who have brought up a lot of children together; we know what to do.

*

Only a few days later Dad came to see me and told me that Molly's mother was dead. She had passed away peacefully, as they say, in bed only one floor below my own ward. Molly had not been there, neither had Granny. Only Molly's father had been with her. Dad had seen the death notice in the paper. The bit about neither Molly nor Granny being there he had heard from a colleague at the Institute who had some small acquaintance with the family. It's just the sort of thing to set people gossiping.

I didn't know what to say. Nor did Dad. I could see that he already had enough to cope with, he couldn't take any more. He had that look in his eyes which said he did not intend to waste any energy on this. I understood him. I couldn't take any more either.

He asked if I didn't think we should send flowers to the funeral. I said I would take care of that from the hospital. He looked relieved, as if a small burden had been removed from his shoulders, almost before he had had a chance to wish he could be relieved of it.

After Dad left I lay and thought. I felt strangely calm and clear. I turned my head slowly towards the bedside table and my eye fell on Molly's black notebook, the one with the elastic band round it. It was lying next to the radio, where she had laid it before she turned into the sorrowful bird. There must have been something in it she wanted to show me, a sketch of Strøm or something like that, but then the bird had taken over and the notebook had been forgotten.

I opened it and looked at her drawings, the dense writing, the arrows and underlinings. I didn't feel I was doing anything wrong; it was as if this notebook had always been mine, as if it was actually me who had made the notes in it.

Most of what was written in it was about Strøm. It looked as though Molly had kept a little diary of the past weeks, filled with little drawings and quotations. I saw nothing there about her mother being ill. Clearly her project at that time was exclusively a Strøm project, it was not a mother project.

I wanted to understand what had happened to Molly. That was all I wanted. I saw the whole thing in my mind, and I let her live for me as I leafed slowly through the notebook. She hadn't told me very much in terms of actual facts about her and Strøm. Mostly, what I got were dreamy descriptions and partially digested philosophizings. The real pictures I had to create myself:

At the start of their affair, Molly and Strøm trod warily with one another. If she was young, with no limits of any sort and game for just about anything, he – when you came right down to it – was not as much of a rake as rumour would have it. He was a member of the old school and I decided that he knew he could hurt this young woman if he pushed her into doing something for which she was not ready.

They went on a lot of walks together. They drove down to the sea, or to the large wooded areas outside of town. Molly asked him about his life, first and foremost about his career as a photographer, but also about the women he had been with, about what he had done with them, what sort of influence they had had on him. He only told her so much, though.

Then came one evening when Molly was about to leave. She had spent the whole afternoon in his flat. With typical teenage presumption she had commandeered his kitchen, made tea for them both and served it in his living-room. He had spent a lot of time commenting on her latest photographs. They were not good, they displayed the most elementary technical faults; and yet there was something about them. He talked to her about this. She took this as a sign that he cared about her, displaying towards her a patience she had never heard mentioned by any of the many people who came to see him.

He had asked her to pick out those pictures which she thought were the best and tell him why. She had been very sure in her selection, but her explanations were poor. He had listened to her with a furrow between his eyes and this put her on edge, made her talk faster and louder. In the end she had swept up all of the pictures from the large desk on which she had laid them. She said she was going home, and that actually it wasn't photography she was into, it was drawing.

And now she was standing in his hall, staring at him. He had not risen out of the deep, battered office chair in which he was sitting, he had swung round so that he had his back to her and his face towards the window, while she fumbled with her jacket and her long, knitted scarf. She put her jacket on, then took it off again. He swung his chair back towards her and eyed her intently. Then he asked if he could keep her pictures for a while. She did not answer.

She heard him get up from the chair and walk across the room towards her. She was standing facing the door now, but she had her jacket in her hands.

All of a sudden something had changed between them, but she didn't know what.

'What is it you see in me that I don't see ?' she asked in a voice that made it impossible not to answer her. He walked right up to her, reached an arm round her and took her jacket. Then he held it open behind her so that she could stick her arms into the sleeves. He turned her round and slowly did up the buttons.

He has nimble fingers for such an old guy, she thought to herself. He wound the long scarf round her neck several times and finished by placing his hands on her shoulders and pressing her, as it were, into her own form.

'You are lovely,' he said softly. 'You shine.'

Some weeks later they were standing close together before the big mirror in the hall, naked. She had been with him like this many times before, she was no longer shy. Now he was standing behind her, she drew his arms round her and leaned back against him.

'Say it again, what you said before,' she said.

'Say what?'

'Say what you said to me. The second time we made love. Just before.

'Oh, that.'

'Say it.'

'You're lovely,' he said.

'Yes, but say the other bit, too.'

'Was there something else?'

'Yes. You said something else.'

'I'm not sure I remember.'

'Don't kid me. You remember. Say it.'

'I . . .'

'Say it.'

He removed his arms from her, took a step to the side, leaving her reflected alone in the mirror.

'You shine,' he said.

'Do I?'

'Yes. And one day you are going to do something great.'

That was the moment when her flame burst into life.

Some things you just know.

But there was another time, too, I told myself, when Molly paid a very different visit to his flat. This time she had no photographs with her; instead she had brought her drawing things. She carried herself with a new air of authority, as if she had the right to ask something of him now, a right which she had not had before. She walked straight into the living room without taking off her shoes first and asked him to pull the office chair over to the window and sit in it.

'Are you going to draw me?' Strøm asked, suddenly seeming shy.

'Certainly. I've decided to apply to the Academy.'

'The Academy, Molly?'

'Yes.'

'And you're going to start by drawing me?'

'Yes.'

'Oh, but I hadn't really thought . . .'

'Didn't you mean what you said? Or maybe you don't remember?'

'I do remember, and I did mean what I said.'

'Then sit still. And you're not allowed to see it. I'm just going to draw you and then I'm leaving. Okay? We are not going to bed.'

'Well, but shouldn't I make some coffee for us first?'

'No. Sit still.'

She had already sat down, balanced her drawing board on her knee, and made a start.

He sat quite still in the chair and stared out of the window for as long as he could. Then he stood up abruptly and tottered towards her: he had been sitting awkwardly, one of his legs had gone to sleep, and he wasn't feeling very well either. He hadn't told her that he had diabetes, nor was he planning to say anything about it now.

She threw the drawing board down and jumped up to catch him as he fell towards her. Without a word she helped him over to the littered sofa, settled him on it and laid the blanket over his knees, as if he were an aged passenger on a pleasure steamer. Then she packed her drawing things into her bag, put on her coat, planted a kiss on his forehead and left the flat.

I think he thought: she's going to leave me. I know more or less what I have to show her and she has an inkling of it too. When I have nothing left in reserve and she realises that I am sick, she's going to leave me.

But what he meant was: I am afraid.

Neither Molly nor I knew much about Strøm's background, except what she had managed to winkle out of him about the women in his life and the few details given in the biographical note in the catalogue to the exhibition which we had seen. He had remarked on this text that time when I visited him at his flat, but I hadn't told her that. In the note it had said that he came from a well-to-do family, that he had been destined to take over the family firm, but had broken all ties with his family and been cut off without a penny. Initially he had wanted to be a painter and had attended a private art school for a while. But then he had changed direction and decided to become a photographer instead. He had gone abroad and very soon made the acquaintance of a great French photographer, one of the greatest of them all, who was by then an old man. There were lots of stories going the rounds about the first meetings between these two and it was hard to know whether they were pure fiction or whether they were in fact true. Strøm seemed uncomfortable talking about that period in his life.

And then came the evening when Molly came racing up the stairs to the flat where Dad and I lived.

She was obviously in shock. Dad wasn't home, he was still at the Institute as he often was in the evenings at that time. I think it depressed him to be with me too much.

I stood in the doorway, staring at her. She stared back. Then I helped her out of her jacket and led her into the sitting-room, set her on the sofa, tucked a blanket round her.

'Would you like a cup of tea?' I asked.

'No.'

'Brandy?'

'Yes.'

I went over to Dad's drinks cabinet, poured a measure into one of Dad's large brandy glasses and handed it to her. She drained it in two large gulps. She didn't even shudder as she swallowed. That didn't worry me, I knew her.

And then she told me. She had been at a café with Strøm and some people whom she thought were just casual acquaintances from the art world. He had seemed out of sorts all afternoon, something was clearly bothering him, but she couldn't figure out what. Eventually he got up and left. She had stayed where she was, she was too proud to go after him, she didn't want to be one of those girls who were always running after their conquests, all clingy and helpless.

After Strøm had gone it was not long before the conversation, not unexpectedly, came round to him.

'But what did they say?' I asked. Molly seemed so miserable, I couldn't think what could have happened.

'They started talking about his past. And suddenly I realised that one of these females at the table used to live with him. She was the one who was talking the loudest, of course.

'Hm, I suppose she would be.'

'I'm sure she did it because she knew that I'm seeing him. And the others followed her lead, coming out with all sorts of stories about him. Those bitches, they're so jealous and they don't even try to hide it, they egg each other on.'

'But what did they say?'

'They said he's married.'

'Uh-oh. Who to?'

'Some woman who lives in France. They met when he was very young, she was some years older than him.'

'And he's never got divorced from her? After all these years?'

'Apparently not. But it doesn't really matter, because she doesn't want anything to do with him.'

'Why not?'

'She has a child by him. A daughter, she's quite big now. About my age.'

'Heavens.'

Then she told me that later that evening Strøm's old lover had followed her into the ladies. She was a woman twenty years older than Molly, an acclaimed singer. She was obviously drunk, and she said it was none of her business, but she thought Molly ought to know that Strøm had been denied all right of access to his daughter in France on the grounds of incest. The acts of abuse had apparently continued over a period of several years when his daughter was small, and Strøm had admitted to them. He had done time for it, she said, some years back. The matter had come to light while this woman was living with him. He had also admitted to her that he had abused the child. Not many people knew about it; she had chosen to keep it to herself, so this was something that the others round the table in the café knew nothing about, and she wasn't going to tell them, she asserted with an air of self-importance. As for herself, she had left Strøm when she learned about the incest charges. She had had no contact with him since then, until she happened to bump into him this evening, here in the café. She didn't think he had told anyone else either.

Molly kept her eyes fixed on me as she spoke. I didn't know what to say. She held the brandy glass out to me and I refilled it.

'The worst of it was that she told me all this while I was sitting there peeing,' she said. 'There was nothing I could do to shut her up and I had had two or three beers, I thought I would never stop and it was hard to hear exactly what she was saying. She was so horrible. I don't know what he saw in her.'

'Are you going to tell him you know about it?'

'No. But he saw she was there, that must have been why he left. He's probably worried sick.'

'I know, things won't be the same between you now, will they! You'll have to stop seeing him.'

'Well, obviously. In a little while. But I'm not finished with him yet,' she said tightly.

'What do you mean?'

'He has to teach me to draw, and to take photographs. There's no one in this town as good as he is and it's too soon for me to go abroad.'

'It seems to me you're using him, Molly.'

'And what do you think he's doing to me?'

'I'd say you're using him just as much as he's using you.'

'Yes, but he flaunts me. Like some sort of trophy. I can see it, he can't hide it, when we're out somewhere and bump into friends of his, like tonight.'

'You've never said anything about feeling like this before.'

'I didn't realise it until this minute.'

She wound up getting pretty drunk and by the time Dad came home she had fallen asleep on the sofa. He helped me carry her through to my bed. Dad didn't ask any questions, he respected me and my life and understood that this was an emergency. But he looked puzzled.

In retrospect, though, I've been thinking that he seemed almost relieved to see that I had something to occupy me.

I watched as he made up a mattress on the floor for me. I would watch over Molly like a dog.

Molly went back to Strøm the next day. I couldn't believe it. I was worried about her. It was clear that she'd had some sort of breakdown, but also that what she had decided to do was stronger than whatever had snapped inside her.

It was a Sunday, she had a hangover and must still have been feeling pretty groggy when she left our flat. I had made some good, strong coffee and fried some bacon for her, I had kissed her clammy brow before she left.

I don't think she confronted Strøm with what she had heard. Maybe she just went on drawing him as if nothing had happened. There's no way of telling how much he knew about her at that time. He may have been a little afraid of her. Afraid of being deserted.

The way I imagine it, it was on the Sunday when she returned from my place that Strøm took her for a long, long walk along one of the beaches outside of town. They strode out side by side without speaking, I would guess. It was a cool autumn day in the middle of October; the weather was wet and blustery, they were both wearing full rain gear, complete with boots and sou'westers, but they still got soaked through and chilled to the bone.

In the car on the way home he turned the heating on full, they had dumped their raincoats and sou'westers on the back seat. The windows steamed up and they had to keep wiping them with a rag from the glove compartment. For once, Molly sat quietly staring out of the window, only stretching across to Strøm's side occasionally to rub clear a patch on the windscreen in front of him, and get pushed away impatiently because she was blocking his view.

I fancy that already there, in the car, he sensed that she had come to a decision. He thought he knew what she had decided to do and that made him uneasy. Without being aware of it he reduced his speed. When they turned off on to the quieter streets of the area where he lived, he asked if he shouldn't just drive her home. She stared at him blankly.

So they drove to his place and parked in the usual spot on the street. She walked ahead of him into the building and up the stairs to his flat. She stood and waited for him outside his door, he handed her the keys and she kicked aside the newspaper which was lying on the mat. She opened the door, pulled off her boots in the hall and disappeared into the bathroom without a word. He heard her lock the door, heard her flush the toilet several times, then came the sound of water running in the shower. He hung up his own rain gear and hers to dry in the hall then went through and sat down at his desk in the living room. He poured a drink for himself, but not for her. He sat there wondering what to do, not touching his drink.

At length she came out. She was naked, her skin flushed and warm after a brisk rub-down with one of his rough, washed-out towels. She had her clothes in a bundle in her arms, her panties and bra tucked neatly inside the sleeve of her sweater. She didn't look at him, but walked stiffly past him and into the bedroom. She laid the bundle of clothes on the floor and flicked the bedcover aside. Then she slid under the duvet.

It was a single bed, quite narrow.

He sat for a while in the living room, not knowing what to do. Then he crossed to the bedroom door and stood there, leaning against the door-frame, looking at her. There was so little of her under the duvet, she was barely visible.

'What do you want me to do now?' he asked eventually.

'Don't ask,' she said. 'Come here.'

Afterwards she cried. Silently at first, then quite openly; she was shaking all over. He tried to put his arm round her, but she pushed him away.

It was impossible to lie very far apart in the narrow bed, but she squeezed up as close to the wall as she could, facing away from him. He stayed on his back with one forearm over his eyes. Perhaps he had the feeling that he had ruined everything now, that this was all his fault. He had been rougher than he had intended and she had been different, he had never seen her quite like that before. He had meant to take his time, be gentle with her, but she had been so aggressive and impatient, and at the same time rather distant, as if she did not want him to get through to her. As if she would really rather be left in peace.

It wasn't the first time they had made love, but it felt as though it was. He had the feeling that this was the one time that counted, that this was the last time, the one which cancelled out all the other times. Like a false step, the one which negates all the other times, the times when you get it right.

'I'm sorry,' he said at last. She made no reply, but sobs racked her body. And it suddenly dawned on him that this crying fit had nothing to do with him. Something had opened up between them, something that had no bottom; he didn't know what it was. But he knew that this was where their ways parted.

Had they stayed together he would have remained like this, beating against the loneliness inside her, that harsh, angry weeping with which she wished to be alone. Neither he nor she had the strength to look down into this thing that had opened up between them.

What he could not know was that all the men with whom she would later become involved would have to go through this same process: follow her for a while and then see her way veer away from theirs in some bed. They would lie on their backs beside her and stare at the ceiling with her trembling body beside them; a body which would not be comforted. It was almost as if she was in fact on her way to somewhere else entirely: travelling along a road, towards a sparse forest.

It took its toll on me, picturing all of this. I suffered along with Molly, and Strøm. I wasn't feeling well; the short period of remission which had prompted the doctors to send me home from the hospital had evidently been nothing but a fluke. Something inside me had glimpsed some hope there, hope of a way out, of a move forward. But then Molly and Strøm stopped seeing one another and this thing inside me that spoke to fate let go, I think. I felt it so clearly in my legs, they withered away under me like two diseased plants, they were not to be trusted, they did not want to go where I wanted to go. They didn't want to go anywhere, all they wanted was to sleep.

More tests were done at the hospital, experiments with new pills with new side-effects, and eventually another spell in hospital which looked like being quite a long one. I felt that I was trickling out of myself, like a dark river that did not know where it was going.

At the same time something had changed between Molly and me, something which in some strange way made me stronger. It seemed to me that my illness gave me greater authority in her life, or maybe it was simply that I was all she had now. At any rate, she turned to me with a lack of restraint that I had never seen her show before: tenderly, as if I were a man. It was almost as if she and I were having an affair.

I suppose what happened was that she allowed me to fill the place that fell vacant when she broke up with Strøm. I became the one who listened to her and observed her, admired her, blew on her flame, gave her good advice and put her in her place when she went too far in one direction or another. That, at least, is how I liked to think of it. The fact that Molly accorded me this role almost led me to acknowledge this authority myself: the authority of illness.

*

She still would not talk about her mother. I never did find out why she had not gone to the hospital to visit her, or to the funeral. I see now that I ought to have brought more pressure to bear on her as far as that was concerned. Maybe that was exactly what she was waiting for me to do the whole time. Maybe that was what her trust in me came down to, although she would never admit it: it was up to me to untie the knot of her mother's sickness and death.

Strøm, on the other hand, she would talk about, even after they broke up. And it was as if even at that point I understood that she was actually talking about her mother when she talked about Strøm. I can't explain it, that's just how it was, some strange form of displacement had occurred inside her. She felt that both her mother and Strøm had let her down badly, but she wasn't going to let them break her. She would just have to do a bit of a mental reshuffle.

For my own part, I felt that I, too, had let her down. Fortunately, though, I didn't think she had noticed. And during all of our conversations about Strøm I kept telling myself that I must never, never let her down again, as I had done that evening when I allowed her to go off and seduce him, become attached to him, even though everything in me was screaming that this affair would not end well.

But if I am really honest, I suppose I realise that I still do not understand what truly happened between her and Strøm in the days after they broke up. I had the feeling that, even while she was pushing him away from her with all her might, in actual fact she was protecting him from something.

Before she broke up with him, Strøm helped her to get into the Academy. Her drawings had impressed him and no doubt he had his contacts: he was a force to be reckoned with in the art world at that time.

Molly took her studies very seriously and did everything to

hide the fact that she was the youngest student at the Academy. She came across as being outgoing and self-assured and she would not have it said that she had got her place at the Academy thanks to a bit of string-pulling on Strøm's part. She still thought of herself as a self-made woman. And she had no trouble getting others to believe her. As a benefactor Strøm no longer existed for her, he was simply someone who had let her down.

Looking back on it, I can see that my second long stay in hospital was to a great extent coloured by my fantasies of what had occurred between Molly and Strøm. That is how I occupied myself while lying in that hospital bed. I certainly wasn't spending my time trying to get well, as Dad was begging me to do.

I thought of them and what they were up to, I saw everything that took place between them so clearly. It was as if I turned the story of Molly and Strøm into my own reality.

It occurs to me now that perhaps those insights into love which I had while in hospital – and which were, of course, only indirectly based on real events – formed the cornerstone of my fate project: it was through these pictures inside my own head that I learned something about reality. I only visited the man in the flat next door to Granny in order to have something concrete to link to these pictures, some sensations.

And to a certain extent it had worked: the odour of half-cooked potatoes and fish fingers hung over the image in my mind of Molly and Strøm in Strøm's narrow bed.

Just as Molly's affair with Strøm ended in a kind of little death, a plunge down into something that was too deep for either of them to fathom, so my affair with Granny's neighbour ended with a child that had to die before it had begun to grow. That child never came to anything more than a seed with a very, very tiny beating heart deep inside it.

The effect was both striking and surprising: something indefinable had been added to the balance between Molly and me, some sort of disparity had been corrected, and I think it came as a relief to us both. We could both breathe more easily.

After the abortion I got it into my head that I had to start doing some life drawing, as Molly and the others at the Academy were doing. I got Dad to buy me drawing materials: sticks of charcoal, expensive felt pens and the finest quality paper, as well as a drawing board which I could use in bed. He was obviously relieved that there was something he could actually do for me and bought the best he could find. But I had no models, everybody who came and went in the ward was on their way somewhere else, there was no one I could ask to stand still long enough for me to draw them. Apart from Dad, of course. He sat there, stock-still on his chair. But he only got upset when I tried to draw him, it was so obvious that I made him feel uncomfortable. I tried a couple of times, but then I gave up.

I found myself wishing that I could meet Strøm again. I had an idea that it was him who was supposed to sit there at my bedside, watching over me. I would have known how to steer clear of his dangerous side, I thought. He just had to help me discover something inside myself, the way he had done with Molly. I needed someone like him to blow on my flame.

But that was as far as it went. On the surface at least. It got to the stage where I had no strength for anything except listening to the radio. I would have to leave it to Molly to go on and become an artist without me, I concluded resignedly. That was how it was always meant to be anyway, ever since primary school.

But now, when I rewind, to look at the film of myself in the days after Molly broke up with Strøm, I see things differently. I see that it was at this point that the first tiny seed of my fate project was formed. It was in the fate project that I myself would become a person who created things. And I did it all by myself, without any man to blow on me.

This time Molly did not come to visit me at the hospital, despite the new bond between us, her belief in my knowledge of her. I don't know why she didn't get in touch. I could have called her, or asked Dad to contact her, but I didn't, not for some weeks.

I missed her. I felt it was up to me to think of something. I tossed and turned in bed until the sheet was all rucked up underneath me, had only half a mind on what the doctors and nurses were doing to me; I was trying to come up with a plan for Molly and me. I had a feeling that time was running out; something was happening to us that I wanted no part of. It was as if something out there was starting to tighten its grip.

I could not let that happen. I had to get back out of the hospital. I had to put my foot down, had to steal a march on my illness. And the only solution I could come up with was for Molly and I to move in with Granny. Somehow I had utter faith that if only we were within Granny's four walls fate would not be able to get at us.

Once I had made up my mind, carrying out my plan seemed merely a formality. That is often the way: the hard part is to conceive of something, once you have that image fixed in your mind the actual implementation turns out to be easier than you had thought. I simply asked to speak to the doctor in charge of my case. I insisted that I should go to him, not the other way round.

I got a porter to wheel me along to his office. It's odd, but at that time my need of a wheelchair varied from day to day. It was as though a switch were being turned on and off on some mechanism that neither I nor the doctors understood.

The doctor was sitting at his desk, waiting for me, he had all my files in front of him, a great pile of them, but he was not looking at these. He offered me a plastic cup of awful coffee from the duty room, I thought that was very nice of him. He had postcards from all over the world stuck up on a notice board behind his desk. I caught myself wondering whether they were from former patients. I couldn't see what it said on the backs of those cards, but it wasn't hard to imagine: *Dear Doctor, Heartfelt thanks for curing me, I am now fit as a fiddle and enjoying life here on the west coast of Africa.*

He had got himself a cup of coffee too, and unwrapped a number of sugar cubes which he had a job getting to dissolve in the lukewarm coffee. It struck me that for a doctor he didn't know much about health and well-being if he thought a plastic cup of bluish, lukewarm coffee and four sugar cubes was what was needed. There are better alternatives. But I made no comment. I suppose not every doctor thinks it's his job to know about health and well-being, or to apply this knowledge to himself. They probably have other things to see to. Like me, for example.

The doctor eyed me keenly as he stirred his coffee, and asked what he could do for me. I smiled and said that what I would really like, of course, was for him to make me well. But since things weren't looking too promising on that front I was wondering whether it wouldn't be better for me to be at home, getting used to the idea of a life in a wheelchair, rather than slowly withering away in the artificial environment of the hospital.

'I mean, the hospital isn't real life,' I said. 'There's nothing one can really practise on here, it doesn't have the smells and sounds and tastes of real life.' And he had to agree with me there. He may well have been a very clever guy, for all his bad coffee habits. At any rate, I think he understood what I was saying, and it wasn't as if he could do that much more for me anyway.

I had my way in everything, on the proviso that I stuck strictly to my medication.

It was me who took the lead in this. As soon as I got home I called Molly and without any preamble announced that she and I had to move in with Granny for a while. She made no objection, even though she was in the middle of her first term at the Academy. She simply followed my lead like a frightened child.

She had grown so thin since the last time I had seen her. There was something shadowy about her, as if she had been wandering around in that sparse forest where I had never been. As if she had been waiting for me to call her back.

It was also me who called and arranged everything with Granny, and me who got Dad to help me to pack what Molly and I would need for our stay. I asked him to pack for both her and me, but in one bag, not two. This enhanced the feeling of us being twins. Then I called Molly's Father and made up an excuse for us having to stay with Granny for a while. I don't remember what I told him, he asked no questions, he just seemed relieved. He must have forgotten that I had been in hospital, he was so wrapped up in himself and his own grief for the wife who had been taken away from him, he couldn't understand why anyone would inflict such grief on him. He didn't want to understand.

Nor did my own Dad ask why I wanted to take Molly with me to Granny's. He just went on pottering about, turning down corners in books, switching the kettle on and forgetting about it for so long that the water was cold again before he got the length of putting a tea-bag in a cup. There was no point in trying to change such things about him. I heard him talking to the doctor on the phone about my condition, it sounded as if he were leaving everything in the doctor's hands.

He offered to drive us to Granny's, but I said we could take a taxi and he didn't argue.

Granny normally never took two guests at one time, I don't know what moved her to make an exception on this occasion. I hoped she would think of Molly and me as sisters. Maybe even as almost one and the same person. Two birds with one stone.

We were in a pretty sorry state when we turned up at her flat. It was a morning in November; the weather was clear and cold, it was ages since I had felt such keen air against my skin as I did during the few minutes between the taxi dropping us off and Molly and I standing in Granny's hall, swinging between us the bag that Dad had packed. We must have looked rather lost, or a bit comical; at any rate, Granny took one look at us and burst out laughing.

'Oh, my little lasses,' she cried. 'What *is* the matter?'

There was something comforting about being Granny's little lasses, as we had been when we were younger.

We were taken through the tea ceremony separately. Molly went first: Granny dispatched me to the bathroom to freshen up while the two of them had tea in the sitting-room. She supplied me with a pile of towels and told me to pamper myself, take all the time I needed, there was no hurry.

Maybe it was what she said about there being no hurry that made me break down. My tears took me completely by surprise. I sat on the white stool next to the bath and wept and wept, staring all the while at my stomach and my flabby, white thighs. I could hear the faint voices of Molly and Granny in the sitting-room and I tried my best not to make any sound.

After a long time, when Molly and Granny had finished their tea, Molly came to the bathroom door and called my name in a soft, anxious voice. I think she realised that there was something seriously wrong with me, far more serious than whatever ailed her. In the end she was crying too. I didn't answer her. I had got undressed and left my clothes in a heap on the floor, put the plug in the bath and turned on both taps. The water gushed down on to the gleaming porcelain, the bath must have been very new, possibly only recently installed by someone who had been staying with Granny prior to us, slept in the guest room which was now mine and Molly's for a few days, drunk Granny's acidic red wine.

*

It was Granny who came in. She stood by the door for a while, considering me, much as the doctor had considered me before discharging me from hospital. Then she walked up to me, lifted my chin so that I had to look her in the face.

Those eyes. I don't know how to describe them.

We ate the first dinner together, all three of us. The tape recorder rolled in the middle of the table. I stared at it, as if it knew something I didn't know. We whiled away the rest of the evening ensconced in our respective deep-red, plush armchairs, flicking through back numbers of dressmaking magazines. Granny had informed us that our task during our stay would be to make her a suit for the autumn. We held pictures of different designs up for each other to see, commented on the cut and the degree of difficulty. Granny lit cigarette after cigarette, popping each one into her elegant cigarette holder. She regarded us silently, she did not seem happy.

Once we had agreed on which suit we would make, she suggested that Molly should be responsible for the jacket, while I took care of the skirt and the jacket lining. But Molly protested and said that of course we would both do the whole thing, jacket and skirt and lining, together. I shot her a grateful look, she has her own special way of raising me up to her level, playing at being twins.

And I'm sure Granny understood that with us it had to be share and share alike. Without any more argument she brought out the fabric for the suit, she had had it lying around for some time, it was a lovely marled tweed from England. She showed us how to take her measurements: gave us each the measuring tape in turn and got us to measure her this way and that, from top to toe; we noted the measurements down on a slip of paper. I had the feeling that we took many more measurements than were strictly necessary, every one was checked at least twice. She clearly enjoyed standing there in the middle of the room with her arms raised, issuing orders while Molly and I wound our way round her to ascertain the distance from shoulder to wrist, around the waist, around the bust, as she called it, from the nape of the neck to the tailbone.

Then she showed us how to ease out the stiff pattern pages in the middle of the dressmaking magazine and copy the parts belonging to the appropriate suit on to pattern-paper. She explained to us how to find out which sections we needed by following a special system of symbols; both Molly and I felt that a whole new world was opening up for us, it was so obvious, almost self-explanatory: we just hadn't known about it until now. Not that we hadn't both done a fair bit of sewing in recent years, but all out of our own heads and all according to rule of thumb. We had never taken measurements and we had had no idea that there was a special world of symbols for such things.

When all the measurements had been taken, she turned gravely to us. We knew that now came the important part. She said:

'Never, ever use dressmaking scissors for cutting paper. Dressmaking scissors are sacrosanct.'

We nodded solemnly, as if we had just been initiated into a secret.

Then we cut out all the sections of the pattern and marked them with the correct numbers and symbols for darts, buttonholes and pleats. But once that was done Granny rose abruptly from her chair and announced rather coolly that it was time for bed. We didn't know what time it was; at Granny's all guests had to deposit their watches in a particular drawer in the chest in the hall, and there were no wall clocks or alarm clocks in the flat. I could tell that I was tired and Molly was yawning too. It didn't matter what hour it was, we had stepped into another time.

At night we slept each in our own bed in the guest room. We had had to move an extra, folding bed in and make it up, I slept on it, just as I had slept on the mattress on the floor of my room the night Molly came to me after learning Strøm's secret.

We both slept soundly and dreamlessly, woozy from Granny's red wine.

I don't know what Granny got up to after we were in bed. It's odd, it never occurred to me at the time, but she must have been in mourning. After all, she had just lost her only daughter.

I was too deeply immersed in my own problems.

After breakfast the next morning we removed the tablecloth and spread the length of marled tweed out on the big dining-table. Granny must have ironed it the night before, there wasn't a crease in it. She didn't look as if she had slept much that night either.

She showed us how to set out the pieces of the pattern so as to save on material.

'It's all a matter of using your head,' she said, laying the section for a cuff inside the curve of the neckline on one of the front pieces.

The key, I soon realised, was to follow the weave of the fabric. There were lots of important points to remember when dressmaking. I drew round the pattern pieces with tailor's chalk, noted down the different symbols with the greatest accuracy at my command and Molly cut out each section. The dressmaking scissors looked to be razor sharp, they were probably quite heavy in the hand. Granny stood next to Molly, showing her how to cut with a wide, steady action.

We took it in turns to baste and to work the sewing machine. One of us would pin and baste a sleeve, then the two of us would take it through to the other room where Granny sat reading, to try it on her. She showed us how to check whether the sleeve was going to sit nicely. Sleeves are always tricky, she told us; the fabric can easily end up being pulled into unsightly creases over the shoulder, or puckering horribly under the arms. There has to be enough room to raise both arms without anything tearing, and at the same time the line of the back should fall neatly into place as soon as the arms are lowered again. The lining helps here, of course. It has to be inserted correctly, and the jacket has to be just long enough to skim the base of the thumb when the arm is hanging straight down. When the arm is lifted forwards or upwards the sleeve will of course ride an inch or so up the forearm.

'But we don't normally walk about with our arms in the air for any length of time, so that usually isn't a problem,' Granny said, in a rather weary attempt at humour. Neither Molly nor I laughed.

After we had gone to bed on the second night, Granny came tiptoeing in to our room and up to my bed. She leant over me like a dark shadow, shook me gently and whispered something in my ear that I didn't catch. I was just nodding off and didn't really know what was happening, I was in that strange landscape that lies between dream and reality. Looking back on it, though, I see that that was a deliberate calculation on Granny's part: it was in this unreal landscape that she wanted to catch me. On the borderline.

She took me by the hand and helped me out of bed, put a finger to her lips and pointed to Molly, a sign that this was just between her and me. Then she led me out of the bedroom and down the hall to the sitting-room. I suppose I must have been a bit of a dead weight on her arm.

In the sitting-room she had set out all her candlesticks, on the tables, the mantelpiece, along the window-ledges, on the floor. She had lit tall, white candles whose flames wavered as we walked into the room: it was like entering a medieval church, candles everywhere, and a strange sort of humming in the air, as if a big machine were churning away in the next room. I felt almost dazzled, certainly confused.

Granny led me over to the sofa and sat me down, she placed a blanket round my shoulders and another on the floor, over my feet. On the table before me stood a picture of Molly's mother in a heavy silver frame, alongside the bulky, old-fashioned tape-recorder. The two reels were turning soundlessly. Next to the tape-recorder lay a deep-red velvet cushion. Arranged on the cushion were a long, slender silver hammer and a silver bell attached to a twisted, red and gold silk cord. I had never seen anything like that hammer. It looked foreign, the slim shaft was finely chased and the head was shaped like a silver elephant. The elephant's trunk was raised and at the very tip of the trunk was a tiny silver ball. Both the hammer and the bell must have been polished in some special way, they seemed to sparkle in the flickering glow of the candles.

For a long time Granny just looked at me, saying nothing. Then she lifted the hammer off the cushion and placed it in my hand. She picked up the little silver bell on its cord and held it so that it hung right in front of my chest. With a little nod of her head she indicated that I should strike the bell with the hammer.

I felt as if I had been doped, I was breathing heavily. I lifted my leaden arm and held it steady for a moment in front of the bell. I stared at the photograph of Molly's mother, it was a picture of her as a girl, she must have been about nineteen, the same age as we were now.

Then I struck the silver ball on the tip of the elephant's trunk off the silver bell. The sound was high and clear, it seemed to go on for ever. When it finally faded away Granny pressed the button and stopped the tape-recorder.

The suit turned out beautifully. The jacket nipped in at the waist, then flared out perfectly from the small of the back, and the skirt sat nicely on Granny's hips. It had a long, generous split at the back so she wouldn't be forced to hobble along.

This, our first stay with her had proved to be an effective training course in suitmaking, no doubt about that. But I also have a notion that it gave us training in something else, something bigger, although neither Molly or I could have said exactly what, some skill which I am still not sure we have succeeded in turning to good account.

Myself, I haven't had much opportunity for using my suitmaking skills, there are limits to what I need in the way of clothes in the life I lead. But Molly does, of course, make the most amazing costumes for her productions and is known in the theatre world as a mean seamstress who doesn't hesitate to send badly sewn garments back to the sewing room. She has acquired Granny's way of whipping a garment inside out to check the seams, then dismissing it with that characteristic little wave of her hand.

Our stay came to an end. There was no more to talk about. It was as if nothing had happened – or maybe I should say: that everything had happened, though none of us could have said what.

We packed our bag and stripped the beds, laid the bedclothes in a neat pile at the foot of Molly's bed and folded mine. Granny was standing ready and waiting in the hall, dressed in the suit, with smart high-heeled shoes to match. She had done her hair and put on lipstick, she looked elegant and foreign. Something had happened to her too, maybe it happened on that night with all the lighted candles. But I didn't know what and I didn't dare to ask. Perhaps her great grief had started to trickle out of her.

'Before we say goodbye, let's go for a little stroll,' she said. 'We deserve it.'

We walked in the direction of the park, Granny stepping out smartly in front and Molly and I following more slowly. I felt weak and unsteady on my feet, but oddly enough much, much stronger than I had felt since being discharged from hospital only a few days earlier. It seemed unreal to think that I had had to get someone to push me to the doctor's office in a wheelchair. It was hard to say what had happened. I was feeling both happy and confused. But it seemed to me that neither of us was truly finished with Granny yet, nor ready to go home.

'Cheer up, girls,' said Granny. 'Now we're going to sit on this bench and feed the ducks, and then we're going to come up with a plan.'

'A plan! Yes!' I thought to myself. 'That's what we need.'

By the time the paper bag full of bread which Granny had had in her handbag was empty, we had agreed that Molly should carry on at the Academy, but keep her eyes open for the first available opportunity to go abroad. To get away would be the right thing for her to do, this country was soon going to be too small for her, on that we were all agreed. Molly was meant for something bigger than anything this country had to offer. Granny would help her with the money and have a word with her father to ensure that he didn't cause any problems. This last was said in a rather caustic tone. With a sudden flash of insight I realised that her relationship with her son-in-law might not be as easy-going as the annual business of moving the piano would have it.

The plan for me was that I should move back in with Dad, proceed with the medical tests and examinations and concentrate on getting well. End of story. That was all I got from Granny. She seemed to want me to suffer in silence.

Before she left she gave me a notebook which she had had in her bag, neatly wrapped in paper that had obviously been used before. It was exactly the same as the one Molly had left behind in the hospital that time, in which I had read her notes about Strøm, and possibly made a few notes myself. She must have been given her book at some earlier point.

Molly got a kiss on the forehead, I got a pat on the hand.

With that Granny left us there on that bench. We watched her brisk figure walk off in the suit that we had made. She seemed to glide along the path beside the duck pond in the park in the November light. The suit jacket hung beautifully from her shoulders, you couldn't fault the cut. She did not look back.

I thought: she must be cold without a coat. And the grief has not left her completely yet. There is still some left. But it's trickling out.

After that I didn't hear much from Molly. Winter came. She appeared to have settled into her life at the Academy again. Those few times when we did speak it was on the telephone; she seemed a little fraught, although she chatted away as if everything were back to normal, and she never mentioned Strøm. She talked only about whatever new projects she happened to be working on, what teachers at the Academy had said or done, and what the other students were like. I felt suddenly tongue-tied and stupid, couldn't think what questions to ask, or how to comment on what she told me. I wasn't even certain that we still had the same sense of humour. She had adopted a different sort of jargon, a way of speaking that seemed strange, her words didn't seem to be directed at me. She talked about art.

So I decided to go back to Granny on my own. I had something I needed to discuss with her in private. I didn't call beforehand to make an appointment, I don't know why, perhaps that brief stay at her flat a few weeks earlier had given me the idea that I could come and go there as I pleased, with as much right as Molly.

I reached the door leading off the courtyard just as one of the other people from her building was coming out. I stepped inside with a smile of thanks. I toiled my way up the stairs, round and round, flight after flight. I was gasping for breath and totally spent with exhaustion. For some reason Granny's front door was unlocked, I assumed she must be sitting sewing; I didn't want to disturb her, just give her a nice surprise. Very quietly I slipped off my outdoor things in the hall and slid my feet into a pair of battered slippers. Then I made my way towards the sitting-room. It wasn't until I got closer to the sitting-room door that I heard the sounds coming from behind it: like little whimpers, the sort of noises a small animal might make. A small furry animal in great distress and great ecstasy.

Granny and the man from the flat next door were lying in a tangled heap on the sofa. I could see Granny's naked white back and her skirt rucked up into a sausage around her waist. She was facing away from me, but she was the one doing the moving, the man from next door was lying almost perfectly still. I could see his hands clenched around Granny's gyrating hips. For a long time I just stood there, stunned, staring at them. It didn't look as if he had removed any of his clothing at all, although he must have undone something a bit at least. As Granny kind of shuddered and gave a little scream he raised his head and looked over her shoulder. He looked straight at me. Granny slumped down and went all small. Then he shut his eyes and groaned.

Only then did I start to move backwards down the hall, as if someone had tugged on the elastic band in my spine. The man opened his eyes again, stared right at me for an instant before I backed away, out of his sight.

I kicked off the slippers, grabbed my coat and boots and stumbled out of the flat and down the stairs. I no longer felt heavy, I was angry and upset and for a few moments I had felt a new sort of fire inside me.

I didn't put on my outdoor things until I was out on the street and only then did I feel the tiredness creeping over me again.

Although I could not have said why, I knew for sure that the man on the sofa would not tell Granny that he had seen me, and also that it was not the first time he had been there.

In my mind I saw him standing at the top of the stairs, directing the moving of the big piano when Molly and I were little girls. He had authority.

I never brought myself to tell Molly about what I had seen, but after several weeks had passed I called her and insisted that she and I should pay Granny another visit. I felt drawn to her flat as if to a magnet, I was restless and tense, I didn't want to bear the knowledge of what I had seen alone. But Molly was no longer as interested in Granny. And she seemed to have shoved everything that could remind her of Strøm into a drawer and locked it with a little key.

She had grown wary and withdrawn, and aggressive in a way I had never seen in her before. This was not the spirited aggression that I knew so well, it had a more bitter, stale taste to it. She had not, after all, gone abroad as we had planned that day in November in the park with Granny, and I could tell that something had happened since the last time I had spoken to her; she was no longer attending lectures at the Academy. She was hopping from one phase to another so quickly at that time that it was hard to keep up. Only a few weeks earlier she had been an ambitious art student, now I had the impression that she spent most of her time lying in her room at her Dad's house, reading novels. She couldn't stomach all the hypocrisy at the Academy, she said, the lecturers were nothing but a bunch of morons, with not an original thought among the lot of them.

She had discovered an endless series of historical novels, volume upon volume of them, you could have spent years buried in those books, or so it seemed to me, they were piled up all round her bed. She had evidently also gone into the mass production, so to speak, of suits just like the one Granny had taught us to make. She had made at least four, all in the same material, they hung on clothes-hangers in her room, in different colours, but otherwise identical. She was always dressed in one of them. She said they were part of a project on identity which she had been working on at the Academy, although it was completely lost on those morons there. Which was just too bad.

I could tell from the suits that she was skating on very thin ice here. Unlike the one we had made for Granny, with which we had taken such pains, these were unlined, and made from a cheap, synthetic fabric that hung badly. There were lots of loose threads and the fabric made her look cheap too. She had also started wearing very heavy, theatrical make-up. It struck me that she looked like someone who had used the dressmaking scissors to cut paper.

But I understood that she was in mourning for something. Her mourning did not take the same form as Granny's, grief did not trickle out of her; her mourning took an aggressive turn. It was impossible to say whether it was her mother's death or Strøm's deceit that had worked this change in her. Perhaps both. Perhaps a combination of the two.

All the more reason to take her back to Granny's, I thought to myself.

As for me, around this same time I found myself growing a lot weaker. The feeling of being stronger, which I had had when Granny said goodbye to us in the park that day, had been fleeting, merely the crest of a little wave. I had had to get into the way of using the wheelchair whenever I had to travel any distance, which was incredibly impractical for someone living in a building without a lift, so for the most part I tended to stay indoors.

I still had the little, black notebook which Molly had left at the hospital that time when she played the mournful bird in Granny's mask. My plan had been to give it back to her, but somehow it hadn't worked out that way. She had never asked about it, and I had the impression that she no longer did any drawing. I told myself that it would be an imposition of the very worst kind if I were to go running to her with the notebook now, when she had so obviously moved into another phase of her life.

Her notebook was exactly the same as the one given to me by Granny in the park. It was easy to get them mixed up. It could be that I actually did mix them up sometimes, and went on to make notes in hers instead of my own.

I spent a lot of time in my room, wishing that Molly would come and see me, but she stayed away. Although she has never admitted it, I don't think she liked being in our flat. I think she felt my room was too ascetic, rather reminiscent of a nun's cell perhaps. But that's how I like it, there's possibly something a bit convent-like about my flat here, too. I can't have pictures on the walls, I need them as screens on to which to project my pictures. Not that anyone has ever remarked on it.

I kept calling her and urging her to go back to Granny's with me and after a deal of persuasion and much against her will she came to collect me and wheel me back to the flat for visit number two. She made it quite clear that we wouldn't be staying long.

Dad had helped me and the wheelchair down the stairs. He had hooked my bag over the back of the chair. The way he did this made me feel like an invalid. He wanted to wait out there on the street with me until Molly arrived, but I sent him back inside. To have him standing there, pale and shivering in his slippers and shirtsleeves, only made the whole scene that much more pathetic.

I saw her a long way off. It was a grey winter's day with sleet in the air, the synthetic yellow fabric of her suit shone with a kind of neon glow. I could tell by the way she moved that she was still not herself, and that there was very little chance of her talking about anything at all, to me or to Granny.

She gave me a quick, distant peck on the cheek, then grabbed my bag and stuffed it behind my back, pushing me into an uncomfortable, hunched position, then put all her will into pushing me along the slushy streets. She barged recklessly along, bumping into high kerbs, charging straight across intersections without waiting for a green light. Given the choice of several modes of behaviour, Molly will always opt for the most dramatic. We must have been an odd sight.

'For Christ's sake,' she fumed, as cars coming in both directions braked sharply and beeped their horns. 'Can't they see this is a handicap vehicle?'

I held on tight to the arms of the wheelchair for fear of being tipped out.

Outside Granny's building she hesitated for a moment. It was obvious that she didn't know how to tackle the task of getting me and the chair up to the third floor. I was much weaker than I had been the last time we had climbed those stairs. I wasn't sure either. I hadn't had much practice in being in a wheelchair at that point, I hadn't planned how we should proceed.

In the end we left the wheelchair in the courtyard. Molly hoisted me on to her back and carried me up all three flights, one floor at a time. It was quite a feat. She has never been particularly muscular, but she has a tremendously strong will, and with that anything is possible. Her will turns her into a bull. I protested, naturally; I could have got up those stairs perfectly well on my own, given enough time. But it seemed as if it did Molly good to go the whole hog like this. All the pent-up fury gradually seeped out of her as we struggled up flight after flight in the light from the coloured panes of glass. And by the time we reached Granny's door on the third floor we were both almost crying with laughter. It was all just too hysterical, such an awful farce. It really was enough to make you howl.

This time Granny looked perfectly normal: the slightly dishevelled hair, loose strands tumbling from her bun, the clear, kind eyes. She gave us a big, beaming smile, as if she knew what we were laughing at, and insisted that Molly let her have a look at her new suit right away. She praised it lavishly while Molly stood there, still hiccupping with laughter, and she refrained from commenting on the poor choice of fabric or the fact that the suit was neither lined nor double-hemmed. She did not know, of course, that Molly had made several of these suits, all identical, but I could tell by her eyes that she understood something about this suit that I had missed. I felt bewildered.

Once Molly and I had hung up our coats and put on our slippers, Granny wrapped one strong arm round my waist and helped me into the sitting-room. The table was all set with the tea service and the special, spicy biscuits which she always served on a silver platter decked with an almost unnaturally white crocheted doily. We sank down into our respective plush armchairs. We weren't laughing now.

Granny looked from one to the other of us, as if our faces told her all she needed to know. As I'm sure they did. I spoke up before she had time to say anything.

'We've come to talk about men,' I said. 'We didn't get round to talking about them last time we were here. There's something you need to explain to us.'

It proved to be a long conversation. That was the day on which Granny told us her theory about men: about their vulnerability, about the extent to which they are controlled by their urges, about their relationship with their mothers, and about the purpose of women in a man's world.

For the most part Molly sat quietly and listened. There wasn't the ghost of a giggle left in her. She poured more tea for all of us and looked from Granny to me and back again, as Granny talked and I asked the occasional question. She looked like a spectator at a tennis match.

Eventually I could tell from Granny's face that she was wondering whether she had said too much. Given away too much of herself, so to speak. She had never spoken so directly to us before, usually it was us who did the talking and her who listened and asked questions.

'I understand what you're saying about men and their mothers,' I said. 'But what about mothers and daughters?' I glanced uncertainly at Molly, who promptly looked down at her hands. So did Granny. And I realised that she and Molly had joined forces to maintain a certain impenetrable silence on this subject ever since Molly's mother's death. They were never going to speak about mothers and daughters, neither to me nor to anyone else. I would have to try another angle.

'Was it because of these things you've told us about men that you didn't live with the father of your child?' I ventured tentatively. But Granny did not answer. I felt irritation building up inside me. This was too important a subject to be kept under wraps.

'You have to answer us when we ask you about important

things, Granny!' I cried. 'Why have you never lived with a man?'

Granny turned her face slowly towards the window and at length answered softly:

'I don't really feel I've had the time for all that. They expect too much.'

'What have you done instead? Been a mother?'

'That's my business.'

'But what about Molly's grandfather? The man whose child you had?'

'I've always had so much else to do. And you can't do everything. I had a baby, that in itself was almost too much. I didn't have time to take care of a man as well.'

I thought of Molly's mother's sad eyes.

I still wasn't satisfied. There was too much here that I didn't understand. I found this secretiveness of Granny's and Molly's very wearing. Somehow I had to try to steer them both towards the heart of the matter.

'But Granny,' I said. 'What are you to do when you don't have your mother any more?'

I nodded towards Molly, who looked away.

'Then you have to grieve,' Granny said, coming back, as it were, from the window. 'You have to grieve very deeply for a very long time, until there is no grief left. Then you have to get drunk, then you sleep it off, then you go abroad – and then you get down to work. And you have to keep doing this, always in the same order.'

I could tell that she was speaking from experience. It struck me that I had never heard anyone say a word about Granny's mother.

'And you certainly shouldn't shut yourself away and read trashy historical novels, should you?' I added insistently. Molly's gaze had lighted fleetingly on our faces, now it slid away again.

'Oh, I'm not denying that you might have to do that,' Granny said. 'For a while. But after that you have to get drunk. Then you have to sleep it off. Then go abroad. In that order.'

Suddenly, and coming as a surprise to all three of us, I think, Molly spoke.

'But what if you don't feel up to it?' she said.

Granny eyed her tenderly and gravely.

'Then you have to grieve a little more,' she said. 'And then you have to go abroad. And once there you have to work.'

'In that order?' Molly asked.

Both Granny and I nodded.

I think it must have been once we were actually finished talking and were out in the hall, getting back into our outdoor things, that Granny came out with her remark about there always being something to learn from men. I don't remember her exact words, but Molly and I have discussed it several times and both believe the gist of her theory is that all the men we meet are like gift-wrapped parcels which we have to remember to unwrap before we leave them. There's nothing as sad as an unopened parcel, Granny said. Or words to that effect.

'But surely they know what's best for them?' I asked.

'Not necessarily,' Granny said. 'Generally speaking they don't. They just follow their dicks.'

Molly and I burst out laughing again.

'Oh, Granny, I didn't think you knew words like that!' Molly screamed. Suddenly she had found her normal voice again and her face had fallen back into its lovely, old folds. Her squirrel look. It was a long time since I had seen that.

'Oh, no?' said Granny.

Since then I've been thinking that Granny only said that to make Molly laugh. She can't actually have meant what she said, not really. But she succeeded in releasing Molly from a room that had been locked up for a long time, and that wasn't bad going, with just one remark. Sometimes laughter is the only thing that helps.

We stood in the hall among the slippers for quite a while, all three of us. I didn't want to leave. I felt there was something still unresolved between Granny and me. As a delaying tactic, I asked her if she would play something on the piano for me. I could see that she was tired and was about to say no, but then it was as if she turned a different gaze on me, that inward-looking gaze, and this caused her to change her mind in mid-sentence.

'I might,' she said.

'I think I'd better go,' Molly said. 'I have a date.'

That was what I had been hoping she would say. I didn't want to leave with her and I didn't want to know what sort of a date she had, or with whom.

'Just you go on,' I said. 'I'll take a taxi. I can get Granny's neighbour to help me down the stairs.'

Then I sat in the sitting-room and listened to Granny playing for me. She had settled me in the red armchair again and packed a red blanket round me. It was just what I needed: her complete, undivided attention. It was like being inside a soft, red-hot cave.

Granny was so focused, her back so straight and yet so fluid. She struck the keys so lightly.

I didn't dare to ask what she was playing. Her cigarette lay in its holder in the ashtray on the piano. It went on burning for a while, but she didn't touch it and eventually it went out all by itself. I stared at the glowing tip as it gradually turned first grey, then black, I was mesmerised by it. Everything was red, and slowly dying out. Beyond the windows darkness had fallen.

When I went to get up from my chair, I thought I was going to faint. Granny helped me into the hall and rang her neighbour's bell. She got him to help me down the stairs. He transported me with authority and care, almost as if I were Granny's piano being conveyed down to a waiting trailer. He didn't look me in the eye once as we staggered down the stairs. It was almost as if he didn't know who I was. He seemed more intent on making sure he didn't lose his grip on me and send me crashing down the stairs with one last, gigantic, jangling chord. It wasn't hard to imagine how this chord would sound: like all the notes being struck at once.

By the time we reached the bottom and he had got me into the wheelchair, he was as sweat-drenched and breathless as I. I remembered another time when I had seen him like that.

Behind us we could hear Granny coming slowly down the stairs. In her hand she held the sheet music from which she had just been playing. It had a pale green cover, the illustration on the front looked to be from around the turn of the last century. She handed it to me.

When I think about it now, it occurs to me that that moment with Granny and the neighbour down on the street, when she gave me that sheet music, was so clearly a fateful moment. So many powerful forces concentrated in one spot. Only now do I see that in handing the sheet music to me, Granny probably meant to show me that she did know something about fate after all.

I think: maybe everything that happened back then is connected in ways that I do not as yet understand. Maybe it was Granny who granted me the experience of going to bed with her neighbour that time. Maybe I was guided by her will. Maybe she was the cause of my becoming pregnant and having the chance to be a mother carrying a child for a few weeks, before my illness gained the upper hand again. To be a woman who knew that a baby could live inside me. Maybe Granny and fate were working together.

But that can't be right, surely? Granny can't possibly have made all of that happen. I mean, it was me who decided to go and see her neighbour back then. I did have a will of my own.

For the first few years after I moved into this flat I had some trouble figuring out with whom I belonged and whom I could trust. There was Dad, obviously, but I think he had enough to do just seeing to himself. I believe it came as a great relief to him when I moved out and he no longer had to be reminded of his own inability to save me from my illness, and of the family he had had when Mum was still living with us. Or of his inability to help anyone with anything at all. Not that he could ever have admitted such a thing, of course – he, who felt that he had had more than his fair share of troubles.

I took a fairly pragmatic view of this, feeling that it was probably better for him to be getting on with his research at the Institute than having to mind me. At least there he received recognition and respect, and could maintain some sense of usefulness by continually planning new research projects which might expand the boundaries a little further. The boundaries of the research front or whatever they were called over at the Institute. I had a mental picture of a military chart on which new boundaries were constantly being drawn in for the two fronts: the red and the blue. The ignorant old guard versus the new, progressive forces. Even if Dad and his colleagues never did anything that most people could understand, at least they did something for science; that was bound to be quite clear from the chart with the flexible boundaries, I told myself.

When he came to visit me, he played the interesting guest and I was the attentive hostess, these were simpler roles for both of us. I asked him informed questions about what was happening on the research front and he spelled out the state of the chart for me. From what he told me I learned a great deal that has since been of help to me in my fate project.

*

To be honest, it was more painful to lose touch with Granny than with Dad. After Molly finally went abroad I didn't feel that I could go on pretending that Granny was my granny too. I was on my own. She never got in touch with me, she never seemed to spare me a thought. That hurt me. I had had the idea that I had in some way become special to her, almost more so than Molly, I sometimes thought. After that day when she played for me and gave me her music book, at any rate. That fateful moment on the pavement with her and her neighbour must have meant something I thought to myself. She must have had a plan for me.

I called Molly's father a couple of times to ask how Granny was. He seemed surprised that I should ask, as if she had kind of slipped his mind. But from what he said about her it was clear that her life had not changed: still a steady succession of lodgers in the flat in winter, and hectic summer days at the house by the shore: house concerts and lots of laughter. There was nothing to suggest that she had aged at all and it never occurred to me that she would one day die, even though the odds were that she would be the first of us to go.

Granny was the oldest, of course, but only very slowly did it dawn on me that it wasn't always the oldest who died first. Granny's daughter had died before Granny. I don't know whether she ever really got over that. But I had no one I could talk to about this, no one I could ask.

And here I am, of course, only indulging in speculation: maybe I'm going too far in weaving everything into my fate project. The question as to who dies first is a classic fate question and as difficult to comprehend as everything else relating to those forces. The rules, if there are any, seem complicated and not very consistent.

For a while I actually got it into my head that Granny was as interested in these questions as I am, and that she had progressed much further with her studies, that *that* was what she was up to in her flat and at the summer house.

But now I'm not so sure. There is plenty to suggest that she was just as much in the dark as I. And if she had known anything, then she must have had the same problem as I have: how to impart what she knew?

The music she gave me that day when her neighbour carried me down the stairs was an arabesque by Debussy, the first. I couldn't understand what her purpose was in giving it to me. I didn't have a piano, I couldn't even *play* the piano. And it didn't look as if fate had a career on the ivories in mind for my fingers, it had let my illness put paid to that. I had a mental picture of my hands turning into two bundles of limp, boiled asparagus.

I tucked the sheet music into the bookcase, under some books. Through all of my remaining years at home with Dad I would see the edge of that pale-green book sticking out from under the reference books on the middle shelf. Obviously there was no point in telling Dad that I would like a piano, and piano lessons with a good teacher.

When I finally moved into a place of my own, into this flat, I made sure that the music book was packed with all my other things. I slipped it into the drawer in this desk.

Only now do I have an inkling of what Granny's purpose was in giving it to me. Something is just about to break through. Like the sun. *Like the first morning.*

I lifted the receiver. In the background, at the other end of the line, I heard a sort of squealing sound. A high-pitched, little-girl's voice: Ine, of course.

'Listen to the racket they're making,' Molly said. 'The first thing they asked was whether I had a TV.'

'You haven't got a TV.'

'What do kids of their age do when they're not sleeping or shouting and screaming or watching TV?'

'I haven't the foggiest idea. But no doubt you'll find out.'

I knew from what Aksel had told me that Eilif and Ine started every morning during the summer holidays with watching cartoons on TV, but I couldn't bring myself to tell her that.

'You've got a computer and you're hooked up to the internet,' I said. 'Maybe you could let them use your computer now and again. There are lots of good games and so on that you can download for free. All perfectly harmless.'

'No way!'

I knew that Eilif was an adept internet user, Aksel had shone with pride when he told me this. But I didn't mention that either. It seemed to me that things ought to be allowed to progress at their own pace.

Molly cleared her throat, as if already gearing herself up for the speech in which she explained to them why she didn't have a television and why they couldn't use her computer.

'Yes, I suppose I'll find out more about their likes and dislikes as we go along,' she said.

'What do you intend to do about the baby?' I blurted. 'Are you going to keep it?'

'I'll talk to you later,' she said shortly. 'It sounds as if they're arguing about something or other out there. They might need me to referee. I'd better go and see what's up.'

'Yes, go see to them,' I sighed.

There was silence again. I heard her light a cigarette: fumbling with the pack, the sharp hiss of the red match-tip igniting off the matchbox. Normally I don't have anything against her smoking, cigarettes suit her, but I felt it was different now that Ine and Eilif were living in the same house.

'Molly?' I said tentatively. 'Were you lighting a cigarette?'

'Mm.'

'D'you think that's wise – I mean, with you being pregnant . . .?'

'Yes,' she snapped, and hung up.

The pictures from the summer house streamed into my mobile the same evening that the children arrived there. Molly must have done as I asked and told them I would like some pictures. It was obvious that she had dutifully taken a couple of shots of Aksel and them after dinner, then got either Ine or Eilif to take one of her and Aksel with their arms round one another. I found this last picture a mite ostentatious. Then she and Aksel had handed the mobile over to Eilif and Ine and sent them out for a walk. They may even have used the term 'photo safari', not remembering that it was me who had come up with that particular name for it. I hoped Molly had remembered to say that I would pay them for the photos.

There they were.

It almost took my breath away when I saw those pictures of the children. With trembling hands I transferred them from my mobile to the computer and projected them on to the wall. The photographs were of excellent quality, they stood up well to being enlarged. In the blink of an eye I had made them enormous, they seemed to swell out into the room: pin-sharp, in clear, bright colours.

And I knew right away that I would have to make a lot of adjustments, both to the cardboard puppets and to the rough portraits I had done of them in my notebook. In neither case did they come anywhere close to the real thing.

Ine with her lovely hair. Eilif in his orange baseball cap. Both wearing sunglasses. They were so . . . real. More real than I had imagined. And older.

In the first picture they were clearly standing beside the table on the veranda at which they had eaten dinner. It wasn't possible to tell from the leftovers on their plates exactly what they had been eating, but it looked like spaghetti with sausage chunks. Good, I thought. She took my advice. And of course they are older than I had imagined, it's so obvious that it never even occurred to me. The photos Aksel showed me before Christmas were taken last summer. It's amazing how much children grow and change in a year. How stupid could I be, not to think of that?

But there were other pictures too. The children had plainly gone for a walk and taken the mobile with them. They had taken a number of shots of the veranda steps, on Molly's orders no doubt, to let me see where the wheelchair ramp would go. After that, though, they must have taken a bit of a wander, because there were also pictures of the garden, of the road running past the summer house, of a cat crossing the road up ahead of them. Lots of pictures of that cat.

Then came a couple of snaps of Eilif's back, Ine must have taken those. And then of a red cottage behind a big rose hedge. They must have been making towards this cottage.

In the depths of the garden in the picture a figure was visible: an old man in a white cotton hat. It looked as though he was peering at the photographer.

The next photograph I projected on to the wall that evening was a close-up of the same man, taken inside a dark, untidy kitchen. It was slightly under-exposed. The man in the cotton hat filled most of the frame.

My heart grew still and dark. I opened my eyes wide and stared at the photograph. The man in the cotton hat. I blew the picture up as much as I could, until it covered the whole of the sitting-room wall. Gradually he grew towards me as I clicked and clicked, making him bigger and bigger.

There was no doubt. It was Strøm.

He was so old. There was something odd about his eyes.

'Molly,' I screamed down the phone, into her answering machine which had just switched itself on. It's quite common for her not to answer the phone when she's working. 'Do you realise who you've been sending the children to? Strøm! Strøm's living in the house next door to you! That's his cat! You've got to go down there right this minute! He's a convicted paedophile! What on earth are you doing down there?'

But the answering machine cut me off with a little beep.

I have to get down there, I have to rescue them! I thought. Because I know what they say about Strøm. He's capable of anything, that man. He's not to be trusted!

And it wasn't hard to imagine how it had all come about:

After dinner and the taking of the photographs on the veranda, Molly pointed to Eilif's mobile and suggested that he and Ine go for a walk and take some photographs for a friend of hers and their Dad's who lived in town and who would shortly be coming down to stay at the summer house. Me. This friend was confined to a wheelchair, she explained, and she would like to know how everything looked down here, so that she could plan how to get around the place on her own. They wouldn't mind helping her with that, would they? She made it clear that her friend would pay them well for their help.

She and Aksel started to clear the dinner table, trying to act casual, but the children sensed that they were up to something and were eager to be gone as quickly as possible. I thought to myself: suddenly they have split into two camps. The adults versus the children. It's a pity, but that's what happens sometimes.

I pictured Eilif and Ine walking down the narrow road towards the sea. The houses round about are a mixture of summer houses and year round homes, I told myself, and the road is winding and laid with gravel. The air is vibrant with the sounds of insects and, somewhere, the sound of a lawnmower, as is always the case, I suppose, in such places in the summer.

They walk along side by side, without speaking. Eilif takes longer strides than Ine, he looks withdrawn and determined, she has to run a few steps every now and again to keep up, but this she does automatically, without thinking; trying all the while to read her brother's face. She has thin, delicate legs, she almost looks as though she's floating. At regular intervals Eilif stops and takes a snap with the mobile. After a while he gives it to Ine.

When they come to the crossroads they pause for a moment, wondering which way to go, which is the quickest way down to the beach. Because it has already been agreed between them that they are going to the beach, even though not a word has been said about this, and even though they know they're not supposed to. That's probably just how it is with brothers and sisters, I think: sometimes words aren't necessary.

And while they are standing there at the crossroads, I went on, a kitten slinks out from under a garden hedge. It is black and white and its paws hardly touch the ground, it seems to drift towards them. The cat stops short when it sees the two children, then it trots over to them, its tail stiff and erect, and rubs itself up against Ine's legs. She doubles over in a fit of tenderness and lifts it up, hugs it to her chest, delighted with this new arrival, which might be something she and her brother can share. The cat immediately starts to purr, it rasps her chin with its rough tongue, making her squeal and drop the mobile phone on to the path. Eilif picks up the phone, shakes it anxiously, then wipes it with a corner of his T-shirt before sticking it into his pocket. But he says nothing, and the cloud over his face is starting to break up, he reaches out to pet the kitten. Then he takes a picture of Ine with the cat in her arms, followed by several close-ups of the cat alone and one just of Ine's face.

'Where do you think it lives?' Ine asks.

The cat gives a sudden squirm and springs out of her arms. It looks back at them, as if answering her question and wanting them to follow it.

I couldn't stop the pictures in my head now, they kept on running all by themselves; it was no longer like a film, it was something of which I was a part. Real life.

I saw:

Strøm is in the garden surrounding his house. Enclosed within the garden. It is becoming completely overgrown, with huge hollyhocks in bloom: white, pink, mauve, sulphur-yellow, violet. His face is becoming overgrown too, with hair, it's a long time since he last shaved, perhaps he feels it's no longer safe to wield a razor himself, now that his sight is so poor. He has the idea that his face has shrunk under the beard, at least that's how it feels when he runs his liver-spotted right hand over his chin, a habit he has acquired over the past couple of years. There is something helpless about this gesture.

He peers down the garden. He is aware that his sight has grown worse even over the last couple of weeks, it's as if a milky film has spread over everything around him. He is wearing his worn, blue flannel shirt and a pair of washed-out beige slacks. Wellingtons on his feet, a white cotton hat on his head.

When he bought this house a couple of years ago he had plans for the old garden; he has kitted himself out with new garden tools: hedge-clippers of varying sizes, a wheelbarrow, shovel and new lawnmower. But then came the job of mounting the major retrospective exhibition that I had read about in the newspaper, I thought. The director of the museum which had invited him to do this was an old friend. You don't say no to an offer like that. And although right from the start he instinctively baulked at the whole idea of the project, he told himself that this time he could at least begin by going through all the old contact sheets from so many years before.

He got himself set up in the sitting-room of the old house, with the battered office chair he had brought from the flat in town, a magnifying glass and a powerful work lamp, as well as cartons and boxes full of photographs. He has his own system. And initially the absorbing process of holding the contact sheets up to the lamp, putting the magnifying glass to his eye and studying the frames, one by one, slowly and unemotionally, sent what felt like a fresh wave of pleasure in his work running through him. An almost giddy sensation, a yearning to create something new, pictures no one had ever seen before, and certainly not anything like this stale old stuff.

At first he had thought that he would call the people at the museum one of these days and warn them that this was going to be an exhibition of totally new work, that he wasn't ready for any retrospective, sentimental, recycled affair. He wasn't sure what these new pictures would be like, but the very feeling of having something still to do transformed him, got him out of the house. Every day for weeks he roamed the surrounding area with his camera, from the house down to the beach by the bathing huts, the same round every day until he knew every step of the way and this route had for him become a world all its own. He always stopped at the same spots and would stand perfectly still for minutes on end, waiting to see whether something would happen; whether the tree, the fence-post, the sturdy clump of cow parsley, the wicket gate, had anything to say.

After some weeks of this it came to him that here he had the subject of his new exhibition: the world as it spoke to him, an old man who was going blind. The world, not through his eyes, but as itself. The world when not being observed. That had to be it. The world when the photographer is blind. The world when the photographer is no longer there.

He wasn't certain how he was going to do this, but he was starting to rediscover his old feeling that something inside the camera knew more than he did, that it wanted something of him.

He has toyed with the notion of using some sort of device which would take photographs of the world when he is not present, at unexpected moments. He envisages such pictures as creeping up on reality from behind, catching it unawares, when it least suspects it. Revealing hitherto unseen aspects of objects chosen at random, such as the fence-post, the gate, the cow parsley or the well-worn ladder from the bathing hut down to the water; deep secrets which would make most museum-goers look away in confusion or disgust.

Everything would depend on the light, naturally. Because at the end of the day it would be the light that created the pictures, not him. The light is forever changing, this he has always known of course, his feel for the shifting of the light and the demands this makes on him is his greatest strength; it is this that has set him apart, all these years, from the mass of mediocre camera jockeys who raced around brandishing the very latest in equipment, and who had latched on to the digital reality as if there was nothing else but that, as if the old craft did not exist.

I gave a little sniff at the thought of such photographers.

Because of the light, on his walks he never stops twice at the same spots or by the same objects, I went on. The light causes everything to drift, blend together, slide in and out of focus. To hide, or suddenly to rip itself wide open for him, raw and wild.

The alterations in the light seem to him to occur more abruptly than when he was younger. As his sight gradually deteriorates he is having to resort more and more to an inner sense of the light. To begin with he had thought that this would be impossible, but over the past few weeks he has begun to feel that he can sense the shifts in the light with his eyes shut, as though the inner and outer worlds are starting to run together, become one.

And always there are changes. They are most easily seen in the young plants which, from one day to the next, can become unrecognisable, twice as tall as the day before, or suddenly with all their flowers gone. His heart sinks a little when he sees this.

Those huge hollyhocks. The blue monkshood with its poisonous flowers.

This set tour of his has come to form a world of its own which always allows him entry, and it has been a relief to be made welcome in such a way. But he has also had to admit that it is a world he finds more and more difficult to leave. He's not even sure he wants to leave it now.

It occurs to him that lately he has almost stopped taking pictures. He just looks. Peers.

That is what he is doing on this particular day. He is just peering. Or working in the garden, pulling up a few weeds and throwing them on to the compost heap, snipping off the odd branch with the garden shears.

Oddly enough, the fact that his sight has become noticeably worse over the past six months has only made it more difficult for him to break out of this world in which he has shut himself away. Already he has become more detached from the preparations for his exhibition. These days he doesn't even take his camera with him all the time. He has made a start on a letter to the director of the museum which invited him to mount the retrospective. In this letter he intends to say, sensibly and firmly, that there is not going to be any exhibition, that they will have to find someone else. He just hasn't come up with the right words yet, and it seems so easy to put off writing it, something always gets in the way.

When he sat down at the kitchen table this morning and flicked through the newspaper, in which he could make out nothing but the headlines, it struck him that he had spent long enough in that other world. Things no longer spoke to him, they talked mainly to each other, or to themselves. And it was time to come out, face up to other people again. If anyone was still out there, if they hadn't all disappeared while he was busy with his own concerns, deep in some dim corner of his mind, he thinks.

He has filled the watering can from the outside tap on the other side of the house and lugged it down the gravel path to what was once a neat flower bed. The hollyhocks are in bloom, despite the fact that no one has tended them; are blooming more profusely than before, almost; seeming to insist on their own form, their own scent, they have become more and more real in the course of the summer, their reality no longer has much to do with his own.

Over the past couple of days he has had the feeling that everything is going downhill. It's as if he has forgotten where the exit is, he thinks, as he pours the water from the can over the flowers. The exit he must walk through in order to find the others has become hard to spot. As if it has been overgrown by vigorous plants, inordinately efflorescent, so real that they are almost too much, almost unbearable.

He wishes those flowers would let go, start to fade.

The hollyhocks have given me one last chance, he thought to himself. One last chance before everything goes downhill. I'd better water them. He picks up the watering can.

They are such a deep, intense colour, they draw him to them. He smells them better than he sees them.

There's no reason why this wilderness can't be cleared up. Get down to some weeding. Lay out a flower bed. Get out the sharp new shovel and dig up the grass along one side of the red cottage. Two or three yards out from the wall, maybe, so the bed won't be under the shadow of the eaves. And one could easily plant peonies here, and other hardy perennials. Down the side of the house he could lay a path, on which he could stroll around the property at his own pace, with a cigarette in his hand.

Yes, that's what he'll do. He could split the big, old peony on the other side of the house, he muses. Or no, maybe the bleeding heart would be better. Peonies don't like being moved. He rubs a hand over his bearded chin again. Actually what he needs is an old-fashioned scythe, the lawn-mower would never be able to cut that long grass.

❊

He feels the cat rubbing against his trouser leg before he sees it, I continue in my head. He can tell by the deep thrumming in the kitten's throat that it has just been stroked by someone who knows what they are about. It is his cat, the only living creature which he sees every day.

Then he becomes aware that there are people in the garden. He straightens up and peers at the spot where he thinks they are standing, just inside the garden gate.

'Yes?' he shouts, a little too loudly.

Ine and Eilif have stepped through the gate, but remain standing down by the hedge. He screws up his eyes, lifts a levelled hand to his brow to shade them from the sun and sees the outlines of two figures, he realises they must be children, they are too short and not broad enough to be adults.

'Can I help you?' he asks softly, almost to himself. They don't hear him. Ine takes a step towards him, but Eilif holds her back. He raises the mobile and points it down the garden, at the man with his eyes screwed up.

'Is that your cat?' Ine calls to him as her brother presses the shutter with a little, digital beep.

'That cat is nobody's but its own,' Strøm calls to the two children down by the gate. 'But it lives here with me!' He feels he can see them more clearly now. 'His name's Henry!' he adds. As if those kids down there are the slightest bit interested, he thinks peevishly.

'Can I hold it?' Ine calls back to him. 'I held it a minute ago, out on the path and it liked it, it wasn't scared.'

That's a high-pitched, little girl's voice, he thinks to himself. Infant-school age, no more than that.

'You're lucky,' he calls back. 'Henry's usually a bit shy with strangers. Come on in, my dear.'

Ine looks quickly at her brother, ignores his warning glance and walks over to the old, white-bearded man and the cat. It makes it easy for her, comes to meet her with its tail in the air. She wraps her slight little form around it and picks it up again, it burrows its head into the hollow of her throat and the underside of her chin.

'Well now, here's a young lady who has a way with cats,' says Strøm, setting down the watering can. Eilif raises the mobile and takes another snap of his sister and the cat. Strøm notices, but doesn't let on. He can see Ine more clearly now, she is a skinny little creature in red shorts, she has already lost herself in the cat's sonorous purring, its movements, smell, sleek coat, all those things that shout 'cat'. Sway-backed with tenderness she stands there, stroking and stroking. Strøm can see that she and the cat are already as one, and that Ine has a great longing inside her for something that can enfold her, hold her tight.

'You two must be new here,' he says. 'I don't think I've seen you around before.'

'We're staying at a house a bit further up the road,' Eilif says. 'But we live in town.'

'Town folk, eh? Is it nice to get away for a while?'

'We don't want to be here.'

'You don't?'

'No, we were really supposed to be going to Italy with our Mum this summer, but then she got sick.'

Eilif has also moved closer now.

'Ah, Italy. Well, well. Lovely country, I actually lived there myself for a while'.

'You did?'

'Yes. But that was a long time ago. Oh, it's nice enough here, especially in the summer, but it's not exactly Italy. Well, for one thing they speak Italian there, and they serve the most wonderful wine, which is more than can be said for folk round here.'

Strøm breaks off this unwonted flow of words, amazed at himself. His voice seems to be that of a stranger, he is conscious of how long it is since he spoke to a child. How long it is since he spoke to anyone at all. It's not often that anyone comes to see him, and never unannounced. And never, never children. The roguish tone I've been affecting doesn't suit me, he thinks. I've never been roguish, and there's little point in starting now.

'Mum's in the hospital,' Ine suddenly bursts out. 'They operated on her.'

Strøm stands quietly, not knowing what to say. He waits for what will come next, but there is no more from Ine, only a stiff, little pause on his part.

'I see,' he says at last. Then he doesn't know what else to say and again there is silence.

'No, that's certainly not something to be taken lightly,' he says eventually, to break the silence. 'But you know, most operations go very well, or so I've heard from the people who know about such things.'

'Do you know them?' Ine asks.

'Know and know. You have to trust the doctors, they know what they're doing. They went to school for lots and lots of years to learn all about these things.'

'Have you ever been operated on?'

'No, there wouldn't be any point in operating on me.'

'Why not?'

'I think I'm probably too sick. And too old. I've got what they call diabetes, I haven't taken very good care of myself and I reckon it's a bit too late to start now. My eyesight's very bad and it's going to get worse. But that's a rather gloomy topic of conversation for such a lovely summer day. Where are you from?'

'We live in town,' Eilif says. 'Mostly with Mum, but a lot of the time with Dad too.'

'An awful lot of the time,' Ine says. 'Our Mum and Dad live just down the road from one another,' she is quick to add.

'We don't really want to be here,' Eilif says. 'We're just waiting for our Dad to come and get us.'

He edges a little closer, his interest in the old, white-bearded man aroused. He feels as though he knows him from somewhere, although he cannot remember where.

'I see. Well, then maybe Henry and I could offer you some light refreshment while you're waiting? We might have some squash in the kitchen for all I know. Although I'm not sure if we have any cake and so on . . .'

'Yes, please,' says Ine. 'Why's he called Henry?'

'Well, it's actually Henri, that's French. He's named after a great teacher I once had. But that's a long story, and folk round here don't speak French anyway, so I think we'll just call him Henry and leave it at that.'

'What kind of teacher was he?'

'He was a photographer.'

'We take photographs too!' Ine exclaims. 'Dad gave us a mobile phone with a camera and Molly says we're to take photographs for somebody she knows who's coming here soon. Somebody who's in a wheelchair. She's going to pay for them.'

'Did you say Molly? Now that's an unusual name. Is she the lady you're staying with?'

'Yes. She's Dad's girlfriend. She says she can only go swimming with us once a day, so we have to find something to do between breakfast and one o'clock, and probably in the evenings too. She doesn't even have a TV, but she was going to do something about that.'

'I see. And what does Molly do?'

'She makes things,' Ine says. 'For the theatre. I can't remember what you call it.'

'Stage sets,' Eilif chips in.

'Well now, is that so?' Strøm murmurs. 'Stage sets, you say.'

'That's why she doesn't have time for us before one o'clock. We don't like her. We'd rather stay here with you. Wouldn't we, Eilif?'

Eilif doesn't reply. Strøm looks thoughtful.

'Molly,' he says. 'It's not a very common name. I used to know a girl who called herself Molly, many years ago. How old is this Molly that you're staying with?'

'Don't know,' Eilif answers. 'About the same age as Dad. Not as old as you anyway, but grown-up.'

'Yes, grown-up,' Ine echoes. 'She used to live in the city, but then she inherited the summer house where we're staying from her Gran. She died. In hospital. Her Gran, I mean.'

'Hmm,' says Strøm.

'What do you mean, hmm?' asks Ine.

'The Molly that I knew was very good at drawing,' he says. 'She was very young then. I taught her to take photographs.'

'We've got a photo of her here!' Eilif bursts out. 'We only took it this morning.' He pulls the mobile out of the pocket of his hooded sweatshirt and proceeds to work his way back to the right picture, past the photographs he has just taken of Strøm, Ine with the cat in her arms, the cat on its own, the path down to Strøm's house.

'Ah-ha, so you have one of those telephone cameras. I wouldn't know where to start with one of those,' Strøm says.

'They're really cool,' Eilif says. 'Look. There she is. That's her next to Dad. It was taken only a few minutes ago, on the veranda of her summer house.'

Strøm takes the tiny, silver-coloured gadget which the boy holds out to him and peers hard at the photograph of Molly, endeavouring to gain some impression of it. He goes very quiet. He is obviously having difficulty seeing. Eilif moves to his side, shows him how best to angle the screen in order to get a good, clear view of it. At last Strøm appears to see something he recognises.

'It's been a long time,' he says.

'Do you know her?'

'Knew her,' Strøm replies.

'We can say hello to her for you! Oh, by the way, what's your name?'

'No, don't do that,' Strøm says. 'I'm not sure she'd be happy to know that I'm here.'

'Why not?'

'Come on,' Strøm says. 'Let's go inside, and I'll show you round the house. We might be able to get a better look at the photo in there, where it's not so bright.'

I could not help speculating further on what happened to the children. I had been caught by a current, a story that swept me along with it. It had a will of its own, it wanted something of me. I sat there in my wheelchair by the telephone, with my eyes closed and my fingers curled round the handles on the chair wheels, ready to push off, set myself in motion.

Strøm wouldn't tell them his name, I thought to myself. Well, of course he wouldn't, he was afraid of being exposed. He knows there are rumours circulating about him, he wonders whether Eilif and Ine could have heard that he is a child molester. You never know how a rumour gets about, whose ears it reaches. A rumour can flare up again in the most unexpected places. He can never feel safe, and he knows it.

And yet it seemed as though the story I was concocting was taking me somewhere other than I had intended. As if it knew more than I. It drew me in, made a place for me. I felt confused.

Strøm is a child molester and he and the children are now strolling through the garden towards his cottage, I thought. They are still chatting away. None of them realises how dangerous this could be. As yet they feel quite safe.

'Did you have a teacher who taught you how to take photographs,' Eilif asks. He has thawed slightly.

'Yes,' says Strøm. 'But he was no ordinary schoolteacher. In those days you didn't go to school to learn how to take photographs.'

'So how did you learn?'

'Just by doing it, and if you were lucky you would meet a really good photographer who was willing to teach you.'

'A bit like when you want to learn to play the piano?'

'A bit like that, yes. It was Henri who made me want to be a good photographer, when I was a very young.'

'And did you become one?'

'Oh, a decent one, I think.'

'But how did you get him to teach you?'

'By doing the best I could, I suppose, and hoping that he would take an interest in me. That he would think I had . . . that bit extra.'

'How do you show somebody that you have that bit extra?'

'What a lot of questions you ask. Well, I suppose all you can really do is be yourself. But the main thing is, of course, that *you* have to believe that you have that bit extra, otherwise it's hard to make others believe it.'

'And how do *you* know if you have it?'

'Oh, you just know,' Strøm says soberly, eyeing Eilif closely. 'You can feel it.'

'A bit like a sort of flame?'

'Yes, something like that. Like a sort of flame.'

'But how do you pay the teacher?'

'Oh, there are all sorts of ways. I repaid Henri by doing various odd jobs for him, working for him in the darkroom, that sort of thing. I freed him to get on with what he needed to do. He was quite an old man by then.'

Ine is starting to lose interest in this conversation, she understands that it doesn't involve her. She shifts restlessly, falls to studying her surroundings. But Eilif isn't finished yet.

'So you moved to France to be with this teacher?' he said.

'Yes, indeed. I lived in Paris for many years. Although I had only been there a couple of years when Henri died. So I didn't have that much time with him.'

'What did you do when he died?'

'I went on taking photographs. What else could I do?'

'But you didn't have your teacher any more.'

'You only need a teacher to begin with. After that you're on your own. Either your teacher dies – that's what usually happens – or you have to leave him.'

'And your teacher died.'

'Yes.'

'Was his eyesight starting to go?' Ine chips in. So she must have been following the conversation after all.

Strøm turns to her in amazement.

'I've never thought about it. But I suppose it must have been. It does with most old folk.'

'Like you,' said Ine.

'Yes, like me.'

'Does Henri have a second name?' Eilif asks.

'Hmm. You're a slyboots. What did you say your name was again?'

'I didn't, but it's Eilif. And that's Ine.'

'A-ha. Ine and Eilif. Fine names, with a nice ring to them. Yes, the cat does in fact have a second name, but it's a secret.'

'Oh, tell us!' Ine exclaims eagerly, totally involved in the conversation again. Strøm catches a glimpse of something slipping from her shoulders. A burden. He wants to make this moment last for her, to allow her a little respite from the fear for which she has not yet found the words. He has seen it. He's the sort who sees things like that; he saw it in me, too, that time when I called on him at his studio. In the days when he and Molly were together.

'No, I don't think I can tell you.'

'Why not?'

'Not all names should be uttered out loud.'

'Why not?'

'There are some things one likes to keep to oneself.'

'And what's your name?'

'My name is Strøm.'

'That's a surname.'

'Yes, it is a surname.'

'Well, what's your first name?'

'Not all names should be uttered out loud,' Strøm says again. 'When you get to be as old as me you'll understand that. Come on, let's see if we can find some squash in there. If nothing else I have coffee, that I know.'

'I drink coffee,' Ine cries eagerly.

'You do not,' Eilif retorts.

'Yes I do!'

'Well, maybe I can offer you a cup of coffee then?' Strøm smiles, slowly leading the way to the house.

Both children follow him up the aged stone steps.

Inside the house is cool and shadowy, and not unlike Molly's place, Eilif thinks: an awful mess, but with a strange order to everything.

I pictured all three of them sitting round the well-worn table in Strøm's kitchen, waiting for the water for the coffee to boil.

The table is strewn with shreds of tobacco, newspapers and breadcrumbs, I tell myself. He is a white-bearded man in a white cotton hat, they are two skinny, long-legged children in trendy summer clothes: Eilif wearing an orange baseball cap and hooded sweatshirt, Ine with her hair in a ponytail. The cat has followed them in and is weaving around their legs under the table.

Strøm makes the coffee weak and warms milk in a pan. Then he half-fills the children's coffee cups with milk before adding a dash of coffee and offering them the sugar bowl. Both children shovel sugar into their cups, then stir it round. In sync, clockwise. They seem content, already comfortable with him.

And he feels that he's beginning to get to know them too, I continue to imagine. He asks no more about their mother; they, on the other hand, quiz him on why he no longer wants to live in town, and he tells them more about the problem with his eyes, which he expects to worsen steadily as the years go on. He doesn't think there is much that can be done for him; he has gone too long without having it seen to, and he's scared of doctors. But until the day when he is plunged into darkness, he feels that he can manage better on his own out here in the country than in town, away from all the traffic and all the demands that the city makes on you; all the disturbance.

Eilif stares at him.

'But what if you go blind?' he asks. 'Wouldn't you have to go into an old folks' home?'

'Oh,' says Strøm. 'They'll never get me into an old folks' home, that's for sure.'

'Me neither,' Ine puts in.

'Well that makes two of us, then,' says Strøm, smiling at her. 'I haven't figured out what to do about that yet. The main thing right now is for me to finish a few things that I want to do before it's too late. I have a couple of jobs that won't wait.'

'What sort of jobs?' Ine asks, dipping her tongue in her coffee and shuddering silently. She has never tasted coffee before.

'I have to take some photographs for an exhibition which someone in town has asked me to put on. But I don't know. When your eyesight is failing . . .'

'Are you sad?' says Ine.

To his surprise Strøm feels embarrassed. This skinny little waif at his side gets to him in some way.

'Don't worry about it,' Ine goes on.

'No. If the exhibition comes to nothing, then it comes to nothing, even though I did sort of promise. To try at any rate.'

'You can only do your best,' pronounces Ine precociously. 'That's what Mum always says when there's something we can't manage.'

'That mother of yours is not stupid.'

'No, she's really clever. Much cleverer than her up at the summer house.'

'You don't say? But I feel I ought to try to come up with something. And we'll just have to see how it goes. In any case I've decided to stop worrying so much about what everyone else will think, or what they'll say about what I'm doing. That's another thing that comes with age.'

'I've decided to stop worrying about it too,' says Ine.

'Good!' Strøm cries heartily. 'Then that makes two of us.'

'Three,' says Eilif.

After this, I went on to myself, Strøm shows the children round the red cottage. It has two floors, but half of the ground floor has been converted into a darkroom, with blacked-out windows and a warning sign on the door lending a rather sinister air to the place. The rest of the sitting-room is taken up by a dining table, some ancient armchairs and a dark, old piano. There are huge, indiscriminate heaps of newspapers, photographic prints and books lying all over the place, interspersed with cups and plates and tools of one sort and another.

'Ooh, what a mess,' Ine breathes. 'It's almost as bad as Molly's place.'

'You've got a piano,' Eilif says.

'D'you play,' Strøm asks.

'Only a little bit,' Eilif replies. 'We don't have a piano at home, not at Mum's or Dad's, neither of them has room for one. But Mum plays. She's good, I've heard her, she plays when we visit people who have a piano.'

'Well, maybe you could play here sometimes,' Strøm says.

'Can you play?'

'I used to. But I seldom sit down at the piano these days. I'm getting too old for it, I think.'

'Were you good?'

'Pretty good. Good enough to get by.'

'Could you teach me?'

'We-ell, I've never tried to teach someone to play the piano, I don't know that . . .'

'I think I could learn.'

'You feel the flame, you mean?'

Strøm chuckles, but Eilif doesn't find it funny.

'Oh, please. And I'll help you with something you need help with. The garden, for instance.'

'Now you mention it . . .' Strøm says thoughtfully. 'I had an idea a minute ago, while we were having our coffee. I was thinking about the exhibition I'm preparing. It's this problem with my eyesight. I need someone to be my eyes. I need to get some more pictures taken.'

'We can be your eyes!' Ine cries excitedly. She has spied a chance to clear a space for herself within whatever is being built between Eilif and Strøm. 'You can just sit back and relax,' she carries on. 'And we'll run around and tell you what you're looking at and take pictures for you. It'll be fun.'

'That sounds great,' Strøm says. 'You'll be like Hugin and Munin. Have you heard of them?'

'No, who are they?' Ine asks.

'Hugin and Munin were two ravens that flew around the world. It was their job to be the eyes of the god Odin.'

'Why?'

'Because he couldn't see so well,' Strøm told her. 'Maybe he had something wrong with his eyes, I don't know.'

'Did he have to go into hospital and have an operation?'

'No, I think it was too late for him to have an operation. He hadn't looked after himself as well as he should.'

'Was he scared of doctors?'

'Something like that.'

'And maybe he was scared of the scalpel, too.'

'It's possible. That's probably why he had to have the ravens. They spent the whole day flying around, seeing what went on in the world and when evening came they lighted on his shoulders and told him about everything they had seen.'

'What sort of things did they see?' Ine asks.

'What do you think?' Eilif says. 'All sorts of things, of course.'

'Exactly,' Strøm says. 'And they told him about all these things, which was why Odin was the wisest of all the gods.'

'But could you teach me to play the piano?' Eilif asks again.

'Bags I'm Hugin!' Ine whoops.

Strøm realises now that Eilif is serious. He looks the boy straight in the eye.

'This means a great deal to you, doesn't it?' he says.

'I want to give Mum a surprise. She's really sick.'

'And you think she'll get better if you can show her that you've learned to play the piano?'

'She would be so happy.'

'Well, being happy may well help people to get better,' Strøm says. 'Of course I'll help you. If you think I'll do as a teacher for you.'

'And Ine and I will take pictures for you with our mobile. Nobody cares what sort of pictures we take with it.'

'No, you can take any kind of pictures you like, you two.'

'And then we can give them to you. As payment. You can do what you want with them.'

'But I don't know anything about these digital cameras.'

'I can transfer the photos to the computer and print them out on proper photographic paper for you. It's no problem, Molly has all sorts of equipment at the summer house, I've seen it. I know what to do.'

'I don't have any music for beginners,' Strøm said. 'We'll have to manage without music.'

'That's okay.'

'Is there anything in particular you would like to play?'

'There's one song that Mum loves. It's Swedish, I can't remember what it's called.'

'Can you sing it?'

'No, the words are really hard,' Eilif replies.

'But I can whistle it!' Ine cries, she obviously knows exactly which song her brother is talking about. 'I've learned to whistle.' And slowly and deliberately she whistles the little melody, all the way from beginning to end. Her brother follows her closely with his eyes, as if ready to step in and take over if she misses a note. When she is done she breathes a long sigh of relief.

'Ah, yes, that's a lovely one,' Strøm says slowly. 'I know it well. 'The butterfly in the garden'. It's by Bellmann.'

'Can you teach it to me?' asks Eilif.

I realised that Molly had not heard my warning on her answering machine and I couldn't bring myself to mention it to her on the phone. I was in such a state; I had become deeply embroiled in a story about Strøm and the children, one that had something to say to me. It was as if I was a narrator again, as I had been that time in fourth grade, standing in Molly's spotlight in the school play. Only this time it felt as though the story being told through me demanded something of me.

As if storytelling was bound up with fate.

I had to press one soothing hand to my own brow to stop me from blurting out what was on my mind to Molly.

'So, how are they anyway?' I asked, speaking a little too loudly into the telephone. 'You are keeping an eye on them, aren't you? Not leaving them to roam around on their own?'

But Molly didn't know what was going on inside me, she said that Eilif and Ine were much bigger and more sensible than she had feared, it was perfectly okay for them to be out on their own.

'Eilif looks out for his sister like a proper little knight in shining armour,' she said, with something approaching pride in her voice. As if it was thanks to her that Aksel had such a reliable son.

She said the children had told her they had met a nice neighbour. They had evidently not said any more about him than that, and she had simply been relieved to know that they had something to keep them occupied and let her get on with her work in peace. She had taken a run into town to pick up the television from Granny's, without popping in to see me, she said. The video machine too, and some films. A faint, jarring note seemed to creep into her voice when she said this. Maybe she was feeling guilty about something.

*

I don't think she could have told Aksel about the baby yet. Despite the fact that I was now the narrator of a story that wanted something of me, I felt as though I had also been seized by a new kind of speechlessness. This speechlessness was related to Molly's pregnancy. It seemed to tie in with the story of Eilif and Ine, in some way that I did not understand.

But this much I understood: fate was in the process of making some sinister moves, and I was the only one who knew, the only one who could stop Strøm from molesting Aksel's children. I might even be the only one who could prevent Molly and Aksel from having a child together: a responsibility which was almost too much to bear.

But I let Molly talk on as if nothing were amiss. On the way to the summer house from town she had stopped at a petrol station and picked up more videos for the kids, she said. I asked her what she had bought and wasn't particularly happy with her answer, it seemed a pretty haphazard selection: rubbishy potboilers designed for much younger children, or younger than Eilif anyway. He was growing into a young man, he needed more than this on which to hone his mind. It annoyed me that she hadn't gone to more trouble to buy decent films for them. She, who was always boasting about what excellent taste in films she has.

But she seemed to be extremely pleased to have acquired a cheap babysitter in the form of the video machine. She gaily announced that she had had an idea for the costumes for the dream play; she had been up in her bedroom, working on some intricate crochetwork in metallic thread with which she had been experimenting, while the children were flopped in front of the television in the sitting-room downstairs. If she could get it right, it would be quite spectacular, she was sure. She tried to explain the crochet technique to me, but I was only half-listening to what she said. It was clear that she no longer needed my help with the dream play quite so badly.

'But have you talked to the children,' I asked, breaking her off. 'I mean, you have to talk to them. Show them that you care. They must have so many terrible thoughts in their heads. Remember their mother. Or they could have had a shocking experience at some point during the day. Something associated with one of the neighbours, maybe? Traumatised children need someone to talk to. For the moment you're their guardian, remember that.'

'Okay, okay,' Molly snapped huffily. 'Don't push me. I need a little time to myself, too, you know. I'm not used to children.'

'What do you do when it's their bedtime?' I asked.

'What do you mean?'

'Do you spend some time with them then? Kids like that.'

'What, with bedtime stories? No, that's not my style. I don't know any bedtime stories. And anyway, they're way too old for all that. They're much bigger than you seem to think. You don't know them.'

'You don't need to tell them bedtime stories,' I said. 'Just sit on the edge of the bed, have a little chat with them. Ask them what they're thinking, what they've seen and done that day. Kids like that. You have to remember, Ine's only six. Think back to when you were six.'

That was a stupid thing to say, of course, that last bit. When Molly was six she was probably a fractious child who wouldn't allow anyone to tell her anything. Unless it was Granny.

'She'll be seven soon,' Molly said. 'On Midsummer's Eve.'

I hadn't known that. That was the sort of thing I should have known about Ine. I would have to remember to find out when Eifil's birthday was.

'Oh, but then you'll have to have a birthday party for her!' I said.

'Well, of course.'

'Have you and Aksel discussed what to do about that? It's only a few days away, you know.'

'Agnes, don't fuss.'

'And I really would recommend that you make sure the

children aren't out on their own visiting neighbours,' I went on. 'You still don't seem to have grasped just who you have living next door. And I want you to come and collect me tomorrow morning. Bring the children with you. There's something I need to tell you. It's very, very important, Molly.'

'Dear, oh dear.' She sounded really annoyed now. 'Well, if it's that important, why can't you tell me now?'

'I have to be with you when I tell you,' I said. 'You're going to need support when you hear.'

Then I hung up.

Time was starting to run out. I had an errand to attend to. The new day was beginning, fate had something it wished to show me. It had something it wished to show Molly, too, and it could be that it was using me as its messenger. I could tell by the trembling of my lips; there was no mistaking it. I had to be there to act as witness, be the one of us who was calm and clear. I had to take care of those children.

I did a few rounds of the room in the wheelchair, then I lifted the receiver and rung Molly's number again. This was so unlike me. I said she had to come and get me right away. I was afraid that the full gravity of the situation had not been brought home to her in that first call, and I was right, I think.

'Molly!' I cried. 'There's no time to lose. You need me there now!'

'Agnes, what's happened? You sound a bit upset.'

I could tell from her voice that she had already put the conversation we had just had behind her and was busy with her metallic crochetwork again.

'I *am* upset,' I said. 'I miss you.'

I don't know what possessed me to say that of all things. It was hard to stay calm and clear.

'I miss you too, pet,' she said. 'I'm so looking forward to having you here. But now I think I'd better get some work done. I've promised the kids that we'll play a game once I've finished all this crocheting. And if you make a child a promise you have to keep it, don't you?'

'Which game?'

'How do you mean?'

'Which game are you going to play!' My voice was out of control now, even I could hear that.

'Oh, what's it called again?' she said, somewhat ruffled by my vehemence. 'Something about a diamond. They brought it with them, I didn't really look at the box properly, they've got it up in their room, I think?'

'The Hunt for the Lost Diamond?'

'Something like that.'

I felt my heart sink. That was my game. I was the one who was supposed to play it with them. That was my plan, and Molly had stolen it. How dare she. She no longer seemed to be able to tell the difference between us, I thought, shaken.

She had just about everything, that was how it had always been, I was used to it. But The Hunt for Lost Diamond was for me and Eilif and Ine. That was my idea.

'But Agnes. What's the matter? Aren't you feeling well?' Molly asked. I thought the concern in her voice sounded rather affected. 'I'm really looking forward to having you here,' she said again.

'Yes, well the only question is when were you thinking of coming to get me!'

'Don't be like that,' she said. 'I'll be there tomorrow morning. I'll make the wheelchair ramp this evening, I know you can't manage without that. I'll work all night if necessary.'

'Good,' I said. 'Then I'll pack my things and get everything ready. But be careful with that bandsaw. The last thing we need is for you to go cutting yourself. You have responsibilities now, remember. Aksel has left the children in your care.'

She must have laid her metallic crochetwork aside and begun on the ramp as soon as we hung up, because late that same evening she mailed pictures of it to me. She can work incredibly fast once she gets started and she's a skilled carpenter.

The ramp had turned out really well. It had no handrails yet, and she hadn't painted it, but we could see to that over the summer, I told myself. If I'm to walk up that ramp I'm going to need handrails. I'll sketch out an idea for them and let her see it. I can do it in the same style as the rail around the veranda, so it will look as if it's always been there. And of course it has to be painted, so that it looks permanent.

But I didn't get round to sketching any handrails. I was in such a flap, it was impossible to keep a clear head. I chased back and forth in the wheelchair, going round in circles; threw myself into work on the model; moved things about inside the house: the tiny telephone and the spotlight, the little scrap of fabric which served as the hammock. I felt around for the cardboard puppets I had made of myself, the children Aksel and Molly, picked them up one after another, moved their arms and legs, carried them towards one another, then away again. I tried to get them to hug one another, but without success, they just got all tangled up; I had to pull Ine away from Molly, pull Aksel away from me, it was a right mess. In the end I threw the puppets away and they landed in a heap on the top of the desk.

I shut my eyes and said to myself, as fervently and as clearly as I could:

'Now. It has to be now.'

And maybe that's what did it. At any rate, Aksel came to me on the evening of Monika's operation.

Yes. He came to me.

All he could think about was Monika and her sick body, that was not hard to see: the anaesthetic, the scalpels, the bandages. He was worn-out, grey-faced. But it was me he came to.

I had forgotten that he had his own key. I almost jumped out of my skin, sitting there in the wheelchair, when I heard the three brisk rings on the front-door bell. I shouted something or other in the direction of the door, I don't remember what, he let himself in before I had time to wheel myself out into the hall. I bent down quickly and switched off the projector, which had been casting the picture of the summer house on to the ceiling, and shoved the cardboard puppets under some books that were lying open on the desk. I don't think he noticed anything.

I had spent all afternoon working on the model. There was something about the way I wielded the scissors, a somewhat frenetic air, which bothered me slightly, but I couldn't stop myself. It was as if I had handed over the controls to a pilot who was heading for somewhere other than I had planned. The room was filled with the crisp snip-snipping of metal on card and the faint clink-clunk every time I let the scissors drop on to the desktop in order to concentrate on the glue or the little pins. And, at odd intervals, my own small sighs when I had to take a big, deep breath.

I had almost finished the bathing hut, and the jetty. I had put the cardboard puppets of Molly and the children and myself on the blue tissue paper representing the water while I put the final touches to the bathing hut. But now they were lying under some books.

*

It was so strange, seeing Aksel like this, with an uncertain look in his eyes and a hesitant huskiness in his throat. He was clearly not my nurse now, he was simply a tired, anxious man in need of a bed for the night. My first thought was: he's not here because of me. And I'll have to get that desk turned round, I can't sit with my back to the door like that when I'm working, it's awful not to know who's walking in on you. It could be someone with a knife.

My eyes must have been just about starting out of my head, because Aksel walked straight up to me, apologised in his quiet way and placed a protective hand over my eyes. I felt the warmth from the palm of his hand flow into my face and heard him say that he hadn't meant to scare me. I wanted him to never let go, my face needed the warmth of his hand so badly.

'I understood from Molly that it would be all right for me to stay the night here,' he said, slowly removing his hand and letting it fall on to my shoulder. 'She called to let me know.'

'Of course,' I said. I kept my eyes closed for a few seconds longer than I needed to. 'Of course,' I repeated. 'I'm really glad you came.'

Then he stepped back and asked if I had any beer. He was so thirsty and tired. I told him to help himself from the fridge. I never drank beer on my own.

He came back carrying two bottles, a bottle-opener and two glasses. He slumped down on to the sofa, I wheeled myself over to him and took the glass he offered me. I've never been very keen on beer, but I almost drained the whole glassful in one great gulp, my head tilted way back. He did the same. Then he lit a cigarette, without asking whether I minded. He used the beer glass as an ashtray. We sat there, looking at one another.

'How's Monika?' I asked eventually.

'I don't know.'

After that he didn't say anything else for a while. I sat in silence with him. I felt how, almost instantly, the alcohol set my blood racing; it had been such a shock to the system. He turned his eyes to the ceiling, on to which the picture of the summer house had been cast only minutes earlier, and went on: 'They said it's too early to tell, they should be able to tell me more tomorrow. But when I pressed the surgeon he did say that he thought they had got the lot. The cancer had spread further than they had expected, but he thought they had got it all.'

'Is she going to . . .?'

'Live?'

'Pull through, is what I meant.'

'We'll have to hear what the doctors say tomorrow. She's sleeping now, she's going to be pretty groggy when she comes round.'

'So you'll be going down to the hospital first thing in the morning?'

'Yes, of course.'

'You must be exhausted.'

'I am.'

I hardly dared to look at him. I didn't want my eyes to seem too prying, and I couldn't pressurise him by showing how glad I was to see him.

'What will happen to her now?'

'They'll give her radiotherapy,' he said. 'Just to be on the safe side. I assume they'll start her on that as soon as she's strong enough. She's going to be in hospital for a while yet.'

'I see.'

'I don't know whether I'm up to driving home tonight. That's why I came here. It was Molly who suggested it. She called me and said you'd told her it would be all right. And I had my key.'

I managed to stifle a little hiccup.

'But of course,' I said hurriedly. 'You can always come here. Any time, and stay as long as you like.'

'Oh, just tonight will do, I think. After that I should be able to stay at home.'

'Of course. But I'm afraid my sofa is a bit on the short side . . .' I faltered. 'You take my bed. I'll sleep on the sofa.'

'No way. You'll just end up rolling on to the floor and not be able to get back up.'

'But I don't have a spare bed,' I argued.

'Well, there's plenty of room in your bed,' Aksel said. 'It is a double bed, after all.'

I was struck dumb. I didn't know what he was talking about.

'I mean for sleeping, Agnes. I'm absolutely worn out. And I have to get up early, I want to be at the hospital when she wakes in the morning.'

'Of course.'

We sat for a while saying nothing, staring into space, both of us.

'I see you've started on a new project?' he said, nodding at the model on the desk.

'Oh, yes,' I gabbled. I was worried that he might realise what it was meant to be. 'Just some bits and pieces I've been working on to pass the time. Have you spoken to Eilif and Ine?'

'Not yet, but I sent them a text message.'

'Then I think you ought to call them right away,' I said. 'I'm sure they must be waiting for you to call.'

'I was thinking I would call them tomorrow. They're probably in bed by now.'

'Don't leave it till tomorrow,' I said. 'Even if they are in bed, I bet you anything they're not asleep. Eilif will have taken the mobile to bed with him.'

'How do you know that?' he asked. But I didn't answer.

'Call them now,' I said.

'You're probably right. But I think I'd better take a shower first,' he said. 'I have to work out what I'm going to say. I don't want to scare them.'

'No,' I said. 'You don't want to scare them, but you have to tell them what's happening, otherwise they'll just start to imagine things. And we always imagine things to be worse than they really are.'

He nodded, heaved himself off the sofa and made his way

towards the bathroom. He was staggering slightly. He didn't close the door, I heard the tinkle of a stiff jet of urine striking the toilet bowl. Then the swish of the shower curtain and the rush of water from the shower, heralded by the familiar clanking in the pipes. I sat as if turned to stone.

A little while later he wandered back to the sitting-room with my towel round his waist and a mobile phone in his hand. His hair was wet. He stood in the doorway, regarded me solemnly.

'I'll call now,' he said. 'I'll do as you say, you're probably right.'

'Good.'

He went through to the kitchen, but he didn't close the door there either, I could watch him through the open door. I don't think he did it deliberately, he was just tired and confused. Aksel is not an exhibitionist.

I saw him key in a number on the mobile. He obviously didn't get through, and suddenly I remembered that it was impossible to get a signal inside the summer house. I wanted to call out to him, but couldn't bring myself to do so, I was as if hypnotised. I saw how he pressed the buttons, trying again and again, saw how the towel slipped from his hips and fell to the floor. I opened my eyes wide. He had his back to me, he was so absorbed in what he was doing he hadn't noticed that I was watching him. He bent down, picked the bath towel off the floor, but it was difficult for him to fix it around his waist with the telephone in one hand. He fumbled with the towel for a few moments and then gave up.

Aksel has a pale back and lovely, tight buttocks with a little dimple on the outer side of each one. I suppose it must have something to do with the muscles there. I've never had dimples like that in the sides of my cheeks. I know I need to exercise the gluteus muscles more and not concentrate solely on my legs and arms. The gluteus muscles are what keep us from tipping over when we sit down, so Aksel has explained to me. Without good, strong gluteus muscles one wouldn't be much good on one's own in a kayak, I'll warrant. The thighs have to be strong too. And the back. And the stomach.

He was still standing with his back to me. I stared and stared, wishing he would turn round.

Then he put the mobile down on the kitchen table and wrapped the towel firmly around his waist again before turning to face the open door. I spun the wheelchair about, so he wouldn't see that I had been observing him.

'There doesn't seem to be any signal,' he said. 'Either that or they've forgotten to charge the mobile. I'm not getting any answer, anyway. It'll need to wait till tomorrow. I think I'll have to go to bed. I'm afraid I'm not the best company today. You'll have to excuse me.'

'Of course,' I said.

'Do you need help getting into bed?'

'No thanks. Just you go ahead. I think I'll stay up a while longer. I've got something here that I'm working on.'

'You're sure?'

'I'm sure,' I said.

'I'll set the alarm on my mobile for half-six. There's a ward meeting at seven, when the day shift come on, and I want to be there for that. I've pretty much worn out the late shift, I think. I'm sure they think I act as though I work there.'

'Don't you mean: as though you were in charge there?' I said, smiling at him.

'Hmm. Yes, that's maybe more like it.'

'You're really fond of Monika, aren't you?'

'She's the mother of my children.'

'And you are really fond of her.'

'Yes.'

'I'm sure she going to be fine,' I continued. 'You said yourself she's as strong as an ox.'

'As a lion. She's really tough.'

'Everything's going to be fine, I'm sure. You just need some sleep, both of you. You've had a lot on your plate these past few weeks. And you're a nurse, you know what's needed. You're an excellent nurse.'

'Thanks for saying so,' he said with a tight, weary smile. 'You're sure you don't need help?'

'Quite sure,' I said. 'I have started a new and better life. I think I forgot to tell you. I'm working out a lot more now. You have to take some of the credit for that, you've taken such trouble with me. I tried to explain it to the temp, but she doesn't listen to me.'

His eyes searched my face. I could see that he really had heard what I had said; it hadn't gone in one ear and out the other as it did with the temp.

'A new and better life,' he said. 'Sounds good. I hope you're remembering what I told you about breathing and taking it nice and easy. Don't force it.'

'I have no problem getting out of bed and over into my chair on my own now.'

'What did I tell you?'

'I know.'

I paused before adding: 'So I don't think it's necessary for the temp to come here any more. I've really tried to tell her this, but I don't think she hears what I'm saying. It's like she's just decided that I'm sick and that's that.'

'The temp's very new to the job, she doesn't have much experience of cases like yours,' he said. 'You'll have to be patient with her.'

'And she ought to listen to what I say!'

'Yes, she should. I'll talk to her.'

'You're on holiday.'

He made no reply.

'Do you have a T-shirt I could borrow for tonight?' he asked. 'I think mine's a bit sweaty. Everything has been happening so fast this last day or so, it never occurred to me to pack an overnight bag.'

'Just take one from the cupboard,' I said. 'I've got lots of big ones. In fact they're all big. And you're welcome to use my toothbrush.'

'I'll pick up an apple or something first thing in the morning. Well, goodnight. Thanks for letting me stay here.'

'I'm glad you came,' I said. 'Everything's going to be fine, you'll see.'

Saying that made me feel like a guarantor: someone has to stand guard. Someone has to stand guard over this man and his fate. He has children. A father must be strong. Someone has to ensure that the good forces are given peace in which to work.

I sat on in the lamplit room, staring at the model. I couldn't go to bed anyway, not until the beer had worked its way through my system. It was too much of a bother for me to have to get up in the middle of the night to pee. People in my situation have to be good at planning ahead.

It was strange to sit there waiting for the beer to run through my body. It took forever, but at last I felt that the time had come. I trundled out to the bathroom, but stopped outside the door and decided to try to get out of the wheelchair and walk the four steps to the toilet unaided. I almost made it. My legs were wobbly, they felt funny; but they were possessed of a will they had never known before. It was as if someone had filled the tank with some new sort of fuel.

By the time I finally sank down on to the toilet seat and could let go, I was tingling with a sensuality I had never felt before. I gazed down at my feet and tried to spread my toes. A feeble little spread, perhaps, but a spread none the less.

It took me almost half an hour to get ready for bed. I washed under my arms with a cloth, sprayed a little perfume into the hollow of my throat then regretted it: it was too much. I tried to wipe the perfume off, but a trace of it still lingered. I smelled like a garden in full bloom.

When I finally wheeled myself into the bedroom, Aksel was fast asleep. He lay curled up and dead to the world, right on the edge of the double bed, with a quilt cover over him. I've never seen a living soul look so exhausted and completely bereft of life.

I eased myself gently out of the chair and over on to my side of the bed, pulled the duvet over myself.

He smelled nice. So did I, to say the least. Gentle Jesus looked down on us from the wall above our heads. I thought I could hear the faint tinkle of the bells round the lambs' necks. A thin, brittle tinkle.

But I did not stand guard. I slept so soundly that night. I don't know how I could have slept so soundly with Aksel there in my bed. I dreamed about Dad again; dreamed that he was shouting something to me, and that I fell into a great, yawning void, a kind of lift-shaft cutting through the heavens.

When I woke, the bed next to me was empty. There was not a sound to be heard in the flat. The curtains were pulled back and the light forced its way into the room in the most insistent fashion. Disappointment spread inside me like a heavy bog. I couldn't understand how he could have gone before I woke up.

The morning papers were lying beside me on the bed. The flat smelled of coffee. Next to the papers was a note from Aksel, scribbled on the back of the envelope from some bill. He had written it in capital letters, without any punctuation whatsoever, as if he were just some workman who had left school at fifteen. I had never seen his handwriting before:

IM GLAD TO HEAR THAT YOURE FEELING BETTER GOOD LUCK WITH GETTING WASHED AND DRESSED ON YOUR OWN WELL GIVE IT A TRY ILL CALL THE TEMP AND TELL HER YOULL SEE TO YOURSELF FOR THE REST OF THE HOLIDAY THATS MY GIRL AKSEL

II

MOLLY

I catch sight of myself. In the mirror in the hall, or in the bathroom; often, in the evening, in the gleaming, dark windows down here in the sitting-room. I am always bigger than I imagine. I think of myself as being below average height, but actually I'm not, I am average height. It's well seen that I cut my hair myself. I look severe.

Sometimes my reflection springs itself on me too suddenly and I falter and step back a little, as if I don't dare. I ask myself: Who is that? And next time I pass the mirror I snap my eyes shut.

I look more severe in the mirror than I do in real life. When I see myself like that, suddenly it no longer seems quite so self-evident that the woman in there wishes me well.

You have to wish yourself well.

If I manage not to shut my eyes, but stand there and consider myself calmly, without looking away, I can find myself thinking: that woman isn't as severe as she looks, maybe she's just a bit lonely.

Eilif and Ine didn't want me. I could tell just by looking at them, the minute they got out of the car: to them I was a stranger, somebody on whom they were being fobbed off.

Aksel drove down with them from town. They had gone with their mother to the hospital, she was to be operated on the next day. Aksel is a nurse to the core, he probably wanted to make sure that everything was okay before he left her. That she was already asleep, or had been given her pills, or whatever it is they give you the day before a big operation for cancer.

I had raced about, tidying up the house and seeing to the food in the kitchen at the same time: the boiling water for the pasta, the pasta lying all ready next to the pot, the sausage chunks in the frying pan.

I tried to think of all the things that it could be dangerous to have lying around with children in the house. Things with sharp points, sharp edges. Chemicals. Badly connected electrical appliances. This was before I discovered how big and sensible they are, of course. Neither Eilif or Ine would ever dream of sticking anything sharp or pointed in their mouth, or of swallowing any chemicals, you don't have to worry about such things with them.

The car drove up in front of the house and I dropped the pasta into the boiling water, as if on cue. Then I went out on to the front steps and saw Aksel put on the handbrake with what seemed like an exaggerated pull of the arm. He turned and said something to the two in the back seat. It didn't look as if either of them answered, they sat still, making no move to get out. It was the first time I had seen them. They were just two blonde and almost faceless heads. They were a lot bigger than I had imagined.

Suddenly it dawned on me that to them I was the scary one, not the other way round. To them, it must feel as though their father was putting them into kennels while their mother had her operation. I was the kennel owner. It wasn't hard to see that they were angry with him and had no wish to meet me. How could they possibly want someone they had never met before, someone whose name they might only have heard mentioned in passing.

Aksel and Monika had been divorced for years before I met him. I would bet that Ine, at least, can't remember a time when her parents were living together. But everything was bound to seem different now that I had appeared on the scene as their Dad's girlfriend; for them it had to be like a door closing, a door which, until now, had stood open on to the possibility of their parents getting together.

I stayed where I was on the steps, made no move. I couldn't remember whether I had switched off the ring under the frying pan in the kitchen, but I couldn't bring myself to turn and go inside to check. It would have looked odd, as if I had changed my mind and didn't want to bid them welcome after all.

I wasn't prepared for them to look so hostile. I thought: they hate me. There's nothing I can do about that, and Aksel has no intention of helping me. I've lost even before I've begun.

But there was no way back for any of us. They climbed slowly out of the car, all three. Aksel was first, he opened the boot and lifted out their bags before coming up the steps to me. He kissed me lightly on the cheek, not on the lips as he usually does. The kids followed behind, dragging their heels.

'Well, here they are – Eilif and Ine,' he said.

Eilif was carrying some boxes of board games, he nodded curtly and looked beyond me, through the door. Ine merely stared at me and mumbled something I didn't catch. She was lugging a large bag stuffed with Barbie dolls. Aksel said my name and pointed to me. That was the extent of the introductions. Both children carried on past us into the house.

It was a strange arrival.

*

I had indeed forgotten to turn off the ring on the cooker when I heard the car. The sausage chunks had a blackened crust on one side. I burned myself on the scorching-hot frying pan when I went to take it off the ring. I yelped and pulled my hand back, but I don't think anyone noticed, and I couldn't bring myself to go hunting for the burns ointment, I just held my fingers under the cold tap, then fanned my hand while thinking to myself that I ought to have done some vegetables, it would have looked good – as if I knew something about feeding children. At the very least I could have sliced some radishes. Aksel is so health- and fitness-conscious, I'm sure he likes the children to eat things with lots of fibre, and strong, natural colours. Aksel is a colour and fibre man.

It was a quiet meal. Afterwards the children thanked me politely and seemed relieved to have that part over and done with. Luckily I remembered that Agnes had asked if they could take some pictures. I told them that she was my friend, as well as being their Dad's patient. Aksel nodded absent-mindedly. I said I had invited her down to the summer house, and that she was in a wheelchair. So she had asked me to let her have some pictures of the house and the surrounding area, to help her plan how she was going to get about. I pointed to the veranda steps.

'I'm going to make a wheelchair ramp for her,' I said.

For the first time I spotted a glimmer of interest in their eyes. Maybe they liked the idea that I could build things.

'She said she would gladly pay you for your help, if you could take those pictures,' I went on.

But just then Aksel seemed to wake up. He wouldn't hear any talk of payment.

'I think this is one favour you can do for Agnes for free,' he said, eyeing them sternly.

We took some snaps of one another. It was all so stilted. Aksel put his arm round my shoulders, then took it away again as soon as Eilif had taken the picture.

Then the children took off, across the garden, through the lilac bushes and on down the road. I looked helplessly at Aksel. The table was a mess, everything looked so unappetising, none of us had cleared our plates. The burn on my finger was smarting and I couldn't help thinking that I should have made more of an effort to smarten the place up a bit, make it nice for them.

Aksel met my eye for a split-second and smiled. Then he jumped up from his chair and ran after the children, shouting something to them. They turned and walked back to him, trailing their feet. He hugged them, I couldn't hear what they were saying, but I guess he was explaining to them that he would be going back to the hospital. And probably telling them to behave themselves.

I walked out to the car with him. I had thought he would have a whole list of things for me to remember to do or not to do with the children, but he didn't say a thing, didn't even ask me to keep an eye on them when they were in the water. Maybe he had come to the conclusion that I knew all that. Maybe it just never occurred to him that I wasn't used to children. I said:

'Is it all right for me to take them swimming?'

'Yes, of course.'

'And is it all right for me to use the bandsaw while they're here?'

'Of course.'

How could I tell him I was pregnant, then, standing next to the car? It wasn't the right moment. He wouldn't have been capable of taking it in. All he wanted was to get back to Monika. I kissed him on the cheek, not on the lips, and that seemed to be fine by him.

The kids didn't come back for hours. By then it was evening; I had cleared the table and washed up and then I had started cutting out the wood for the wheelchair ramp with the bandsaw in the sitting-room. They had lain in the hammock for a while after wandering back through the garden, I heard them out on the veranda, but couldn't bring myself to go out to them.

Then they came to me, in the sitting-room. They came up on me from behind; I always think it's so unpleasant to be taken by surprise like that. I jumped and straightened up too quickly, switched off the saw. Suddenly things went so quiet round about me. I think I must have looked cross, maybe they thought that already I had almost forgotten that they existed. I drew a hand across my brow, but couldn't think what to say to them.

They turned on their heels and left the room again, I heard them running up the stairs, up to the room where Aksel had left their bags. I don't know whether they went to bed right away, I didn't hear another sound from up there. They must have kept their voices low, talked in little more than whispers.

I didn't see how I could go up to them. I hadn't even shown them their beds as I had meant to do. But they had obviously found them for themselves, beds didn't really need any explanation.

I wondered if it was normal to go up and say goodnight to children of their age, check that they had brushed their teeth and all that. But I dismissed the thought. I didn't feel I had any right to interfere.

I don't think it took very long for me to become engrossed in my work again. It was almost as if I truly had forgotten them now; as if I managed to make myself believe that I didn't really have two children who were not my own sleeping in the spare room.

My mind was a complete blank, I was simply in motion, raising and lowering my arms, reaching for pieces of wood, guiding them towards the screeching saw-blade.

The floor around the bandsaw gradually became covered in sawdust. I could see the criss-cross tracks of my feet in it, it looked as though a whole army had been tramping around in the pale, powdery shavings. I thought to myself: what is all this? The place never looked like this in Granny's day, I really ought to start hoovering, cleaning up after myself.

But I prefer woodworking to cleaning. I worked on for hours and forgot all about the hoovering. I forgot the time too, I worked until my back was stiff and my arms like lead. The garden was in darkness by the time I finished.

I went to get the digital camera, took a photograph of the completed wheelchair ramp, using the flash. It looked as if it were flowing down the veranda steps and on into the garden. It had turned out well, as if to plan, except that I had planned on something quite different. It's often the way. I only realise what I have actually had in mind when I see how it turns out. That's probably why my models tend not to look much like the end result. Or the other way round. This can be frustrating for people at the theatre who have to work with my models.

There was plenty of space at the side of the ramp for walking up the steps.

The picture of the wheelchair ramp was one of the first I had taken with my new camera. I had bought two before Christmas, one for Agnes and one for myself. I haven't quite got used to it yet: I'm used to taking photographs that I can work on in the darkroom, not on a computer screen. I like the pent-up concentration of the darkroom, and I like the mechanical shutter on a proper camera: the metallic click, the resonance and hollowness of that sound. I like the fact that with a little practice one can tell the shutter speed by the length of the click, by the way the click is drawn out; prolonged, hollow.

That sound is rather like the one you get when you click the tongue off the back of the mouth to imitate the sound of galloping horses. Like we did as children.

I had understood from Agnes that she urgently needed to come down here. Her voice on the phone had brooked no argument, she wanted me to build the ramp and send her a photograph right away. She has a very strong will, sometimes I can sense it way down here without her saying a word.

I didn't have a wheelchair with which to test the ramp, but I went out to the tool shed and found Granny's wheelbarrow. It was pitch-black out there by then. Suddenly I remembered what it had been like to step into the gloom in there as a child, from a day of dazzling light and warmth. How I would stand there, half-blinded, letting my eyes get used to the darkness, how I could only just make out the shapes of the tools hanging in their allotted places: Scythe. Axe. Hedge-clippers. Crowbar. Hoe. The big, rust-spotted, steel shovel and the little, sharp, aluminium one. I remembered that I used to think the two shovels were brothers. Hefty, rusty big brother – light, gleaming little brother.

Next to big brother hung Granny's old life-vest.

I only had to reach out my hand and I could touch all of Granny's things. But I didn't, I simply bent down, grasped the handles of the wheelbarrow, backed it out of the shed and wheeled it over the grass around the house, up to the veranda. Then I made a run at the ramp and rolled straight up it. It seemed to work well, it was just steep enough and it didn't creak; it had a nice give to it.

I sat down in one of the wicker chairs and thought: I won't paint it yet. First we have to see how long Agnes intends to stay. She may change her mind, in which case I can use the ramp for something else, maybe as part of a stage set, you never know what you're going to need. And the materials are the theatre's property anyway.

I left the wheelbarrow on the veranda and went back into the sitting-room, lit some lamps and switched on the computer. My eye fell on the sawdust and all the footprints again, but I didn't go for the hoover this time either.

I am in the process of creating a new era here at the summer house. I'm trying to push the old me out of the way, to let the new me in. But I'm not entirely sure how to do this.

*

There were several mails from the theatre. I sat in the pale, bluish light from the screen and skimmed through them, but wrote no replies. I never know how to deal with being hassled; it just confuses me. When people hassle you, should you hassle them back? Why don't they solve the problems themselves, when they know they can?

No mail from Aksel. It must be ages since he went anywhere near a computer. He's had other things to think about. And no mail from Agnes. It struck me that it must have been hard for her to learn that I was pregnant over the phone. I should have waited until she came to visit, just as I wanted to wait with telling Aksel until he could come down here and we had time to ourselves. I could have told them both at the same time, I tried to tell myself. But I knew that would not be right. It's Aksel's baby, not Agnes's.

I clicked on the icon with the white letter and envelope in the left-hand corner of the screen and wrote Agnes's e-mail address in the panel provided. In the panel underneath I wrote: 'Here you are. It's finished. I'll be there around eleven. Be ready.' I attached the pictures of the wheelchair ramp and pressed 'Send'. The button glowed red, the tiny, digital hourglass that is never completely full or completely empty flashed up on the screen for a second, the sand slowly trickling through it. I thought to myself: now time stands still, as the sand runs and runs through the hourglass without anything emptying or filling, and my message to Agnes flies in an arc through the air, from this house all the way to her flat in town. Everything is in motion.

When I got up from the chair after switching off the computer I felt suddenly faint; I lost my balance for a second and had to support myself against the wall, take a deep breath and let it out again in little puffs. There was a rushing sound in my ears and I felt a fresh wave of nausea rolling upwards from my stomach to my throat. I just made it on to the veranda, leaned over the rail and spewed semi-digested pasta and sausage chunks all over the rose bushes. My mouth smelled sour.

*

Not until my stomach had settled down and I felt well enough to lock the front door and the veranda door for the night and plod up the stairs to bed did it strike me that the bandsaw I had been using in the sitting-room and all the hammering out on the veranda must have kept the children awake far into the night. Maybe they had been frightened by the noise, frightened or annoyed. But they hadn't come down to ask me to stop. They must have dropped off eventually.

The next morning I got up early. I felt as if I had hardly been gone at all, as if I had lain with my eyes open all night. I heard no sounds from the spare room, the children were probably still asleep. I had the feeling that something important had happened during the night. I strode out into the expectant air and on round the side of the house to have a look at the wheelchair ramp.

It looked different in daylight. It was as if it had already grown accustomed to being there, it had settled in. Both the garden and the veranda appeared to have welcomed it with open arms. I placed my foot on the ramp, took a couple of steps up it to check the give; it felt just as good this morning. The wheelbarrow was still on the veranda.

I went into the kitchen and put on the coffee machine, then sat at the kitchen table gazing out of the window at the drive and the road down to Håvard's cottage. You can't see it from here, it's hidden behind the trees, you can only just make out the smoke from the chimney when he burns newspapers.

I had learned, that morning, that it was him who lived in that house. Agnes had told me, she had left a message on my answering machine. She had sounded quite hysterical, not at all like her usual self. It worried me: not what she said, but the way she said it. I thought about her illness. I knew that in some people it also affected their personalities.

I felt I needed time to think. Something seemed to be happening to her, something I didn't understand.

Agnes is observant. She's rather like a detective, digging up information in the strangest places and putting it together all by herself to form a new and surprising picture. Even so, though, she doesn't always hit the nail right on the head. She thinks too much. She needs to get out, meet people, get involved in the real world. I try to help her, but it's not always easy. I think she has difficulty dealing with real life. Sometimes it's as though she doesn't want to see.

I often think about Håvard. I've always known he would come back into my life, that it was only a question of time. That I only have to reach out my hand and he'll be there, on the other side of a veil, so to speak.

I knew, of course, that he was no child molester, that I had discovered long ago. But I was confused by the fact that Agnes didn't know this. Had I really not told her that those rumours about him had all been a web of lies? Surely not. I tell Agnes everything.

But what worried me just as much as Agnes's shrill voice shrieking at me that Håvard was living next door, was the fact that I had no idea what to do with the children while they were staying with me. How to get close to them. I felt that it was my job to get them to like me. That I needed a television, a video machine, some films. But that wasn't enough! I had to come up with something better, something really special. Something they would never forget.

Poor little kids, I said to myself. They have to have something to do down here. I haven't time to think about Håvard right now.

After some time I heard someone coming down the stairs. It was Eilif. He trod very softly, as if he didn't want to give me a fright, but I heard him anyway. He didn't say anything when he came into the kitchen, just stood at one end of the table looking at me. He was wearing a different face from the one he had had on the day before, I didn't recognise it, he looked as though he had had a dream from which he hadn't quite surfaced. He didn't smile. I had the feeling that he had had the same thought as me during the night: that from now on everything was going to be different.

I smiled and said good morning, making it clear that I was pleasantly surprised to see him up so early. He pulled a chair out from the table and sat down. He had clearly been to the bathroom for a quick wash and had slicked his hair back with the gooey, glistening hair gel which someone had unpacked and left there the night before. I had seen it when I went in, stiff and tired, to brush my teeth. I recognised the smell of it, I had squeezed a little out of the tube and sniffed it. I had been trying to imagine how one might use such a shiny substance, visualised how it might be possible to produce some interesting effects with a thick layer of this stuff spread between two sheets of Perspex: experimenting a bit with light, projecting the images on to the wall behind; with everything moving to a particular rhythm. A lazy jazz rhythm, perhaps. But you would need an awful lot of tubes for that, I told myself.

Eilif had painstakingly slicked his fair hair up into lots of little spikes. He was possibly a bit vain, unlike his Dad, who doesn't seem to be aware of his looks at all. I liked the fact that Eilif wasn't a carbon copy of his Dad.

I could see his scalp. It was easy to tell that he had been packed off to the hairdresser right before this holiday. Maybe it was his mother who had decided that it was high time he had a haircut. There was still a paler band of skin running all the way round his head at the hairline. I realised that this marked the old line of his hair, and that he didn't use hair gel every day, that his hair didn't normally stick straight up into the air.

It was as if his hair were the sea, and it had gone out a little, leaving a band on the sand. The sun hasn't got to work on that band yet, I thought. It's a bit vulnerable right now. But we'll soon mend that. A few days in the fresh air down here at the summer house, and lots of swimming, and it will all be a lovely, even colour again.

He was gathered in on himself and his own body in a careless, almost nonchalant way. In that he resembled his father. It touched my heart, but I didn't let on. I didn't want to embarrass him or scare him away. I was so pleased that he had come downstairs, that he wanted to be with me.

I got up and fetched a glass of milk which I placed in front of him. He didn't look up, nor did he touch the glass, it struck me that he might not like milk. I remember thinking that I would have to ask Agnes whether she thought they would expect me to buy cocoa powder to put in their milk. I assumed that was the sort of thing she would know.

We sat quietly for a while, saying nothing. Then I asked him if he had slept well and he nodded. I asked whether he would like me to make him a sandwich, and he said he could do it himself. But he didn't rise from his seat on the other side of the table.

I asked what he and Ine had done the previous afternoon, while I was working. And he proceeded, rather solemnly, to tell me about the old man they had met in the house next door, about the pictures they had taken of him and sent to Agnes from their mobile phone. He pulled the phone out of the pocket of his hooded sweatshirt, brought up one of the pictures on to the screen and handed it to me while reaching out with his other hand for my lighter, the one I have painted with nail polish, which was lying on the table between us. He examined it carefully, but made no comment.

So we sat there, each with our little gadget in our hands, studying them. I spent some minutes gazing at the phone's tiny, bright screen, nodding and endeavouring to smile as if in recognition, to let him understand that I also remembered what had gone on between us the day before, that he and I felt the same way about that photograph session: as something we had gone along with because we felt we were obliged to. That we had grinned and borne it.

The first photograph was the one of Aksel and me on the

veranda. It looked stiff and unnatural, Aksel's mind was so clearly elsewhere. Eilif showed me which button to click to view the other snaps and I clicked forward to the ones of him and Ine posing in front of the hammock, and then their pictures of the garden, the gravel path, a cat with its tail held aloft like a pennant. And then, suddenly, I was sitting with a picture of Håvard in the palm of my hand. I already knew that it had to be him, I had heard the message on the answering machine. But still I felt my breath catching in my throat when I saw him. Something stopped for a moment, and then something had to be started up again, the way you sometimes have to do with a computer. Restart.

It's a long time since I decided to stop calling him Strøm and start saying Håvard instead. Strøm is such a stupid name, it's part of his flirtatiousness, something he hides behind, to save anyone finding out who he really is. I can see no reason not to use the name his mother gave him, since that's what she would have whispered to him when he was four weeks old, all wrapped up in towelling nappies and crocheted rompers, howling and howling: he'd had colic. I've seen that picture of him hundreds of times. He likes to use it alongside the biographical notes in the catalogues ot his exhibitions, a tiny little photograph, always placed right at the end. He's too self-absorbed to see how he gives himself away with this, and to be honest I rather like him for it. It shows that there's nothing calculating about him. He just wants everyone to see that he is still a howling, colicky infant. Self-absorbed, often despairing, but never calculating. A man who is waiting for someone to come and comfort him, lay a warm hand on his stomach, take the pain away.

'There, there, Håvard,' his mother whispers to him. 'Ssh. There, there.'

I got up and crossed to the fridge. I took out cheese and jam. I placed everything on the table in front of Eilif, sliced some bread, remarked that it was a good idea to eat something in the morning.

He looked straight at me and said that in twenty minutes the surgeons were going to start operating on Monica. I glanced at my watch and nodded gravely.

'Are you scared?' I asked.

'A bit,' he said.

'I can well understand that,' I said. 'It's kind of hard to know what to do.'

And then, without any warning, his face broke into a shy, little smile. It wasn't the smile of a child, it came from a man almost grown, who looked at me and saw how difficult this was for me; that it was almost as difficult for me as it was for him. I realised that he was fully awake now, and that he had come to a decision: all that was best in him had chosen to make the effort to take the first step towards me. He paved the way for me. That was very good of him, he didn't need to do it, he could have immersed himself in his longing for his mother, left it at that.

'Your Dad's bound to call as soon as he knows something,' I said.

'Do you think so?'

'Of course.'

'But the mobile doesn't work in here. He might not be able to get through to us.'

'Have you tried out in the garden?'

'Some places. Not them all.'

'Come on then. Let's go out and check,' I said. I picked up my own mobile and rose from the table. Eilif put down the lighter and followed me.

We worked our way silently and systematically around the garden, our eyes glued to the little bars on our mobile screens indicating the strength of the signal: I walked round the garden shed, he checked the patch down among the apple trees.

At last we met up outside the gazebo. Both telephones were picking up a decent signal there. We looked at one another and nodded earnestly, then we stepped inside the gazebo and sat down on the bench among all the cushions.

*

'This is really nice,' Eilif said, looking around and nodding approvingly.

'Yes. It's the sort of thing my Granny – the one I told you about yesterday – was so good at. She designed it herself, I think she was quite young at the time. She liked things to be a little bit different, as you can see.'

'Unusual roof,' he said. 'It looks like an onion.'

'I know, it's actually called an onion dome. They're usually seen on churches. My grandmother was a rather special person. Maybe she should have been an architect. She was an actress too, as a young woman.'

'Lovely cushions.'

'She had a thing about cushions,' I said. 'Cushions and blankets.'

'And colours, it looks like,' he said. 'I think I'll wait here till Dad calls.' He glanced at his watch again. 'They'll just be starting the operation now.'

'Then I'm sure it'll help if you think about her,' I said. 'Do you want me to keep you company?'

He shook his head.

'Well, I'll get you your breakfast then,' I said. 'It's nice to eat down here. Granny and I often did that in the summer when I was your age.'

I didn't get up from the bench, though.

'I know the man you met yesterday,' I said hesitantly, motioning with my head towards his mobile, on which I had seen the picture of Håvard. 'He used to be my teacher.'

'Strøm?'

'He likes people to call him Strøm, but I call him Håvard, just to annoy him a bit. He was an excellent teacher.'

'Oh, that's right. He said he used to know someone called Molly.'

'He did?'

'Yes.'

'Did he say anything else?'

'He said he wasn't sure you'd be happy to know that he was living here.'

'Oh? Why not?'

'He didn't say. But he's promised to teach me to play the piano,' Eilif went on.

'Really? That's great,' I said. 'He was pretty good on the piano, as I recall, although he didn't play much when I knew him.'

'He told us that he had taught you to take photographs,' Eilif said. 'And that you were good at drawing.'

'He said that?'

Eilif nodded.

'Why do you want to play the piano,' I asked.

'Mum says she's always wanted a piano. And that if we had one she would teach me to play it.'

'So your Mum can play the piano?'

'Uh-huh, but she hardly ever does, because we don't have a piano at home. We don't have room for one.'

'And you want to surprise her by learning to play without her knowing?'

'Something like that.'

I stared at him in delight and amazement. So many words suddenly pouring from his lips! I hoped he would keep on talking to me, I liked hearing the sound of his voice.

'What a brilliant idea,' I cried, a little too brightly. 'She'll be so surprised. What sort of music does she like?'

'There's this one tune . . .,' he said. 'But I don't know what it's called.'

He whistled a couple of bars.

'Oh, okay – that one,' I said. 'It's a song by Bellmann. It's lovely, a real summer song.' I sang the first couple of verses from 'The butterfly in the garden' for him. That was all I could remember, the Swedish lyrics are quite tricky.

'Do you think Strøm is right when he says he can teach me to play it?' Eilif asked.

'I'm sure he can, as long as you're willing to practise,' I said. 'Get him to show you the chords.'

'What are chords?'

'They're like groups of notes played together. It's easier to learn them than all the individual notes. Strøm's good at that sort of thing. He used to be a pretty decent jazz pianist.'

'The main thing is that it shouldn't take too long to learn.'

Then there was silence between us again. Eilif gazed at his mobile. I could tell that he wanted to be alone to think about his mother. I ought to leave him in peace now. But it was hard to leave.

In the end I decided to go and pick up the paper. And his breakfast.

I stood for a moment by the postbox, thinking. I needed to let it sink in that it was Håvard who was living over there behind the trees. That he had spoken about me. I was aware that I wasn't ready to see him just yet. All in due course. Suddenly I no longer knew what he meant to me. And it was Eilif I wanted to think about. Eilif taking that step towards me.

Then I had an idea: Granny's piano! I could have it brought down here to the summer house, as she always did in the summer. Then Eilif would have something to practise on. That would be a grand, good thing to do for him, something he would never forget. And then he wouldn't have to go over to Håvard's to play.

I was relieved to have come up with an idea. I strode back to the kitchen to fetch Eilif's breakfast. I got out a clean glass and filled it with orange juice. I poured the milk down the sink.

A fair bit of time must have past before I returned to the gazebo with his breakfast and the folded newspaper, fifteen minutes maybe. But he was sitting exactly as I had left him. He looked calm and clear. The gazebo tends to have that effect on people. It's as if they sink into something. As if it opens up to receive them.

I set the tray down in front of him. It was the one I had made at the time when I was really into Twenties-style designs. He mumbled a quick, diffident 'Thanks' and did not touch the newspaper.

'What should I say to Ine when she wakes up?' I asked. 'She must be thinking about your Mum and her operation too.'

'Send her down to me,' he said. 'Then we'll both be here when Dad calls.'

He didn't say whether he wanted me to be there. But that was okay.

I went back up to the house. I felt so much lighter; my skeleton seemed to me to be completely weightless, with only a paper-thin layer of skin covering my feather-light organs. I was suffused with light, as if I had just been X-rayed.

I had to do something useful now, I felt. Something for all of us. I got out the hoover and made my way through to the sitting-room to clear up the sawdust around the bandsaw. My footprints in the shavings seemed to have multiplied during the night. I didn't recall there being so many of them. I put the plug into the socket and ran the nozzle over my footprints: it sucked them up. With one sweep I erased all trace of myself. It was a weird feeling. Normally I suppose I'm more interested in making tracks than erasing them.

I couldn't get that tune of Eilif's out of my head. It's such a lovely summer melody, I felt it fitted just perfectly for that day. I whistled it while trying to remember all of the unfamiliar Swedish words to the first verse.

I had been at this for quite some time before I sensed someone standing behind me in the room. I immediately stopped whistling and pressed the stop button on the hoover with my foot. Suddenly everything went very quiet. I turned round. Ine was standing there.

Her arms were full of Barbie dolls and she was still in her nightie. She glared at me.

'Why do you have to make such a noise!' she cried. 'You were making a terrible noise last night too, we couldn't get to sleep. Where's Eilif?'

'Oh, Ine, I'm sorry,' I said, a little thrown by this. 'I wasn't thinking.'

'Where's Eilif?'

'He's gone down to the gazebo, he can get a signal on the mobile down there. He's waiting for your Dad to call and say how your Mum's operation has gone.'

'Then I'm going down there, too!'

'Yes, but maybe you'd better get dressed first,' I said. 'And have some breakfast? I don't think there's any hurry, an operation like that takes a long time, and they've only just started.'

'Not hungry,' Ine muttered gruffly and ran out on to the veranda. I stood and watched as she stomped furiously down the wheelchair ramp, barefoot and still in her nightie, then trotted off across the grass to the gazebo. I felt such a bungling idiot.

I went on cleaning and hoovering for a good while before daring to go down and see how they were. It was mid-morning when I headed back down to the gazebo. I took Granny's blanket from the sofa with me. I paused outside for a moment with the fine wool throw over my arm, to give them the chance to spot me through the window before I walked in.

They were sitting close together on the bench. Ine looked blue with cold, she had her feet tucked in between her brother's legs. They were hunched over the mobile phone, Eilif was clearly keying in a text message.

'Hi, you two,' I said, clearing my throat as I stepped into their territory. 'How's it going? Have you heard from your Dad?'

'He hasn't called,' Eilif said without looking up.

'No?'

'But he sent a text message.'

Ine stared at me and the blanket. I could tell just by looking at her that she wanted it desperately, but that she certainly wasn't going to let me wrap it around her.

'So, how did the operation go?' I asked, taking a pace forward and placing the blanket next to her before sitting down at the end of the bench among all the cushions, as far away from them as possible.

'He says it went fine,' Eilif said. 'Mum hasn't woken up from the anaesthetic yet. But they've sewn her up again and all that.'

'With a needle,' Ine added.

'Dad's going to stay with her today and tonight,' Eilif went on. 'He's going to stay over in town. At your friend's place, I think. The lady in the wheelchair, the one we sent pictures to.'

'That's great,' I said with a little cough. 'It's a relief to hear that your Mum's doing all right. I've been so worried.'

As one, they both turned to look at me, with amazement in their eyes, as if they simply could not believe that I could actually be worried about what happened to their mother.

'I've had an idea,' I continued, pursuing the line I had forged with these words. 'Eilif, I was thinking that you should send a message to your Dad, asking him to tell your Mum, as soon as she wakes up from the anaesthetic, that she has to get back on her feet as quickly as possible, because you have a surprise for her.' I winked at him. 'In town I have a piano that my Granny left me. I can ask the people who work at the theatre to bring it down here. That way you'll have a piano to practise on while you're here. We could put it out here, in the gazebo, I thought. There's just enough space for it, don't you think?'

I watched both children size up the room with their eyes. They were expert eyes, that I could see. I could also see that they reached the same conclusion as me: there was room for a piano in the gazebo.

'And once Håvard has taught you that tune your Mum likes so much,' I went on, 'we can call her on the mobile. And you can play it for her. That way she can hear it while she's actually lying in her bed in the hospital. What do you think? I mean, we can get a signal down here, right?'

'Cool,' said Eilif.

'What about me?' Ine asked.

'What do you mean?'

'Well, what will I do?'

I hadn't thought about that. I wasn't used to children back then; I didn't know that if there's more than one of them you have to treat them all exactly alike. On that first morning it was Eilif whom I felt I knew, not Ine. She and I hadn't really met one another properly at that point.

'Ah, for you I have even bigger plans,' I said, trying to look sure, but secretive, my mind working frantically. 'I just have to sort out a few details first.'

Fortunately, this lie seemed to work. Ine reached for the blanket which I had laid next to her and pulled it over herself. I saw her relax with a little sigh of contentment at the feel of the soft flannel against her skin. She kind of caved in on herself.

Granny had always had such lovely blankets. For her they were like an art form: sooner or later everyone who walked through her door, whether at the summer house or the flat in town, got wrapped in a blanket. They were light and warm, those blankets, and they came in all sorts of colours. They must on no account be prickly. Sometimes the reverse was lined with soft flannel, as with this throw, a white one.

I sent a grateful thought to Granny as I saw how Ine immediately made a cave for herself under the blanket. She drew in her feet and closed off all the openings until all that could be seen was her eyes. Eilif smiled at me; he was seeing the same as me. Then he bent over the mobile again and carried on keying in the text message to his Dad.

He liked my idea! I thought exultantly. And I will think of something for Ine too!

*

When I got back to the house I stood at the sitting-room window, half-hidden behind a pale curtain, and gazed at them down there. They couldn't see me from the gazebo, and I could only just make them out because of the reflection from the windows.

After a while I saw Ine come trotting up to the house with the blanket wound round her like a toga. I stepped back smartly from the window. I could hear her skipping up the wheelchair ramp, on to the veranda, through the other room, then up the stairs with a series of little thuds. Minutes later I heard her running down again, taking big, confident steps this time. In the glimpse of her I caught through the open door I noticed that she was now dressed. She ran off down the garden again, to where her brother was standing waiting for her. Together they disappeared into the lilac bushes and on down the road to Håvard's house.

I could well see why they would rather be with Håvard than with me. They liked him. They didn't like me yet. Well, Eilif might, I dared to think. Maybe Eilif liked me a little bit. Or could grow to like me. If he just had time to get used to me.

It's not so surprising that they should prefer Håvard, I told myself. There was a time when you were won over by his charm too. You also called him Strøm, just as he has them doing. You also believed that there was something he could teach you. That he was the only person who could teach you this. But that was a long time ago.

It was hard to believe that Håvard was an old man.

I thought: how does he look now, when he moves about? Does that strange, almost invisible jolt still run through his body when he sees something he's never seen before? As if he'd had a little shock?

Of course it does.

And I was right. When he sees something he has never seen before, he looks as though an electric current has run through him.

It was still early in the day, but I felt oddly tired. I felt as if I had been doing some big, tough job, like cutting through a very hard piece of wood with the bandsaw. But I wasn't done yet. Now I had to drive into town and fetch Agnes. It was just as well, really, that Håvard was close by and could keep an eye on the kids.

That's one of the things it takes time to get used to with children: you always have to make sure that there's someone there to look after them.

Mind you, I can't actually recollect anyone looking after me when I was a child. Although that can't be right. Maybe I didn't want to be looked after. I don't rightly recall. Maybe I ran away.

I felt queasy. There was hardly any traffic on the road, it wasn't even midday yet. Most of the time I was driving over the speed limit, but I know where the speed control points are. I slowed down and waved to the cameras as I always do. I had the car stereo playing full blast, but I was halfway to town before the music got through to me, puncturing the nausea and flowing through to the darkness inside.

I was going to pick up Agnes. But somewhere along the way something inside me changed its mind. I had the feeling that it might be better to wait; maybe I was afraid that Aksel would be at her flat when I got there.

I raised one hand and ran it through my hair again and again, back and forth, trying to shake up my thoughts. I probably wasn't the most alert of drivers that morning.

I realised that it was still far too soon to bring Agnes to the summer house. I didn't even know Eilif and Ine yet; I needed to have them to myself for a little while before introducing them to her. I thought: she can have a pretty mesmerising personality. It's bound to work on the children too. She could win them over to her side quick as a wink, do something to them. I needed to have them feel more secure with me first, like me better, otherwise I would lose them before I was even begun. And I have to think of something for Ine. Something impressive.

So I took another route once I reached the city centre. I didn't make for the hospital area and Agnes's flat; I turned off long before that and drove to Granny's flat instead. I have the key on my key-ring. It was as though I hadn't quite known what use I had for it until that moment.

I let myself into the flat and sat for a long, long time in one of Granny's red armchairs, looking and looking at all of her things. There was no longer anything of her in them. Her things had lost her, they were blank and dull. Left me speechless and sad.

Even the piano seemed dead. It could do with a change of scene, I thought. I'll nip round to the theatre, have a word with the guys there, ask them to give me a hand. It shouldn't be a problem.

I took Granny's television, the video machine and a little bag of videos, lugged the whole lot down the stairs. I had to make several trips. It was only a small TV, but it was awkward to carry.

I popped into the theatre, gave the receptionist a quick nod and stole along the corridors, hoping no one would see me. I didn't want to bump into Jan or anyone else who was liable to ask me how the work was going. I didn't have anything to report right now, as far as work was concerned.

I made it to the stagehands' room unnoticed. They were pleased to see me, I think, although they're not the sort to show it. They like me. They didn't ask how the work was going, they just offered me a cigarette. I arranged for them to help me move the piano from Granny's flat to the summer house. They didn't seem to have that much to do. Maybe they were actually on holiday, but preferred to hang out in their room backstage.

On the way back I stopped at a petrol station to fill the tank, and picked up some films for the children. I had glanced quickly through the tapes I had taken from Granny's, there were film versions of some of Shakespeare's plays and a couple of experimental black-and-white movies from the Sixties. Not exactly kids' stuff, perhaps.

*

I got back to find that the children had still not returned from Håvard's. I hope he's taking good care of them, I thought. And that he has the sense to give them something to eat. He has a tendency to forget about mealtimes, as I recall.

And I was right: he had forgotten to give them something to eat. When they finally appeared they seemed pleased to see me, but they were both starving. I made them an omelette, cut some radishes with the scalpel, as artistically as I could, made them into roses. I put the roses on their plates. I could tell they were impressed. Maybe they didn't know anyone else who could make roses out of radishes.

After dinner I took them down for a swim. We were all a bit shy. I let them get changed in the bathing hut while I waited outside, then I went in to change. Suddenly I noticed how old and stiff and shapeless my bathing suit was. It struck me that they must think I looked kind of funny. Old-fashioned. Like some aged aunt.

I let them spend the rest of the evening watching the videos I had bought. I told Agnes about this on the phone. I got the feeling she wasn't particularly happy about it.

Neither of us mentioned the message she had left on my answering machine. Nor the fact that Aksel was thinking of spending the night at her place after he left the hospital.

The next day I found, however, that I couldn't put it off any longer. I went back into town and picked her up.

When I got to her flat she was all ready and waiting in the wheelchair. I assumed that Aksel had gone back to the hospital, he certainly wasn't anywhere in the flat. We didn't mention him.

Agnes was wearing a new, cream-coloured coat, one I hadn't seen before. It was very stylish, beautifully cut; it can't have been cheap. I could see that she was agitated, she didn't seem herself.

She had packed a big bag, it was sitting next to her on the floor. She had spread a sheet over something big and lumpy on the desk behind her. I didn't ask what it was, something told me that would have been the wrong thing to do. But once I had wheeled her out to the car and got her settled in the front, then folded the chair and put it in the boot, I said I needed to pee before we left. She gave me the key and I ran back upstairs to the flat.

I lifted the sheet carefully and looked underneath.

She had made a model of the summer house. It was very nicely done. She does everything so precisely, despite the fact that she doesn't always have the best control over her hands.

But I didn't quite understand what her aim was in building it. I thought: the idea is not clear, Agnes. It's essential to have a clear idea of what you are making. You have to know what you want to say. It should be there in the hands, in the way you work. Otherwise it's no use.

Her model didn't look much like the real summer house either. I realised that she was working from an old photograph, she had taped it to the desk, right next to the model. I sent her that photograph years ago, just after I got my first Nikon, when I was pretty much living in the camera club's darkroom at the university. It was taken before Granny had the new extension built. The house looks completely different now. The extension altered the whole character of the façade.

Alongside the model lay a bundle of little cardboard puppets she had made. They were quite delicate and they had movable joints, for these she had used paper fasteners. I didn't look too closely at them, I had to be getting back down to the car, but I popped them into my bag on impulse. I might be able to use them in *The Dream Play*, I thought. They were actually rather nice. Maybe I could work up some sort of shadow play? That must be possible, surely. I'll have to remember to speak to Jan about it. Jan is the director, he knows how to respond to a fledgling idea without strangling it at birth. He knows the thing is to say: 'You might be on to something! Work on it a bit and see what happens.'

Although I won't, of course, use the idea before I've asked Agnes if it's all right with her, I told myself firmly. That goes without saying.

I didn't notice the two big, black cardboard birds she had made until I had placed the sheet over the model again and was turning to leave. They scared me. I left them where they were.

The old photograph taped to Agnes's desk alongside the model reminded me of the summer after Mum died. That was the summer when Granny started building the extension to the summer house. It was as if she needed to do some restructuring of her life. As if she had to make a fresh start. We were both equally raw, I think, and only we two could understand how the other one was feeling. Only we could help one another.

I helped Granny with the drawings for the extension. She was convinced that I could be an architect, so that is what I became. You became whatever Granny saw in you. It was a simple as that. Maybe she thought that I had inherited her gifts.

It seems I had almost forgotten that summer.

It was around this time that Agnes became ill. So it was no wonder it had escaped her attention. It was a bit sad, though, that she should have made such a mistake with her model, when she had put so much work into it.

But I couldn't tell her any of this. I had obviously not been meant to see either the model or the photograph. I was beginning to sense that she had secrets from me.

It's actually very rare for Agnes to show me what she gets up to in her flat. Usually when I visit her she acts as though she's been sitting watching television all day. But I know that can't be true. She has to be doing something else.

I also understand that it's best to let her be. She hates it when she can sense that someone feels sorry for her, that they're only interested in her because she has this insidious disease.

I locked the flat door behind me, went down to the car and got into the driver's seat. I turned to Agnes and smiled.

'I'm so glad you wanted to come,' I said. 'I need you at the summer house now.'

Then I curled my hand round the back of her neck and we pressed our brows together for a moment. Our brows wished each other welcome.

She was strangely tense the whole way down here. She stole glances at me when she thought I wasn't aware of it. I suppose she was looking for signs of the pregnancy, as if she had expected me to show up sporting a great pot-belly.

She asked, in the high, rather shrill voice that I remembered from the message on the answering machine, where the children were that morning. I said I thought they were probably down seeing someone she had met once, years ago.

'Strøm?' she asked.

I nodded.

At that she began to tremble so uncontrollably that I had to stop the car in a bus lay-by and hold her for a while. Then, like a bolt out of the blue, it hit me: I never *had* told her about the time I met Håvard at his exhibition in Berlin. The time I confronted him with the rumours I had heard about him committing incest with his daughter. Agnes obviously still believed him to be a child molester.

I don't know how I could have forgotten to tell her. Maybe I didn't want her to know the full story regarding those spurious stories of child abuse. Maybe I wanted her to stop being so interested in him. Start thinking about something else. Maybe I wanted to hold her back from him a bit.

It took me ages, there in the car, to get her calmed down enough for her to take in what I was saying.

'He's not a child molester, Agnes,' I whispered into her hair as I stroked her back. I had undone her seatbelt so that I could get my arms round her properly. 'It was just something that woman said, to scare me away. That singer in the ladies, his old girlfriend – don't you remember I told you about it? She was just jealous, I think. Wanted him all to herself. So she spread those rumours about him.'

Agnes didn't answer me. But she gradually seemed to soften. She relaxed and began to breathe more evenly. Eventually I was able to belt her in again and drive on.

We pulled up outside the house. It stood there before us, shining in the sunlight.

'Well, here we are,' I said. 'It's so good to have you here.'

But Agnes just stared. I realised that it must all look very different from what she had imagined.

The first thing she said was:

'It's grown.'

'Yes,' I said, cautiously clearing my throat. 'A new wing has sprouted on the sunny side, isn't that funny? It's an extension that Granny had built years ago. It was me who designed it, actually. After Mum died. You were ill at the time. Do you like it?'

I asked her to wait in the car, then I went round and got the wheelchair out of the boot. That gave her a little time to digest her first impression of the house, before I got her into the chair and wheeled her round to the veranda. The wheelchair was set up and waiting for her.

She was white as a sheet.

'There's the gazebo,' I said, pointing down the garden to the sparkling onion dome. 'Now wait till you see this!'

I took a run at it, rolled her up the ramp and on to the veranda.

That ramp had a lovely give to it, it really did.

When we entered the sitting-room she fixed her eye on the bandsaw, pointed and said:

'That thing's got to go.'

She looked almost as though she had received a shock.

Things weren't helped by the fact that the children weren't there to meet her. It was well into the afternoon before they dawdled back up the road from Håvard's. I had Agnes installed in the sitting-room by then and we had agreed that it would be okay for her to sleep on the sofa. She had also made a trip over to the bath-room door to check whether there was space for the wheelchair next to the toilet. I could see that that was the moment when she decided to manage without the wheelchair. Sometimes she is almost depressingly easy to read. She tenses her muscles in a particular way and a determined look comes into her eyes.

Suddenly the children appeared in the doorway. I saw how Agnes started. The sight of them had obviously given her another shock.

I don't know exactly what she had been expecting. That they would be smaller perhaps, or bigger. She stared at their eyes as if she had never seen real eyes before. I thought of the cardboard puppets I had taken from her flat. There were still in my bag. All of a sudden I realised that they were meant to be us: the children, Aksel, Agnes and me. I hadn't taken them out of the bag, some instinct told me it would be best to keep her away from those puppets. I was beginning to regret having taken them, in fact. I had been too hasty.

Later I realised, of course, that before coming to the summer house she had only seen pictures of Eilif and Ine, and in those pictures they had both been wearing sunglasses. She'd had no idea of how their eyes looked in reality.

'There you are, you two,' I said to the kids. Suddenly it felt as though we had known each other for ages. 'Come and say hello to my friend Agnes.'

Once, when Agnes and I were in fourth grade, I was allowed to stay the night at her house. Her parents were away. Her mother had won some award, and her father had gone along to sit in the audience and applaud. I could just see him, nodding shyly to right and left and smiling the lost little smile he always wore when there were a lot of people around. Generally speaking, those two never went away anywhere together, not as far as I know. Agnes's Dad was happiest at home.

We had been given permission to bake a cake. The kitchen worktop was splattered and sticky, and flour had sifted down on to the floor, we had trod in it and spread it all over the place. We were laughing and pushing and shoving one another. I had decorated the cake with some big blossoms from a huge bouquet in a vase on the hall table. It looked kind of scraggy afterwards, that bouquet; I think Agnes was a bit worried about it, but she didn't say anything.

We put the cake on a big glass cake dish with a foot and I carried it into the sitting-room. Agnes followed on my heels, she had taken the silver cake forks from the sideboard. We weren't going to use plates, we meant to eat straight from the cake dish.

I remember how we made our way through the spacious rooms of their flat with that blossoming cake. All the walls were lined with bookcases. Much of the floor and all the tabletops were covered with stacks of her mother's books and piles of manuscripts, it was hard to find a good spot for the cake dish. It was dark outside and the tall, white-framed windows were curtainless. The large panes of glass were black and gleaming. I stopped and stared at one of them. In it I saw my own skinny frame; a slim figure behind the enormous, flower-bedecked cake. Then I saw Agnes come up behind me and stand right at my back. She was breathing down my neck.

She pointed to the window, at our reflection. She said there were people living in there in that pane of glass. It might look like a reflection of her and me, but it wasn't. What we were seeing were our mirror sisters. They might *look* like us, but in fact they led a completely different life from us. They didn't have the same names as us either. Sometimes when it was dark outside our mirror sisters stepped up to the windows to look in on us. They were curious to see what we got up to. As I could perhaps see, they had a cake too, but theirs wasn't decorated with flowers, because no flowers grew in their world, she said.

Then she put a hand on my shoulder and swung me away from the window before I had a chance to take a closer look at the cake in there and see if there were any flowers on it. We oughtn't to stare at our mirror sisters for too long, she said. They might get scared and stop coming forward to observe us. They would think we were out to get them. Or worse: they might come and get us.

All at once I felt so frightened. We managed to clear a space on the coffee table and sat down to eat our cake, but I no longer had any notion for it, I didn't feel very well.

For weeks after that evening I made sure that all the curtains at home were drawn when darkness fell; I couldn't face learning any more about what went on in the windows. Couldn't face thinking about it. If I did start to think about it a drowsiness seemed to come over me and I felt as though I could fall out at any minute, sink down into something soft and dark. I knew it was important to stay awake.

Since I moved down here to the summer house some of the old fear of reflections has returned. Although it's not quite the same, I don't think. I have the feeling that I'm afraid, but also a little curious. Maybe Agnes was right and there is a secret world within the windows. With people living there, in a kind of village maybe; folk who are content with their lives: they hardly know anything else. These villagers only appear when they see fit. The time has to be right for them to show themselves.

And yet I've been thinking that it's not quite the way Agnes described it when we were young. The difference is that I myself am one of the villagers. That I actually live in there, that it is me who steps into the mirror every now and again, when the time is right, to peep out for a moment, almost by accident. It's not my sister I see, it's myself. In a minute I'll go back to what I was doing: pulling water out of the well; sitting at a big, stone table, shelling peas into a bowl; shouting something about food to some children running across a yard and into a field.

And I do not picture myself as looking severe when I'm doing such things, nor lonely, it's only when I choose to look out of the mirror that I appear severe or lonely. But I'll never be able to catch a glimpse of her when she is off-guard, that Molly in the mirror who is not severe and not lonely. She is only her normal self when she is not looking out, when she is absorbed in herself and the life of the village. That Molly who is not severe and not lonely is hidden from me. But not from herself.

It ties you in knots, thinking like that. It doesn't quite add up. When I've been doing it for a while I have to say to myself: Stop that now. Agnes is the one who indulges in this sort of speculation, not you. You're a doer. You have your feet on the ground. You are like Granny.

I had made up my mind to tell Aksel about the baby the minute I saw him, the first time he came to see us after Monika's operation. But the right moment never seemed to present itself then either. I felt we needed peace and quiet for this. He would need time to think about it; becoming a father again, that must be a big thing for a man. We needed space in which to be gentle with one another, listen to what the other one had to say, keep all options open. We had to talk about Eilif and Ine, how would they take the news? I had to be prepared for him to bring up Monika's name, to say that we would have to consider her feelings. I believed I had thought of everything. But nothing went the way I thought it would.

He drove down from the hospital late in the evening. I managed to arrange my features in an appropriate expression, put on a warm, neutral smile. I felt stirrings in parts of me that I hadn't been conscious of in a long time, but my heart was still a spare part.

Agnes and the children and I were sitting on the veranda when he arrived. The children jumped up with such force that their chair legs scraped the veranda floor. They raced to meet him. Ine reached him first, leapt up at him, flung her arms round his neck and her legs round his waist. He swung her round a few times then put an arm out to Eilif, pulled him close and ruffled his hair. He murmured something to them. Probably a message from Monika: Agnes and I weren't meant to hear it. Then he put Ine down and came over to my chair, still with his arm round Eilif. He bent down and kissed me on the forehead. Eilif had to bend down with him, it was odd, to say the least of it. I thought: Oh, Aksel. Don't go dragging the boy into this. Then he let go of Eilif too and stood looking down at Agnes in her wheelchair. He gave her a big smile, it was hard to interpret it in any other way than that he was glad to see her.

'Hello there,' he said. 'So you're on your summer holidays too, eh? That's great. I have something for you. It's in the car. Come on, kids!'

Eilif and Ine went after him, they hopped and skipped around him, looking positively frisky. Agnes and I sat in silence during the few minutes they were away. I could already feel that something had changed.

When they returned from the car each of the children was brandishing a crutch. Ine had discovered that she could use hers as a long-jump pole, she went leaping off across the lawn, probably making dreadful holes in the grass, but their father wasn't the sort to bawl them out for things like that.

'Crutches?' Agnes said. 'No. You must be kidding.'

'Nope, no kidding,' Aksel answered with a laugh. 'Weren't you the one who wanted out of that wheelchair? Well, then you need crutches.'

The children laid the crutches in her lap. They stood there, eyeing her expectantly, as if hoping she would give them a demonstration right there and then. But Agnes sat where she was, looking at the ground.

'Don't pester Agnes, you two,' Aksel said. 'You know very well she's going to need time to practise with them.'

He sat down at the table and began to talk about how things were going with Monika at the hospital, speaking in a way which made it all right for Agnes and I to listen too, his words were not aimed solely at the children this time. Monika was doing fine, he said. She was still in intensive care, but they would soon be moving her to another ward. The children's eyes never left his face all the time he was talking. They drank it all in, but they didn't ask any questions.

*

Aksel wasn't allowed to sit for long. Eilif wanted him to come down the garden with them. I stood on the veranda and watched them as they sauntered off towards the gazebo. They looked so alike from behind. Somehow I felt I had seen them like this before. Aksel had lifted Ine on to his shoulders, her spindly legs dangled down his front, and she rocked recklessly back and forth, almost making him lose his balance. He gripped her thighs and began to charge about the lawn, acting as though he was trying to shake her off. Ine giggled and squealed and clung to his head, covering his eyes so that he couldn't see and bumped into a tree. They fell over and lay in a wriggling heap on the grass. Eilif was screaming with laughter; he threw himself on top of them and the three of them lay there for long enough, laughing and tickling one another.

Seeing them like that, my heart swelled. That's how a Dad should be! I thought exultantly. Just like that! Bumping into things! Falling over! Laughing!

I turned and smiled at Agnes.

'Aren't they wonderful?' I said.

But she was looking at the ground.

I realised that Aksel meant to stay the night. And I knew that I would really have to tell him soon about the baby. I had already told Agnes on the phone so I had to break the news to him too, and in a more genuine manner than that in which I had informed Agnes. He was the father, after all.

But that was the night when Agnes got herself out of the wheel-chair and on to crutches. It must have taken an enormous effort of will on her part.

I think she derived the strength from not being able to stand the thought that Aksel and I would be going to bed together in my room upstairs. She sat at the kitchen table glowering at us while we washed the dishes and cleared up for the night. And when we said goodnight and made to go upstairs to my room she said she would sit up for a while longer. She meant to go back out to the veranda and practise using the crutches, she said. Aksel nodded encouragingly to her, I suppose that's the sort of thing nurses like to hear.

We went to my room, she stomped up and down the veranda, making a hell of a racket. She stumbled and fell, hauled herself back on to her crutches, cursing and swearing.

Aksel watched her, baffled, from behind the bedroom curtains. I don't think he understood what was going on down there on the veranda. How was he to know that she was using every means at her disposal to prevent me from telling him what I had to say?

'But look at her,' he said. 'She really has built up the strength in her arms, hasn't she? It almost makes you feel quite proud. But she's overdoing it. I've tried to tell her not to strain herself when she's exercising.'

I felt so sorry for her. And for him. It hurts when you can see that someone doesn't understand. You say to yourself: 'The truth would be too much for you to bear.'

Sometimes I feel that I'm too complex for Aksel.

He slept like a log all night, he never touched me. I knew he was worn out, that his head was full of worry about Monika. He was just one big head, there was no room in him that night for a body. I cried as softly as I could.

Early the next morning he drove back to the hospital and Monika. I could tell that in his mind he was already there with her.

I knew I could rely on him to take good care of her. When you are as scared as he was, you are very careful. You don't forget to give a person their pills. Or to run a soothing hand over a person's cheek.

The next day was a strange one. Eilif and Ine had got up with Aksel and waved him off, they looked a bit down in the dumps when they came back into the kitchen. I thought: Right, now you have to think of something, Molly. It's time for you to take charge. Cheer them up.

I didn't dare to go into the sitting room, where Agnes was sleeping. I had already peeked round the door and seen her lying flat out on the sofa, fully dressed, with a wine bottle and a smeared glass beside her on the coffee table. It looked to me as though she had sat up drinking all night, after she had worn herself out getting on to those crutches and making such a hell of a racket underneath my bedroom window. It had been too much for her.

I gently closed the door from the sitting-room to the kitchen and told the children that she needed to be left in peace. Eilif nodded and promptly announced that he was going down to Strøm's to play the piano. Ine wanted to go too, she wanted to say hello to the cat. I don't think she wanted to be with me.

They dutifully ate a quick breakfast. Then, with a couple of tight little nods, they disappeared out of the kitchen door. I couldn't find it in me to stop them. They still preferred Håvard to me.

I tidied away the breakfast things, wiped the table and benches with the dishcloth and went up to my room to work.

I got out the cardboard puppets I had taken from Agnes's flat and placed them on the table in front of me. I studied them. I had been right, they really were meant to represent us: Agnes herself, Aksel, me and the children. I noted the care she had taken over the little details: Eilif's neatly coloured baseball cap, and the different shades in Ine's hair. They really were quite lovely. I thought: I could almost use them in *The Dream Play* just as they are. With Ine as Victoria, Eilif as the lawyer, Aksel as the officer. Me as the poet. And Agnes as . . . Agnes. One by one I gingerly lifted each puppet and slowly swivelled the garden canes to which their arms and legs were attached. It was not hard to see where the flaw in the construction lay; there was no way, with these, that one could ever achieve the flowing, ethereal movements which I thought the theatre's choreographer might be able to produce. I had some ideas for how to improve on the construction, how to make the figures bigger and more distinct, give each one its own distinctive features, alter expressions to make them more theatrical. I got out my scalpel, a pencil and some stiff card and set to work. I need a puppet to represent the mother in the play, I thought. The woman who knows that she is dying.

Hours must have passed before there was any sound of movement downstairs in the sitting room. I heard Agnes wake with an audible moan, heard her fumbling about, heard her crutches falling to the floor as she tried to get up from the sofa.

After a while I went down to her, she obviously needed help. I stood in the doorway and regarded her.

'Morning, Agnes,' I said gently. 'Did you sleep well?'

'Fucking hell,' Agnes muttered. She did not look happy.

'Do you need some help?'

'Absolutely not.'

'Are you sure you don't want me to get the wheelchair?'

'Quite sure.'

'Can you manage to get to the bathroom on your own with the crutches?'

'Of course I can.'

The scene which followed is difficult to describe. Agnes seemed so disconsolate, so determined, and was so obviously suffering from a terrible hangover, but she refused to have any help. I retreated to a chair in a corner of the sitting room and observed her from there, ready to step in should she ask for assistance. She hissed at me that I had no business sitting there gawping at her as if she was a fish in a bowl. I took her at her word and went through to the kitchen, from where I could hear how she somehow managed to stump out to the bathroom with the aid of the crutches. She must have toppled over several times in there, I heard clattering and banging, but eventually the rush of water told me that she had pulled the chain; then I heard the tap running, for a long time. There is no shower on the ground floor, only in the bathroom upstairs, next door to my room, and the idea of climbing the stairs under her own steam must have seemed quite beyond her at that point.

At long last she joined me in the kitchen. Her face was pale and scrubbed looking; she sank down into a chair at the kitchen table. I pushed the coffee jug towards her along with a cup which she eagerly filled.

'Where're the kids?' she asked.

'Down at Strøm's.'

'You're not serious! Not today as well!'

'Yes.'

'Do you realise who they're with?'

'Look, Agnes,' I said. 'I told you, those rumours of incest, it was all a pack of lies. Have you forgotten?'

'Have you met Strøm recently?'

'No.'

'So how can you be so sure he's harmless?'

'I know him,' I said. 'And besides, I saw the picture Eilif took of him. He's an old man now.'

Sometimes it has occurred to me that Agnes was more fixated on Håvard than I was back then, when we were teenagers. I remembered how worked up she would get at the mere thought of him. She didn't want to talk about anything but him, or so it seemed to me. On the few visits she made to my room at Mum and Dad's, I had the feeling that she had only come to see me so that I would tell her about him. I was very taken with him too, but in a different way, I think. I was infatuated, but she was bewitched.

'Listen to me, Agnes,' I said. 'Calm down, now. I told you all this in the car on the way down here. Don't you remember? I've known ever since my time in Berlin that Håvard is not a child abuser. We got all of that straightened out years ago.'

She didn't answer.

'Will I go over it again for you?' I asked.

She nodded dumbly.

'Okay,' I said, placing both my hands on the table between us. 'Let's run through it once more. Do you remember that time when I was so upset, and I broke it off with him? When we were nineteen?'

'How could I forget? It was me who had to look after you,' she mumbled morosely.

'Well, it took me some years to pluck up the courage to check whether what that woman had told me in the ladies' toilets back then was actually true. I was living in Berlin at the time, as you know, and I knew he had an exhibition running in the city. I had read about it in the paper. So I went to the gallery and saw his pictures. He had obviously begun on a new project; these were urban images: drifters, down-and-outs, truck drivers, hookers and fat men in service stations. I felt a certain sentimentality had crept into his work which I did not like.'

'You've always been so critical of him.'

'Technically, though, he was still a master, as he had always been, that I had to admit, and no one could say that he didn't have a good eye.'

'Yes, well it was him who taught you to see, as you're so fond of pointing out,' Agnes remarked.

'I had such a job finding the gallery,' I broke in. 'It was a grey and rather chilly day, I had biked over from the other side of the city. I'd forgotten my gloves, my fingers were blue with cold. I cycled round and round the area where, according to the address and the A-Z, the gallery ought to have been, but there were no signs for it and no one could tell me where it was. Everyone I asked seemed almost offended that I should dare to approach them and ask the way.

'In the end I had to call the gallery from a telephone box and ask the woman who answered the phone to give me directions. Even she seemed reluctant to admit that the place really existed, and that it was actually possible to get to it. But eventually it transpired that I wasn't far away from it at all, only a few yards. I parked my bike in a gloomy back-court which looked like a factory yard, and pressed the buzzer on the door. I was admitted.'

I paused for a moment.

'Go on,' Agnes said. I could tell that she was starting to get caught up in the story. She has always had a very vivid imagination.

'The gallery consisted of just one room,' I continued, thinking to myself that I had better describe everything as clearly as I could, to bring it to life for her. 'It was absolutely huge, like a factory painted white, it was lofty as a church, with skylights in the ceiling. I could not fathom how it was possible for such a vast room to be situated so high up. The space seemed to expand round about me as I advanced further into it; it stretched out in all directions.

'There was no one there except myself and the woman who had answered the telephone. I guess no one else had been able to find their way to the place. The woman looked as if she lived there, as if this was the only world she knew.

'I paced slowly from picture to picture, accompanied by the sound of my trainers on the concrete floor – a sort of spongy squelch. I warmed my hands inside my sweater sleeves while trying to learn from the pictures who Håvard had become in the years since I had left him.'

'Why do you call him Håvard,' Agnes asked.

'Because that's his name.'

'You want to rechristen him. You want him to yourself. You want to be his mother.'

'Listen to what I'm telling you,' I said. 'Don't interrupt.'

'Go on.'

'It was strange to see all his pictures, old and new, together in one room. It seemed obvious to me that this exhibition had been staged just for me. I was probably the only one who would ever find the way there. And it wasn't hard to see from the pictures that Håvard really had done all he could to give me the impression that he had become a man of the city. But I think I saw more than he intended me to see. I saw that he had become more sentimental with the years; many of his later pictures had a conciliatory air about them. At the same time I had to admit that he had grown more aggressive in his approach to his subjects. I also noticed that there were almost no photographs of young girls – the sort of shots for which he had once been so famous.'

'He took a lot of you at one stage.'

'But here the subjects were almost all men, mainly decrepit, elderly men. I thought: they need comfort, and this the photographer gives them.'

'God, you don't half go on,' Agnes sighed.

'I said don't interrupt!'

She put a hand over her mouth and tried to look apologetic.

'I spent ages in that gallery. Eventually I saw the woman to whom I had spoken looking at her watch: it was almost closing time. I went over to her and persuaded her to tell me which hotel the artist was staying at; and to give me a large envelope. She complied without a murmur, she must have thought that anyone who had actually found the gallery despite all the obstacles in their way, deserved a medal.

'Then I picked up a catalogue and wrote a message on it. There was a picture of him inside, one in which he was leaning against a wooden fence. I knew who had taken that photograph, a woman he went out with long before me, she has gone on to become quite a big name in Sweden, I've seen her work cited by critics I respect.'

'I doubt if there's a single female photographer he hasn't bedded,' Agnes commented.

'Cool it,' I said. 'I drew a beard and horns on his picture and blackened out a few teeth, then I scribbled my phone number underneath. I was pretty sure he would know who had sent it, and that he would call me. Then I biked back to my studio and lost myself in my work again.'

'I bet you did,' Agnes said.

'It was a couple of days before I heard from him,' I went on. 'He called. His voice was hesitant, he spoke faltering German, asked to whom he was speaking, sounded extremely nervous. I laughed and said in Norwegian that surely he must know who I was. I could tell he was relieved to be able to speak his own language.

'He said he had had a suspicion it was me who had sent the catalogue. We arranged to meet at the gallery the following day. He was going back to Norway the day after that. I told him that it had been almost impossible to find the gallery and he said that the exhibition had not been well attended. I replied that he had only had the one visitor. And he laughed.

'But the reviews had been good.'

'Did you keep them,' Agnes asked.

'No,' I said. 'You know I don't hang on to things like that. I'm not exactly a filing clerk, you know.'

'No, not exactly,' she said.

'When I visited the gallery for the second time the woman wasn't there,' I continued. 'I couldn't see Håvard either, but I could feel in my bones that he was there. I didn't say anything, I simply marched into the room and began to walk round the pictures. I affected to study each photograph very closely. After a while I became aware that he had come up behind me. I stopped in front of one picture and examined it at length. But he said nothing. I don't know whether he was nervous, or worried about what I might do. Then I turned very slowly to face him. "Hi, Håvard," I said.'

'You only said that to provoke him. He likes people to call him Strøm.'

'Maybe.'

'What did he say?'

'I don't recall. But I do remember that we sat down side by side on the floor in that vast, white room, with our backs against the wall. And his pictures hanging above our heads. It was as if we picked up a conversation that had been rudely broken off when I left him.'

'Oh boy, do I remember that . . .'

'He asked me what I was working on,' I continued. 'And it was so easy to tell him about it, all of a sudden I remembered what it was like not to have to use a lot of words when talking about things that really mattered. I didn't feel I had anything to prove to him, and I found it easy to open up, be direct. That was when I asked him about it.'

'About the incest business?'

'Yes. About what his drunk ex-girlfriend had told me in the ladies that night.'

'What did he say?'

'Well, he looked straight at me and said that what she had told me was not true, but that she was not the only one to have heard these rumours, which had been started by his wife. And he had not done anything to quash the rumours. He felt that he was guilty, even though he had not abused his daughter.'

'You're joking.'

'No, that's what he said.'

'How weird.'

'Well, the way he put it, he had abused his daughter, to the extent that he had failed her.'

'You can say that again.'

'Yes, but not the way you think. He had left her and her mother when she was just a baby, and had not kept in touch. Hadn't remembered birthdays, hadn't called, hadn't offered to take her on holiday – all the sorts of things that even absent fathers do still do. And when he discovered that his wife was spreading rumours that he had abused his daughter he did nothing to stop them. In a way he felt she was right. He had shouldered the guilt and thus, in a way, branded himself as a child molester. And his wife was awarded custody of their daughter, which is what she had been after.'

Agnes remained silent and thoughtful for a while, she looked as though she was trying to shake herself out of the story I had told her.

'And you believed that crap,' she said eventually.

'Yes.'

'And you don't think that was incredibly naïve of you?'

'No. I know he's telling the truth.'

'How can you know that.'

'I know him really well, Agnes. We used to be lovers. We knew one another inside out. We still know one another inside out, I think. People like us, we can't fool one another.'

But it seemed that those last words were the very ones that Agnes did not want to hear. I saw how she closed in on herself again. A curtain fell over her face.

I don't remember exactly what she said after that. Something to the effect that she couldn't trust either Strøm or me any more, that she would have to take matters into her own hands. That she would have to go down there right away, that it was clear that I did not intend to do anything at all to protect Eilif and Ine from a pædophile with a conviction for incest behind him. There ought to be a law against anyone being that naïve.

I watched as she struggled out of the chair and groped for the crutches.

I realised that I was never going to be able to get through to her. She simply was not capable of accepting the facts, even though I was doing my very best to present them to her in a way she could understand. It could be that she had been living too long inside her own fantasies, or whatever it is she occupies herself with in that flat of hers.

I suggested, as calmly as I could, that if she was thinking of going to see Håvard then it would be better for her to use the wheelchair and not the crutches. It was a fair distance down to his cottage. I pointed to the trees at the bottom of the road and offered to push her. But she wouldn't hear of it.

'Do you have any drawing things?' she asked.

'What do you mean?'

'Fuck what I mean! Do you have any drawing things?'

'Yes, of course. Shall I get them?'

'Yes, get them. Don't stand there gawping.'

Only minutes later I was able to stand at the kitchen window watching her rolling down the road to Håvard's cottage in the wheelchair. She wasn't exactly tearing along. On her hands she wore fingerless leather gloves to give her a better grip on the wheels.

In her lap she had my drawing board, a block of good quality drawing paper and a pencil case containing pencils and sticks of charcoal.

She had tremendous power in her upper body when she spun those wheels. She was like a machine.

I think that was the moment when it finally hit me that I was pregnant. Hit me so hard that a shudder ran through my body. Hit home in a way that said there was no way back.

I roamed restlessly around the house, filled with a sense of how everything was changing, both around me and within me. I was no longer in control, I was losing Agnes and I could not help feeling that Aksel and the children would be sucked into her wake. That something else was in the process of taking over inside me. Something.

This baby required me to make a decision; I had to find out whether it should live or die. Whether it was to go on growing inside me, taking up more and more space in there with each day that passed, or be expelled and sent back where it came from.

I wasn't used to feeling so afraid and yet so incapable of action.

I walked through to the sitting-room. Through the open veranda door I caught sight of Granny. She was sitting out there in a wicker chair. I flinched. At first I couldn't think who it was: she looked much younger than I ever remembered her being. She was a tall woman of my own age, with dark hair pinned up into a bun, a slender, elegant neck and the distinct shadow of a dark moustache on her upper lip. She was wearing a light-coloured dress and high-heeled shoes. She didn't look at me, simply sat there surveying the garden with one leg crossed over the other, one shoe dangling from her toes.

It seemed as if she wanted to give me time to realise who she was. When it finally dawned upon me she turned slowly towards me and smiled. It was her nice Granny smile, the one that was directed outwards, not inwards. There was no mistaking it, it flashed across her face.

'Oh, Granny,' I said. She didn't answer, merely turned to face the garden again and nodded impassively and rather absently. I think she wanted me to say how beautiful everything was there at that moment, on that summer's day. With everything in full bloom, the garden bursting with growth.

'Granny,' I said again, more softly. 'I'm pregnant. And Agnes is about to leave me. I don't know what to do.'

Granny didn't look surprised. Maybe she hadn't heard what I said. Maybe she couldn't speak. She simply sat there staring at the lilac bushes. I wanted her to fill me with a warm, peaceful glow. But no. I understood that she had heard me, but that she was not going to answer, that I would have to sort it out by myself. But I also understood that she had no plans to leave me.

The next time I dared to look out on to the veranda, she was gone. But an air of peace pervaded the house, the veranda and the garden. I didn't feel that I could go and lie down when Granny's smile inhabited every room and was drifting down there around the lilac bushes like a soft, white haze. Not a breath stirred, and yet the garden seemed to be hovering.

I crossed to the bookcase and took one of the old photograph albums from its shelf. It was full of photos of people who had visited the summer house, during my own time and earlier. I found lots of pictures of myself there. I always look so dour and sulky in photographs, even as a child.

I flicked back to one of the first pages in the album. Here I found a snap of Granny in the same dress I had just seen her wearing out there in that chair on the veranda. She must have been a few years younger than me in that photo, she was standing next to an old-fashioned pram, one of those old, low-slung ones with the little wheels.

It must have been Mum who was in that pram. Mum as a baby; new-born, maybe.

*

It was then that I had the idea for how to make the rising castle in *The Dream Play*. I'll use shadow play, I thought. And I'll make the castle out of glass.

It would be easiest to use Perspex, I can cut that with the bandsaw. I would use light to project the castle on to a plain background. That way I could make it look as though it was growing and growing. I'd be able to produce all sorts of effects with light and shadow, I thought to myself. And I could continue working on the puppets for which Agnes had given me the idea. I'll make the doorkeeper look like Granny as I have just seen her. And the door that everyone in the play talks about, all wondering what lies behind it, *that* I would make out of mirror. I would just have to figure out where to place it on the stage and how to use lighting to prevent the audience from seeing their own reflection.

In the door there should be a hatch through which daylight would filter.

It occurred to me that cutting out that hatch would be tricky, it wasn't something I could do by myself with the bandsaw.

I was going to need a glazier.

Agnes and the children did not return from Håvard's house until late in the afternoon. Eilif was pushing Agnes and Ine was walking beside the wheelchair, holding her hand – they all seemed to be on very good terms. Agnes had my drawing things in her lap, but it was hard to tell whether she had used them. They looked a little surprised when they spotted me, as if they had almost forgotten that I existed. They weren't unfriendly, but they said nothing about what they had been doing.

For the first time it crossed my mind that Agnes might not mean well by me. That she might be . . . jealous. Or something.

Over dinner Ine cheerfully announced that she was planning to buy a new Barbie doll when she got back to town. It appeared that Agnes had paid her and her brother a small fortune for the pictures they had taken for her with their mobile. Now they were both flush with pocket money. I refrained from making any comment, simply smiled and said that sounded nice.

But after the children went to bed that evening, Agnes and I had our first real quarrel. It started with me pointing out to her that Aksel had said he didn't like the children taking money from strangers.

'What do you mean: strangers?' Agnes demanded. 'I'm no stranger to them. We're great friends. And anyway, Aksel hasn't said anything to me about them not being allowed to accept money.'

'Well, it's not like you're the first person he's going to consult when it comes to bringing up his children, is it?' I retorted.

'How do you know?'

'It looks to me as if you're trying to buy them.'

'Buy them? Because I kept my promise to pay them for a little job they did for me? I don't know what you're talking about.'

'No, that's obvious.'

'You're going on as if you were their mother. But you're not. Not as far as I know,' Agnes snapped.

So it began. As the evening wore on the argument grew more and more heated. We were beyond keeping our voices down, we shouted things at one another that I had never thought possible for two people who are so fond of one another. Agnes was pale and set-faced. She accused me of having stolen her ideas, of having been feeding off her all these years. She had allowed herself to be used by me, I was selfish and self-centred, with no thought for anything but my own projects. According to her, I had no consideration for other people.

'And what do you think you are?' I yelled back. 'What do you call shutting yourself away in a flat and wallowing in your own misery all day long? That's not exactly contributing to society either, is it!'

'You have no idea of what I do to contribute to society,' Agnes said through clenched teeth.

'Have you ever once, in the whole of your adult life, tried to get yourself a real job? To learn something about the real world?'

She seemed to gather herself:

'What the hell would you know about what I get up to in that flat!' she screamed. Her face was chalk-white now. 'You're never there! And you never phone me, either!'

'Well, tell me about it,' I said, trying to keep my voice steady. 'Tell me what you get up to there that is so fucking special. Tell me what I'm missing.'

Agnes was silent. I could see that she was really angry now. But I couldn't control myself, there was something inside me that needed outlet:

'Tell me what you do in there that is so important!'

'Shut up!' Agnes shouted. 'Shut up, for Christ's sake! You don't know what you're talking about! What I do in that flat is of greater importance to the world than anything you will ever manage to achieve with your self-centred theatrical productions.'

'Oh, is that right? Okay, so enlighten me. I'm all ears.'

'I am charting fate,' Agnes hissed.

That was an odd thing to say.

'I see,' was all I could think of in reply. 'Charting fate. Wow. No wonder you're busy.'

But by then she was already on her way out the door. Just as she was leaving she turned and said she was going back down to see Håvard. On her way past the bandsaw she switched it on at the plug and the saw began to whine. She let the crutches fall to the floor, bent down, picked up a sheet of Perspex and guided it towards the blade. The noise was excruciating.

'Oh, well done!' I yelled. 'Why don't you see what else you can ruin before you leave! And go and see Håvard again by all means. You make a fine pair, you two.'

She didn't answer.

That night Ine came to my room. She stood in the doorway, slight and scared-looking. She hardly seemed to touch the floor. It seems only fitting that her birthday should fall on Midsummer's Eve, she is a light, bright child, there is a great openness about her.

She must have been woken by all the shouting and the screeching of the saw.

But that was hours ago, I thought. Had she been lying awake since then?

'Oh, Ine, is that you,' I said softly, sitting up in bed. 'What are you doing up so late? Did you get a fright?'

'It's too noisy here,' she said. 'I can't sleep when you make so much noise. Where's Agnes?'

'Agnes went for a little walk down to Strøm's house,' I said. 'I think there was something she wanted to talk to him about. Maybe she decided to stay the night.'

'Did you two fall out?'

'No, no. Nothing like that,' I answered quickly. 'Agnes and I are the best of friends. We know one another so well that sometimes we have to have a bit of an argument just to remind us of the difference between us.'

Ine didn't smile, but she seemed to understand what I was talking about.

'I miss Dad,' she said. 'I wish Dad was here.'

'But your Dad's in town, looking after your Mum at the hospital,' I said. 'Your Mum needs him too, you know. Right now I think she needs him more than you do.'

'He's my Dad,' Ine said. 'Not yours.'

'Of course he's your Dad,' I said. 'I had my own Dad, when I was a little girl.'

'Where is he now?'

'He lives in town. He's an old man.'

'Is he nice?'

'Yes.'

'Do you miss him?'

I hesitated.

'Yes,' I said.

'I want Mum too,' Ine mumbled. I could tell by her voice that she was scared, but that she was trying to hold on to herself, act angry instead.

'Come here to me,' I said. 'You can come in beside me for a little while if you want. Are you cold?'

'A bit,' Ine replied. But she didn't venture all the way over to the bed, merely sat down in one of the chairs. She drew her feet up underneath her and wrapped her arms round her thighs, as if knotting herself together. She was so small.

'Where's Henry?' she asked.

'Out hunting, I should think,' I said. 'He is a night creature, you know.'

'Why can't he be here?'

'Well, he might pop in during the night,' I said. 'He does that sometimes. I think he's tumbled to the fact that you and Eilif are living here.'

'We don't live here! We live in town, with Mum.'

'Are here on holiday, I meant. He's tumbled to the fact that you two are on holiday here at the summer house. That's why he comes here,' I said. 'Is Eilif asleep?'

'I tried to get into his bed, but he just kicks me,' she said. 'He's a real pain when he's asleep.'

She was quiet for a moment. I understood that there was something she was trying to say.

'Do you feel he's a bit of a pain during the day too?' I asked.

'Yes!' she exclaimed. 'He's always down at Strøm's house playing that piano, he doesn't do anything else! Is that all he can talk about! Nobody ever thinks that I might want to play the piano too! I want to show Mum that I can play too!' She was a little tearful now.

'I know,' I said.

'It's always Eilif, Eilif, Eilif! That's all any of you can talk about.'

I had to smile to myself a little, but I don't think it could be seen in the dim light.

'Would you like the light on?' I asked.

She shook her head.

'Shall I tell you something,' I said. 'When Agnes and I sit and talk after you two have gone to bed, it's mostly about you. Ine, Ine, Ine, we say.'

'No you don't,' she retorted. 'All you do is argue.'

'Only very, very rarely do we argue,' I said. 'And we certainly don't argue when we're talking about you. Because that makes us feel good.'

'Really?' She sniffed and straightened up slightly.

'Absolutely.'

'And then what? What else do you say?'

'We talk about how nice it is to have you here, how lucky we are to be able to spend the summer with you. How dull it would be here at the summer house without you. And how lovely it will be for you when your Mum is all well and you can be together again.'

'But Mum isn't going to get well quick enough for us to go to Italy,' Ine said. 'So I'm not going to learn to swim this summer. Mum promised she would teach me.'

A thought struck me.

'I have an idea,' I said. 'Maybe I could teach you to swim? It could be our secret?'

Ine gazed at me. She seemed to brighten up a little.

'Would you?' she asked.

'Of course I will,' I said. 'We can practise down at the bathing hut when nobody's around. When Eilif is practising the piano. We could start tomorrow.'

Ine said nothing for a moment. Then she smiled wanly to herself, as if she were already picturing the scene.

I felt so happy. I could see that now she felt we had a plan.

'Just think how surprised they'll all be,' I said. 'I bet you'll get the hang of it in no time. And then they'll all be calling your Mum to tell her!'

'And she'll be so glad,' said Ine.

Then she crossed the room and climbed on to my bed. I lifted the light summer duvet for her and she snuggled into me. I felt how cold she was.

It was a strange sensation, having a child snuggling into me like that. Her body was slight and rather angular, but in a soft way. She smelled of toothpaste.

'Do you feel a little better now?' I asked. 'Do you think you could get some sleep? It's the middle of the night, you know. Everyone else is asleep.'

'Not Agnes and Strøm,' she said.

'No, those two might not be,' I said. 'But everyone else.'

'I want Mum,' she said again, in a whisper. 'When's Mum coming home? How long do we have to stay here?'

'Not that much longer,' I said. 'And you have to remember that your Dad is with your Mum all the time. He's looking after her, just as he looks after you when you're not well.'

'Is he sleeping at the hospital too?'

'I think he's sleeping at Agnes's flat, she lives right next to the hospital. She said he could stay there for as long as your Mum needs him. She's probably given him his own key.'

'Then he can run right back if Mum wakes up or anything?'

'That's right,' I said, doing my best to sound calm and reassuring. 'If she wakes up during the night and wants him to be there, they'll call him and he'll run right over. He has his mobile phone, right?'

'How long does it take?'

'A minute at most. Certainly no more than that. Agnes's flat is right next door.'

'But what if Mum gets scared,' Ine wailed, bursting into tears again. I stroked her back. I could feel every vertebra in her spine through her nightie. I could have counted them.

'It'll be okay,' I said softly. 'I'm sure everything will be okay. If your Mum gets scared your Dad will run to her side right away, and he'll take care of her. He is a nurse, you know. He knows just what to do when someone is feeling lonely and frightened. He'll comfort her and hold her hand and get her something to drink and . . .'

'Tell stories,' Ine said.

'Yes, exactly. Tell stories, or one story that your Mum likes to hear . . .'

'Which one?'

'Oh . . . a nice story, the kind that can make someone feel well and happy.'

'But which one?'

'Well, there are so many stories you can tell someone who is feeling frightened or sad,' I said. My brain was working frantically to come up with a story I could tell her, but I couldn't think of any. It suddenly occurred to me that it was a long, long time since anyone had told me a story that was suitable for children.

We both lay quietly again for a while. I felt her take several deep breaths. She was growing a little more relaxed.

'Shall I tell you something?' I whispered eventually. 'I think I know how you're feeling right now, Ine. I was also scared of losing my Mum once. I was so scared that I didn't know what to do with myself. I didn't know where to turn.'

'Was she sick?' Ine asked.

'Yes.'

'Was she in the hospital?'

'Yes.'

'Did she have an operation?'

'Yes.'

'But what about your Dad?' Ine whispered. 'Wasn't he there?'

'He's not like your Dad,' I replied. 'He's totally different. He didn't know how to comfort me. He had enough trouble just seeing to himself, he was scared too. I think he missed her more than I did.'

I was astonished by what I had just said. I had never thought of it like that before.

We both fell silent again. I was conscious of Ine absorbing what I had said, and knew that it had made her long for Aksel even more, but that she would not say anything to me about this longing. All of a sudden I felt I knew her well, that I could read her like an open book.

Now she and I are friends, I thought. It doesn't take as long to make friends with a child as one might imagine at the start.

Then it was as if I suddenly became aware of something over by the window. I turned my face towards it. There lay the shadow puppets I had started making for the play. I felt a little stab of delight.

Of course! I thought. There they are. *That's* the story.

And so I began. I told Ine the story that I knew so well, the one to which I was trying to give visual form in my work. I told her the story of *The Dream Play*.

'Once upon a time, in an old town,' I began, 'there was a great theatre.' Ine looked up at me with dark eyes that said: 'I'm listening.'

'It was a venerable and well-loved theatre, and the people who lived in the town had been going to it for generations. Both tragedies and comedies were performed there, plays for adults, for children and for the old folk. All sorts of people worked at the theatre. Some made the scenery, some worked the lights and some sold tickets. But most popular of all were the actors, especially the theatre's leading lady, Victoria. She was the loveliest of them all, with long, fair hair which she curled with curling tongs into ringlets that hung down her back. She wore little, pink satin shoes and her waist was so slender that a grown man could almost get his hands to meet around it. Victoria had a great many suitors, but there was one who was more ardent than all the rest.'

'What are suitors?'

'Suitors are men who want to win the love of a lady. And the most ardent of all her suitors was the officer. He was a dashing young man in a uniform with fringed épaulettes.

'Each evening after the performance the officer would come round to the stage door with a bouquet of red roses, intent on offering his heart to Victoria. He was so in love. But each evening he was met by the doorkeeper who sat there to make sure that no unauthorised persons managed to slip into the theatre. The door-keeper was a sweet old lady who was working on a big crocheted blanket covered in stars, and those who had worked at the theatre longest said that this star-covered blanket contained the sorrows of all who had confided in her in the course of her long life in the theatre. Which is to say almost everyone, for in the theatre everybody had their secret sorrows.

'But the officer did not give up. He loved Victoria, so each evening he appeared at the stage door, hopeful as always, to present her with his flowers and pledge his eternal troth. And every time he was denied admittance he was just as disappointed, although he tried to hide it as best he could. The doorkeeper consoled him gently and sweetly and, unbeknownst to him, she crocheted his disappointments and sorrows into the big, starstrewn blanket too.

'Now it so happened that in this theatre there was a door which had never been opened. The door was made of mirrored glass, and behind it lay a secret, or so it was said. Over the years many people had wondered what that secret might be, but no one had ever seen the door opened. And each evening, when the officer was standing outside the theatre, waiting for Victoria, he wondered what lay behind that door. He asked lots of the people who passed by if they knew, but none could tell him. Even the doorkeeper did not know what lay behind that door, and the officer grew more and more determined to open it. It got to the stage where he almost forgot Victoria for a while, if he was thinking about the door.

'Now, in this part of the world there lived the daughter of a god. She had come swooping down from heaven to dwell with the mortals on earth. She had been out playing with a bolt of lightning, shooting across the sky, revelling in the speed, but she had allowed herself to be carried a little too far. Her father had started calling for her, worried that he was going to lose her:

"Daughter, daughter, where are you?"

"Here, father, here."

"Be careful, child, you have gone astray,' her father cried anxiously. 'You are sinking . . . what happened?"

"I was only following the lightning, and using a cloud as a carriage on which to ride," his daughter called back. "But then the cloud began to sink and now I'm falling down and down. Tell me father, where shall I end up? Why is it so difficult to breathe down here?"

"Because you have left my world and entered that other world, that is why," her father called to her. "You have passed the morning star and will soon be entering the Earth's gravitational field. Take care, daughter, you are going to fall to Earth! Take care!"

"Do not worry, father," the daughter called back. "I have a mind to see what it is like to be on this Earth. Who lives there?"

"Human beings," her father said.

"But it looks so dark down below," his daughter said. "Tell me, does the sun never shine there? And what are those sounds I hear?"

"Oh yes, the sun does shine sometimes, but not always," her father replied. "At the moment it is dark because it is night, but during the day the sun shines. And what you are hearing are the sounds of people talking, weeping and wailing."

"But why do they do that?"

"Because once upon a time something happened to their planet, perhaps. Who knows – I don't understand it myself."

"Oh, now I can see!" his daughter cried joyfully. "I can see green forests, blue water, white-capped mountains and yellow fields. I can hear rumbling and rolling. It's so lovely here. I want to stay! Oh, father, please let me! Just for a few days! Just a while."

"I'm not sure that you will like it, my dear," replied her father from the heavens. "There is so much care and woe among human beings, I don't think it's quite the thing for you."

"Oh, no, it's *just* the thing for me, truly it is!" said his daughter. "You judge human beings too harshly, father. I can hear laughter and singing now, and someone playing the piano, and I can see someone swimming and someone lighting a bonfire . . ."

'And the god's daughter went on falling, down and down, until she was caught by the Earth's gravitational pull and her father could no longer stop her. So he shouted a blessing to her, and added that if she really wanted to know what it was like to be mortal then she might as well stay down there for a while and find out. But she was to be sure to call to him when she had learned what she wanted to know and wished to return to heaven. He would be watching over her.

'Then, with a bump, the god's daughter landed on Earth. When she opened her eyes she saw that she had landed in a garden. In the middle of the garden was a great castle with an onion for a dome, and all round the castle grew the most wonderful flowers. There were huge hollyhocks in full bloom: white, pink, mauve, sulphur yellow and violet. There were roses, too, and blue monkshood. And the castle was a strange castle, it did not look like any other castle on Earth, although the god's daughter didn't know that, of course, because she had never been there before.

'This castle grew like a plant; on the sunny side a new wing had just sprouted, a splendid extension.

'Dazed, the daughter picked herself up off the ground, dusted off her dress and checked to see whether she had hurt herself in the fall. But her father must have arranged for a soft landing for her, because she was completely unscathed. When she took a closer look around she noticed a man walking towards her. It was the glazier. He seemed to be lost in his own thoughts, he probably had no idea that she was the daughter of a god and that she had never been here before.

"Good morning, Agnes," the glazier said, nodding to her. And she realised that she was now a human being, and that her name was Agnes.'

Ine interrupted me:

'Was her name really Agnes?' she asked doubtfully.

'Oh, yes. Agnes was most definitely her name,' I said.

'But she wasn't the Agnes that we know? She wasn't in a wheelchair, was she?'

'No, it can't have been the Agnes we know,' I said. 'This one was the daughter of a god. And I think it's safe to say she wasn't in a wheelchair. No, there's nothing in the story about a wheel-chair.'

This answer seemed to satisfy her.

'Go on!' she said.

And I went on:

"See how much the castle has grown since last year!" Agnes cried happily to the glazier.

"That's odd," the glazier muttered to himself, "I've never heard of a castle that grew." But to Agnes he said: "Yes, it's actually grown about four feet, but that's because they've given it plenty of fertiliser . . . and if you look over there you'll see that a piano has just shot up in the gazebo."

And so it had.

"But who lives in the castle?" Agnes wanted to know.

The glazier creased his brow and looked as though he was thinking hard.

"I used to know," he said. "But I've forgotten."

"I think there's a prisoner in there!" Agnes exclaimed. "I'm sure of it! I just know it!"

"A prisoner? No, I don't think so," the glazier said.

"Yes," she cried. "I can feel it in my bones! There's a prisoner in there, and she's waiting for us to come and set her free! Let's go in and find her!"

"Well, if you say so," the glazier said. "I suppose we'd better go in. But are you sure it's safe?"

"You can never be absolutely sure," Agnes said cheerfully. "Come on, let's go in and see!"

'And then what happened?' Ine asked excitedly. Her body was warm now. Her breath mingled with mine; I could almost see it, a column slowly rising from us to the ceiling over our heads. I turned my face away from her and looked back at the window.

'Answer me! What happened next?' she persisted, putting her hand to my face impatiently and turning it back towards her. 'Did they go into the castle?'

'Yes, they went into the castle,' I said slowly.

'And then?'

'Oh, what was it now?' I murmured. 'You know I think I've almost forgotten.'

'I think there was a prisoner in there,' Ine said.

'Yes, I'm sure you're right,' I said. 'There probably was a prisoner in there.'

'Don't say it like that! Just tell me what happened!' she hissed in frustration. Her voice sounded tired now, faltering and faint.

'No, it's late,' I said. 'It's the middle of the night, Ine. And this looks like being a very long story. I think we'd better get some sleep now. We'll finish it another day.'

And strangely enough she went to sleep. She must have been exhausted.

But I couldn't sleep. I lay and stared at the window until first light. Thinking about the story I had been telling.

I was waiting for Agnes to get back from Håvard's.

I must have fallen asleep, though, in the grey light of dawn, because when I woke again Ine was gone. She must have woken up before me and gone down to the sitting-room to see Agnes. So Agnes must have got back from Håvard's somehow or other during the night. She and Ine were evidently up and doing already; I could hear them talking in the sitting-room.

I could still feel the weight of Ine all down my one side.

That morning to which I woke. How can I describe it? The sounds. All the light. The feeling that Granny had just been there, that she wanted something of me.

Something I was on the point of discovering, but which I urgently needed to get clear in my mind.

She had laid it out for me.

'Is that you, Granny?' I whispered. 'I think I need a little help. I don't know what you mean.'

I got up, went down to the kitchen and busied myself in there for a while. I assumed that Eilif had already run down to Håvard's house to practise on the piano. I made coffee, poured orange juice into two glasses and made up some rolls, garnished them with parsley. Then I put the whole lot on a tray and took it through to Agnes and Ine in the sitting-room.

'Good morning, ladies!' I said, as blithely as I could. They both turned to me in surprise, as if they had completely forgotten I was in the house. I felt as though I was interrupting something important, something that concerned no one but the two of them.

Ine had brought down all her Barbie dolls and spread them out on the sofa and the coffee table. She and Agnes were talking in low voices, their heads close together; they were each dressing a doll. Neatly lined up along the edge of the table were lots of tiny Barbie shoes, so small that the slightest breath would have blown them away. But I didn't blow on them, I simply walked up to Ine and Agnes, carrying the tray at chest height, and asked them where they would like their breakfast served. Agnes pointed to the floor at her feet; I could leave it there.

I put down the tray, but I didn't want to leave, I wanted to be let into their secret. But what could I say? I didn't dare ask what Agnes had been doing down at Håvard's that night. It was as if the evening before had never happened. It had been erased.

At last I cleared my throat and put the question in a different way:

'What exactly were you three doing down at Håvard's yesterday morning? You were gone for ages.'

'D'you mean Strøm's?' Agnes asked innocently.

'Yes, Strøm's. You spent almost the whole day down there.'

Agnes passed the question on:

'How do you feel things went at Strøm's yesterday, Ine?' she asked the child, with a little nod in my direction.

'Great!' Ine said. 'But I don't think he liked having his picture drawn!'

And that was all I got out of them.

I set down the tray and backed out of the room.

'Oh, and thanks, Molly!' Agnes called after me. 'Nothing quite like breakfast on a tray! Ine and I are really going to enjoy this. Don't you want some?'

I went back to my room and did not come out again for hours. I didn't know how to tackle this situation. Something was starting to take shape inside me and all I could was work.

The day passed. I seemed to lose myself in what I was doing. I was working on the shadow puppets and on the rising castle. I had been getting on so well with them since telling Ine the story the night before.

I need to have something to show the people at the theatre soon, I told myself. It's no use just having it in my head.

I began to make a model.

As I worked I thought about Aksel. The last time he had spent the night with me I had lain watching him and waiting for him to come to bed too. He had been standing at the window, looking down on to the veranda, at Agnes staggering about on her crutches. Beyond him, outside the window, I could see the bright, empty summer sky.

It just went on and on: there was nothing for the eye to fix on, no clouds, only a light haze; nothing to hold you fast, only a faint sighing.

I knew that if had chosen that moment to tell Aksel I was pregnant he would have said, from the spot by the window from which he looked set to disappear into that empty sky:

'But Molly. I don't want another child. I've had all the children I'm going to have.'

*

Eventually, though, I had to pull myself together and go downstairs and join the others. By then it was evening.

Agnes had things well under control. She was hobbling around the kitchen on the crutches, giving the children their dinner. When I appeared in the doorway she gave me that searching look that I knew so well, her eyes seeming to see past me, focusing on my contours.

But she didn't say anything. She pulled out a chair for me, I took it and sat quietly at the end of the table, watching them.

Eilif and Ine paid me no attention. They had clearly got used to having Agnes there; they had already swapped me for her. That hurt me more than I could admit. I had the feeling that it was them against me now.

After a while Agnes nodded amiably, as if to say that I had done the right thing in coming down and that if I had anything to say to her I should just come right out with it, she was open to whatever comments I might have. As open as a blank canvas was how she seemed to be presenting herself. But I didn't believe her.

She kept glancing over at me as she bustled around the kids. I could see that she was trying hard not to make too much of a to-do with the crutches – it was amazing how good she had become at getting about on them in such a short time. Aksel had obviously done an excellent job with her. She could get in and out of the bathroom without any problem, and moved around the kitchen with ease.

I had to force myself not to stare at her. But I felt my eyes being drawn to her against my will, as if she were a magnet, and I wanted her to say something to me, interpret my feelings for me. She does that sometimes.

'You seem very down today,' she was liable to say when we spoke on the phone. Or: 'It's not hard to hear that you're happy, Molly.'

I find it both annoying and soothing when she talks to me like that. But this time she was leaving me to do the interpreting myself. I thought: I seem very down today. I need someone to come and comfort me soon.

Through the sitting-room door I could see that the Barbie dolls had been cleared away. The box for The Hunt for the Lost Diamond was sitting on the coffee table. The three of them must have been playing it before dinner.

It was Ine who broke the silence:

'But if Mum *doesn't* come home,' she said suddenly. Her words were cut out with scissors and blown into the air. They drifted slowly to the floor without anyone saying anything.

I saw Eilif and Agnes exchange glances, as if they were her parents: loving and attentive.

'What if she dies at the hospital,' Ine went on, louder now. 'What if something happens?'

'What are you talking about?' I said. I was surprised by the sound of my own voice, I hadn't used it since I had taken their breakfast tray in to them.

I could tell by my voice just how much it mattered to me to be part of whatever it was that was going on between Agnes and the children; these three seemed to constitute the only human society left in the world. The one place where there might be a slot for me. 'Of course your Mum isn't going to die,' I said. 'She's on the mend already. Your Dad said so when he was here, you heard him.'

All three turned to look at me with surprise in their eyes. Only now did they really seem to notice me, when I opened my mouth.

'Maybe she's feeling lonely, though, and scared!' Ine said. 'Right now! Maybe she's thinking about us and wishing we were there. What if she's wishing we were there to look after her? What if she's so scared that she dies?!'

I realised that this was my chance. I gave Agnes a hard stare, a look that said I was taking charge now, and she should just shut up and listen.

'Ine,' I said gently. 'Your Mum may be scared. But she's not going to die.'

'How do you know!'

'Come here for a minute,' I said. 'Come here to me.'

To my surprise she came over to where I sat on the other side of the table from Agnes. I parted my knees and she placed herself between them, I put my hands on her hips. She was so skinny; I remembered from the night before. I felt her hip-bones digging into the palms of my hands. I thought: Agnes is looking at us. She sees Ine's fair head and my darker one. She's thinking to herself that we look like mother and daughter. And her stomach tightens. Because she knows now that I'm going to keep the child I'm carrying, that in only a few months I will be the mother of Aksel's baby. Of a little one like Ine.

'Your Mum is not going to die,' I say firmly, looking Ine straight in the eye.

'You don't know that.'

'Yes, I do.'

'You're just kidding,' Ine shouted, wriggling free of my grasp. 'You're only saying that to shut me up. You don't care about Mum.'

'You think I don't care about your Mum?'

'No. You just want her to die so that you can marry Dad.'

Across from me I saw Agnes's eyes widen. All of a sudden I felt a blackness inside my head, like the distinct, clearly defined dark spot left by a tiny explosion.

'Ine,' I said. 'What are you talking about?'

'You just want Mum to die,' she said again. She went over to her brother and huddled up against him. 'You don't care about her at all, you don't even know her. You only want Dad. Agnes says so, too. She says that you want Dad and that the two of you are going to have a baby. It's true, I know it is. I heard you arguing about it last night. You're trying to trick Dad into making a baby with you. But you can't trick him.'

'What the hell have you been saying to these children!' I yelled at Agnes. But she merely regarded me sternly, the look of a mother saying: Don't use that tone of voice in front of the children.

I saw Eilif place a protective arm around his sister. He didn't like it when I got angry and shouted. He glanced appraisingly from me to Agnes, seeming unnaturally grown-up at that moment. It was as if he were trying to distance himself from what was going on, to observe the situation without becoming emotionally involved. To assess it according to his own standards. He looked so much like his Dad at that moment.

'Ssh, Ine,' he said. 'Let Molly speak.'

I stared at him in amazement. So did Agnes. We both realised that he was offering me a big chance. He was on my side now.

I had not been imagining it, that bond I had felt between us on the morning before Agnes came to the summer house.

I cleared my throat again, thoughtfully. I knew I had to make the best use of this chance he had given me.

'I don't want your Mum to die,' I said softly. 'And I do want to be your Dad's girlfriend. But that is something quite different. Your Dad and I are not going to get married.'

'Promise?' said Ine.

'Promise.'

'And you're not going to have any babies?'

I had to pause again for a moment.

'It's far too early to say, Ine,' I said. 'But we're definitely not going to get married.'

'You promise?' she said again.

'I promise,' I said. 'I don't think your Dad wants to marry again, and I have no great notion to get married either. I don't think I'm cut out for marriage.'

'No, there's no point in it,' Ine said. 'Everybody who gets married just gets divorced. There's no point.'

*

I put all the love I had into the look I gave Ine. But out of the corner of my eye I saw Agnes struggle to her feet and hobble through to the sitting-room on her crutches. I don't know what had come over her. I think maybe she sensed a sea change on the way.

It was the children and me against her now. She couldn't bear that.

I realised it was up to me to put an end to this madness.

'Come,' I said to Eilif and Ine. 'I don't think we should let Agnes walk off and leave us. There's something we have to talk to her about, I think. Something to do with mums'.

We followed Agnes into the sitting-room. But she wasn't there, she had hobbled on out to the veranda on her crutches. She was standing next to the hammock, trying to get into it. It was no easy task for her, her balance wasn't good enough, she looked as if she was fighting with the voluminous length of fabric, as it twisted and turned and swung back and forth uncontrollably.

'Hang on a second,' I said. 'Hang on, I'll give you a hand.'

Together, the children and I managed to lift her into the hammock. It was the first time she had ever lain in one. She looked like a little girl in it; a little girl weak of body and strong of will, suspended in a large, gently swaying piece of cloth. After a moment's hesitation Ine clambered in beside her and put her arms around her.

I went back to the sitting-room for Granny's mauve blanket and laid it over them. Eilif and I settled ourselves in the wicker chairs and took it in turns to give the hammock a little push, as if it were a cradle. We sat like that for a long time, all together. And peace gradually settled over us again. It felt good.

'I've been thinking,' I said slowly, in a calm, low voice.

I was conscious that the others were listening, the two up in the hammock as well. 'Sometimes it feels as though we are completely caught up in the workings of fate,' I continued. 'As though it is driving and controlling us.'

I saw Agnes's head rise over the edge of the hammock. She stared at me.

'What makes you say that?' she said in a small voice.

'Oh, I've been giving it a bit of thought,' I said, not letting the look in her eyes put me off. I went on rocking the hammock. Pushing her away from me, towards me. Away from me, towards me. 'I know there is someone in this house who is on the verge of making a very important discovery about fate,' I went on. 'She told me herself.'

'Who did?' Agnes asked.

'What does 'fate' mean?' Ine chimed in, sticking her head up too. Eilif said nothing, but he was eyeing me intently and had now left me to set the hammock's tempo.

'Fate is the word for whatever it is that decides what is going to happen,' I explained to Ine. 'Fate is a story that wants something of us. A story which contains the grand plan for us; it follows our progress and notes how we move in relation to it. I have a friend who knows a great deal about fate.'

'Who?' Ine asked. Agnes's head had sunk into the shade of the hammock once more.

'That character lying next to you,' I said.

'Agnes?'

'Mmm.'

'Do you know what Molly's talking about, Agnes?' Ine asked.

'Kind of, I suppose,' Agnes muttered from under Granny's blanket.

'Well, if you know so much about fate, you must know what's going to happen to Mum,' Eilif put in. Agnes did not answer.

'Yes, I do believe Agnes does know,' I said. 'She has been studying this whole subject of fate for years, she was telling me this only the other day. So she must have a pretty broad frame of reference.'

'What's a frame of reference?' Ine asked.

'Well it means that you've seen lots of other things that are something like whatever it is you are studying,' I said. 'That you have seen enough and studied enough to start drawing inferences.'

'What're inferences? You use such hard words.'

'An inference is a conclusion,' Eilif said.

'And now I think Agnes might like to tell you something of what she has discovered,' I said. 'Am I right, Agnes?'

Agnes brought her head out from under the blanket again. I forced her to meet my eye. The look I gave her said: Don't let me down.

You and I are one.

We have shared everything.

Don't let these children down. Let's not fight over them, this is bigger than the two of us, bigger than the gulf that lies between us at the moment.

There was a long silence while we regarded one another. I think both Eilif and Ine understood that something crucial was taking place between us.

'Why doesn't Agnes say anything,' Ine asked.

'Ssh,' said Eilif.

And at last Agnes began to speak. She heaved herself up into a half-sitting position in the hammock and pushed the mauve blanket aside. Ine crawled up beside her and tucked herself in under her arm: not affectionately, just expectantly.

'Yes,' she said. 'What Molly says is true. Or some of it anyway. For years now I've been studying fate. It's just about all I do up there in my flat, I have plenty of time to give to that sort of thing. And I have learned to rely on my instincts to tell me when something is true. To believe that fate will take the turn which I sense it will take.'

'I know you're going to say that Mum will get better,' Eilif said doubtfully.

'You're right, as always, Eilif,' Agnes said. 'All my instincts tell me that you're Mum is going to get well.'

'Are you quite sure about that?'

'Quite sure.'

'Definitely?'

'Definitely.'
'And you're never wrong?'
'Never.'
I breathed a sigh of relief.

Agnes and I were on the same side again. Agnes and the children and me. All on the same side. What a relief. I had a sudden flash of inspiration:

'And I know something else that's quite definite,' I said, looking straight at Agnes.

'What?' said Ine.

'No mother ever dies,' I said.

'Of course they do,' Eilif countered.

'Not completely,' I said. 'It's impossible, it goes against the laws of fate.'

'How can you say that?' Eilif said.

'Well,' I went on. 'Because even if your mother did die now – which she is certainly and most definitely not going to do – she would never, never leave her children. You're a part of her, you see. You grew inside her. It was her who gave you life. There was a time when each of you was one with your mother. Fate decided that that was how it should be, otherwise it wouldn't have happened.'

'How do you know that?' Eilif asked.

'Oh, it's just one of those things you learn as you get older,' I said. 'It was like one of the great tales of fate into which you two and your mother fitted perfectly. A tale that was already written.'

I had one eye fixed on Agnes as I said this. She was shifting restlessly in the hammock; she removed her arm from the back of Ine's head and laid the lower half of it over her eyes, as if shielding them from the non-existent sunlight.

'I don't know what you're talking about,' Ine piped up.

'Ssh,' Eilif said.

'You and Eilif lay inside your Mum, right?' I said. 'Deep inside her tummy. And when she put her hand on her tummy she could feel the baby moving in there. And she was so amazed! She understood that she was going to be somebody's Mum. And the only thing you need to understand, Ine, is the lovely feeling it gives you to think that she is your Mum.'

'Mum,' Ine whispered in a very small voice.

'Exactly,' I said. 'Your Mum will never leave you, because there is a little part of her in you, just as you were once a little part of her.'

'Is Mum in here?' Ine asked, placing her hand on her tummy.

'Yes, there, or maybe more like here,' I said, lightly moving her hand up to her narrow chest.

'Here?'

'That's right.'

'Are you quite sure?'

'Positive,' I said. 'You don't think I'd make up something like this, do you?'

'I don't know,' Ine said.

'Well, I'm not making it up, I'm just telling you how it is,' I said. 'That feeling that your Mum will always be there – you'll never lose that. When you're a grown-up lady like Agnes and me, you'll still have that feeling: that your Mum is there with you, that she's a part of you. Enfolding you, you might say.'

'What does enfolding mean?'

'That she's around you all the time, wherever you go,' I said. 'And when your Mum does die, many years from now, that feeling of being enfolded by her will stay with you. So she can never die completely.'

'Never?'

'Never.'

'But what will she be when she's dead?' Ine asked.

I hesitated.

'Then she'll become . . . something all her own, a little thing,' I replied.

'A little thing? Now you're joking.'

'I most certainly am not,' I said. 'You're Mum will be a little thing all her own. A little . . .'

I hesitated again. 'A little nut,' I finished decisively.

'A nut?' Ine repeated sceptically.

'A nut,' I said. I was almost starting to believe it myself. 'Not very big, but beautifully formed.'

'Okay, so what sort of a nut?' Eilif broke in. He sounded more suspicious now, more childlike, but he no longer looked embarrassed. He had got quite carried away by all this. I had got quite carried away myself. I'd never talked like this before. I don't know where the words came from.

'Oh, it's hard to say exactly what sort of nut it is,' I said. 'An acorn, maybe?'

'An acorn? You must be joking.'

'No, I'm not joking, I said. 'You both know what an acorn looks like, don't you?'

'Small and round and hard,' Ine said.

'Exactly,' I said. 'But the most important thing is that in the middle of the nut there is a little seed. And that seed contains everything that's needed to make another oak tree. If you plant it in the earth a new tree will grow. It's a miracle!'

Eilif gave a little smile. I think he felt it was nice of me to try so hard.

'The new tree will never be exactly the same as the tree on which the nut grew,' I continued. 'It is its own tree. And yet you can tell that it sprang from the mother tree. There is always a resemblance.'

Ine giggled.

'Mum's not going to become an acorn when she dies,' she said. 'Isn't she?'

'No. I think probably she'll be an almond.'

'An almond?' I said. 'Well, almonds are nice too.'

'An almond,' Ine said again. 'White. Like the ones in our rice pudding on Christmas Eve. White so that you can't see it among all the rice. Nobody knows where it is, but it's there! It was me who found the almond last year.'

'Well, there you are then,' I said.

'Maybe we could take Mum's clothes off so she'd be all white, and then hide her in the rice pudding!' Ine cried. 'Where it's all lovely and warm and soft. And then after a while we would find her.'

'Great idea,' Eilif commented drily. 'You're always coming out with the most brilliant suggestions, Ine.' He glanced across at Agnes and she smiled and rolled her eyes a little demonstratively. It was meant to be a secret exchange between him and her. Maybe she didn't think I would notice.

Then she sat up so abruptly that the hammock tipped. Both she and Ine tumbled out on to the floor. Ine landed on top of Agnes. She didn't hurt herself, but I could see that Agnes had taken a knock. She let out a little whimper, the sort of sound a small child would make.

Ine jumped to her feet and she and I bent over Agnes and got our arms round her. We tried to lift her, but had to give up. She suddenly went all limp in our grasp, like a rag doll.

We sat there like that on the floor of the veranda, all three of us. Eilif stood a little apart, gazing in bewilderment at us.

'Did you hurt yourself?' Ine asked anxiously. Agnes answered with another whimper.

'I'll go and get the wheelchair,' Eilif said.

'Good,' I said. 'But we can't go on like this. We have to do something. Tomorrow we're going into town to fetch that piano.'

And that is what we did. It was high time; it had long been high time. Granny's piano belonged at the summer house, I simply had not understood that it was my job to see that it got there. In any case, it was also high time the four of us had a little outing. The atmosphere at the summer house had become rather close. It was having a stupefying effect on me.

Not much was said on the drive up to town. But the mood was lighter than it had been the day before, it felt as though a thunderstorm had passed over. Agnes sat up front next to me, gazing out of the window on her side. I sneaked a peek at her every now and again and noticed the children doing the same.

Maybe it's not such a bad thing to air one's feelings every now and again. I mean, they're there inside you, so why not give vent to them. To prevent the atmosphere from becoming too close.

I wasn't entirely convinced, though. That feeling of stupefaction was still there.

I had called ahead and arranged when to meet the guys from the theatre at Granny's flat. It sounded as though they had been sitting in their room, waiting for me to call, ever since I had last been to see them and smoked a fag with them. As if they were there just for me.

They had moved a piano before, that was clear. They seemed more like removal men than stagehands. There were three of them: big, burly characters, all of them with beards. They had huge, hard fists and communicated mostly in words of one and two syllables; none the less their words had a distinct lilt to them.

I stood on the top step outside Granny's flat and listened to the rhythms of their speech, thinking that now I could almost be Granny. I had gone up to the storage room in the loft and found the harnesses which she kept up there specifically for this purpose, and I had insisted on packing the piano in cushions and blankets so that it wouldn't get scratched, exactly as she used to do.

Eilif lent a hand with the lifting like a real man and Ine hopped excitedly round about them like a little bunny rabbit. I could tell that the children liked the men too, they lapsed into the same mode of speech, speaking to one another in curt, mumbled mono-syllables and looking as though they were having a whale of a time.

Agnes sat at the bottom of the stairs in her wheelchair and held the door open for them when they came down the last flight with the piano. She seemed much calmer now, she didn't try to sabo-tage any of my arrangements. I believe she must have slept deeply and peacefully the night before, despite being a little tender after her fall from the hammock. It always helps to get a good night's sleep, Granny taught me that.

The guys never once questioned how they came to be moving a piano from a flat in town to a summer house miles away, for the theatre's scenographer, when they were supposed to be at work. It occurred to me that perhaps they had the same respect for me that people had had for Granny in her day. It was the sort of respect that forbade you to question her decisions. You simply did as she said; it never felt like an order.

Down in my untidy little car I had a bag containing schnapps glasses and a bottle of aquavit which I had found in the drinks cabinet at the summer house. The plan had been for me to do as Granny had done and serve a little glass, so we could drink a toast once the piano was safely down the stairs. But I hadn't considered the fact that two of us would be driving, two were children who did not drink alcohol, and another two were men who were not allowed to drink during working hours. That left Agnes, and she appeared to have had more than enough booze to last her for a while, that night when she drank herself into a stupor on the sofa.

Stupid of me.

I was glad that I hadn't packed the bottle and glasses into a basket, that would have looked a bit too obvious. I just left the bag in the boot, I didn't let the others see it.

The van with the theatre's logo on the side sat right behind us like a reassuring shadow all the road to the summer house. I drove in front to show the way. Agnes sat silently by my side; she kept twiddling the knob on the radio and changing the station, she didn't want to listen to anything but news.

Now and again I looked in the mirror and smiled at Eilif in the back seat. He met my eye and smiled back. Ine had been allowed to ride with the stagehands. She was sitting between them in the cab and waved happily to her brother every time he turned and raised an arm to her. I flashed my lights occasionally to let her know that I was happy too. Even Agnes looked round from time to time. I could tell that we all adored Ine. That was something we had in common.

I think the guys from the theatre were a bit surprised, when we got to the summer house, to find that the piano was to be put in the gazebo. But they said nothing. I could hardly start explaining that the gazebo was the only spot on our ground where we could get a signal on the mobile phone, and that a functioning mobile was absolutely necessary if Eilif was to play his tune for his mother in hospital.

As soon as the piano was in place Eilif sat down and played the first bars of 'The butterfly in the garden'. It sounded awful.

'Hm,' I said. 'I think we're going to have to have it tuned. It doesn't really like being moved. I remember that from Granny's time. She had this one piano tuner she always rang.'

'That's okay,' Eilif said. 'I can go on practising at Strøm's for now.'

'Are you sure?'

'Yeah, 'course. It's better that way, anyway. I need him there to show me what to do. With playing the chords and what not.'

'Oh, of course,' I said. 'The chords and what not. You do need your teacher around.'

'At least to begin with,' said Eilif.

'At least to begin with,' I said.

Not long afterwards he headed off down to Håvard's house.

I was aware that I was disappointed. I had had this image of Eilif practising the piano in the gazebo, maybe with Håvard ensconced among the cushions on the bench along the wall, directing him. I wanted to entice them into my garden. But it seemed they weren't so easily enticed.

The guys had lunch with us before driving back to town. By the time they left it was late afternoon; they had hung out in the gazebo, drinking coffee, for over an hour after they had eaten. They couldn't seem to drag themselves away. Ine hovered around them, in her element. She had charmed the socks off all three of them, I think. I said to myself: that's how little girls are when they have a father who is strong and happy.

When they finally drove off in the empty van, Agnes said she was going to lie down. She wasn't feeling all that great.

'You're not coming down with something, are you?' I asked.

'No, no. Days like this just take so much out of me. I'm not used to shuttling back and forth all the time. There's just so much to take in.'

'I know,' I said. 'Off you go and lie down. Ine, do you think you could give Agnes a hand?'

Ine was solicitude personified. She helped Agnes back to the house and up the wheelchair ramp. I sat where I was and watched them disappear through the veranda door. Then I closed my eyes. I may have dropped off for a moment.

I woke with a little start: someone was stroking my cheek. I opened my eyes and peered in confusion at Ine.

'That's her settled in bed,' she said, with old-fashioned gravity.

'She was absolutely worn out, poor soul.'

'That was sweet of you,' I said, smiling at her. 'I think I nodded off myself.'

'I think I know why you're both so tired,' she said. 'It's because you had that argument. Why are you always arguing, you two? I thought you were friends.'

'We *are* friends,' I said.

'But you just have to find out what the difference is between you?'

I couldn't help but smile. Clearly you had to be very careful what you said to this little girl. She had the memory of an elephant.

'Do you remember what you promised me?' she asked. Only now did I notice that she had one hand behind her back.

'You mean about teaching you to swim?'

She nodded meaningfully.

'Of course I remember!' I said. 'Come on, let's go get our bathing costumes!'

'Ha-ha! I've got them here!' she cried triumphantly, revealing the hand clutching the two costumes and waving them under my nose.

'You're quite a girl, Ine,' I laughed.

'And now I'm going to learn to swim!' Ine whooped.

When Ine and I got back, after over an hour of swimming practice down by the bathing hut, Aksel was there. He and Agnes were sitting on the veranda talking in hushed voices. Eilif was back from Håvard's, he was lying in the hammock reading a Donald Duck comic.

Agnes was in the wheelchair now. She must have risen when she heard Aksel's car. Or maybe she got him to help her off the sofa and into the chair. Had she really grown so much weaker again, or was it all just an act designed to get his attention? I snapped my eyes shut and tried to shake off both thoughts.

That was the afternoon when we wheeled her down to the beach and sent her out in the kayak. It was Aksel's idea. He had the boat strapped to the roof of the car; it was red and slender and looked very dynamic. I gathered from the way they talked that he and Agnes had a deal that she was to go out in the kayak, as a kind of reward for something or other – quite what, I didn't know.

I thought to myself that this was possibly not the best day for it – she might be too weak to paddle out on the fjord on her own. She had had to go and have a lie down, after all. I wasn't happy about it. But I said nothing.

Aksel and Eilif had gone down to the bathing hut ahead of us, carrying the kayak between them. Ine and I followed behind with Agnes in the wheelchair.

She didn't say much and she didn't help the chair along by spinning the wheels with her hands as she usually did. I pushed the chair, it was pretty hard going on the loose gravel without her putting a bit of arm power behind it.

Ine carried Granny's life-jacket. It was an old make, not particularly sporty looking, it didn't really go with the kayak at all. Aksel had brought along his own streamlined, fluorescent life-jacket and seemed a little surprised by Agnes's insistence on wearing Granny's, but this was obviously something she had decided on ages ago. I had seen her going out to the tool shed to inspect that life-jacket several times since she arrived at the summer house.

When we reached the bathing hut we saw a figure standing watching Aksel and Eilif, who were down at the water's edge, getting the kayak ready. A jolt ran through me: it was Håvard. No doubt about it. Half a second is all it takes for me to recognise him, quicker than blinking, always. He is still there inside me.

He looked so old. So thin. So white of hair and beard. And so much himself.

I brought the wheelchair to an abrupt halt and stood quite still. Just at that moment Ine caught sight of him, she ran up to him and gave him a hug, she was obviously pleased to see him. Then she took him by the hand and dragged him over to us. Agnes raised a hand in salute, I stood as if turned to stone.

And then there he was, right in front of me. He greeted us gravely. He bent down and clasped Agnes's hand, Ine put an arm round his neck and gave him another hug. When had they become so close? He straightened up and looked me right in the eye.

'Hello, Molly,' he said.

'Hello, Håvard,' I said.

'I gather that we are neighbours.'

'Looks like it.'

'You're all grown up, I see.'

'So are you,' I said.

He gave a little chuckle, squinted at me and put out his hand. He must have sensed just how confused I was. Håvard has always been very quick to size up situations.

I could tell that he was trying to help me, and I don't quite know why, but for some reason it angered me to see him like that, with his hand outstretched.

Håvard has seen me angry before. He lowered his hand, I could see that he was already having thoughts about me. He bent over Agnes in her wheelchair again:

'So,' he said, smiling at her, 'this is the big day, I see.'

I didn't know what he was talking about. How could he know that Agnes and Aksel had planned for her to go out on the kayak on this particular day? Was this the sort of thing they had talked about that night she spent down at his place? Or had they spoken on the phone, unknown to me?

Together we made our way down to where Aksel and Eilif were standing by the kayak. Eilif's face lit up when he saw Håvard, he ran up, thumped him on the shoulder and led him back to his father.

'This is Strøm,' he said. 'My piano teacher.'

Håvard and Aksel shook hands and greeted one another as men do: cagily, respecting one another's territory.

I, on the other hand, was going frantic. The wheelchair had got stuck on the shingle. I tugged and tugged, but couldn't pull it free, and Agnes was no help.

Both Aksel and Håvard turned to look at me, then came over to lend a hand. They pushed me out of the way. I stood off to one side, watching as they assisted Agnes out of the wheelchair and into the kayak, which was bobbing at the water's edge.

'Careful!' Aksel warned.

She had a bit of a struggle getting herself properly installed in the kayak, finding the right position. I could tell by the set look on her face that she was starting to realise that this was not going to be as easy as she had thought. Keeping her balance was harder than she had expected. Aksel, Håvard and the kids helped her all they could, and when at long last she was settled, Ine was ready with the life-jacket, which Agnes put on, with a serious, concentrated expression on her face.

Aksel showed her how to ply the oars: both hands gripping the paddle firmly, a shoulder's breadth apart. A smooth, steady action. The narrow edge of the blade slicing the surface of the water. But she didn't appear to be paying much attention; all she wanted was for someone to push her out on to the water so she could get on with it. I don't think I was the only one who was a bit overwrought at that particular moment.

She seemed to be feeling the same anger as me, and the same impatience to be off, away from everything that was holding her back. Off and into something else, something new.

I looked on as they sweated and strained, making no move.

'Who wants to push her off?' Aksel asked.

'I do,' I said. And with two great bounds I was down by the kayak and had given it such a shove that it shot away from the shore, far too fast and tilting to one side. Agnes glided away from us across the water, looking none too steady as she started waggling the paddle about, her upper half lurching back and forth.

'Careful!' Aksel shouted. 'Easy does it now! You have to find your balance or you'll tip over!'

'Yeah, right,' I said tightly. 'She'd better find her balance!'

I took a couple of strides into the water, all set to give her another push, but she was already a fair distance away from me. I was conscious of Håvard coming up behind me and laying an admonitory hand on my arm.

'That'll do,' he said. 'She's going fast enough now. I think you should come with me.'

And then the kayak capsized. It turned over, right before our eyes. She was quite a long way from the shore. The children screamed, Aksel dived into the water and swam out to rescue her. I was left standing: numb, blind, dumb, and aware that Håvard was trying to lead me away, but I pulled my arm free. I had no voice, not even the last shreds of anger were left to me. I felt stunned.

*

I don't recall all the details of that incident. But everything ended well. Agnes did not drown; Aksel must have managed to flip the kayak over and pull her out, haul her back to shore. I'm sure he knows all about life-saving.

I think it must also have been Aksel who saw to bringing the kayak back in afterwards. He's such a practical person, and it *is* his kayak, he wasn't likely to just let it go like that. That kayak is his freedom. That much I have understood.

A man must be allowed to enjoy his freedom in peace, that's what Granny would have said. You mustn't meddle with a man's freedom.

The others had retreated to the bathing hut, where they set up a sort of field hospital. Here they tended to Agnes. I learned later that they got her calmed down to the point where she actually dared to go out in the kayak again. That must have been Aksel's idea. He's not the type to give up at the first attempt.

Meanwhile, Håvard took care of me. He put his arm round my shoulders and led me firmly away. We walked up to his house. I had had no idea that he could move so surely and so resolutely. As for me, I could barely put one foot in front of the other, my legs were like jelly.

I stayed with him all evening. He made me coffee, and later he gave me a glass of sherry. I sat in his kitchen and gazed and gazed at him. I was trying to absorb the fact that he was an old man. He gazed at me too; neither of us has ever shown any restraint when it comes to looking at people. We stare at them the way an animal will stare at another of its own race. We didn't quite sniff each other's rear ends, but we weren't far off it.

Maybe no time at all has passed for us, I thought. Maybe everything is exactly the same as when I was nineteen. Maybe we can pick up where we left off.

But no.

As usual he came right to the point. I knew how direct he could be. I don't think I had ever really forgotten.

'You look like yourself,' he said.

'Is that supposed to be a compliment?'

'No. It's a fact. But you seem tense. You're trying to control too much. You didn't used to be like that.'

'I don't know what you mean,' I said.

'What's going on between you and Agnes?' he continued. 'I remember her. Her condition's worse now than when she was young. It's sad to see. But she's managing all right.'

'Oh, yes,' I said. 'Her condition has worsened. But she's certainly managing all right.'

'Is there anything you want to tell me?' he asked. 'Because there's something going on here.'

'I don't quite understand it myself,' I said.

'No, evidently not. But I suggest that you get it sorted out. Otherwise you two are going to kill one another.'

'Don't joke,' I said. 'It's not funny.'

He did not reply. He merely gazed at me.

'I think there's something you want to tell me,' he said.

'Go away,' I retorted.

'Try.'

'I can only think of one little thing – but it's totally irrelevant.'

'Okay, so what is this irrelevant little thing, then?'

'It's something that happened a long time ago,' I said. 'But it's got nothing to do with Agnes and me.'

'Tell me anyway.'

'It's something I saw once.'

'I see.'

'Something to do with a mother and a daughter.'

'A-ha. I had a suspicion it might be something like that.'

'They were dancing in a café.'

'Tell me about it,' Håvard said.

*

So I told him about the time I had seen Monika in a café in town. She had Ine with her. Ine can't have been more than three or four at the time; she had probably come to the café in a pushchair which her mother had brought inside and parked discreetly by the door.

'This was long before I met Aksel,' I said. 'I was sitting at a table with some people from the theatre, drinking wine – I used to do that a lot in those days, I was going through a restless patch.'

'You'd had restless patches before that too,' Håvard said. 'And you drank wine.'

'That's as may be,' I said. 'I didn't know what I wanted to do with my life, I didn't seem to be getting anywhere with the job I was doing. We were working on *The Seagull* by Chekhov, that was the time when I ended up using Agnes's ideas for the model. It was never really a success, that production. There was something about it that wasn't quite right.'

'There was a band playing on a little stage in the café. Simple, rather jolly jazz music, one of the band was singing, a number of the people at my table knew the words to all the songs and they were singing along, while some of the others kept shushing them because they were trying to have a conversation. I was fiddling with a camera that I had on my lap, and wasn't taking much interest in the music or the conversation. Suddenly I saw a woman who was sitting at the next table with a little girl get up, lift the child off her chair and carry her out on to the floor in front of the stage. She started to move to the music. After a while she put the little girl down and she danced too. She had so much rhythm in her little body, that child, but I noticed how she kept her eyes fixed on her Mum and copied all of her movements, as if her mother was the original and she was a copy.

'The talk around the table gradually died away and everybody stared at the two dancing in front of the musicians: the big woman and the little one. I raised my camera and began to take pictures. I stood up, moved round the room. I, too, kept time to the music, sank into the rhythm. I took shots from every angle. The woman noticed me, saw what I was doing, but it didn't seem to embarrass her; she looked as if she enjoyed having her photograph taken, she went on dancing as naturally as before, as if she and her daughter were alone in the room. And her daughter did just as her mother did, she too flashed a dazzling smile at the camera before fixing her eyes on her mum once more.

'All of a sudden I felt unwell, I had to sit down on a chair. The music kept on playing, I don't think anyone noticed that I had stopped taking photographs. From one minute to the next I had been filled with such a huge . . . I don't know, something was running out of me. I picked up my jacket and muttered something about having to go home. Then I dashed out of the café.'

'It was such a weird experience. I don't know what came over me.'

'Do you need to know?' Håvard said.

'The pictures turned out well. I used them in a production some years later. I projected the dancing mother and daughter on to the walls in the background in a rather spooky forest scene.'

'I saw that.'

'Did you?'

'Oh, I have been known to go and see your productions, you know.'

'Then you'll remember the programme for that play.'

'Vaguely.'

'There was a little note in it. At that point I had no way of knowing how to get in touch with my subjects, to ask their permission to use the pictures in the show; I didn't know who they were and I hadn't laid eyes on them since that day in the café. In the end I put a little note in the programme giving the name of the café and the date on which the pictures were taken, and thanked the two who had danced so beautifully. No one ever got in touch with me about those photographs.'

'When I saw that play I remember thinking that you had grown. You had become more independent. More yourself,' Håvard said.

'I'd known Aksel for some months before he invited me home to his place,' I went on. 'Eilif and Ine weren't home, but there were signs of them all over the little terraced flat, of course. The whole flat had plainly been designed with children in mind. There was a rope ladder hanging from the ceiling in the sitting-room and the floor was strewn with big cushions and a mattress on which certain people must have been in the habit of rolling and tumbling. Aksel had told me how good the children were at gymnastics. He was probably pretty good at it himself, of that I had no doubt.'

'Yes, he looks the gymnast type.'

'There was little to suggest that this place was home to a motherless family. On the walls in the hall hung framed photographs of all four of them, and several of Monika and the children alone. It was from them that I recognised her.'

'Did you tell Aksel?' Håvard asked.

'No,' I said.

'Why not?'

'It seemed too private, somehow. I've never found a way of introducing it naturally into the conversation,' I said.

'But you can tell me?'

'Yes,' I said, 'You I can tell.'

'What good does that do?' Håvard said.

'Go away,' I said.

It was late when I got back to the summer house. I was feeling a lot easier in my mind. Håvard had not said any more about the incident with the kayak down on the beach. Instead, he had begun to tell me about the exhibition he was putting together, and how he had asked the children to help him with it. I felt my interest quickening. I had forgotten how easy it was to talk to him. He and I had our own language from all those years ago, certain codes that neither of us had forgotten.

Aksel was sitting on the veranda waiting for me when I got back. I walked slowly towards him, through the garden and up the wheelchair ramp.

'Ah, you're here are you?' I said.

'Ah, you're there, are you?' said Aksel, smiling at me. Then he got up and came over to me.

'You've made a nice job of this,' he said, nodding at the ramp on which we were both standing. 'You really have.' He rocked back and forth a little, feeling the give in it.

Then he put his arms around me.

I could hardly remember the last time I had felt the warmth of him.

'Have you been waiting for me?' I murmured into his chest.

'Waiting and waiting,' he said. 'Come on, let's go to bed.'

The thought flashed through my mind: He's been sitting here waiting for me. Maybe he's jealous too.

Next morning no one at the summer house mentioned what had happened on the beach the previous evening. Aksel ate a quick breakfast, kissed me on the lips when no one was looking and set off back to Monika at the hospital.

Agnes spent most of her time on the sofa, sleeping. This was what Aksel had urged her to do, and she would never have dreamed of not doing as he said. His last words before he left were:

'Take good care of my patient, now. Make sure she gets plenty of rest. She's not to overexert herself. Don't forget she's sick. It was all a bit too much for her yesterday.'

The children and I nodded solemnly.

Sometimes, when no one saw me, I tiptoed into the sitting-room and considered her while she was sleeping. I could see by her face that some change was taking place inside her in her sleep. I couldn't quite put my finger on what it was.

I asked the children to stay out of the sitting-room, so as not to disturb Agnes.

Eilif went back over to Håvard's place for another piano lesson. Ine and I strolled down to the bathing hut for some more swimming practice and afterwards we parked ourselves in the gazebo to play patience. It was me who taught her to play patience, she'd never heard of it before.

She picked it up very quickly. I explained the function of the ace to her and about the kings and queens. And I showed her how to shuffle the cards, something which she found most intriguing. I'm pretty good at shuffling cards, I can do all sorts of tricks; stuff I've picked up from various old boyfriends: guys who were dab hands at shuffling cards and opening beer bottles in a dozen different ways, none of which involved using a bottle opener – useful skills like that.

Ine wanted to learn how to shuffle the cards too, but she found it hard to do. Her hands were too small, even she had to admit that. I had already perceived that she was like me in that respect: she couldn't stand it when she tried something and it didn't come out right. I found it hard not to smile.

She turned her back to me so that I wouldn't see her botched attempts. By way of encouragement I began to tell her all about patience and how my granny used to play it when I was a little girl on holiday at the summer house. Granny often used to sit out there in the gazebo in the evening, surveying the garden while slowly turning the cards picture-side up.

'Was she nice?' Ine asked, still with her back to me. I noticed how the salt water from her swim was dripping down her back and soaking her T-shirt. She had refused to let me rub her hair dry.

'Very nice.'

'But why did she play patience?'

'I think she did it in order to discover the outcome of whatever case she happened to be mulling over in her head at that particular time,' I said.

'What's an outcome?'

'An outcome is a result,' I replied. 'How something turns out. If Granny was wondering how something was going to turn out, she would ask a question, toss it into the air, so to speak. It had to be a question that could be answered with either a yes or a no. Then she played a game of patience while she considered the case. If the game came out, the outcome would be good. If it did not come out, the outcome would be bad.'

'So the cards sort of knew what fate would bring?' Ine said.

I stopped shuffling and stared at her in astonishment. She had clearly taken in everything I had said that day when she and Agnes were lying in the hammock.

'Sort of,' I said. 'But maybe that's something you should ask Agnes. She knows more about fate than I do.'

As I said these words, I felt a tremendous surge in my breast, it felt like something had shrugged and turned over. I had the urge to lean forward and plant a kiss on Ine's brow: she was so lovely, I thought. But I didn't. Instead, with trembling hands I laid out the cards for a game of Klondike and showed her how to turn first one card, then another. She followed my every move with her eyes, making no comment. I could see that she was taking it all in.

'I want this game of patience to show us how things are going to go with Mum!' she suddenly burst out.

'Ah, no, I don't think we should do that,' I answered quickly.

'Why not?'

'Because . . . because it's time to go in and start making lunch. Eilif will be back soon, and he's bound to be starving.'

I made lunch and served it to Agnes and the children on the veranda. With plenty of vegetables this time.

Agnes was very quiet. She seemed groggy with sleep, and yet somehow clearer than before. A new kind of tranquillity, I thought. A new air of tranquillity had settled over her while she slept.

After lunch Eilif wanted to try playing the piano in the gazebo. Ine and Agnes were going to play with the Barbie dolls.

'Or read a book, maybe?' Agnes suggested.

'No, Barbie dolls,' Ine said. 'We have to build a bit more of their house.'

It was late afternoon. All at once I realised how tired I was, totally drained in a way I couldn't remember ever feeling before. It had to be because of the baby. There were more and more signs now. Eventually I would just be one big sign that said: expectant mother.

I knew of only one place I could go. There was no rest for me in the summer house now. Agnes had passed her agitation on to me. She, on the other hand, seemed to have achieved some sort of balance.

For a moment, when I found myself at Håvard's front door for the second time, my courage failed me. I sat down on the bench outside his house and took a deep breath. From the top of the road I could just hear Eilif playing the piano in the gazebo. It still sounded awful. The air was so clear and the sound carried well, in little gusts of music, you might say. As if the wind were playing with the sound – possibly trying to remind me that the piano was out of tune.

Through the kitchen window I could see Håvard ambling across the room. I think he knew I was sitting there. When at last he came out on to the steps he didn't look surprised. He stood at the door and regarded me with narrowed eyes as I got up from the bench and went to him, up the short flight of stone steps. My head was spinning.

I think he had known the minute he saw me down by the bathing hut the evening before that I was pregnant. But he hadn't said anything; that wasn't his way.

We talked for hours. Outside, the light slowly faded. We sat each on our own side of the kitchen table, each fiddling with our own coffee cup. This time it was his turn to talk.

Håvard spoke in a soft, warm voice. Occasionally I broke in with a question, as if I were a journalist. I understood there was a story that had to be told, one which was for my ears only.

He told me the thoughts that had gone through his head when I left him, back when I was nineteen, after hearing the rumours of incest. Told me how he hadn't known what to do with himself. And how he had thought we would get back together, that time when I contacted him in Berlin. That he had been so happy, but nervous. And so disappointed when I left him for the second time.

He said he was glad, but not surprised, that I had come back into his life.

'You never used to talk like this,' I said. 'You never spoke about your feelings when we were together.'

'No, when we were together I was merely middle-aged,' Håvard said. 'Now I am old. Your idea of what is important changes as you get older.'

'I don't know how you can say you're old. According to my calculations you haven't even turned seventy yet.'

'Ah, but your calculations don't allow for the fact that I haven't taken very good care of myself,' he said. 'I'm paying for that now. I've let my illness go too long untreated, I'm afraid.'

'Have you spoken to a doctor?'

'I don't like doctors.'

'You can't go through life talking only to people you like,' I said.

'Oh, yes you can.'

'Were you ill when we were together?' I asked. 'Because I certainly wasn't aware of it.'

'Well, I had so many other things to think about in those days,' he said. 'I was tough, I thought I could handle anything. And taking insulin injections wasn't really my style.'

'So now you find that you can't, in fact, handle anything?' I teased, wrinkling up my nose at him.

But the joke fell flat. He didn't reply, but simply rested his head against the wall behind him and closed his eyes.

No more was said about his illness, or about the two of us. For a while there was silence in the kitchen. Then I rose slowly and walked round the table to the man sitting on the cushioned bench.

'I was just wondering if you could hold me for a minute,' I whispered. 'I'm so tired. I need to rest.'

He opened his eyes and regarded me steadily.

'Come here,' he said, and turned so that he was leaning against the cushions at the end of the bench, with his face to the window. I wriggled in between the table and the bench and climbed up beside him. He spread his knees to make room for me and I arranged myself between his long, skinny legs with my back to him. Then he bent forward and put his arms around me. Rested his chin on my shoulder.

I could feel his bristly chin against my ear, and the great warmth that flowed from him.

Being close to him has always been like sitting next to a big tiled stove.

'I can see you haven't shaved in a while,' I murmured.

'And it'll be a while before I do, too,' he said. Then he leaned back, propping himself up against the cushions.

'Do you feel rested now?' he asked.

'Don't rush me. I'll tell you when.'

'You musn't feel that I'm pressuring you.'

'I never feel pressured.'

'Good. But just remember to let me know.'

'Okay . . . now. Now I think maybe I'm a little rested.'

'Only a little?'

'Don't rush me.'

We were right back where we had been fifteen years earlier: the same close, almost claustrophobic, to and fro of questions, the tiny shifts in the rhythm of our exchanges.

And the smell of him, just the same: warm and sweet. Like a baby, perhaps, I thought. But I wasn't sure how a baby smelled.

Little by little I let the tension in my back and shoulders relax, and sank back against him.

We sat like that for a long time. I rested.

I remembered a game we had often played when we were lovers. It was a game of question and answer: each of us had to ask the other one three questions, the only rule being that the questions had to be answered with complete and utter honesty. The aim was to leave the other person lost for an answer. It was up to the winner to decide on the forfeit for not answering. Usually it was fixed at a certain number of kisses. But that was then, I thought.

'Do you remember Three Questions?' I asked.

'Three Questions? Oh, that.'

'Are you ready?'

'What, now?'

'Yes, now.'

'Here?'

'I asked if you were ready.'

'Okay. I'm ready. Who's going to start?'

'I am, of course.'

'As always.'

'Right, here we go,' I said. 'First question: what did you think when you saw me down by the bathing hut yesterday?'

'I thought: there she is.'

'Were you surprised?'

'Not at all.'

'How did you think I looked?'

'Older. Angry.'

'Angry in what way?'

'Ha!' he cried. 'That's your fourth question. Now it's my turn. You've got to stick to the rules, girl.'

'Your turn.'

'Why aren't you up at the summer house with the others?'

'Because I don't feel at home there any more.'

'Why not?'

'Because Agnes is in the process of taking over up there.'

'And what do you intend to do about that?'

I paused for a moment.

'Pass,' I said.

'I get the impression you're not feeling particularly competitive today,' Håvard remarked.

'No need to sound so smug,' I said. 'Okay, you won. You'll have to come up with a suitable forfeit.'

But he had no answer to that.

It was dark outside. I knew I ought to be getting home, but I couldn't bring myself to leave.

Our reflection loomed into view in the kitchen window. Who's that? I asked myself. Well I never. A woman in her thirties snuggled up in the arms of a bearded, old man?

But what that reflection showed was: rest.

'I feel my competitive instincts returning,' I told Håvard. 'New round. I'll start: who's that?' I raised my hand slowly and pointed to the window-pane.

'That's Håvard and Molly,' he said.

'And what are they doing?'

'Sitting one behind the other on the bench, looking at the window.'

'Why are they doing that?'

'Pass.' he said.

'Okay. I'll give you another chance.'

'Is this a new rule? The winner can give the loser another chance?'

'Yes,' I said. 'Hasn't that always been in the rules?'

'Definitely not. The loser never used to get another chance.'

I realised that he was talking about us now. 'Well, fire away. Ask your question,' he said. He made a circular motion with one hand, as if wanting the film to roll faster.

'Why am I sad?' I asked.

'Because you have a secret,' Håvard said.

'Why don't I tell you my secret?' I said.

'Because you've already decided what you are going to do, and you don't want me telling you you're wrong,' he said.

'And what is the secret?'

'Pass.'

'Don't fool about! This is important. I'm not playing any more.'

'Hey, it's not just up to you to say when the game's over,' he said. 'My turn to ask. Why are you sad?'

'Because I have a secret.'

'And what is that secret?'

'I'm pregnant by a man who may not want to have children with me,' I said. 'And he doesn't know yet.'

'I see. And what do you intend to do about that?'

'I've decided to keep the baby.'

'No more questions,' he said. 'Game over.'

I felt a faint twinge of disappointment. I did want to go on playing after all.

*

I opened my eyes. Håvard nodded at my reflection in the window. I didn't know what he meant by that nod.

'Time to decide on our forfeits?' I said.

'Yes.'

'I think we should say that we each won one round,' I said. 'Me first.'

'As usual, yes.'

'Your forfeit is for you to come to Ine's birthday party. She's going to be seven. We have to have a party for her.'

'Who else will be there?'

'You'll be the only guest. Her birthday's on Midsummer's Eve.'

'Aksel will be there, though, won't he?'

'Yes, Aksel will be there. But he's her father.'

'And the father of the child you are expecting, I take it?'

'Yes. He counts as family, not as a guest. Please come. It would mean so much to Ine to have a guest there too.'

'Ine's afraid her mother is going to die,' Håvard said. 'Have you any idea how she's doing?'

'Not really. But Aksel's with her the whole time. He says the operation went well, but that they're going to give her radio-therapy, just to be on the safe side.'

'Well, we'll have to keep our fingers crossed.'

'Yes. And you can see why it's so important for Eilif to learn to play that Bellmann piece on the piano?'

'Of course,' he said. 'His idea is to make his Mum so happy that she'll have to get better.'

'Right. I thought maybe I should suggest that he call her and play it for her on Ine's birthday. That would be the perfect occasion. Do you think he's ready for it?'

'Not quite. I'd best go over it with him again tomorrow.'

'And I need to get the piano tuned.'

'Yes. He said it was out of tune.'

'And you promise to come to her birthday party?'

Håvard kept his eyes fixed on my reflection in the mirror. He promised nothing.

He's not the type to make promises., but he is the type to listen to what one says.

'Now it's my turn to decide your forfeit,' he said. 'Listen carefully, because I'm only going to say this once: you have to invite Eilif's and Ine's mother to the party. It's not me Ine needs there as guest, it's her mother.'

'But Monika's ill. She's in hospital, she's just had an operation. They would never let her out so soon.'

'I know. But invite her anyway. You can only do your best. Make sure that the children get to see her as soon as possible. Show them that she's alive.'

I wandered slowly homewards. It was completely dark by this time. My legs felt like lead and I was still tired. But unlike earlier in the day I felt at peace, both in my body and my mind.

When I entered the garden I saw that Agnes and the kids had lit candles in every room. The summer house looked like a shimmering castle.

Inside I could see the three of them sitting round the coffee table, bent over a game. They looked as though they were laughing.

I had but one thought in my mind the next day, and that was to get the piano tuned. That was one way of making a space for myself in the summer house again; something I could do for all of us. Something I could do for Eilif and his mother.

After a less than chatty breakfast, Agnes announced that she and Ine had another date with the Barbie dolls on the veranda. They were gradually building a whole village out there.

Eilif muttered something about having to practise a bit more, and left for Håvard's as soon as he had finished eating. It was almost as though he felt time was running out.

I sat down at Granny's desk and found the piano tuner's name in the telephone book. I didn't stop to think, but quickly keyed in his number, using three fingers. He answered right away. He had a tiny, wrinkly piano-tuner voice. He had to be a very old man by now.

I introduced myself and explained why I was calling. He clearly knew who I was, he remembered both the piano and Granny. But he couldn't come.

'My mother is dead,' he said brusquely in that wrinkly voice. It sounded as if he hadn't used it in ages. 'I don't get out any more. I'm blind.'

'I know,' I said. 'But this is very important. Are you sure there's no one else who could drive you down?'

'No one.'

'Well, maybe you could take a taxi?'

'A taxi? That would be very expensive.'

'I'll pay,' I said.

The taxi pulled up outside the house and dropped off the doddery old man, and it was as if he brought with him another time; a time

I could only just recall, but to which, somehow, I belonged. Granny's time.

He was even smaller in the flesh than he sounded on the phone. I didn't remember him being so small. I helped him out of the car, paid the driver and was given the number to call when he was to be collected.

The first thing the piano tuner said to me after I said hello was:

'So you're the granddaughter. I remember you. You look like your grandmother.'

What a strange thing to say: I mean, the man was blind!

And then he started talking about Granny. It felt a bit odd to hear her being described by someone who had known a completely different side of her. I realised that there had to have been some truth in the rumours that he had stayed for a while at Granny's flat after his mother died. How else could he have known her so well, I thought. He must have drunk Granny's red wine and slept in her guest room. I imagined that his voice must still be on one of the tapes in her flat.

I put a hand under his arm and led him gently over to the gazebo. He felt his way with his white stick and seemed none too willing to walk through the garden.

It was plain that he was not happy about where we had put the piano. He felt the instrument would be far too vulnerable to shifts in temperature down there. Granny had always put the instrument in the sitting-room. The instrument ought never to be positioned next to an outer wall, far less an uninsulated one. He never used the word piano, he simply called it the instrument. I liked him for that. He was not to know that the gazebo was the only spot on the property where we could get a signal on the mobile phone, or that the piano had been put there for one reason and one reason only: so that Eilif could perform his mobile-phone concert for Monika. I assured him that it would not be left out there in the winter.

After a lot more talk about Granny and what a marvellous woman she was, I managed to persuade him to tune the instrument, even though its situation was not ideal. I promised him that I would have it sent back to town as soon as the holidays were over. That he could tune it again then, and that it would never, never be moved again.

He spent hours working on it. I sat among the cushions, watching him. He had left a tuning-fork lying on the table. I sat fingering it, then tapped it lightly against my kneecap, as I had seen him do. It produced an incredibly strong, clear sound, that little steel instrument, it seemed to set the whole gazebo vibrating. I held it to my ear, shut my eyes and felt the sound reverberating inwards and downwards, deep down into my stomach.

'Did you hear that, Tiny,' I whispered under my breath. The piano tuner turned to look at me, as if he had heard what I said.

'Concert pitch,' he said.

Ine and Agnes spent the whole morning on the veranda, playing with the Barbie dolls. They were still at it when the piano-tuner left in the taxi. I could hear them talking and laughing, they were obviously having a lovely time. It sounded as if they were building yet another house for the dolls: I heard something about them needing another cardboard box. Every now and again I walked up the garden towards the veranda, to listen to them. They never noticed me standing there and I always returned to the gazebo. I stayed there until Eilif got back from Håvard's place.

I jumped up and ran to meet him.

'Eilif!' I cried. 'I've got a surprise for you!'

He stopped and smiled at me.

'I've had the piano tuned! Now you can play all you like!'

He followed me into the gazebo, sat down at the piano.

'I'll sit here on the bench,' I said. 'And you can pretend that I'm your Mum, lying in bed at the hospital with the mobile beside her, listening to you play. This'll be like a little dress rehearsal. I thought maybe we could call her tomorrow. It's Ine's birthday tomorrow, isn't it?'

He nodded.

Then he sat down at the piano and played 'The butterfly in the garden' for me. It was a beautiful little concert. He played so well. He had a lovely touch. Håvard had done a very good job with him. Splendid chords.

I clapped my hands.

'Well done, Eilif!' I said. 'You'll be the star turn at the birthday party.'

'No,' he said.

'No?'

'I want to do it now. There's no time to lose. I can't wait until tomorrow. I'm ready now.'

So we went up to the veranda to get Agnes and Ine.

This is what we did: first, Eilif sent a text message to Aksel, asking if he was at the hospital with his mother. Which, of course, he was. Then Eilif sent his father another message, asking him to find the ear-piece for the mobile and stick it in Monika's ear. I saw the speed with which he wrote the messages, his thumbs rattling over the keypad on the tiny mobile. He seemed quite galvanised; he read out what he had written to Ine and me: *The next call you receive will be a concert. It's a surprise for Mum.*

He showed us the message he received back from his father, written in capitals, with no punctuation:

OK THIS IS EXCITING MUM IS LYING HERE ALL READY WITH THE EARPIECE IN GOOD LUCK DAD

Ine and I took it in turns to hold the mobile. We held it at what we thought would be a suitable distance from the instrument. Agnes had taken her seat right alongside Eilif, as if she was all set to step in and help the pianist, should it be necessary. Take over the keys.

But Agnes, I thought to myself, you can't play the piano. What good would you be?

We keyed in the number of Aksel's mobile and Ine checked that we had got through to him. Then we nodded to Eilif. He began to play.

It sounded so beautiful.

'*A butterfly in the garden seen, wings through mists of frost and down,*' I breathed, '*to make therein its bower green, and its bed in a blossom's crown.*'

'What's a bower?' Ine whispered.

'A bedchamber,' Agnes said, turning to us.

When Eilif finished playing we, the audience, remained silent for a few moments, before I handed him the phone. We heard him talking to his mother. Ine was sitting beside me, rigid and tense, feet anxiously tapping the floor. I bent down to her and whispered:

'I think you should invite your Mum to your birthday party tomorrow.'

She gazed at me, wide-eyed.

'D'you think so? But she's in the hospital. Doesn't she have to stay there for a while longer?'

'Why don't you have a word with her,' I said. 'Just suggest it. It's up to her, anyway. She won't do anything she doesn't feel she can manage, or that she's not allowed to do.'

She walked over to Eilif, stood right next to him and stared hard at him, as if she might be able to tell what her mother was saying from his expression. After a minute or two he gave her the mobile.

'Hello Mummy,' she said.

Oh, the sound of those words. The longing.

I turned to Agnes. She had closed her eyes. Something wet was running down her cheeks.

*

Ine had a long coversation with Monika. Eventually she looked at me and handed me the phone.

'Mum wants to talk to you,' she said.

'To me?'

She nodded. I put the mobile to my ear.

Monika was crying. She must have been so moved. Her voice was weak and hoarse, not unlike the piano tuner's. I could tell by the way she spoke that she was on very strong painkillers.

She thanked me from the bottom of her heart for taking such good care of her children. And for organising this concert. She understood that I had got hold of a piano for her son. That was so kind of me, she said.

'It was the least I could do,' I told her.

Then she begged me to bring the children to the hospital. Right away. She needed to see them. She missed them so much.

'Well . . .' I said. 'Do you think you're strong enough?'

Then Aksel took the phone. I could hear the emotion in his voice, too, but he seemed to be trying hard to sound brisk and nurselike when he spoke to me. That's because Monika's there, I thought.

Aksel asked me to pack the kids into the car and take a run up to the hospital right away. He thought Monika could cope with a five-minute visit. It was really important that she got to see them as soon as possible. I had never heard him sound so insistent before, he couldn't hide the urgency in his voice. He must have been longing to have his family all together again.

'We're on our way,' I said. 'We'll be there in an hour.'

'Thanks,' he said. 'This means a lot to Monika.'

'And to you,' I said. But he didn't answer.

Agnes insisted on coming with us to the hospital.

'Are you sure you're up to it?' I asked. She nodded mutely.

'Well,' I said. 'In that case we'd better fold up the wheelchair and take it with us. You're not to go tiring yourself out on those crutches. I promised Aksel I would look after you.'

She nodded again.

When we got to the hospital, Agnes and I waited outside in the corridor and observed the scene being enacted in Monika's room. Agnes was in the wheelchair, I stood behind her, stock-still, with my hands on the handles. We both stared through the open door.

It was a four-bedded ward, like the one Agnes had been in that time when I visited her because I didn't dare to go and see Mum, who was on the floor below. That was just before Mum died.

But this was another ward, with another Mum. This Mum was going to get well. She had to.

Ine and Eilif were thrilled to bits to see Monika. They all but crawled into bed beside her, although I could see that they were doing their best to be careful. There was a framed photograph of them on her bedside table. They were sitting in a boat, gazing solemnly at the camera. It must have been taken the summer before.

We saw Aksel wrap his arms round Monika and the children on the bed; he looked as though he was trying to tie his family together like a knot. Presumably they were talking excitedly about the concert and how well it had gone; and how fantastic it was that Eilif had learned to play 'The butterfly in the garden'. Eilif looked so proud, he was positively glowing.

I thought: I hope Ine gets a chance to say that she's learning to swim. She has to have something to give her Mum, too.

I gripped the handles of the wheelchair and proceeded to push Agnes along the corridor, away from this scene.

'Are we leaving?' she asked quietly.

'We'll just take ourselves off for a while,' I said. 'Give them some privacy. It's not a stage show, you know.'

On impulse, I nipped round in front of the wheelchair and bent down so I was level with her. I saw what a big effort she made to pull herself together. She must have been exhausted. I ran a hand over her wet cheek.

'Everything's going to be fine,' I said. 'Monika is not going anywhere. She'll pull through all right. And so will you. You've just had a lot on your plates recently, the pair of you. You both need to rest.'

When we got back from the hospital that evening, and after the children had fallen asleep, happy and exhausted, I sat on the veranda among the houses in the little village that Agnes and Ine had built out there. It's Ine's birthday tomorrow, I thought to myself. I have to bake a cake. I have to get this house cleaned and tidied. I have to decorate the place for the party. I have to make everything look bright and gay. I have to make up for Monika, since she can't come to the party. I have to be her stand-in.

And tomorrow morning I need to get Agnes up the stairs to the kids' room with me and the cake. How am I going to manage that? I'll need to carry her on my back.

I sat out there for ages. I felt as though I was becoming one with the soft gloom. It was the second shortest, second lightest night of the year.

Eventually I went into the kitchen and started baking. I found Granny's recipe book and looked up her hand-written recipe for sponge cake. I'm hopeless when it comes to making cakes, it's not something I've done much of.

After a while, Agnes came rolling in in the wheelchair.

'What are you up to?' she asked. But when I told her I was making a birthday cake she went all huffy and peculiar. I realised that she must have been planning to make her own cake, after I had gone to bed.

'Why don't we make one together?' I said. 'You're bound to be better at this then I am.'

She nodded irritably.

And she did try to help, still sitting in the wheelchair, but only succeeded in getting into a right muddle; her hands started shaking and she dropped the whisk on to her knees. I was starting to get irritable myself.

I tried to pull the baking bowl away from her, remarking a mite too sharply that I'd obviously be better doing it myself after all. I happened to graze her hair with the spatula, leaving behind a thick, sticky streak of batter. She immediately let go of the bowl and sat with her hands lying limply in her lap.

And then it struck me: she was absolutely worn out. I felt a sudden stab of tenderness for her: Agnes wasn't well. What a way to behave!

'I'm sorry, Agnes,' I said. She eyed me in bewilderment, as if she couldn't believe that I was actually apologizing to her. She looked as though she had considered making some sarcastic riposte, but didn't have the strength.

I put the cake in the oven. While it was baking, I gave her a hand to take her top off and helped her into the bathroom. I filled the wash-basin with lukewarm water and arranged a chair in such a way that she could sit astride it in front of the basin.

She bowed her head over the washbasin and let me wash her hair. I looked at the skinny, white neck which had to bear all the heavy thoughts inside her head. I ran a finger over it, before giving her a good, gentle shampoo. Afterwards I wrapped her hair in a towel, then gave her some assistance in combing it out. Finally, I helped her to get settled in her bed on the sofa in the sitting-room.

But I had forgotten about the sponge cake in the oven. It was a total disaster: runny in the middle and dark-brown on top.

I sat looking at the cake for a long time that night, before eventually going to bed. I was so tired. I'll decorate it in the morning, I told myself. I'll just have to make sure to pile on so much whipped cream and berries that nothing else will be visible. And I'll need to pick some flowers.

After a few hours of restless sleep I got up and went outside. The sky was already light. I wandered around the garden barefoot in my nightgown, armed with the kitchen scissors and snipping off red and pink flower-heads. I suddenly noticed how many weeds had sprung up in the flower beds over the past few weeks.

I'll have to do something about that, I thought. It looks as though I'm going to have to learn how to weed. Maybe Håvard knows something about weeding.

I went back to the house and decorated the sponge. It looked great; you couldn't see that it was burnt. I spent a long time completely engrossed in this task: it was like working on an idea at the theatre. There, I thought. At least there's something I can do.

I remembered the cake that Agnes and I had baked when we were in fourth grade and I spent the night at her place. That time when she told me about the sisters in the mirror.

Once the cake was finished I went up to my room to rest for a while before getting dressed. I must have nodded off for a couple of minutes, because I woke with a start at the sound of Aksel's car pulling up outside the house. I ran over to the window. Down in the sitting-room I could hear Agnes fighting to get off the sofa and dropping the crutches on to the floor with a bang in the process.

Aksel had a carrier bag from a toyshop in town with him, there were a number of parcels sticking out of it. When he saw me standing at the bedroom window he waved, but made no attempt to smile at me. Then he evidently caught sight of Agnes at the sitting-room window on the floor below me, and waved to her too.

I was so relieved to see him. I thought: Agnes feels the same. She's so relieved to see him. We can't do this alone.

We made a really nice birthday morning ceremony out of it, we three. I carried the cake. Aksel helped Agnes up the stairs. On the way up he whispered to us that Monika had asked him to buy a present from Agnes and me too, he assumed we hadn't had a chance to pick up anything down here. He had bought a mouth organ.

I paused on the landing, pressed my cheek to his for a moment and quietly thanked him. Agnes thanked him too. Neither of us had really given any thought to a present. Outside the door of the spare room we stopped and looked at one another, all three. I cleared my throat and began to sing:

'Hooray, hooray . . .'

'. . . it's your birthday today,' Aksel chimed in, in his deep voice. Agnes didn't sing, she's never had much of a singing voice. But she let go of Aksel, opened the door and hobbled ahead of us into the room on her crutches, cutting right in front of me. I came behind, carrying the sumptuous cake with its seven candles.

Both Ine and Eilif were sitting up in Ine's bed, bright-faced and wide-awake. They smiled.

After a birthday-cake breakfast I sent Aksel, Agnes and the kids off to the beach for a morning dip. Once they had gone I threw myself into the car and drove up to the local shop to get the stuff for the party that evening. I bought beer and sausages and everything I could find that was brightly coloured and looked as if it would taste good or could be used for decoration.

Back at the house I carried everything into the kitchen, and then some impulse prompted me to walk down to the bathing hut and spy on them. I guessed they would still be out swimming.

They didn't see me. Aksel had pushed Agnes down to the beach in the wheelchair. She was parked out on the jetty. Eilif and Ine were in the water underneath her. I couldn't see Aksel, he had to be in the hut.

I stood a little way off, watching them. I hadn't brought my costume, I had just wanted to see what they were doing. Evidently Agnes had not taken her costume with her either, she was sitting fully dressed in the wheelchair.

'Why don't you just swim in your bare skin!' I heard Ine shout.

'No way,' Agnes called back with a laugh. 'You're not getting me in that fjord with nothing on! I'm quite happy sitting here watching. And anyway, didn't you have something you wanted to show your dad?'

'Hey, Dad!' Ine called from the water to her father in the bathing hut. 'Hurry up! I've got something to show you!'

Aksel stepped out on to the little ladder down to the water. He looked a little self-conscious, as if he didn't really feel like parading himself in front of Agnes. His body gleamed white in the sun. He was just as I remembered. That lovely, strong body. He hadn't had much sun this summer, that was clear. But he looked good, all the same.

I saw how Agnes stared at him.

'Come on, Tarzan!' she cried. 'Hop in! Ine has something to show you!'

'It looks a bit cold to me,' Aksel called back, pretending to shudder at the thought.

'It's not cold at all,' the children yelled from the shallows. 'Just dive in!'

And Aksel dived in. It wasn't the most elegant of dives, he made a pretty big splash. The spray hit Agnes up on the jetty.

'You beast!' she squealed. 'What are you trying to do – drown me?'

I thought: This is not for my eyes.

I went back to the house.

I had to tidy up and make things nice for the party. I decorated the place with all the things I had bought at the shop, together with whatever else I happened to come across in the house. I built the whole thing around the houses that Agnes and Ine had made for the Barbie dolls. This is the village, I thought. It is inhabited.

It was a bit theatrical, but very colourful. I hoped Ine would like it.

The others hung out around the jetty for most of the morning. Eventually Aksel came up to the house to see me. His hair was wet. He ran an eye over the veranda and the garden.

'Wow,' he said. 'Somebody's having a party, I see!'

'Uh-huh. Is it a bit much, do you think?'

'No, it can never be too fancy for Ine's birthday party,' he said. 'As I see you have discovered. Oh, by the way – we had a little accident down by the bathing hut. But everything's fine now.'

'How do you mean?'

'I just thought I'd better tell you now, so you're warned. We'll have to go easy on Agnes this evening. She fell off the jetty into the water. She's all right now, though. I pulled her out. I need a blanket, and she could probably do with a bit of cossetting.'

'Again? What is all this?' I cried angrily. 'God, you've got a full-time job of it, being that woman's own personal lifeguard!'

He didn't say anything. Just eyed me closely. Then he came up and put his arms around me.

'Thanks for doing all this for Ine,' he said. 'For us. She's going to have a wonderful birthday. And thanks for bringing them to the hospital yesterday. It meant the world to Monika. She was so happy.'

I loosened his arms, stepped into the sitting-room and fetched a blanket.

'I wish you'd have a word with Håvard when you get the chance,' I said. 'He's terrified of doctors, and he's decided that he's fated to go blind because he has diabetes.'

I noticed how the nurse in Aksel instantly came to the fore.

'Well, if you live long enough with diabetes, without getting treatment, it's bound to leave its mark,' he said. 'I did notice he was looking rather frail. Has he had a slight stroke, by any chance?'

'I don't know,' I said. 'But he needs to see a doctor.'

I stood and watched as he walked off through the garden with Granny's blanket over his arm.

And there, coming through the lilac bushes towards him as if on cue, was Håvard. He was carrying something big – I couldn't see what it was. The two men stood chatting for quite some time.

'Good,' I whispered to myself.

Aksel slapped Håvard on the shoulder before carrying on down to the beach with the blanket. That's the sort of thing men do when they've just made a deal, I thought.

Håvard made his way slowly up to the veranda, where I was setting the table. I acted as though I wasn't pleased to see him. He put down the bundle he was carrying, took a seat in one of the wicker chairs and regarded me. I said nothing.

'You're in a bad mood again,' he said. 'You're more given to bad moods now than you used to be. What is it?'

'I'm not in a bad mood,' I said. 'I'm just a bit annoyed at Agnes. She makes herself out to be so helpless.'

He made no comment.

'What have you got there?' I motioned towards his bundle.

'None of your business. Do you need a hand?' he asked, with a nod at the table.

'You can see very well that I don't.'

'Good.'

'Are you here for the party, or merely making a tour of inspection?'

'For the party,' he said.

'I saw you talking to Aksel down there,' I said, nodding in the direction of the garden.'

'We had a quick word, yes.'

'What did you talk about?'

'None of your business.'

'Oh, don't be like that.'

'We had a little chat about my health. He thinks I ought to see a doctor. According to him, they might be able to stop my eyesight from getting any worse by means of laser treatment.'

'Ah, you don't want to go blind, after all?' I said.

'Well, obviously, if there's an alternative . . .'

'Then you'll have to go to the doctor.'

'I suppose so.'

'I can drive you there. But you'll have to call and make the appointment yourself,' I told him, binding tissue-paper roses round the balustrade of the veranda with wire as I spoke. 'You'll have to learn to ask for help when you need it.'

'Speak for yourself,' he said.

'Move your butt,' I said. 'You're in the way.'

'Move your own butt,' he retorted cheerfully, taking a swipe at me.

At long last the others arrived back from the bathing hut. They made a strange sight. Agnes was in the wheelchair, with Aksel pushing her. He and the children must have pulled her wet clothes off her and dressed her in Aksel's trousers and T-shirt. They had got her back into the chair and tucked their towels and the blanket around her. She looked half-drowned and as well packed in as a parcel stamped 'Handle With Care!'

From the children's garbled, incoherent account I gathered that she had fallen in the water just after I had been spying on them down by the jetty. Ine had been eager to show her father the strokes I had taught her, and Aksel had supported her while she showed him what she had learned. Eilif told me that it hadn't taken her long to get the hang of it: her Dad had let go of her and she had swum three strokes unaided.

'Nearly four!' Ine chimed in.

'But Agnes got a little too carried away, I think,' Eilif went on. 'She wheeled herself right up to the edge of the jetty and leaned over to get a better look. And then she fell in.'

'She made a huge splash!' Ine cried excitedly. 'It was really scary.'

'And then Dad had to go in and save her again,' Eilif continued. 'He must be getting used to it by now.'

That was no accident, I thought to myself. She did it on purpose. She wanted to be rescued by Aksel again. Feel his arms around her.

It wasn't hard to imagine it:

The loud splash as she hit the water. The pressure on her body. The grey and green hues, everything dissolving round about her. Sounds fading away. The strange feeling of her limbs threshing under water. The undercurrent seeming to drag her down.

'Maybe I'm going to die,' she might have thought.

I think she must have felt oddly calm and content. Time may have stopped for her, the water become still, it was possibly quite pleasant not to hear any noise.

And then someone grabbed hold of her and pulled her back to the surface: Aksel's strong, white body.

He told us that she had struck out at him down there on the bottom, she was waving her arms about. But perhaps she sensed that he was stronger than her, perhaps it even felt as though the sea-bed itself wanted them to rise to the surface; with a mighty heave it sent Aksel and Agnes shooting upwards.

In my mind's eye I saw her wide, staring eyes as they broke the surface. His strength. How scared they must have been, both of them. And the children.

Afterwards I imagine that she lay on the pebble beach, coughing up water. The children must have bent fearfully down to her. Felt her all over.

Everyone who was there has cited what came next in exactly the same way. The first thing she said once she had got her breath back was:

'Four strokes all by yourself! Ine, we have to call your Mum.'

Then she hawked up a great gob of slime.

'I saw her boobies when we changed her clothes,' Ine sniggered confidentially. 'They're enormous.'

Håvard got up off the chair behind me, from which he had listened to the story of Agnes's ducking.

'Happy birthday, Ine,' he said with grave courtesy. 'Seven years old, I hear? Well, well.' He handed her the bundle he had brought with him. He obviously hadn't had any wrapping paper: only now did I notice that he had wrapped the present in the oilcloth from his kitchen table. And tied the belt from a threadbare dressing-gown around it.

Ine giggled and took the parcel from him. She opened it straight away. It was a watering can. Håvard's watering can. It was pretty filthy, and the bottom was thick with dirt and twigs and leaves, he had made no attempt to clean it before wrapping it up.

'What a funny present!' Ine cried gleefully. 'Can I take it back to town with me?'

'Of course, you can,' Håvard said.

I noticed how Agnes turned her face up to his, almost against her will. It broke in a little smile. I could tell that she liked this gift which Ine had been given, and the manner in which he had presented it. You'd think it was meant for her, I said to myself.

Then I had an idea.

'Tonight we're going to build a bonfire!' I said. 'It is Midsummer's Eve, after all! We all have to go and gather wood! And Strøm's is an excellent place to start! You'll find loads of rubbish down there that's perfect for burning. Take the wheelbarrow!'

'Rubbish? At my place? I don't know what you're talking about,' Håvard said.

Aksel and the children and I went down to Strøm's and helped him to clear the house and garden of all sorts of old junk. We wheeled several barrowloads up to my garden for the bonfire. Agnes lay in the hammock, resting, while we worked. When we got back to the house she appeared to be asleep.

'Nobody builds a Midsummer bonfire in their garden,' Aksel said. 'Midsummer bonfires should be built on the beach. You're going to have a great pile of ashes in the middle of your lawn. It won't look very nice.'

'That's as maybe,' I said. 'But no one here is going back to the beach for a while. There's to be no more falling into the water, and no more lifesaving. Twice is quite enough.'

I glowered at him.

'There,' I said, pointing to a spot on the lawn in front of the gazebo. 'That's where the bonfire is going to be. So you can start piling everything up over there.'

It was a splendid birthday dinner. We sat round the big table on the veranda and drank toasts and had a perfectly lovely time. Everyone admired my decorations and Eilif took photographs of us with his mobile. We sang the birthday song to Ine again; she had to stand on a chair while we sang and clapped and toasted her. She was beaming from ear to ear, but I could see that she was getting tired. Eventually she fell asleep on Aksel's lap. He carried her in to the sofa in the sitting-room.

I saw Agnes turn and look longingly after them. I'm sure she wouldn't have minded being carried in, too.

'Maybe you could do with a lie-down too,' I suggested. 'You've had an eventful day.'

She nodded.

Eilif and I helped her into the hammock again and soon she was sleeping like a baby.

During dinner I had had an idea. Instead of starting on the washing-up, while Ine and Agnes were resting and the boys were putting the finishing touches to the bonfire, I went down to the gazebo, to organise a special birthday show. With me I took the big roll of canvas, a hammer and nails. I nailed canvas over all the gazebo windows, then I pushed the double doors on to the garden wide open and hung a length of canvas over the doorway too, so that it looked like a cinema screen.

'What are you doing?' Eilif inquired, coming up with his arms full of junk for the bonfire which he had found in Granny's tool-shed.

'I thought I would put on a little show for Ine, seeing as it's her birthday,' I said. 'I'd like to try out some ideas I have for the production I'm working on.'

'Are you going to show a film?' he asked, nodding at the canvas screen.

'No, better than that, I hope,' I said. 'Wait and see. I'll tell you when I'm ready. How's it going with the bonfire?'

'It's nearly finished. Strøm found a can of petrol in the shed. It's going to be brilliant.'

I went up to my room to fetch the shadow puppets I had made, inspired by the dolls I had taken from Agnes's flat. And the model of the rising castle.

It was late in the evening. The light was starting to fade.

Very gently, I woke first Ine, then Agnes. Both were drowsy and cranky, and in all likelihood would rather have been left to sleep. But that was how I wanted them: I wished to meet them on the borderline.

Meekly they allowed me to escort them down to the gazebo. Aksel, Eilif and Håvard were already there.

I checked that Håvard had matches in his pocket.

'Were you going to have a cigarette?' he inquired doubtfully.

'No, but I want you to light the bonfire the minute the show is over,' I said. 'So you need to have some matches handy. Timing is of the essence here. Okay?'

'Okay,' Håvard said.

It was pitch-black inside the gazebo now that I had covered the windows. One by one I let them in by lifting a corner of the canvas covering the doorway. Ine first. Then Eilif. then Aksel. Then Håvard. He patted the matchbox in his pocket and winked at me, as if giving me a secret sign. I smiled.

Finally I let Agnes in. I helped her out of the wheelchair and half-lifted her on to the bench among the cushions. She seemed dazed and slightly disoriented.

*

Once everyone was seated among the cushions, I got the show under way.

'Ladies and gentlemen,' I began. 'Welcome to this little late-night theatrical entertainment in honour of Ine's seventh birthday. Can we have a round of applause for the birthday girl? And can I ask the birthday girl to stand up and take another bow?'

Everyone clapped and Aksel lifted Ine up on to the bench. She curtsied, gave a little giggle and sat down again. She seemed more wide awake now. I stepped outside the gazebo and positioned myself on the other side of the canvas.

'What you are about to see is a brief extract from a long story with many twists and turns to it,' I went on. 'It is the story of the daughter of a god who left her father once, long ago; she fell through the heavens and came down here to Earth to learn what it was like to be mortal. Her name was Agnes. She learned lots of different things, and not all of what she learned was pleasant. But this is also the story of two children. Which is why our play begins in quite a different way:

'Once upon a time there was a village. And in this village there lived a boy and his little sister. They were very poor, and every day their parents had to go to work in the factory and the two children were left on their own. Then one day something strange happened. A god's daughter came tumbling out of the heavens . . .'

I could hear Ine tittering knowingly on the other side of the screen. And I hoped that Agnes remembered the story from the school play we had put on when we were eleven. The one in which she played the narrator and spoke these words. I was pretty certain that she would remember them. How could she forget? That play marked the beginning of our friendship. I had trained the spotlight on her.

I switched on my powerful little torch and aimed it at the shadow puppets and the screen behind them. Slowly and smoothly I lifted the rising castle. Then I told the story of *The Dream Play*, slightly revised. One by one I picked up the puppets and made them move; I carried them towards one another, then away from one another.

I made one of them a mother. A sick mother who was lying in hospital. She was the prisoner in the castle. I showed the bed, the mother, the quilt. Then I performed a dramatic operation, using all the tricks one can do with such shadows: the scalpel making great, slashing cuts; a long rope being pulled out of the patient's stomach, yard after yard of it. I played it as a comedy and added all sorts of funny sounds. The audience in the gazebo were roaring with laughter.

Suddenly I remembered how Granny had taught me to make shadow figures with my hands, so I put down the puppets, hooked my hands together and sent a big, black bird on lazy wings swooping over the castle. It looked pretty spooky, even I could see how effective it was.

And then I had the bird open the locked door with its beak.

I couldn't see the audience inside the gazebo – well, how could I when I was outside. Nor could I hear anyone saying anything in there on the other side of the screen.

Here is what I presented as being on the other side of the locked door:

I picked up the puppets again and showed how, after the dramatic operation, the mother jumped out of bed, having made an immediate and complete recovery; and how the two children and her husband came drifting into the castle and hugged her.

'Where have you been, Mummy,' I said in a piping little voice.

'I've been here all the time,' the mummy doll said. And then they hugged one another again.

I whistled 'The butterfly in the garden' while holding up all four dolls together: Eilif, Ine, Monika and Aksel. All you could see was a jumble of arms and legs, but I don't think it mattered too much. The audience inside got the point anyway.

I don't know what happened after that, though. I must have tripped or something. I kind of crumpled up. The torch fell from my hand and hit the ground so hard that the bulb smashed. I think I dropped the puppets too. The performance came to an abrupt halt. The startled faces of the others appeared around the side of the screen.

All of a sudden I felt so tired.

I think it must have been Aksel and Håvard who picked me up, carried me into the gazebo and laid me down among Granny's cushions.

Before she left, Ine came to me, stroked my cheek and spread the white blanket over me. Then Aksel led her and Eilif off in the direction of the house.

'I think we should leave Molly in peace,' I heard him say to the others. 'She's worked so hard to organise this party, I don't think she got much sleep last night. She must be absolutely exhausted, poor thing.'

The last thing I remember saying was:

'The bonfire, Håvard. You have to light the bonfire.'

And as I drifted off to sleep I saw a huge flame shoot up on the other side of the canvas screen.

I think I may have cried. Or maybe I simply slept. When I woke it was still dark inside the gazebo. I had made a good job of covering the windows.

I rose unsteadily from the bench and put both hands to my head. Then I pushed the canvas over the doorway aside and stepped into the garden. The morning surrounded me on all sides.

The first thing I saw was the remains of the Midsummer bonfire. It must have been fantastic. I hoped the others had enjoyed it.

The embers were still glowing. My eye fell on the charred remnants of Agnes's shoes lying among the blackened bits of wood. I can only imagine that she must have flung them on to the fire after the show. What an odd thing to do. I'm beginning to see that there's a lot I don't know about Agnes.

*

I stood looking up at the house. Nothing moved up there. Most likely they were all still fast asleep. Slowly I wended my way across the garden, between the lilac bushes and down the road to Håvard's house.

Only when I got to his garden did I realise that I needed to pee. I squatted down.

Then I saw him. He was standing perfectly still next to the hollyhocks by the garden gate. He peered at me. He had the sun right behind him; it was impossible to tell whether he was smiling. Then he raised his hand.

The others left that morning. The children insisted on going home, so they could visit their mother at the hospital every day. She was well enough to have visitors now, they had seen that for themselves. I think Eilif was convinced that it was 'The butterfly in the garden' which had done the trick.

Agnes said she was ready to go back to town too. She offered to move in with Aksel for a couple of days to keep an eye on the children when he was at the hospital. Monika was about to start radiotherapy.

I helped them all to pack. It didn't take long. Aksel had washed the dishes and tidied up after the party. The kids had cleared away the Barbie village. Everything looked pretty much as it had done before they came, apart from the great pile of ashes at the bottom of the garden.

I stood on the steps and waved them off.

There followed several days of hard work. I lost myself in a sort of fog of concentration. Sometimes it's good to work like that – you forget about everything else: eating, grieving.

I finished the shadow puppets and the model of the glass castle. I took the whole lot in to the theatre and presented it to the people in the workshop. Over the next few days I pretty much lived there with them. I was the first to arrive in the morning and the last to leave at night. I worked closely with the lighting technician: we experimented with all sorts of different set-ups. It felt good to be back in the control room. I think he might even have missed me too.

I could tell that Jan was relieved. Well, it was understandable: it's not easy being the man in charge. The director always has to have an eye for the bigger picture, even when things don't seem to be falling into place.

*

I haven't heard from Agnes since she left. Her stay at the summer house was not such a long one, but I've decided to leave the wheelchair ramp where it is for the moment. She might want to come back.

I've also decided to stay on into the autumn. Granny used to wait until at least the middle of October before returning to the flat in town.

In any case, I can't leave before I've taken Håvard to the doctor. And then I suppose it'll be up to me to talk him into going through with the laser treatment that Aksel mentioned. I can hardly stand by and watch him go completely blind. He's so bloody stubborn, that man. Just like me.

I think perhaps Agnes needs a break from me and everything connected with the summer house. I can understand that. I can sense that she's thinking about me, just as Ine does. But the force of Agnes's thoughts is much greater than that of Ine's.

Sometimes the force emanating from Agnes tends to unsettle me. I have the feeling that she wants Aksel for herself, possibly his children too. It has occasionally crossed my mind that I will have to guard myself and my baby against her; that she might want this child so badly that she would take it away from me, draw it to her. She has such a strong will, it's like a magnet.

But I don't want to think like that. It has to be possible to turn that thought around. Agnes and I are very close.

And yet I suspect this may be why I still haven't told her that I'm going to keep the baby. I thought I would wait until the next time I see her. This isn't the sort of thing one talks about over the phone. I haven't forgotten that time when I told her I was pregnant.

I remember once, about four or five years ago, when I turned up at her flat unannounced. I'm not very good at letting people know beforehand when I'm thinking of dropping in: I mean to call, but something always seems to get in the way. I don't think she likes me landing in on her out of the blue like that, but I'm sure it's not that she isn't glad to see me, it's probably more because she likes to be in control of things. Maybe I should try to shift some of that control away from her. I believe she might get on better if she didn't have so much control.

She was sitting in the middle of the sitting-room in her wheel-chair. The blinds were down and she had a video projector wired up to her computer. A slide of some underwater creature, a sea anemone or something of the sort – vastly enlarged – was gliding over the wall, down on to the floor and then up to the ceiling on the other side of the room. She sat motionless in the chair, following the picture with her eyes. Her head followed the move-ment of the projector beam: turning slowly, wonderingly.

When she did eventually register my presence, she was furious. I could see that I had startled her. She flinched, as if she had been pulled back from something. I crossed the room to her in three long strides and flung my arms around her. She burst into tears.

I hope she'll come to the premiere. I thought perhaps I could tell her right after the performance that I was going to keep the baby. Then I'll take her and Aksel and the kids out to dinner, give her a chance to collect herself. I will tell her that I have decided to be a mother, but that I don't expect Aksel will want to take on the role of father, not to begin with, anyway.

It's probably going to come as a shock to her, but I hope she'll support me. I'll tell her that I need her to help me come to terms with this, as she has always helped me to come to terms with diffi-cult situations. I have to get her back on to my side.

So I'll leave it till after the premiere, and trust that all goes well: that she will have enjoyed the play; that Jan and I, the actors, the lighting technician and everyone else at the theatre will succeed in providing her with images in which she can take refuge and find rest. And once the applause has died down – if there is any applause – I'll go to her, bend over her and tell her what I have decided to do.

I'm not quite sure how she will react, but I'm hoping that, after she's had time to gather her thoughts, she will say she thinks it's great that I've decided to keep the baby, and that Aksel is bound to take on the role of father eventually. That he is a good man, and that he loves children. Well, she knows him, why wouldn't she say that?

I want her to tell me that one day he'll be happy with the choice I've made. And, she will add, Eilif and Ine will be delighted by the prospect of a baby sister or brother, and their delight will rub off on Aksel.

And finally I want her to assure me in heartfelt tones that she is very, very much looking forward to becoming a godmother. That she has always wanted to have a child who would play around her in the garden, while she sat in her wheelchair, keeping an eye on it.

Then I would say: And I'll go up to the house for a jug of squash, then we can sit in the gazebo, sipping it.

I think she'll like the dress I've made for the première. It's mauve velvet. She knows a thing or two about dressmaking. And she'll love the colour. Håvard helped me. We decided on a high-waisted style. When I had finished it, I went down to his place to let him see the end result. He eyed me up and down and said:

'Lovely maternity dress.'

Once I have Agnes's blessing, I will tell Aksel about the baby. And then we'll all go out to dinner.

Jan has been coming down a lot recently, to keep me posted on how the rehearsals are going and to discuss various practical matters with me. Jan is the consummate theatre director, you can tell by the way he addresses you. As if there is something he is trying to get you to express, something you're not even aware of having inside you.

He usually arrives late in the afternoon, after rehearsals and all his meetings with the technicians.

He looks tired. I realise, of course, that there are so many practical problems to be overcome, there always are when he and I work together. I haven't made his job any easier with my shadow play. Not only that, but this time there is some trouble with the floor of the set, which has proved to be too slippy. The actors are skidding and sliding all over the place, he tells me. He has to laugh when he describes it to me, and I can't help chuckling too at the image of the lawyer, the god's daughter and the doorkeeper in full, metallic-crocheted costume, going headlong in mid-line.

I'm not as worried as he is. Things always tend to fall into place at the last minute, just before the première. It's a lot of work, and you always end up having to make the odd compromise, of course, but it's nothing I haven't done before.

Jan likes to involve everyone in the process, and he has learned to trust me. He had wanted me to stay in town, to be on hand for the final rehearsals: talk to the people in the workshop, show them how I wanted things to be done, help them find some way of making the floor less slippy. Adjustments always have to made once the sets have been mounted on-stage, you can't expect the model to be perfect.

But I wanted to be here. I'm in constant contact with them by phone, and of course I'll be there when it really matters. They'll have to make do with that. I rarely reply to e-mails.

Sometimes a whole morning can be taken up with telephone calls about technical matters. I end up feeling so sick and tired of the whole thing, and it takes me ages to settle down again afterwards. Sometimes I have to take a glass of Granny's red wine. I have a cellar full of the stuff.

Occasionally, when Jan works himself up into a state, I have to get him slightly tipsy and talk about nothing for a while, until he sees that it's best for me to stay here, and not be around the theatre too much, poking my nose into everything.

'Now and again, yes; and a lot at the beginning, naturally, when things are taking shape on stage,' I say. 'To make any major, and absolutely necessary, changes. But after that it has to find its own form.'

When I do finally get through to him, he nods his head wearily, plainly befuddled by the wine, and paces up and down the room, considering the model from every angle. I can see that he is worn out, but that he has no intention of giving up. He is like me in that respect.

I've made an extra model of the rising castle which I have kept here at the summer house. The other, its twin, is at the theatre of course. I keep my copy here so that I can show him exactly how to set the lighting, and how the shadow play with the puppets has to be executed. It is my job to seduce him with this model; show him how magical it can be, that it is worth all the effort, all the hassle. That it will work.

Sheets of Perspex lie scattered all over the sitting-room. I feel I can make as much mess as I want now that the children are gone.

Jan is a decent enough director. We have our little disagreements, but I can see he understands that I have a plan, and that he would do well to trust me. The same goes for him: he has a plan, too, and I would do well to trust him.

I haven't told him that I'm pregnant, but he may have noticed that I'm often a little under the weather when he is here. He's pretty perceptive – well, he's used to working with actors. I like people like him, the sort who are not easily fooled.

This I see now: the sand in the digital hourglass on the screen runs and runs but goes nowhere. Gradually I become visible to myself. Everything becomes clear. Somewhere here there is a wave, I think it wants something of me.

I try to tell myself: not what I want, but what fate wants.

I would have liked to talk to Agnes about this, but she doesn't call. And maybe I'm afraid of what she might say. She knows so much more than me, I see that now. She knows things that you can only know if you have been very frightened and in pain for a long, long time. When you can never be quite sure whether there will ever be an end to the fear and the pain, but have no intention of giving into it, no matter what.

She may not want to share everything she knows with me.

It hurts to think such a thing.

None the less, I think it again: she may not want to share everything she knows with me.

I haven't heard much from Aksel and the children. A couple of text messages from Eilif, amusing messages suggestive of a certain fondness, as if he knows I want him to be thinking about me. Eilif doesn't say how Monika is doing. I think he wishes to keep his mother to himself, would rather not involve me in her affairs. Mainly for my sake, I think. But he tells me about other little things he has been doing, that he thinks might interest me.

He doesn't bring Ine into his messages to me, either. This thing that he does is just between the two of us. This makes me feel glad and warm inside: he doesn't have to do it, I'm only his dad's girl-friend, he could have chosen to go on thinking of me as the enemy, the way he did at the start.

Ine is too small to send text messages, but I know that she is thinking about me, too. I can feel it. Her thoughts have a slender, steadfast force.

She left one of her Barbie dolls behind. I found it on the veranda among what was left of the village. I hope she'll come back to get it herself.

I called the guys at the theatre and asked them to come and pick up the piano and deliver it to Agnes's flat. It was one of the first things I did after she left. The guy who took the message spoke with exactly the same lilt as before. I wasn't sure which one of them I was actually talking to, but it didn't matter. He said they would be down in a day or so.

I brought Ine's Barbie doll into the house and tucked it up under a blanket here in the sitting-room, so that only the skinny neck and the head with its mass of blond hair are sticking out. The hair is all tangled; I can see how Ine has tried, unsuccessfully, to straighten it out with the hairbrush. In my mind I can see her throwing the brush away in exasperation and calling to her brother to come and fix it for her. Ine has quite a temper, she's a little like me in that way. But Eilif isn't about to be wrapped round anyone's little finger, he decides for himself when he will come and what he will fix. Patiently he teaches her to sort things out for herself. It is a gift he has.

The phone rang a couple of days ago, but there was no one on the other end wishing to speak to me. When I put the receiver to my ear I could hear the faint rustle of voices and other sounds in the background. I knew it had to be somebody who had called my number on their mobile by mistake. I listened and listened, as if hypnotised, and after a while it dawned on me that it was the children's mobile which had rung me without them knowing. It was probably lying in the pocket of Eilif's hooded sweatshirt: I could hear the distant, muffled sounds of his footsteps and his and Ine's voices, they seemed to be coming from under water. It sounded as if they were discussing something, I could hear that insistent note in Ine's voice. She never backs down in a discussion, especially not when it's with her brother. I had to smile.

I tried to get through to them. I shouted their names down the phone, but they couldn't hear me. In the end I gave up and put down the phone, but a while later when I went back and picked it up again, they were still there. And there was me thinking that the connection was broken when one of the parties hung up.

I've been thinking a lot about Monika. I've been wondering how she felt when she was pregnant with Eilif, over ten years ago. Was she happy? Was she confused, like me? Was she sure that Aksel would be pleased? Did she think that the two of them would be together for the rest of their lives. Did she feel that everything was as it should be? Or did she also wonder whether she might be carrying Something?

I picture her, the first time she felt the baby move. I envisage her being alone that day: somewhere in a forest, perhaps. By a little stream. Leaning against a tree trunk, a pine; sitting on the warm hillside, feeling the sun on her face, on the top of her head. Sticking her hand into the waistband of her trousers and placing it low down on her belly, letting it rest there, a little squashed by the straining fabric. Feeling for the first time the faint little flutter that is Eilif. A very tiny Eilif, a minuscule fishtail doing a quick flip in the water before swimming onwards, deeper inside her.

Now he is a big lad who sends messages on his mobile phone. Sends them to me.

I think Monika must have been conscious of how that fishtail caused a little wave of nausea to well up, only to sink down again to that imperceptible spot from which all nausea rises, much like that spot at sea from which the tide ebbs and flows. She took her hand out of her trousers and transferred it to her breast, under her sweater. It already felt tender.

Monika thought: now it lives inside me.

Up to now I haven't felt any movement, but my breasts are tender. It will be the same for me as it was for her. But this is a different baby. It isn't Eilif, or Ine, I musn't forget that. I don't know who it is yet, but I mean to find out.

I wonder whether I will simply go on being myself as the foetus gets bigger. Maybe I will start to feel that I am two people? One body inside the other, like those Russian nesting dolls – and each body with a will of its own.

So far it feels as though I am just one.

The floor here is littered with all sorts of small, sharp objects and odds and ends of material. I'm forever tripping or stabbing myself when I walk across the floor barefoot. I tell myself I'll have to be careful, there could be bits of broken glass lying about. I stand in the middle of the room, looking at my feet. They're pretty filthy, I never stay long enough in the shower to get them really clean. Poor things, I think. They deserve better, but they know what I'm like.

The spare room where Eilif and Ine slept is so empty now. I stripped their beds, rolled the the bedclothes into a big ball and dumped it in the laundry room in the basement, but I haven't been able to bring myself to put them into the washing machine yet. At one point I went downstairs and buried my nose in that ball of linen. This was right after the others had left. It was cool down in the basement, it smelled of apples and washing powder and brick. No particular scent clung to the bedclothes, it was more of a texture – smooth, densely-packed fibres, and the hint of a taste: of something chalky. I haven't been down there since.

The children, when they were here: they were very different in their way of sleeping. A couple of times I tiptoed into the room where they both lay, each lighting their way into slumber. Neither of them noticed that I was there in the room with them. Ine wriggled and squirmed until her nightie was twisted around her body like a wrung-out dishrag, her knees seemed to me to be too big for the rest of her. Not much, just a little. Eilif looked more solid, and his knees were more in keeping with all his other limbs.

I think I tried to get to know them while they were sleeping. As they really were. Almost as if I felt that everything else about them, the sides that the day brought with it, didn't actually have anything to do with them. As if the day was but a minor intrusion.

They're in the village now, I thought. They run past me as I sit outside my house, shelling peas. They are racing across the meadow. Beyond them I see the setting sun. My own child is running after them, a little way behind. It looks like them, but is much smaller, it has only just learned to walk, it has such short legs, and shiny, red shoes. Ine stops and waits for the toddler, she takes its hand. Then they run on.

I have been down to Håvard's place several times since the others left. He barely looks up when I walk in. He is working on his project for the exhibition. I can see that he has made up his mind to finish it.

I think Håvard's the sort who would go on taking pictures even if he did go blind. For a while, at least. He would probably create his own genre: 'Pictures from a Blind Man', or 'Landscape of the Blind' or something of the sort. A bit of a cheap shot, maybe, but not hard to imagine. I'm sure he'd be quite willing to carry a white stick if he thought it would add to the effect. I can just picture it: a lovely photograph in the newspaper of the aging photographer with his camera dangling over his stomach and a white stick tapping the ground ahead of him, on his way to an exhibition of his own pictures, catchily entitled *Images of Blindness*. He has a pretty good idea of just what it takes. He has always been good at spinning myths around himself, and he's still as big a flirt as ever. He'll be flirting till the day he dies. I think I'm the only one who can see it. I doubt if there are too many people who know that he has had diabetes since he was a teenager and that he has not taken proper care of himself; that his eye disease is a result of that. He's not as old as he looks, he has simply driven himself very hard. I don't hold it against him. Diabetes doesn't fit with his image of himself. Blindness does.

In order to call the doctor and ask for help, he will have to alter his image of himself. He may find that hard.

He still doesn't like the fact that I refuse to call him Strøm, but he'll have to get used to it if we two are to go on being neighbours.

Eilif has sent me the pictures which he and Ine took for Håvard with the mobile when they were here. He asked me to print them out and give them to him. They are for his exhibition, he asked the kids to help him. This, I gathered, was his payment for the piano lessons. I took the photographs down to Håvard, but he said I should keep them. I might be able to use them, he thought. They are lying here in front of me on the table. They're good. Especially the one of the cat.

It's not only the spare room that is empty and quiet, the whole house is so still. To begin with, it made me uneasy, but now I'm used to it. Everything is reverting to a state in which it is possible to work.

I have taught myself how to weed. Granny's flower-bed was almost completely overgrown. Weeding is really pretty self-explanatory: you simply pull out everything that looks as if it shouldn't be there.

Maybe that is actually what Granny was trying to show me that time I saw her on the veranda. That I ought to get down to some weeding.

III

AGNES REDUX

It feels good to be back in the flat. When I dragged myself through the door after having stayed at Aksel's house for a few days to look after the children, I thought to myself: Home. This is a home. I am built into the bricks of this flat, it has missed me. It's so nice with white walls, bare of pictures. And so good to be alone again.

I laid the crutches on the floor and sat down in the wheelchair, which Aksel had placed in the middle of the room before kissing me on the forehead and going off to take the children over to Monika's place. He plans to live there with them until she comes home from hospital, and for a while after that as well, probably. To keep an eye on her operation wound, among other things. I gave him a big smile and said I thought that was a very sensible decision.

It took a little time for me to get back into my fate project. It was almost as if my brain needed to rest for a while after everything that had taken place at the summer house. I had the feeling that I would have to approach it in a different way.

But one thing is for sure – I see it more clearly than ever: all these disasters want something of us. They throw everything into disorder and always, afterwards, comes a new beginning. We are forced to think differently, our set ideas start to flow. Everything becomes sharp and clear.

What I remember best from my days at the summer house is my trip in the kayak.

When Molly pushed me off so hard that I capsized and Aksel had to rescue me, I was terrified. More frightened than I've ever been in my whole life. It was like I became someone else, someone who no longer had any future.

But Aksel and the children helped me up to the bathing hut and wrapped me in towels and their own clothes. I felt their hands all over my body, they patted and stroked me, Ine rubbed up my hair, Eilif massaged my feet. Aksel went for a blanket which he tucked round me. He talked to me in a soft, calm voice; said he thought I should try again right away. Otherwise I would never dare to go out in a kayak again.

He and Eilif tipped the water out of the kayak and got it ready for me. I stayed in the bathing hut with Ine until they had it back in the water.

They had a bit of bother getting me into the kayak this time, too, but not as much as the first time. Once I was installed, everything went surprisingly smoothly. Eilif handed me the paddle and gave me a very, very gentle push – just enough to send me skimming out across the smooth surface of the fjord, away from him. Ine whooped with delight when I got myself balanced; all three were shouting instructions at me. It took me no time to get into the rhythm of it this time. I could hear them clapping and cheering behind me.

'That's it!' Aksel cried happily. 'Straight and steady. Excellent!'

It was a strange feeling, sitting below the water line like that, deciding for myself where I would go. And it moved so fast, I scudded across the waves! At my back I could vaguely hear Eilif shouting something to me. He's not worried about me, I told myself. He's okay, that young man. He knows that I know where I'm going.

I paddled between some rocky islets. The water was so clear. I'd had no idea there was so much life under the water. So many things moving about.

A seal popped its head up right in front of the kayak's bow. I stopped short. Froze. We stared at one another. The seal wasn't very big, it had to be a pup. Then I cautiously dipped the paddle into the water again and sent the boat shooting forwards. The seal ducked back under the water. It was gone for a while, then it came up again, further ahead. It almost looked as though it was laughing.

Someone called from the theatre to say that they would be bringing Granny's piano over some time today. They just wanted to make sure I was home. I recognised the voice of the man who called: it was the one with the big beard.

'I said: 'Come any time. I'm never out.'

Then he laughed that deep, rumbling laugh which I liked so much and said something about it being high bloody time I got out for an airing.

It was a nice thought of Molly's, sending me the piano. It will be my legacy from Granny. Molly got everything else. Which is only reasonable: she is her grandchild.

When I put the receiver down after talking to the guy from the theatre, I had a thought about my fate project. Until now, my theory has been that fate and suffering go together like Fritz and Hans, the Katzenjammer Twins. But maybe there is an element missing:

Joy. I seemed to have forgotten to factor in joy.

When you least expect it, there it is: popping its little head up, right behind Knoll and Tott, suffering and fate. Winking and blinking. Like a little seal pup.

The day after I got back to town, I went over to Granny's flat
alone. I took a taxi. The driver was the same one as on that night
when I saw the African man and the baby on the stairs. He gave
me a quick nod and a hello: he obviously recognised me. He
remembered the address, I suppose, and the wheelchair. Or
maybe he remembered me.

I knew that the man next door had the keys to Granny's flat. I
rang his doorbell. He didn't seem surprised. Maybe he remembered me, too.

'There's just something I have to find in Granny's flat,' I said.
'Something that belongs to me.'

He gave me a long, hard look, as if he knew what I was talking
about. Then he let me into her flat and left me alone.

Everything looked exactly the same as when Granny was alive. It
didn't even look as if any dust had gathered. Someone had
stopped time and saved all this for me. There was a great, gaping
space where the piano had stood. Nothing to be done about that.
The piano is coming to me now. It will have to be tuned. I'll call
the piano tuner. I'll get the number from Molly. And I'll get him
to take a taxi, too, as she did. I'll let him take all the time he needs.

I had some idea of where Granny's tapes were stored. And I
found the tape recorder. But there was only one tape. I had imagined that there would be one for each person who had stayed with
Granny, that she had kept a kind of archive of her guests' confi-
dences. But there was just the one.

So all the conversations are lying one on top of the other, I
thought.

I carried the tape-recorder into the sitting-room and set it
on the table in front of the capacious red armchairs. I had no

difficulty in getting it started. But I could hear nothing on the tape except a deep hum which sounded as if it were coming from some big machine in the next room. No voices. No other sounds. I sat as if hypnotised, listening.

Aksel has been granted compassionate leave, to look after Monika, so it looks like being just the temp and me for a while yet.

I had to call her a few days after I got back from the summer house. It wasn't as easy to manage without the wheelchair as I had thought. There had been a couple of incidents when I had fallen and not been able to get back up on my own; I had to admit that this crutches project of mine might not be entirely wise.

I sense a change in the temp. I don't know what's been going on behind my back, although it could well be that Aksel has had a serious talk with her. She still buttons that frumpy coat all the way up to the chin when she's leaving, but she has begun to look at me in a different way, there's a new look in her eyes. She doesn't babble on the way she used to and she has begun to take note of whatever I happen to have lying on my desk. A couple of days ago she came right out and asked me what I did all day at the computer. And I don't know what came over me, but to my surprise I heard myself telling her about the fate project. I didn't go into details, obviously, but I managed to explain the essence of what it is I am endeavouring to discover: what does fate want with us? What language does it use? How should one answer, how can one show that one has understood?

To my great amazement, the temp seemed to understand exactly what I was talking about. She didn't make a big thing of it, but it was clear that she had some experience of fate herself. She told me about her little daughter who had been born with a serious illness – no one had expected her to live more than a couple of years. She was seven now and had just started in second grade. She required a lot of help, and needed to have her mother close by most of the time. Which is why the temp works as a temp: she has to be able to decide for herself when she can work, that way she can be there for her daughter when necessary.

'Then it's always a good sign, when you can be here with me,' I said. 'If you're at work, that means you're daughter is well and at school.'

The temp smiled at me and nodded rather shyly. Then she pointed to the model of the summer house, which I had consigned to a corner of the sitting-room. It was still covered with the sheet, the one I had thrown over it just before Molly came to take me to the real summer house earlier in the summer.

I bent down, pulled the sheet off and explained to her that it was a model I had made as part of my fate project, but that it had proved to be a less than fruitful avenue of investigation, a dead-end. I was considering getting rid of it. Maybe she could take it down and chuck it in the skip in the courtyard for me?

But that she would not do. She loved the model, it was full of details on which she remarked: the hammock on the veranda, the spotlight, the itty-bitty computer and telephone in the sitting-room. Did I seriously mean to throw it away, she asked incredulously.

'Certainly,' I said. 'As it turned out, it was nothing like the real thing.'

The temp laughed at that, and asked if she could take the model home with her, for her daughter. She could use it as a dolls' house. When she said that, I sensed a warm wave welling up inside me. It felt almost like tears. The temp eyed me in alarm.

'By all means,' I said, and had to swallow again and again. 'If someone can play with it, that's all to the good. I've no more use for it.'

After she had left with the model in her arms, I sat by the window in the wheelchair, looking out at the street. It seemed I still had some tears left to cry. I reached for the box of tissues and laid it in my lap. Then I let it all out.

And again I felt the sediment sink to the bottom of the troubled waters. I could see the tall hospital buildings down at the end of the road. The sky was overcast, but according to the weather forecast it was liable to clear up in the course of the evening, so there was a good chance of a lovely sunset.

It occurred to me that perhaps it was time for a slight expansion of the research methods employed in my fate project. It might be an idea to start interviewing people, instead of basing my knowledge purely on what I picked up from the internet and the news media. I could start with the temp, I thought. Ask her how she feels about fate. Well, I mean – she has a sick daughter, she must have given some thought to fate and what it wants with us. And maybe I could make occasional visits to the hospital and talk to some of the people confined to bed down there, get their feelings on the matter too. I am pretty well known down there, after all.

Maybe some time a patient will describe their situation to me, and I will listen attentively. And afterwards, maybe I will say, like Granny:

'Are you quite sure about that?

How can you know that that is what fate wants?

Are you quite sure that you are disappointed? Maybe you are actually relieved.

Maybe you're not really angry, but afraid?

Maybe you're not afraid, but angry?'

And perhaps one day I will wheel myself into a ward where a young woman of nineteen is lying, unable to feel her feet; a girl who doesn't know whether she will ever live a normal life. One of the doctors has told her that she may lose the use of her limbs, her memory, the power of speech, everything. A girl whose hands lie lifelessly on top of the duvet, as if they no longer trust her.

Perhaps I could wheel my chair right up to her bedside. Bend in over her, place my hand over hers, look gravely at her and say:

'My dear. Things are as they are.'

Aksel is sure to be doing a great job with Monika. I can just picture him helping her out of bed and over to the training mat, slipping off his nurse's shoes and getting down beside her to show her the exercises designed to gently build up her pelvic muscles, her back, all of that delicate area they have cut into and removed things from. That area which no longer houses a womb, where no more babies will ever form and grow. But that's okay: Monika has had all the children she's going to have.

'Easy now!' Aksel says. 'Take it nice and steady. And don't forget to breathe. Yes, that's it.'

Molly's play has its premiere this evening. It has had lots of advance publicity in the press. Great things are expected of the director and of the scenography. Those journalists who were allowed a sneak preview have more than hinted that what we are about to see is something truly spectacular.

I thought I might invite Molly and Aksel and the children to dinner here at the flat after the premiere. I'll make spaghetti and meatballs for them. A bit basic, perhaps, but I'm not out to impress them. And I'm planning a big surprise for them: for dessert I am going to give them baked ice-cream.

I had a conversation with Eilif about this; apparently he had seen a television programme in which some chef had talked about a dessert which involved baking ice-cream in the oven. The thought of this must have been bothering him: that logical, boy's brain of his had no doubt told him that ice-cream could not possibly be baked in an oven. We had had a chat about this, late in the evening on Ine's birthday. We had sat in our respective wicker chairs, wrapped in blankets and gazing at the dying embers of the Midsummer bonfire. The others had gone to bed. Molly was fast asleep in the gazebo.

I don't know how the subject of desserts came up. After all that had happened that evening you'd think we would have had more important things to discuss. Nonethless, Eilif and I were talking about desserts. There was no way ice-cream could be baked in an oven, he declared indignantly. But I smiled at him and said that I seemed to remember having seen a recipe for baked ice-cream somewhere. In fact I was quite sure of it.

'Okay, so how do you do it?' he asked. But I couldn't explain how it was done. He snorted at me impatiently, the way his dad does sometimes during our work-outs when he thinks I'm being difficult. I couldn't help smiling even more broadly, I had to turn my face away for a moment. I was so happy that he felt I was someone he could snort at. I pulled one arm out from under my blanket and thumped him gently on the back. He put out his arm and thumped me back, on the shoulder. His thump was harder than mine.

I found the recipe on the internet: *glace au four* it's called. Oven-baked ice cream. It's the meringue that makes it possible. You beat the egg whites with sugar until they are stiff and cover the ice cream with this light, fluffy, sweet mass. The meringue insulates the ice cream against the heat of the oven. Hot on the outside and cold on the inside when it's eaten. They're going to love it, I'm sure.

Ine walks in without ringing the doorbell first.

She kicks off her shoes in the hall and crosses the room to me; she has such a light, lovely step, thanks to her ballet training, I suppose. Sometimes she hardly seems to touch the ground.

I am at my desk. I feel my cheeks twitching when I see her coming towards me.

'Dad and Eilif will be here shortly with the car,' she says. 'They couldn't find a parking space, so they drove round to the petrol station to see if they could pick up some flowers for Molly. Dad says he thinks people always take flowers to theatre premieres.'

'Hi, Ine,' I say. 'How nice to see you.'

'Aren't you taking flowers?'

'Of course, I am,' I say, pointing to the big, oblong parcel from the florist's lying on the desk.

'Mum's been out today,' Ine announces, walking over to the flowers and taking them in her arms. 'She and I went for a ride on our bikes. It went fine.'

'Really? That's wonderful. I knew she would be okay.'

'Did you?'

'Mmm.'

'But she had to lie down on the sofa when we got back. She was feeling a bit dizzy.'

'Well, that's not surprising,' I say. 'It doesn't take much to make you dizzy to begin with. She musn't overdo it, she still needs to rest. But she'll improve in leaps and bounds now that she's back home and has your Dad and you two to look after her. Mums need a bit of looking after too, you know. Especially when they've been ill.'

'I know that,' Ine says. 'Was your Mum good at riding a bike when you were little?'

I stare at her in surprise.

'My Mum?' I say. 'Why do you ask that?'

'I was just wondering.'

'No, my Mum wasn't particularly good at riding a bike,' I say. 'Not as far as I remember.'

'What *was* she good at?'

'Well, she was very, very good at writing.'

'What did she write? Stories and things?'

'Yes.'

'Is she dead?'

'No, she's not dead. But I haven't seen her in many, many years.'

'Why not?'

'She left us. She lives abroad now.'

'But you must miss her terribly!'

'Oh, I don't know. I don't think about her that often these days.'

'You don't think about her? But you have to think about your Mum! Otherwise she'll be sad.'

I'm beginning to feel a little flustered.

'But it's not always that simple,' I say.

'Don't you remember what you and Molly said, that time you fell out of the hammock at the summer house?' says Ine sharply. 'It was you two who said that a Mum is never really gone.'

'Did Molly and I say that?'

'Yes!'

'What else did we say?'

'You said that a Mum is like an almond in a dish of rice pudding. Or something like that.'

I had to smile.

'Ah, yes – like an almond in a dish of rice pudding. That's right. I remember now.'

I realise that Ine remembers every word of what was said at the summer house, even if she hasn't understood it all, or doesn't remember who said what. I suspect that Molly and I sometimes tend to become one person as far as she is concerned. All the same, I'm surprised and happy to hear her say it. When a girl like Ine remembers something it can never be lost. It goes on existing, even if it is not fully understood.

'Quite right,' I say. 'A Mum is like an almond in a dish of rice pudding.'

'Yes, because you don't know it's there, you can't always see it! And then – hey presto! – it's there on your spoon.'

She chortles happily.

'Yes, hey presto!' I say.

'Dad knows just how to look after Mum,' she goes on.

'You bet he does,' I say. 'He's incredibly patient and clever, your Dad.'

'And I think you should call your Mum,' she says. 'What if she needs help? Or misses you? You've got the phone right there!'

I don't quite know what to say to this.

'Are you taking your crutches to the theatre?' she asks.

'No, I think I'll take the wheelchair,' I say. 'To be on the safe side. It takes a lot out of me, using the crutches. I find them a bit awkward. And besides, they have special places at the theatre for wheelchair users. Very good places. The best.'

'Can I sit next to you?'

'You most certainly can,' I say, and feel a warm, little thrill in my breast.

'What's that?' Ine asks, putting down the parcelled-up flowers. Her eye has fallen on the red velvet cushion and the little hammer with the silver bell from Granny's flat. Molly gave them to me. She popped them into my bag when I was leaving the summer house, along with the cardboard puppets I had made, and which she had borrowed. I didn't discover them until I got home and started unpacking my things.

She had wrapped the cushion, the bell and the hammer separately, in tissue paper – she must have found this last in Granny's flat the day we went there to pick up the piano. I recognised the colour: mauve. One of the drawers in Granny's bureau was full of tissue paper like that.

'It's a kind of a secret,' I say. 'It's something I inherited from Molly's Granny.'

'The lady who used to live in the summer house?'

I nod.

'Can I have a shot?'

I nod again.

Down in the street we hear the sound of a car horn tooting. Probably Eilif and Aksel telling us to hurry up.

'Yes, you can have a shot,' I say. 'But then we have to go.'

Ine's face becomes very still. She has such powers of concentration, her small body totally focused – as if this were a matter of life or death.

Gingerly she picks up the little silver hammer with the head shaped like an elephant. Holding the cord between finger and thumb she slowly lifts the bell into the air above the deep-red, velvet cushion.

'Now?' she asks, looking at me as though I were a conductor.

I nod.

Ine raises the hammer and gently strikes the tiny silver bell.

The sound is faint, but it hangs in the air for a long time. It seems to swell; it forms a chamber.

Down in the street, it almost seems as though Aksel has heard the sound; he responds with yet another toot on the horn.

I smile at Ine and wink slyly.

And I picture it thus:

The auditorium is gradually filling up. People buzz their way to their seats. A woman in a wheelchair is being shown to one of the places reserved for wheelchair users. She is accompanied by a seven-year-old girl with shoulder-length hair in a pastel-coloured dress. The girl takes the seat next to the wheelchair and passes the woman a copy of the programme: inside, to her surprise, she has found photographs of herself and her brother, as if they were a part of the play. She and her brother took these photos with a mobile phone some weeks ago. There, too, is a picture of a cat; the girl beams in recognition.

The woman in the wheelchair leans towards her to whisper an explanation of how these pictures come to be in the programme. She flicks to the back, to find that she and the girl and the girl's brother are all thanked in the acknowledgements. She points to the place where they are mentioned and the girl nods: she can read a little bit, she recognises their names.

A couple of rows further back sits a fair-haired man of around forty. He wears a short-sleeved, checked shirt buttoned up to the neck. He doesn't look as if he is used to having to get dressed up. He is a little nervous: he has just been backstage to deliver two bouquets of flowers for the play's scenographer. Beside him sits a boy with the same fair hair, only his has been slicked up into lots of little spikes all over his head. He appears to be about ten years old, maybe eleven.

Behind the window of the lighting booth, high up on the back wall of the auditorium, one can just make out two figures bent over the control panel: the lighting technician and the scenographer, a short-haired woman in her thirties, clad in a mauve velvet dress. They are deep in conversation.

Then the scenographer straightens up for a moment and glances down into the stalls. At that very second, as if on cue, the woman in the wheelchair turns round. The girl sitting next to her, and the man and the young boy a few rows behind also turn and look up at the control room. Their eyes meet those of the scenographer.

The woman in the wheelchair lifts her hand in the beginnings of a wave.

Then the lights go down. The play begins.

Nothing is ever the same as they said it was.
It's what I've never seen before that I recognise.

Diane Arbus